Fantastic Tales
of Time and Space

Signet Double Science Fiction:

THE REBEL WORLDS
and
A KNIGHT OF GHOSTS
AND SHADOWS

THE
REBEL WORLDS

AND

A KNIGHT OF GHOSTS AND SHADOWS

by Poul Anderson

A SIGNET BOOK

NEW AMERICAN LIBRARY

TIMES MIRROR

SIGNET TRADEMARK REG. U.S. PAT. OFF. AND FOREIGN COUNTRIES
REGISTERED TRADEMARK—MARCA REGISTRADA
HECHO EN CHICAGO, U.S.A.

SIGNET, SIGNET CLASSICS, MENTOR, PLUME, MERIDIAN AND NAL BOOKS
are published by The New American Library, Inc.,
1633 Broadway, New York, New York 10019

First Printing (Double Science Fiction Edition), November, 1982

1   2   3   4   5   6   7   8   9

PRINTED IN THE UNITED STATES OF AMERICA

THE
REBEL WORLDS

~~~~~~~~~~

Make oneness.

I/we: Feet belonging to Guardian Of North Gate and others who can be, to Raft Farer and Woe who will no longer be, to Many Thoughts, Cave Discoverer, and Master Of Songs who can no longer be; Wings belonging to Iron Miner and Lightning Struck The House and others to be, to Many Thoughts who can no longer be; young Hands that has yet to share memories: make oneness.

(O light, wind, river! They flood too strongly, they tear me/us apart.)

Strength. This is not the first young Hands which has come here to remember the journey that was made so many years before he/she was born; nor shall this be the last. Think strength, think calm.

(Blurred, two legs, faceless . . . no, had they beaks?)

Remember. Lie down at ease where leaves whisper beneath hues of upthrusting land coral; drink light and wind and sound of the river. Let reminiscence flow freely, of deeds that were done before this my/our Hands came to birth.

(Clearer, now: so very strange they were, how can the sight of them even be seen, let alone held in me/us? . . . Answer: The eye learns to see them, the nose to smell them, the ear to hear them, the tongue of the Feet and the limbs of the Wings and the Hands to touch their skins and feel, the tendrils to taste what they exude.)

This goes well. More quickly than usual. Perhaps i/we can become a good oneness that will often have reason to exist.

(Flicker of joy. Tide of terror at the rising memories— alienness, peril, pain, death, rebirth to torment.)

Lie still. It was long ago.

But time too is one. Now is unreal; only past-and-future has the length to be real. What happened then must be known to Us. Feel in every fiber of my/our young Hands, that i/we am/are part of Us—We of Thunderstone, Iron-workers, Fellers and Builders, Plowers, Housedwellers, and lately Traders—and that each oneness We may create must know of those who come from beyond heaven, lest their dangerous marvels turn into Our ruin.

Wherefore let Hands unite with Feet and Wings. Let the oneness once again recall and reflect on the journey of Cave Discoverer and Woe, in those days when the strangers, who had but single bodies and yet could talk, marched overmountain to an unknown battle. With every such reflection, as with every later encounter, i/we gain a little more insight, go a little further along the trail that leads to understanding them.

Though it may be that on that trail, We are traveling in a false direction. The unit who led them said on a certain night that he/she/it/? doubted if they understood themselves, or ever would.

I

The prison satellite swung in a wide and canted orbit around Llynathawr, well away from normal space traffic. Often a viewport in Hugh McCormac's cell showed him the planet in different phases. Sometimes it was a darkness, touched with red-and-gold sunrise on one edge, perhaps the city Catawrayannis flickering like a star upon its night. Sometimes it was a scimitar, the sun burning dazzlingly close. Now and then he saw it full, a round shield of brilliance, emblazoned on oceans azure with clouds argent above continents vert and tenné.

Terra looked much the same at the same distance. (Closer

6

in, you became aware that she was haggard, as is any former beauty who has been used by too many men.) But Terra was a pair of light-centuries removed. And neither world resembled rusty, tawny Aeneas for which McCormac's eyes hungered.

The satellite had no rotation; interior weight was due entirely to gravity-field generators. However, its revolution made heaven march slowly across the viewport. When Llynathawr and sun had disappeared, a man's pupils readjusted and he became able to see other stars. They crowded space, unwinking, jewel-colored, winter-sharp. Brightest shone Alpha Crucis, twin blue-white giants less than ten parsecs away; but Beta Crucis, a single of the same kind, was not much further off in its part of the sky. Elsewhere, trained vision might identify the red glimmers of Aldebaran and Arcturus. They resembled fires which, though remote, warmed and lighted the camps of men. Or vision might swing out to Deneb and Polaris, unutterably far beyond the Empire and the Empire's very enemies. That was a cold sight.

Wryness tugged at McCormac's mouth. *If Kathryn were tuned in on my mind,* he thought, *she'd say there must be something in Leviticus against mixing so many metaphors.*

He dared not let the knowledge of her dwell with him long. *I'm lucky to have an outside cell. Not uncomfortable, either. Surely this wasn't Snelund's intention.*

The assistant warden had been as embarrassed and apologetic as he dared. "We, uh, well, these are orders for us to detain you, Admiral McCormac," he said. "Direct from the governor. Till your trial or . . . transportation to Terra, maybe . . . uh . . . till further orders." He peered at the fax on his desk, conceivably hoping that the words it bore had changed since his first perusal. "Uh, solitary confinement, incommunicado—state-of-emergency powers invoked—Frankly, Admiral McCormac, I don't see why you aren't allowed, uh, books, papers, even projections to pass the time. . . . I'll send to His Excellency and ask for a change."

I know why, McCormac had thought. *Partly spite; mainly, the initial stage in the process of breaking me.* His back grew yet stiffer. *Well, let them try!*

The sergeant of the housecarl platoon that had brought the prisoner up from Catawrayannis Port said in his brassiest voice, "Don't address traitors by titles they've forfeited."

The assistant warden sat bolt upright, nailed them all with a look, and rapped: "Sergeant, I was twenty years in the Navy before retiring to my present job. I made CPO. Under His Majesty's regulations, any officer of Imperials ranks every

7

member of any paramilitary local force. Fleet Admiral McCormac may have been relieved of command, but unless and until he's decommissioned by a proper court-martial or by direct fiat from the throne, you'll show him respect or find yourself in worse trouble than you may already be in."

Flushed, breathing hard, he seemed to want to say more. Evidently he thought better of it. After a moment, during which a couple of the burly guards shifted from foot to foot, he added merely: "Sign the prisoner over to me and get out."

"We're supposed to—" the sergeant began.

"If you have written orders to do more than deliver this gentleman into custody, let's see them." Pause. "Sign him over and get out. I don't plan to tell you again."

McCormac placed the assistant warden's name and face in his mind as carefully as he had noted each person involved in his arrest. Someday—if ever—

What had become of the man's superior? McCormac didn't know. Off Aeneas, he had never been concerned with civilian crime or penology. The Navy looked after its own. Sending him here was an insult tempered only by the fact that obviously it was done to keep him away from brother officers who'd try to help him. McCormac guessed that Snelund had replaced a former warden with a favorite or a bribegiver—as he'd done to many another official since he became sector governor—and that the new incumbent regarded the post as a sinecure.

In any case, the admiral was made to exchange his uniform for a gray coverall; but he was allowed to do so in a booth. He was taken to an isolation cell; but although devoid of ornament and luxury, it had room for pacing and facilities for rest and hygiene. The ceiling held an audiovisual scanner; but it was conspicuously placed, and no one objected when he rigged a sheet curtain for his bunk. He saw no other being, heard no other voice; but edible food and clean fabrics came in through a valve, and he had a chute for disposal of scraps and soils. Above all else, he had the viewport.

Without that sun, planet, constellations, frosty rush of Milky Way and dim gleam of sister galaxies, he might soon have crumbled—screamed for release, confessed to anything, kissed the hand of his executioner, while honest medics reported to headquarters on Terra that they had found no sign of torture or brainscrub upon him. It would not have been the sensory deprivation *per se* that destroyed his will in such short order. It would have been the loss of every distraction from the thought of Kathryn, every way of guessing how long a time had gone by while she also lay in Aaron Sne-

8

lund's power. McCormac admitted the weakness to himself. That was not one he was ashamed of.

Why hadn't the governor then directed he be put in a blank cell? Oversight, probably, when more urgent business demanded attention. Or, being wholly turned inward on himself, Snelund perhaps did not realize that other men might love their wives above life.

Of course, as day succeeded standard day (with never a change in this bleak white fluorescence) he must begin wondering why nothing had happened up here. If his observers informed him of the exact situation, no doubt he would prescribe that McCormac be shifted to different quarters. But agents planted in the guard corps of a small artificial moon were lowly creatures. They would not, as a rule, report directly to a sector governor, viceroy for His Majesty throughout some 50,000 cubic light-years surrounding Alpha Crucis, and a *very* good friend of His Majesty to boot. No, they wouldn't even when the matter concerned a fleet admiral, formerly responsible for the defense of that entire part of the Imperial marches.

Petty agents would report to administrative underlings, who would send each communication on its way through channels. Was somebody seeing to it that material like this got—no, not lost—shunted off to oblivion in the files?

McCormac sighed. The noise came loud across endless whisper of ventilation, clack of his shoes on metal. How long could such protection last?

He didn't know the satellite's orbit. Nevertheless, he could gauge the angular diameter of Llynathawr pretty closely. He remembered the approximate dimensions and mass. From that he could calculate radius vector and thus period. Not easy, applying Kepler's laws in your head, but what else was there to do? The result more or less confirmed his guess that he was being fed thrice in 24 hours. He couldn't remember exactly how many meals had come before he started tallying them with knots in a thread. Ten? Fifteen? Something like that. Add this to the 37 points now confronting him. You got between 40 and 50 spaceship watches; or 13 to 16 Terran days; or 15 to 20 Aenean.

Aenean. The towers of Windhome, tall and gray, their banners awake in a whistling sky; tumble of crags and cliffs, reds, ochers, bronzes, where the Ilian Shelf plunged to a blue-gray dimness sparked and veined with watergleams, that was the Antonine Seabed; clangor of the Wildfoss as it hurled itself thitherward in cataracts; and Kathryn's laughter when

9

they rode forth, her gaze upon him more blue than the dazzlingly high sky—

"No!" he exclaimed. "Ramona's eyes had been blue. Kathryn's were green. Was he already confusing his live wife with his dead one?

If he had a wife any more. Twenty days since the housecarls burst into their bedchamber, arrested them and took them down separate corridors. She had slapped their hands off her wrists and marched among their guns with scornful pride, though tears rivered over her face.

McCormac clasped his hands and squeezed them together till fingerbones creaked. The pain was a friend. *I mustn't*, he recalled. *If I wring myself out because of what I can't make better, I'm doing Snelund's work for him.*

What else can I do?

Resist. Until the end.

Not for the first time, he summoned the image of a being he had once known, a Wodenite, huge, scaly, tailed, four-legged, saurian-snouted, but comrade in arms and wiser than most. "You humans are a kittle breed," the deep voice had rumbled. "Together you can show courage that may cross the threshold of madness. Yet when no one else is near to tell your fellows afterward how you died, the spirit crumbles away and you fall down empty."

"Heritage of instinct, I suppose," McCormac said. "Our race began as an animal that hunted in packs."

"Training can tame instinct," the dragon answered. "Can the intelligent mind not train itself?"

Alone in his cell, Hugh McCormac nodded. *I've at least got that damned monitor to watch me. Maybe someday somebody—Kathryn, or the children Ramona gave me, or some boy I never knew—will see its tapes.*

He lay down on his bunk, the sole furnishing besides washbasin and sanitizer, and closed his eyes. *I'll try playing mental chess again, alternating sides, till dinner. Give me enough time and I'll master the technique. Just before eating, I'll have another round of calisthenics. That drab mess in the soft bowl won't suffer from getting cold. Perhaps later I'll be able to sleep.*

He hadn't lowered his improvised curtain. The pickup recorded a human male, tall, rangy, more vigorous than could be accounted for by routine antisenescence. Little betrayed his 50 standard years except the grizzling of black hair and the furrows in his long, lean countenance. He had never changed those features, nor protected them from the weathers of many planets. The skin remained dark and leathery. A

10

jutting triangle of nose, a straight mouth and lantern jaw, were like counterweights to the dolichocephalic skull. When he opened the eyes beneath his heavy brows, they would show the color of glaciers. When he spoke, his voice tended to be hard; and decades of service around the Empire, before he returned to his home sector, had worn away the accent of Aeneas.

He lay there, concentrating so furiously on imagined chessmen which kept slipping about like fog-wraiths, that he did not notice the first explosion. Only when another went *crump!* and the walls reverberated did he know it was the second.

"What the chaos?" He surged to his feet.

A third detonation barked dully and toned in metal. *Heavy slugthrowers*, he knew. Sweat spurted forth. The heart slammed within him. What had happened? He threw a glance at the viewport. Llynathawr was rolling into sight, unmarked, serene, indifferent.

A rushing noise sounded at the door. A spot near its molecular catch glowed red, then white. Somebody was cutting through with a blaster. Voices reached McCormac, indistinct but excited and angry. A slug went *bee-yowww* down the corridor, gonged off a wall, and dwindled to nothing.

The door wasn't thick, just sufficient to contain a man. Its alloy gave way, streamed downward, made fantastic little formations akin to lava. The blaster flame boomed through the hole, enlarging it. McCormac squinted away from that glare. Ozone prickled his nostrils. He thought momentarily, crazily, *no reason to be so extravagant of charge.*

The gun stopped torching. The door flew wide. A dozen beings stormed through. Most were men in blue Navy outfits. A couple of them bulked robotlike in combat armor and steered a great Holbert energy gun on its grav sled. One was nonhuman, a Donarrian centauroid, bigger than the armored men themselves; he bore an assortment of weapons on his otherwise nude frame, but had left them holstered in favor of a battleax. It dripped red. His simian countenance was a single vast grin.

"Admiral! Sir!" McCormac didn't recognize the youth who dashed toward him, hands outspread. "Are you all right?"

"Yes. Yes. What—" McCormac willed out bewilderment. "What is this?"

The other snapped a salute. "Lieutenant Nasruddin Hamid, sir, commanding your rescue party by order of Captain Oliphant."

11

"Assaulting an Imperial installation?" It was as if somebody else used McCormac's larynx.

"Sir, they meant to kill you. Captain Oliphant's sure of it." Hamid looked frantic. "We've got to move fast, sir. We entered without loss. The man in charge knew about the operation. He pulled back most of the guards. He'll leave with us. A few disobeyed him and resisted. Snelund's men, must be. We cut through them but some escaped. They'll be waiting to send a message soon's our ships stop jamming."

The event was still unreal for McCormac. Part of him wondered if his mind had ripped across. "Governor Snelund was appointed by His Majesty," jerked from his gullet. "The proper place to settle things is a court of inquiry."

Another man trod forth. He had not lost the lilt of Aeneas. "Please, sir." He was near weeping. "We can't do without you. Local uprisin's on more planets every day—on ours, now, too, in Borea and Ironland. Snelund's tryin' to get the Navy to help his filthy troops put down the trouble . . . by his methods . . . by nuclear bombardment if burnin', shootin', and enslavin' don't work."

"War on our own people," McCormac whispered, "when outside the border, the barbarians—"

His gaze drifted back to Llynathawr, aglow in the port. "What about my wife?"

"I don't . . . don't know . . . anything about her—" Hamid stammered.

McCormac swung to confront him. Rage leaped aloft. He grabbed the lieutenant's tunic. "That's a lie!" he yelled. "You can't help knowing! Oliphant wouldn't send men on a raid without briefing them on every last detail. *What about Kathryn?*"

"Sir, the jamming'll be noticed. We only have a surveillance vessel. An enemy ship on picket could—"

McCormac shook Hamid till teeth rattled in the jaws. Abruptly he let go. They saw his face become a machine's. "What touched off part of the trouble was Snelund's wanting Kathryn," he said, altogether toneless. "The Governor's court likes its gossip juicy; and what the court knows, soon all Catawrayannis does. She's still in the palace, isn't she?"

The men looked away, anywhere except at him. "I heard that," Hamid mumbled. "Before we attacked, you see, we stopped at one of the asteroids—pretended we were on a routine relief—and sounded out whoever we could. One was a merchant, come from the city the day before. He said—well, a public announcement about you, sir, and your lady being 'detained for investigation,' only she and the governor—"

12

He stopped.

After a while, McCormac reached forth and squeezed his shoulder. "You needn't continue, son," he said, with scarcely more inflection but quite softly. "Let's board your ship."

"We aren't mutineers, sir," Hamid said pleadingly. "We need you to—to hold off that monster . . . till we can get the truth before the Emperor."

"No, it can't be called mutiny any longer," McCormac answered. "It has to be revolt." His voice whipped out. "Get moving! On the double!"

II

A metropolis in its own right, Admiralty Center lifted over that part of North America's Rocky Mountains which it occupied, as if again the Titans of dawn myth were piling Pelion on Ossa to scale Olympus. "And one of these days," Dominic Flandry had remarked to a young woman whom he was showing around, and to whom he had made that comparison in order to demonstrate his culture, "the gods are going to get as irritated as they did last time—let us hope with less deplorable results."

"What do you mean?" she asked.

Because his objective was not to enlighten but simply to seduce her, he had twirled his mustache and leered: "I mean that you are far too lovely for me to exercise my doomsmanship on. Now as for that plotting tank you wanted to see, this way, please."

He didn't tell her that its spectacular three-dimensional star projections were mainly for visitors. The smallest astronomical distance is too vast for any pictorial map to have much value. The real information was stored in the memory banks

13

of unpretentious computers which the general public was not allowed to look on.

As his cab entered the area today, Flandry recalled the little episode. It had terminated satisfactorily. But his mind would not break free of the parallel he had not uttered.

Around him soared many-tinted walls, so high that fluoropanels must glow perpetually on the lower levels, a liana tangle of elevated ways looping between them, the pinnacles crowned with clouds and sunlight. Air traffic swarmed and glittered in their sky, a dance too dense and complex for anything but electronic brains to control; and traffic pulsed among the towers, up and down within them, deep into the tunnels and chambers beneath their foundations. Those cars and buses, airborne or ground, made barely a whisper; likewise the slideways; and a voice or a footfall was soon lost. Nevertheless, Admiralty Center stood in a haze of sound, a night-and-day hum like a beehive's above an undergroundish growling, the noise of its work.

For here was the nexus of Imperial strength; and Terra ruled a rough sphere some 400 light-years across, containing an estimated four million suns, of which a hundred thousand were in one way or another tributary to her.

Thus far the pride. When you looked behind it, though—

Flandry emerged from his reverie. His cab was slanting toward Intelligence headquarters. He took a hasty final drag on his cigaret, pitched it in the disposer, and checked his uniform. He preferred the dashing dress version, with as much elegant variation as the rather elastic rules permitted, or a trifle more. However, when your leave has been cancelled after a mere few days Home, and you are ordered to report straight to Vice Admiral Kheraskov, you had better arrive in plain white tunic and trousers, the latter not tucked into your half-boots, and belt instead of sash, and simple gray cloak, and bonnet cocked to bring its sunburst badge precisely over the middle of your forehead.

Sackcloth and ashes would be more appropriate, Flandry mourned. *Three, count 'em, three gorgeous girls, ready and eager to help me celebrate my birth week, starting tomorrow at Everest House with a menu I spent two hours planning; and we'd've continued as long as necessary to prove that a quarter century is less old than it sounds. And now this!*

A machine in the building talked across seething communications to a machine in the cab. Flandry was deposited on the fiftieth-level parking flange. The gravs cut out. He lent his card to the meter, which transferred credit and unlocked the door for him. A marine guard at the entrance verified his

14

identity and appointment with the help of another machine and let him through. He passed down several halls on his way to the lift shaft he wanted. Restless, he walked in preference to letting a strip carry him.

Crowds moved by and overflowed the offices. Their members ranged from junior technicians to admirals on whose heads might rest the security of a thousand worlds and scientists who barely kept the Empire afloat in a universe full of lethal surprises. By no means all were human. Shapes, colors, words, odors, tactile sensations when he brushed against a sleeve or an alien skin, swirled past Flandry in endless incomprehensible patterns.

Hustle, bustle, hurry, scurry, run, run, run, said his glumness. *Work, for the night is coming—the Long Night, when the Empire goes under and the howling peoples camp in its ruins. Because how can we remain forever the masters, even of our insignificant spatter of stars, on the fringe of a galaxy so big we'll never know a decent fraction of it? Probably never more than this sliver of one spiral arm that we've already seen. Why, better than half the suns, just in the microbubble of space we claim, have not been visited once!*

Our ancestors explored further than we in these years remember. When hell cut loose and their civilization seemed about to fly into pieces, they patched it together with the Empire. And they made the Empire function. But we . . . we've lost the will. We've had it too easy for too long. And so the Merseians on our Betelgeusean flank, the wild races everywhere else, press inward. . . . Why do I bother? Once a career in the Navy looked glamorous to me. Lately I've seen its backside. I could be more comfortable doing almost anything else.

A woman stopped him. She must be on incidental business, because civilian employees here couldn't get away with dressing in quite such a translucent wisp of rainbow. She was constructed for it. "I beg your pardon," she said. "Could you tell me how to find Captain Yuan-Li's office? I'm afraid I'm lost."

Flandry bowed. "Indeed, my lady." He had reported in there on arrival at Terra, and now directed her. "Please tell him Lieutenant Commander Flandry said he's a lucky captain."

She fluttered her lashes. "Oh, sir." Touching the insigne on his breast, a star with an eye: "I noticed you're in Intelligence. That's why I asked you. It must be fascinating. I'd love to—"

Flandry beamed. "Well, since we both know friend Yuan-Li—"

They exchanged names and addresses. She departed, wagging her tail. Flandry continued. His mood was greatly lightened. *After all, another job might prove boring.* He reached his upbound point. *Here's where I get the shaft.* Stepping through the portal, he relaxed while the negagrav field lifted him.

Rather, he tried to relax, but did not succeed a hundred percent. Attractive women or no, a new-made lieutcom summoned for a personal interview with a subchief of operations is apt to find his tongue a little dry and his palms a little wet.

Catching a handhold, he drew himself out on the ninety-seventh level and proceeded down the corridor. Here dwelt a hush; the rare soft voices, the occasional whirr of a machine, only deepened for him the silence between these austere walls. What persons he met were of rank above his, their eyes turned elsewhere, their thoughts among distant suns. When he reached Kheraskov's suite of offices, the receptionist was nothing but a scanner and talkbox hooked to a computer too low-grade to be called a brain. More was not needed. Everybody unimportant got filtered out at an earlier stage. Flandry cooled his heels a mere five minutes before it told him to proceed through the inner door.

The room beyond was large, high-ceilinged, lushly carpeted. In one corner stood an infotriever and an outsize vidiphone, in another a small refreshment unit. Otherwise there were three or four pictures, and as many shelves for mementos of old victories. The rear wall was an animation screen; at present it held an image of Jupiter seen from an approaching ship, so vivid that newcomers gasped. He halted at an expanse of desktop and snapped a salute that nearly tore his arm off. "Lieutenant Commander Dominic Flandry, reporting as ordered, sir."

The man aft of the desk was likewise in plain uniform. He wore none of the decorations that might have blanketed his chest, save the modest jewel of knighthood that was harder to gain than a patent of nobility. But his nebula and star outglistened Flandry's ringed planet. He was short and squat, with tired pugdog features under bristly gray hair. His return salute verged on being sloppy. But Flandry's heartbeat accelerated.

"At ease," said Vice Admiral Sir Ilya Kheraskov. "Sit down. Smoke?" He shoved forward a box of cigars.

"Thank you, sir." Flandry collected his wits. He chose a cigar and made a production of starting it, while the chair

16

fitted itself around his muscles and subtly encouraged them to relax. "The admiral is most kind. I don't believe a better brand exists than Corona Australis." In fact, he knew of several: but these weren't bad. The smoke gave his tongue a love bite and curled richly by his nostrils.

"Coffee if you like," offered the master of perhaps a million agents through the Empire and beyond. "Or tea or jaine."

"No, thanks, sir."

Kheraskov studied him, wearily and apologetically; he felt X-rayed. "I'm sorry to break your furlough like this, Lieutenant Commander," the admiral said. "You must have been anticipating considerable overdue recreation. I see you have a new face."

They had never met before. Flandry made himself smile. "Well, yes, sir. The one my parents gave me had gotten monotonous. And since I was coming to Terra, where biosculp is about as everyday as cosmetics—" He shrugged.

Still that gaze probed him. Kheraskov saw an athlete's body, 184 centimeters tall, wide in the shoulders and narrow in the hips. From the white, tapered hands you might guess how their owner detested the hours of exercise he must spend in maintaining those cat-supple thews. His countenance had become straight of nose, high of cheekbones, cleft of chin. The mobile mouth and the eyes, changeable gray beneath slightly arched brows, were original. Speaking, he affected a hint of drawl.

"No doubt you're wondering why your name should have been plucked off the roster," Kheraskov said, "and why you should have been ordered straight here instead of to your immediate superior or Captain Yuan-Li."

"Yes, sir. I didn't seem to rate your attention."

"Nor were you desirous to." Kheraskov's chuckle held no humor. "But you've got it." He leaned back, crossed stumpy legs and bridged hairy fingers. "I'll answer your questions.

"First, why you, one obscure officer among tens of similar thousands? You may as well know, Flandry, if you don't already—though I suspect your vanity has informed you—to a certain echelon of the Corps, you aren't obscure. You wouldn't hold the rank you've got, at your age, if that were the case. No, we've taken quite an interest in you since the Starkad affair. That had to be hushed up, of course, but it was not forgotten. Your subsequent assignment to surveillance had intriguing consequences." Flandry could not totally suppress a tinge of alarm. Kheraskov chuckled again; it sounded like iron chains. "We've learned things that *you*

17

hushed up. Don't worry . . . yet. Competent men are so heartbreakingly scarce these days, not to mention brilliant ones, that the Service keeps a blind eye handy for a broad range of escapades. You'll either be killed, young man, or you'll do something that will force us to step on you, or you'll go far indeed."

He drew breath before continuing: "The present business requires a maverick. I'm not letting out any great secret when I tell you the latest Merseian crisis is worse than the government admits to the citizens. It could completely explode on us. I think we can defuse it. For once, the Empire acted fast and decisively. But it demands we keep more than the bulk of our fleets out on that border, till the Merseians understand we mean business about not letting them take over Jihannath. Intelligence operations there have reached such a scale that the Corps is sucked dry of able field operatives elsewhere.

"And meanwhile something else has arisen, on the opposite side of our suzerainty. Something potentially worse than any single clash with Merseia." Kheraskov lifted a hand. "Don't imagine you're the only man we're sending to cope, or that you can contribute more than a quantum to our effort. Still, stretched as thin as we are, every quantum is to be treasured. It was your bad luck but the Empire's good luck . . . maybe . . . that you happened to check in on Terra last week. When I asked Files who might be available with the right qualifications, your reel was among a dozen that came back."

Flandry waited.

Kheraskov rocked forward. The last easiness dropped from him. A grim and bitter man spoke: "As for why you're reporting directly to me—this is one place where I know there isn't any spybug, and you are one person I think won't backstab me. I told you we need a maverick. I tell you in addition, you could suck around the court and repeat what I'm about to say. I'd be broken, possibly shot or enslaved. You'd get money, possibly a sycophant's preferment. I have to take the chance. Unless you know the entire situation, you'll be useless."

Flandry said with care, "I'm a skilled liar, sir, so you'd better take my word rather than my oath that I'm not a very experienced buglemouth."

"Ha!" Kheraskov sat quiet for several seconds. Then he jumped to his feet and started to pace back and forth, one fist hammering into the other palm. The words poured from him:

"You've been away. After Starkad, your visits to Terra

18

were for advanced training and the like. You must have been too busy to follow events at court. Oh, scandal, ribald jokes, rumor, yes, you've heard those. Who hasn't? But the meaningful news—Let me brief you.

"Three years, now, since poor old Emperor Georgios died and Josip III succeeded. Everybody knows what Josip is: too weak and stupid for his viciousness to be highly effective. We all assumed the Dowager Empress will keep him on a reasonably short leash while she lives. And he won't outlast her by much, the way he treats his organism. And he won't have children—not him! And the Policy Board, the General Staff, the civil service, the officers corps, the Solar and extra-Solar aristocracies . . . they hold more crooks and incompetents than they did in former days, but we have a few good ones left, a few. . . .

"I've told you nothing new, have I?" Flandry barely had time to shake his head. Kheraskov kept on prowling and talking. "I'm sure you made the same quiet evaluation as most informed citizens. The Empire is so huge that no one individual can do critical damage, no matter if he's theoretically all-powerful. Whatever harm came from Josip would almost certainly be confined to a relative handful of courtiers, politicians, plutocrats, and their sort, concentrated on and around Terra—no great loss. We've survived other bad Emperors.

"A logical judgment. Correct, no doubt, as far as it went. But it didn't go far enough. Even we who're close to the seat of power were surprised by Aaron Snelund. Ever hear of him?"

"No, sir," Flandry said.

"He kept out of the media," Kheraskov explained. "Censorship's efficient on this planet, if nothing else is. The court knew about him, and people like me did. But our data were incomplete.

"Later you'll see details. I want to give you the facts that aren't public. He was born 34 years ago on Venus, mother a prostitute, father unknown. That was in Sub-Lucifer, where you learn ruthlessness early or go down. He was clever, talented, charming when he cared to be. By his mid-teens he was a sensie actor here on Terra. I can see by hindsight how he must have planned, investigated Josip's tastes in depth, sunk his money into just the right biosculping and his time into acquiring just the right mannerisms. Once they met, it went smooth as gravitation. By the age of 25, Aaron Snelund had gone from only another catamite to the Crown Prince's favorite. His next step was to ease out key people and obtain their offices for those who were beholden to Snelund.

19

"It roused opposition. More than jealousy. Honest men worried about him becoming the power behind the crown when Josip succeeded. We heard mutters about assassination. I don't know if Josip and Snelund grew alarmed or if Snelund foresaw the danger and planned against it. At any rate, they must have connived.

"Georgios died suddenly, you recall. The following week Josip made Snelund a viscount and appointed him governor of Sector Alpha Crucis. Can you see how well calculated that was? Elevation to a higher rank would have kicked up a storm, but viscounts are a millo a thousand. However, it's sufficient for a major governorship. Many sectors would be too rich, powerful, close to home, or otherwise important. The Policy Board would not tolerate a man in charge of them who couldn't be trusted. Alpha Crucis is different."

Kheraskov slapped a switch. The fluoros went off. The breathtaking view of Jupiter, huge and banded among its moons, vanished. A trikon of the principal Imperial stars jumped into its place. Perhaps Kheraskov's rage demanded that he at least have something to point at. His blocky form stood silhouetted against a gem-hoard.

"Betelgeuse." He stabbed one finger at a red spark representing the giant sun which dominated the borderlands between the Terran and Merseian empires. "Where the war threat is. Now, Alpha Crucis."

His hand swept almost 100 degrees counterclockwise. The other hand turned a control, swinging the projection plane about 70 degrees south. Keenly flashed the B-type giants at that opposite end of Terra's domain, twinned Alpha and bachelor Beta of the Southern Cross. Little showed beyond them except darkness. It was not that the stars did not continue as richly strewn in those parts; it was that they lay where Terra's writ did not run, the homes of savages and of barbarian predators who had too soon gotten spacecraft and nuclear weapons; it was that they housed darkness.

Kheraskov traced the approximately cylindrical outline of the sector. "Here," he said, "is where war could really erupt."

Flandry dared say into the shadowed silence which followed, "Does the admiral mean the wild races are going to try a fresh incursion? But sir, I understood they were well in check. After the battle of—uh—I forget its name, but wasn't there a battle—"

"Forty-three years ago." Kheraskov sagged in the shoulders. "Too big, this universe," he said tiredly. "No one brain, no one species can keep track of everything. So we let the bad seed grow unnoticed until too late.

20

"Well." He straightened. "It was hard to see what harm Snelund could do yonder that was worth provoking a constitutional crisis to forestall. The region's as distant as they come among ours. It's not highly productive, not densely populated; its loyalty and stability are no more doubtful than most. There are only two things about it that count. One's the industrial rogue planet Satan. But that's an ancient possession of the Dukes of Hermes. They can be trusted to protect their own interests. Second is the sector's position as the shield between us and various raiders. But that means defense is the business of the fleet admiral; and we have—had—a particularly fine man in that post, one Hugh McCormac. You've never heard of him, but you'll get data.

"Of course Snelund would grow fat. What of it? A cento or two per subject per year, diverted from Imperial taxes, won't hurt any individual so badly he'll make trouble. But it will build a fortune to satisfy any normal greed. He'd retire in time to a life of luxury. Meanwhile the Navy and civil service would do all the real work as usual. Everyone was happy to get Snelund that cheaply off Terra. It's the kind of solution which has been reached again and again."

"Only this time," Flandry said lazily, "they forgot to allow for a bugger factor."

Kheraskov switched the map off, the fluoros on, and gave him a hard look. Flandry's return glance was bland and deferential. Presently the admiral said, "He left three years ago. Since then, increasing complaints have been received of extortion and cruelty. But no single person saw enough of those reports to stir action. And if he had, what could he do? You don't run an interstellar realm from the center. It isn't possible. The Imperium is hardly more than a policeman, trying to keep peace internal and external. Tribes, countries, planets, provinces are autonomous in most respects. The agony of millions of sentient beings, 200 light-years away, doesn't register on several trillion other sophonts elsewhere, or whatever the figure is. It can't. And we've too much else to worry about anyway.

"Think, though, what a governor of a distant region, who chose to abuse his powers, might do."

Flandry did, and lost his lightness.

"McCormac himself finally sent protests to Terra," Kheraskov plodded on. "A two-star admiral can get through. The Policy Board began talking about appointing a commission to investigate. Almost immediately after, a dispatch came from Snelund himself. He'd had to arrest McCormac for conspiracy to commit treason. He can do that, you know, and select an interim high commander. The court-martial must be held on a Naval base or vessel, by officers of suitable rank. But with this Merseian crisis— Do you follow me?"

"Too damn well." Flandry's words fell muted.

"Provincial rebellions aren't unheard of," Kheraskov said. "We can less afford one today than we could in the past."

He had stood looking down at the younger man, across his desk. Turning, he stared into the grand vision of Jupiter that had come back. "The rest you can find in the data tapes," he said.

"What do you want me to do . . . sir?"

"As I told you, we're sending what undercover agents we can spare, plus a few inspectors. With all that territory to deal with, they'll take long to compile a true picture. Perhaps fatally long. I want to try something in between also. A man who can nose around informally but openly, with authorizations to flash when needed. The master of a warship, posted to Llynathawr as a reinforcement, has standing. Governor Snelund, for instance, has no ready way of refusing to see him. At the same time, if she's not a capital ship, her skipper isn't too blazing conspicuous."

"But I've never had a command, sir."

"Haven't you?"

Tactfully, Kheraskov did not watch while the implications of that question sank in. He proceeded: "We've found an escort destroyer whose captain is slated for higher things. The record says she has an able executive officer. That should free your attention for your true job. You'd have gotten a ship eventually, in the normal course of grooming you and testing your capabilities. We like our field operatives to have a broad background."

Not apt to be many broads in my background for a while, passed through the back of Flandry's mind. He scarcely noticed or cared. Excitement bayed in him.

Kheraskov sat down again. "Go back to your place," he said. "Pack up and check out. Report at 1600 hours to Rear Admiral Yamaguchi. He'll provide you with quarters, tapes, hypnos, synapse transforms, stimpills, every aid you need. And you will need them. I want your information to be as complete as mine, inside 48 hours. You will then report to Mars Prime Base and receive your brevet commission as a full commander. Your ship is in Mars orbit. Departure will be immediate. I hope you can fake the knowledge of her you don't have, until you've gathered it.

"If you acquit yourself well, we'll see about making that temporary rank permanent. If you don't, God help you and maybe God help me. Good luck, Dominic Flandry."

III

The third stop *Asieneuve* made on her way to Llyna-thawr was her final one. Flandry recognized the need for haste. In straight-line, flat-out hyperdrive his vessel would have taken slightly worse than two weeks to make destination. Perhaps he should have relied on records and interviews after he arrived. On the other hand, he might not be given the chance, or Snelund might have found ways to keep the truth off his headquarters planet. The latter looked feasible, therefore plausible. And Flandry's orders granted him latitude. They instructed him to report to Llynathawr and place himself under the new high command of Sector Alpha Crucis "with maximum expedition and to the fullest extent consistent with your fact-finding assignment." A sealed letter from Kheraskov authorized him to detach his ship and operate independently; but that must not be produced except in direst need, and he'd have to answer for his actions.

He compromised by making spot checks in three randomly chosen systems within Snelund's bailiwick and not too far off his course. It added an extra ten days. Two globes were human-colonized. The habitable planet of the third sun was Shalmu.

So it was called in one of the languages spoken by its most technologically advanced civilization. Those communities had been in a bronze age when men discovered them. Influenced by sporadic contacts with traders, they went on to iron and, by now, a primitive combustion-powered technology which was spreading their hegemony across the world. The process

23

was slower than it had been on Terra; Shalmuans were less ferocious, less able to treat their fellow beings like vermin or machinery, than humankind is.

They were happy to come under the Empire. It meant protection from barbarian starfarers, who had already caused them grief. They did not see the Naval base they got. It was elsewhere in the system. Why risk a living planet, if matters came to a local fight, when a barren one served equally well? But there was a small marine garrison on Shalmu, and spacemen visited it on leave, and this attracted a scattering of Imperial civilians, who traded with the autochthons as readily as with service personnel. Shalmuans found employment among these foreigners. A few got to go outsystem. A smaller but growing number were recommended for scholarships by Terran friends, and returned with modern educations. The dream grew of entering civilization as a full-fledged member.

In return, Shalmu paid modest taxes in kind: metals, fuels, foodstuffs, saleable works of art and similar luxuries, depending on what a particular area could furnish. It accepted an Imperial resident, whose word was the ultimate law but who in practice let native cultures fairly well alone. His marines did suppress wars and banditry as far as practicable, but this was considered good by most. The young Imperials, human or nonhuman, often conducted themselves arrogantly, but whatever serious harm they might inflict on an innocent Shalmuan resulted, as a rule, in punishment.

In short, the planet was typical of the majority that had fallen under Terran sway. Backward, they had more to gain than lose; they saw mainly the bright side of the Imperial coin, which was not too badly tarnished.

Or so the case had been till a couple of years ago.

Flandry stood on a hill. Behind him were five men, bodyguards from his crew. Beside him was Ch'kessa, Prime in Council of the Clan Towns of Att. Ch'kessa's home community sprawled down the slope, a collection of neat, whitewashed, drum-shaped houses where several thousand individuals lived. Though peaked, each sod roof was a flower garden, riotous with color. The ways between houses were "paved" with a tough mossy growth, except where fruit trees grew from which anyone might help himself when they bore and no one took excessively. Pastures and cultivated fields occupied the valley beneath. On its other side, the hills were wooded.

Apart from somewhat weaker gravity, Shalmu was terrestroid. Every detail might be strange, but the overall effect spoke to ancient human instincts. Broad plains, tall moun-

24

tains, spindrift across unrestful seas; rustling sun-flecked shadows in a forest, unexpected sweetness of tiny white blossoms between old roots; the pride of a great horned beast, the lonesome cries descending from migratory wings; and the people. Ch'kessa's features were not so different from Flandry's. Hairless bright-green skin, prehensile tail, 140-centimeter height, details of face, foot, hand, interior anatomy, exoticism of his embroidered wraparound and plumed spirit wand and other accouterments—did they matter?

The wind shifted. On planets like this, the air had always seemed purer than anywhere on Terra, be it in the middle of a nobleman's enormous private park. Away from machines, you drew more life into your lungs. But Flandry gagged. One of his men must suddenly vomit.

"That is why we obeyed the new resident," Ch'kessa said. He spoke fluent Anglic.

Down the hill, lining a valleyward road, ran a hundred wooden crosses. The bodies lashed to them had not finished rotting. Carrion birds and insects still made black clouds around them, under a wantonly brilliant summer sky.

"Do you see?" Ch'kessa asked anxiously. "We did refuse at first. Not the heavy taxes the new resident laid on us. I am told he did that throughout the world. He said it was to pay for meeting a terrible danger. He did not say what the danger was. However, we paid, especially after we heard how bombs were dropped or soldiers came with torches where folk protested. I do not think the old resident would have done that. Nor do I think the Emperor, may his name echo in eternity, would let those things happen if he knew."

Actually, Flandry did not answer, *Josip wouldn't give a damn. Or maybe he would. Maybe he'd ask to see films of the action, and watch them and giggle.* The wind changed again, and he blessed it for taking away part of the charnel odor.

"We paid," Ch'kessa said. "That was not easy, but we remember the barbarians too well. Then this season a fresh demand was put before us. We, who had powder rifles, were to supply males. They would be flown to lands like Yanduvar, where folk lack firearms. There they would catch natives for the slave market. I do not understand, though I have often asked. Why does the Empire, with many machines, need slaves?"

Personal service, Flandry did not answer. *For instance, the sort women supply. We use enslavement as one kind of criminal penalty. But it isn't too significant. There isn't that big a percentage of slaves in the Empire. The barbarians, though,*

25

would pay well for skilled hands. And transactions with them do not get into any Imperial records for some officious computer to come upon at a later date.

"Continue," he said aloud.

"The Council of the Clan Towns of Att debated long," Ch'kessa said. "We were afraid. Still, the thing was not right for us to do. At length we decided to make excuses, to delay as much as might be, while messengers sped overland to Iscoyn. There the Imperial marine base is, as my lord well knows. The messengers would appeal to the commandant, that he intercede for us with the resident."

Flandry caught a mutter behind him: "Nova flash! Is he saying the marines hadn't been enforcing the decrees?"

"Yeh, sure," growled an adjacent throat. "Forget your barroom brawls with 'em. They wouldn't commit vileness like this. Mercenaries did it. Now dog your hatch before the Old Man hears you."

Me? Flandry thought in stupid astonishment. *Me, the Old Man?*

"I suppose our messengers were caught and their story twisted from them," Ch'kessa sighed. "At least, they never returned. A legate came and told us we must obey. We refused. Troops came. They herded us together. A hundred were chosen by lot and put on the crosses. The rest of us had to watch till all were dead. It took three days and nights. One of my daughters was among them." He pointed. His arm was not steady. "Perhaps my lord can see her. That quite small body, eleventh on our left. It is black and swollen, and much of it has fallen off, but she used to come stumping and laughing to meet me when I returned from work. She cried for me to help her. The cries were many, yet I heard hers. Whenever I moved toward her, a shock beam stopped me. I had not thought there could be happiness in seeing her die. We were instructed to leave the bodies in place, on pain of bombing. An aircraft flies over from time to time to make sure."

He sat down in the whispering silvery pseudograss, put face on knees and tail across neck. His fingers plucked at the dirt. "After that," he said, "we went slaving."

Flandry stood silent for a space. He had been furious at the carnage being inflicted by the more advanced Shalmuans on the weaker ones. Swooping down on a caravan of chained prisoners, he had arrested its leader and demanded an explanation. Ch'kessa had suggested they flit to his homeland.

"Where are your villagers?" Flandry asked at length, for the houses stood empty, smokeless, silent.

"They cannot live here with those dead," Ch'kessa replied. "They camp out, coming back only to maintain. And doubtless they fled when they saw your boat, my lord, not knowing what you would do." He looked up. "You have seen. Are we deeply to blame? Will you return me to my gang? A sum is promised each of us for each slave we bring in. It is helpful in meeting the tax. I will not get mine if I am absent when the caravan reaches the airfield."

"Yes." Flandry turned. His cloak swirled behind him. "Let's go."

Another low voice at his back: "I never swallowed any brotherhood-of-beings crap, you know that, Sam'l, but when our own xenos are scared by a vessel of ours—!"

"Silence," Flandry ordered.

The gig lifted with a yell and trailed a thunderbolt across half a continent and an ocean. Nobody spoke. When she tilted her nose toward jungle, Ch'kessa ventured to say, "Perhaps you will intercede for us, my lord."

"I'll do my best," Flandry said.

"When the Emperor hears, let him not be angry with us of the Clan Towns. We went unwillingly. We sicken with fevers and die from the poisoned arrows of the Yanduvar folk."

And wreck what was a rather promising culture, Flandry thought.

"If punishment must be for what we have done, let it fall on me alone," Ch'kessa begged. "That does not matter greatly after I watched my little one die."

"Be patient," Flandry said. "The Emperor has many peoples who need his attention. Your turn will come."

Inertial navigation had pinpointed the caravan, and a mere couple of hours had passed since. Flandry's pilot soon found it, trudging down a swale where ambush was less likely than among trees. He landed the gig a kilometer off and opened the airlock.

"Farewell, my lord." The Shalmuan knelt, coiled his tail around Flandry's ankles, crawled out and was gone. His slim green form bounded toward his kin.

"Return to the ship," Flandry instructed.

"Doesn't the captain wish to pay a courtesy call on the resident?" asked the pilot sarcastically. He was not long out of the Academy. His hue remained sick.

"Get aloft, Citizen Willig," Flandry said. "You know we're on an information-gathering mission and in a hurry. We didn't notify anyone except Navy that we'd been on Starport or New Indra, did we?"

The ensign sent hands dancing across the board. The gig

27

stood on its tail with a violence that would have thrown everybody into the stern were it not for acceleration compensators. "Excuse me, sir," he said between his teeth. "A question, if the captain pleases. Haven't we witnessed outright illegality? I mean, those other two planets were having a bad time, but nothing like this. Because the Shalmuans have no way to get a complaint off their world, I suppose. Isn't our duty, sir, to report what we've seen?"

Sweat glistened on his forehead and stained his tunic beneath the arms. Flandry caught an acrid whiff of it. Glancing about, he saw the other four men leaning close, straining to hear through the throb of power and whistle of cloven atmosphere. *Should I answer?* he asked himself, a touch frantically. *And if so, what can I tell him that won't be bad for discipline? How should I know? I'm too young to be the Old Man!*

He gained time with a cigaret. Stars trod forth in viewscreens as the gig entered space. Willig exchanged a signal with the ship, set the controls for homing on her, and swiveled around to join in staring at his captain.

Flandry sucked in smoke, trickled it out, and said cautiously: "You have been told often enough, we are first on a fact-finding mission, second at the disposal of Alpha Crucis Command if we can help without prejudice to the primary assignment. Whatever we learn will be duly reported. If any man wishes to file additional material or comment, that's his privilege. However, you should be warned that it isn't likely to go far. And this is not because inconvenient facts will be swept under the carpet," *though I daresay that does happen on occasion.* "It's due to the overwhelming volume of data."

He gestured. "A hundred thousand planets, gentlemen, more or less," he said. "Each with its millions or billions of inhabitants, its complexities and mysteries, its geographies and civilizations, their pasts and presents and conflicting aims for the future, therefore each with its own complicated, ever-changing, unique set of relationships to the Imperium. We can't control that, can we? We can't even hope to comprehend it. At most, we can try to maintain the Pax. At most, gentlemen.

"What's right in one place may be wrong in another. One species may be combative and anarchic by nature, another peaceful and antlike, a third peaceful and anarchic, a fourth a bunch of aggressive totalitarian hives. I know a planet where murder and cannibalism are necessary to race survival: high radiation background, you see, making for high mutation rate coupled with chronic food shortage. The unfit must

28

be eaten. I know of intelligent hermaphrodites, and sophonts with more than two sexes, and a few that regularly change sex. They all tend to look on our reproductive pattern as obscene. I could go on for hours. Not to mention the variations imposed by culture. Just think about Terran history.

"And then the sheer number of individuals and interests; the sheer distance; the time needed to get a message across our territory— No, we can't direct everything. We haven't the manpower. And if we did, it'd remain physically impossible to coordinate that many data.

"We've *got* to give our proconsuls wide discretion. We've *got* to let them recruit auxiliaries, and hope those auxiliaries will know the local scene better than Imperial regulars. Above all, gentlemen, for survival if nothing else, we've *got* to preserve solidarity."

He waved a hand at the forward viewscreen. Alpha Crucis blazed lurid among the constellations; but beyond it— "If we don't stick together, we Terrans and our nonhuman allies," he said, "I assure you, either the Merseians or the wild races will be delighted to stick us separately."

He got no reply: not that he expected one. *Was that a sufficiently stuffy speech?* he wondered.

And was it sufficiently truthful?

I don't know about that last. Nor do I know if I have any right to inquire.

His ship swam into sight. The tiny spindle, well-nigh lost beside the vast glowing bulk of the planet she circled, grew to a steel barracuda, guns rakish across the star clouds. She was no more than an escort destroyer, she had speed but was lightly armed, her crew numbered a bare fifty. Nevertheless, she was Flandry's first official command and his blood ran a little faster each time he saw her—even now, even now.

The gig made a ragged approach. Willig probably didn't feel well yet. Flandry refrained from commenting. The last part of the curve, under computer choreography, was better. When the boat housing had closed and repressurized, he dismissed his guards and went alone to the bridge.

Halls, companionways, and shafts were narrow. They were painted gray and white. With the interior grav generators set for full Terran weight, thin deckplates resounded under boots, thin bulkheads cast the noise back and forth, voices rang, machinery droned and thumped. The air that gusted from ventilator grilles came fresh out of the renewers, but somehow it collected a faint smell of oil on the way. The officers' cabins were cubbyholes, the forecastle could be packed tighter only if the Pauli exclusion principle were repealed, the

29

recreation facilities were valuable chiefly as a subject for jokes, and the less said about the galley the wiser. But she was Flandry's first command.

He had spent many hours en route reading her official history and playing back tapes of former logbooks. She was a few years older than him. Her name derived from a land mass on Ardèche, which was apparently a human-settled planet though not one he had ever chanced upon mention of. (He knew the designation Asieneuve in different versions on at least four worlds; and he speculated on how many other Continent-class vessels bore it. A name was a mere flourish when computers must deal with millions of craft by their numbers.) She had gone on occasional troopship convoy when trouble broke loose on a surface somewhere. Once she had been engaged in a border incident; her captain claimed a probably hit but lacked adequate proof. Otherwise her existence had been routine patrols . . . which were essential, were they not?

You didn't salute under these conditions. Men squeezed themselves aside to make way for Flandry. He entered the bridge. His executive officer had it.

Rovian of Ferra was slightly more than human size. His fur was velvet at midnight. His ponderous tail, the claws on his feet and fingers, the saber teeth in his jaws, could deal murderous blows; he was also an expert marksman. The lower pair of his four arms could assist his legs at need. Then his silent undulant gait turned into lightning. He habitually went nude except for guns and insignia. His nature and nurture were such that he would never become a captain and did not want to be. But he was capable and well liked, and Terran citizenship had been conferred on him.

"S-s-so?" he greeted. His fangs handicapped him a little in speaking Anglic.

Alone, he and Flandry didn't bother to be formal. Mankind's rituals amused him. "Bad," the master said, and explained.

"Why bad?" Rovian asked. "Unless it provokes revolt."

"Never mind the morals of it. You wouldn't understand. Consider the implications, however."

Flandry inhaled a cigaret to lighting. His gaze sought Shalmu's disc, where it floated unutterably peaceful in its day and night. "Why should Snelund do this?" he said. "It's considerable trouble, and not without hazard. Ordinary corruption would earn him more than he could live to spend on himself. He must have a larger purpose, one that requires moonsful of money. What is it?"

30

Rovian erected the chemosensor antennae that flanked the bony ridge on his skull. His muzzle twitched, his eyes glowed yellow. "To finance an insurrection? He may hope to become an independent overlord."

"M-m-m . . . no . . . doesn't make sense, and I gather he's not stupid. The Empire can't conceivably tolerate breakaways. He'd have to be crushed. If necessary, Josip would be deposed to clear the track for that operation. No, something else—" Flandry brought his attention back. "Get patrol clearance for us to go in half an hour. Next rendezvous, Llynathawr."

Hyperdrive vibrations are instantaneous, though the philosophers of science have never agreed on the meaning of that adjective. Unfortunately, they damp out fast. No matter how powerful, a signal cannot be received beyond a distance of about one light-year. Thus spaceships traveling at quasivelocity are not detectable by their "wakes" at any farther remove than that. Neither are the modulations that carry messages quicker than light; and the uncertainty principle makes it impossible to relay them with any hope that they will not soon degenerate into gibberish.

Accordingly, *Asieneuve* was within two hours of her goal before she got the news. Fleet Admiral Hugh McCormac had escaped to the Virgilian System. There he had raised the standard of rebellion and proclaimed himself Emperor. An unspecified number of planets had declared for him. So had an unspecified proportion of the ships and men he formerly commanded. Armed clashes had taken place and full civil war looked inevitable.

IV

~~~~~~~~~~

When the Empire purchased Llynathawr from its Cynthian discoverers, the aim had been to strengthen this frontier by attracting settlers. Most of the world was delightful in climate and scenery, rich in natural resources, wide in unclaimed lands. Navy sector headquarters were close enough, on Ifri, and housed enough power to give ample protection. Not all the barbarians were hostile; there existed excellent possibilities of trade with a number of races—especially those that had not acquired spacecraft—as well as with Imperial planets.

Thus far the theory. Three or four generations showed that practice was something else again. The human species appeared to have lost its outward urge. Few individuals would leave a familiar, not too uncomfortable environment to start over in a place remote from government-guaranteed security and up-to-date entertainment. Those who did usually preferred city to rural life. Nor did many arrive from the older colonies nearby, like Aeneas. Such people had struck their own roots.

Catawrayannis did become a substantial town: two million, if you counted in the floating population. It became the seat of the civil authority. It became a brisk mart, though much of the enterprise was carried on by nonhumans, and a pleasure resort, and a regional listening post. But that was the end of the process. The hinterland, latifundia, mines, factories, soon gave way to forests, mountains, trafficless oceans, empty plains, a wilderness where lights gleamed rare and lonely after dark.

Of course, this has the advantage of not turning the planet as a whole into still another cesspool, Flandry thought. After

32

reporting, he had donned mufti and spent a few days incognito. Besides sounding out various bourgeoisie and servants, he had passed through a particularly ripe Lowtown.

And now I feel so respectable I creak, his mind went on. *Contrast? No, not when I'm about to meet Aaron Snelund.* His pulse quickened. He must make an effort to keep his face and bearing expressionless. That skill he owed less to official training than to hundreds of poker games.

As a ramp lifted him toward an impressive portico, he glanced back. The gubernatorial palace crowned a high hill. It was a big pastel-tinted structure in the dome-and-colonnade style of the last century. Beneath its gardens, utilitarian office buildings for civil servants made terraces to the flatland. Homes of the wealthy ringed the hill. Beyond these, more modest residences blended gradually into cropground on the west side, city on the east. Commercial towers, none very tall, clustered near the Luana River, past which lay the slums. A haze blurred vision today and the breeze blew cool, tasting of spring. Vehicles moved insectlike through streets and sky. Their sound came as a whisper, almost hidden in the sough of trees. It was hard to grasp that Catawrayannis brawled with preparation for war, shrilled with hysteria, tensed with fear—

—until a slow thundering went from horizon to horizon, and a spatial warcraft crossed heaven on an unknown errand.

Two marines flanked the main entrance. "Please state your name and business, sir," one demanded. He didn't aim his slug-thrower, but his knuckles stood white on butt and barrel.

"Commander Dominic Flandry, captain, HMS *Asieneuve*, here for an appointment with His Excellency."

"A moment, please." The other marine checked. He didn't merely call the secretarial office, he turned a scanner on the newcomer. "All right."

"If you'll leave your sidearm with me, sir," the first man said. "And, uh, submit to a brief search."

"Hey?" Flandry blinked.

"Governor's orders, sir. Nobody who doesn't have a special pass with full physical ID goes through armed or unchecked." The marine, who was pathetically young, wet his lips. "You understand, sir. When Navy units commit treason, we . . . who dare we trust?"

Flandry looked into the demoralized countenance, surrendered his blaster, and allowed hands to feel across his whites.

A servant appeared, bowed, and escorted him down a corridor and up a gravshaft. The décor was luxurious, its bad taste more a question of subtly too much opulence than of

33

garish colors or ugly proportions. The same applied to the chamber where Flandry was admitted. A live-fur carpet reached gold and black underfoot; iridescences swept over the walls; dynasculps moved in every corner; incense and low music tinged the air; instead of an exterior view, an animation of an Imperial court masquerade occupied one entire side; behind the governor's chair of state hung a thrice life-size, thrice flattering portrait of Emperor Josip, fulsomely inscribed.

Four mercenaries were on guard, not human but giant shaggy Gorzunians. They stirred scarcely more than their helmets, breastplates, or weapons.

Flandry saluted and stood at attention.

Snelund did not look diabolical. He had bought himself an almost girlish beauty: flame-red wavy hair, creamy skin, slightly slanted violet eyes, retroussé nose, bee-stung lips. Though not tall, and now growing paunchy, he retained some of his dancer's gracefulness. His richly patterned tunic, flare-cut trousers, petal-shaped shoes, and gold necklace made Flandry envious.

Rings sparkled as he turned a knob on a memoscreen built into the chair arm. "Ah, yes. Good day, Commander." His voice was pleasant. "I can give you fifteen minutes." He smiled. "My apologies for such curtness, and for your having to wait this long to see me. You can guess how hectic things are. If Admiral Pickens had not informed me you come directly from Intelligence HQ, I'm afraid you'd never have gotten past my office staff." He chuckled. "Sometimes I think they're overzealous about protecting me. One does appreciate their fending off as many bores and triviators as possible— though you'd be surprised, Commander, how many I cannot escape seeing—but occasionally, no doubt, undue delay is caused a person with a valid problem."

"Yes, Your Excellency. Not to waste your time—"

"Do sit down. It's good to meet someone straight from the Mother of us all. We don't even get frequent mail out here, you know. How fares old Terra?"

"Well, Your Excellency, I was only there a few days, and quite busy most of them." Flandry seated himself and leaned forward. "About my assignment."

"Of course, of course," Snelund said. "But grant me a moment first." His geniality was replaced by an appearance of concern. His tone sharpened. "Have you fresh news of the Merseian situation? We're as worried about that as anyone in the Empire, despite our own current difficulties. Perhaps more worried than most. Transfer of units to that border has

34

gravely weakened this. Let war break out with Merseia, and we could be depleted still further—an invitation to the barbarians. That's why McCormac's rebellion must be suppressed immediately, no matter the cost."

Flandry realized: *I'm being stalled.* "I know nothing that isn't public, sir," he said at a leisured rate. "I'm sure Ifri HQ gets regular couriers from the Betelgeusean marches. The information gap is in the other direction, if I may use a metaphor which implies that gaps aren't isotropic."

Snelund laughed. "Well spoken, Commander. One grows starved for a little wit. Frontiers are traditionally energetic but unimaginative."

"Thank you, Your Excellency," Flandry said. "I'd better state my business, though. Will the governor bear with me if I sound long-winded? Necessary background . . . especially since my assignment is indefinite, really just to prepare a report on whatever I can learn. . . ."

Snelund lounged back. "Proceed."

"As a stranger to these parts," Flandry said pompously, "I had to begin with studying references and questioning a broad spectrum of people. My application for an interview with you, sir, would have been cancelled had it turned out to be needless. For I do see how busy you are in this crisis. As matters developed, however, I found I'd have to make a request of you. A simple thing, fortunately. You need only issue an order."

"Well?" Snelund invited.

He's relaxed now, Flandry judged: *takes me for the usual self-important favorite nephew, going through a charade to furnish an excuse for my next promotion.*

"I would like to interview the Lady McCormac," he said.

Snelund jerked upright where he sat.

"My information is that she was arrested together with her husband and has been detained in Your Excellency's personal custody," Flandry said with a fatuous smile. "I'm sure she has a good many valuable data. And I've speculated about using her as a go-between. A negotiated settlement with her husband—"

"No negotiation with a traitor!" Snelund's fist smote a chair arm.

How dramatic, Flandry thought. Aloud: "Pardon me, sir. I didn't mean he should get off scot free, simply that—Well, anyhow, I was surprised to discover no one has questioned the Lady McCormac."

Snelund said indignantly, "I know what you've heard. They gossip around here like a gaggle of dirty-minded old women.

35

I've explained the facts to Admiral Pickens' chief Intelligence officer, and I'll explain them again to you. She appears to have an unstable personality, worse even than her husband's. Their arrest threw her into a completely hysterical condition. Or 'psychotic' might not be too strong a word. As a humane gesture, I put her in a private room rather than a cell. There was less evidence against her than him. She's quartered in my residential wing because that's the sole place where I can guarantee her freedom from bumbling interruptions. My agents were preparing to quiz McCormac in depth when his fellow criminals freed him. His wife heard, and promptly attempted suicide. My medical staff has had to keep her under heavy sedation ever since."

Flandry had been told otherwise, though no one dared give him more than hearsay. "I beg the governor's pardon," he said. "The admiral's staff suggested perhaps I, with a direct assignment, might be allowed where they aren't."

"Their men have met her twice, Commander. In neither case was she able to testify."

No, it isn't hard to give a prisoner a shot or a touch of brainshock, when you have an hour or two advance notice. "I see, Your Excellency. And she hasn't improved?"

"She's worsened. On medical advice, I've banned further visits. What could the poor woman relate, anyway?"

"Probably nothing, Your Excellency. However, you'll appreciate, sir, I'm supposed to make a full report. And as my ship will soon be leaving with the fleet," *unless I produce my authority to detach her,* "this may be my lone chance. Couldn't I have a few minutes, to satisfy them on Terra?"

Snelund bristled. "Do you doubt my word, Commander?"

"Oh, no, Your Excellency! Never! This is strictly *pro forma.* To save my, uh, reputation, sir, because they'll ask why I didn't check this detail also. I could go there straight from here, sir, and your medics could be on hand to keep me from doing any harm."

Snelund shook his head. "I happen to know you would. I forbid it."

Flandry gave him a reproachful stare.

Snelund tugged his chin. "Of course, I sympathize with your position," he said, trading a scowl for a slight smile. "Terra is so far away that our reality can only come through as words, photographs, charts. Um-m-m. . . . Give me a number where you can be contacted on short notice. I'll have my chief doctor inform you when you can go to her. Some days she's more nearly sane than others, though at best she's incoherent. Will that do?"

36

"Your Excellency is most kind," Flandry beamed.

"I don't promise she'll be available before you depart," Snelund cautioned. "Small time remains. If not, you can doubtless see her on your return. Though that will hardly be worth the trouble, will it, after McCormac has been put down?"

"*Pro forma*, Your Excellency," Flandry repeated.

The governor recorded a memorandum, including a phone exchange which would buck a message on to *Asieneuve*, and Flandry took his leave with expressions of mutual esteem.

He got a cab outside the palace and made sure he was heard directing it to the shuttleport. It was no secret that he'd been on the ground these past several days; his job required that. But the fainéant impression he wanted to give would be reinforced if he took the first excuse to return to his vessel. Ascetical though his cabin there might be, it was a considerable improvement on the flea circus dormitory which was the best planetside quarters a late arrival like him had been able to obtain. Catawrayannis was overflowing at the hatches with spacemen and marines, as ship after ship made rendezvous.

"Why here?" he had asked Captain Leclerc, the member of Admiral Pickens' staff to whom he actually reported. "Ifri is HQ."

Leclerc shrugged. "The governor wants it this way."

"But he can't—"

"He can, Flandry. I know, the Naval and civilian provincial commands are supposed to be coordinate. But the governor is the Emperor's direct representative. As such, he can invoke Imperial authority when he wants. It may get him into the kettle on Terra afterward, but that's afterward. On the spot, the Navy had better heed him."

"Why the order, though? Ifri has the main facilities. It's our natural center and starting point."

"Well, yes, but Llynathawr doesn't have Ifri's defenses. By our presence, we guard against any revengeful raids McCormac may plan. It makes a degree of sense, even. Knocking out the sector capital—or preferably occupying it—would put him a long way toward control of the entire region. Once we get started, he'll be too busy with us to think about that, although naturally we will leave some protection." Leclerc added cynically: "While they wait, our men on liberty will enjoy a good, expensive last fling. Snelund's careful to stay popular in Catawrayannis."

"Do you really think we should charge out for an immediate full-dress battle?"

"Governor's directive again, I hear. It certainly doesn't fit

37

Admiral Pickens' temperament. Left alone, I'm convinced he'd see what could be done first by dickering and small-scale shooting . . . rather than maybe end up bombarding Imperial worlds into radioactive rubbish. But the word is, we've got to blast the infection before it spreads." Leclerc grimaced. "You're an insidious one. I've no business talking like this. Let's take up your business!"

—When he stepped out at the terminal, Flandry received the not unexpected information that he must wait a couple of hours for a seat on a ferry to Satellite Eight, where he could summon his gig. He phoned the dormitory and had his luggage shunted to him. Since this consisted merely of one handbag, already packed, he didn't bother to check it, but carried it along into a refresher booth. From there he emerged in drab civvies, with a hooded cloak and slouching gait and bag turned inside out to show a different color. He had no real reason to think he had been followed, but he believed in buying insurance when it was cheap. He took a cab to an unpretentious hotel, thence another into Lowtown. The last few blocks he walked.

Rovian had found a rooming house whose clientele were mostly nonhumans: unchoosy ones. He shared his kennel with a betentacled hulk from an unpronounceable planet. The hulk reeked of exuded hydrogen sulfide but was personally decent enough; among other sterling qualities, it did not know the Eriau language. It rippled on its bunk when Flandry entered, mushed an Anglic greeting, and returned to contemplation of whatever it contemplated.

Rovian stretched all six limbs and yawned alarmingly. "At last!" he said. "I thought I would rot."

Flandry sat down on the floor, which carried no chairs, and lit a cigaret more against the stench than because he wanted one. "How goes the ship?" he asked in the principal Merseian tongue.

"Satisfactorily," Rovian answered likewise. "Some were curious at the exec absenting himself before the captain returned. But I passed it off as needful to our supplying and left Valencia in charge. Nothing can really happen while we idle in orbit, so no great comment followed."

Flandry met the slit-pupilled eyes. *You seem to know more about what your human shipmates think than a xeno should,* he did not say. *I don't pretend to understand what goes on in your brain. But . . . I have to rely on somebody. Sounding you out while we traveled, as well as might be, I decided you're least improbably the one.*

"I didn't ask you to locate a den, and tell me where, and

38

wait, for sport," he declared with the explicitness required by Eriau grammar. "My idea was that we'd need privacy for laying plans. That's been confirmed."

Rovian cocked his ears.

Flandry described his session with the governor. He finished: "No reasonable doubt remains that Snelund is lying about Lady McCormac's condition. Gossip leaks through guards and servants, out of the private apartments and into the rest of the palace. Nobody cares, aside from malicious amusement. He's packed the court, like the housecarls and the residencies, with his own creatures. Snooping around, getting sociable with people off duty, I led them to talk. Two or three of them got intoxicated till they said more than they would have normally." He didn't mention the additives he had slipped into their drinks.

"Why don't the regular Intelligence officers suspect?" Rovian inquired.

"Oh, I imagine they do. But they have so much else to deal with, so obviously vital. And they don't think she can tell anything useful. And why collide with the governor, risking your career, for the sake of the arch-rebel's wife?"

"You wish to," Rovian pounced.

"*Kraich.*" Flandry squinted into the smoke he was blowing. It curled blue-gray across what sunlight straggled through a window whose grime seemed of geologic age. The rotten-egg gas was giving him a headache, unless that was due to the general odor of decay. Faintly from outside came traffic rumble and an occasional raucous cry.

"You see," he explained, "I'm on detached service. My nose isn't committed to any of the numberless grindstones which must be turned before a Naval expedition can get under way. And I have more background on Aaron Snelund than provincial officers do, even in my own corps and in his own preserve. I've been free and able to sit and wonder. And I decided it wasn't logical he should keep Kathryn McCormac locked away simply for the purpose the court is sniggering about. The admiral's staff may think so, and not care. But I doubt if he's capable of feeling more than a passing attraction for any fellow creature. Why not turn her over for interrogation? She might know a little something after all. Or she might be handy in dealing with her husband."

"Scarcely that," Rovian said. "His life is already forfeit."

"Uh-huh. Which is why my harried colleagues didn't check further. But—oh, I can't predict—her, in exchange for various limited concessions on his part—her, persuading him to give up—Well, I suppose it takes a cold-blooded bastard like

39

me to consider such possibilities. The point is, we can't lose by trying her out, and might gain a trifle. Therefore we ought to. But Snelund is holding her back with a yarn about her illness. Why? What's in it for him, besides herself? His sector's being torn apart. Why isn't he more cooperative in this tiny matter?"

"I couldn't say." Rovian implied indifference.

"I wonder if she may not know something he would prefer didn't get out," Flandry said. "The assumption has been that Snelund may be a bad governor, but he is loyal and Mc-Cormac's the enemy. It's only an assumption."

"Should you not then invoke the authority in your second set of orders, and demand her person?"

Flandry made a face. "Huh! Give them five minutes of stalling at the gate, and I'll be presented with a corpse. Or ten minutes under a misused hypnoprobe could produce a memoryless idiot. Wherefore I walked very softly indeed. I don't expect to be summoned before the fleet leaves, either."

"And on our return—"

"She can easily have 'passed away' during the campaign."

Rovian tautened. The bunk where he crouched made a groaning noise. "You tell me this for a purpose, captain," he said.

Flandry nodded. "How did you guess?"

Again Rovian waited, until the man sighed and proceeded:

"I think we can spring her loose, if we time it exactly right. You'll be here in town, with some crewmen you've picked and an aircar handy. An hour or so before the armada accelerates, I'll present my sealed orders to the admiral and formally remove us from his command. It's a safe bet Snelund's attention will be on the fleet, not on the palace. You'll take your squad there, serve a warrant I'll have given you, and collect Kathryn McCormac before anybody can raise the governor and ask what to do. If need be, you can shoot; whoever tries to stop you will be in defiance of the Imperium. But I doubt the necessity will arise if you work fast. I'll have the gig waiting not too far off. You and your lads flit Lady McCormac there, haul gravs for space, rendezvous with *Asieneuve,* and we'll depart this system in a hurry."

"The scheme appears hazardous," Rovian said, "and for slight probable gain."

"It's all I can think of," Flandry answered. "I know you'll be getting the operative end of the reamer. Refuse if you think I'm a fool."

Rovian licked his saber teeth and switched his tail. "I do

not refuse my captain," he said, "I, a Brother of the Oath. It does seem to me that we might discuss the problem further. I believe your tactics could be made somewhat more elegant."

V

Ship by ship, Pickens' forces departed orbit and moved outward. When the sun of Llynathawr had shrunk to a bright point, the vessels assumed formation and went into hyperdrive. Space swirled with impalpable energies. As one, the warcraft and their ministrants aimed themselves at the star called Virgil, to find the man who would be Emperor.

They were not many. Reassignments, to help confront Merseia, had depleted the sector fleet. A shocking number of units had subsequently joined McCormac. Of those which stayed true, enough must remain behind to screen—if not solidly guard—the key planets. It was estimated that the rebels had about three-fourths the strength that Pickens would be able to bring to bear on them. Given nuclear-headed missiles and firebeams powered by hydrogen fusion, such numerical comparisons are less meaningful than the layman thinks. A single penetration of defenses can put a ship out of action, often out of existence.

On that account, Pickens traveled cautiously, inside a wide-flung net of scoutboats. His fastest vessels could have covered the distance in a day and a half, his slowest in twice that time; but he planned on a whole five days. He had not forgotten the trap his former commander sprang on the Valdotharian corsairs.

And on the bridge of *Asieneuve*, Dominic Flandry leaned forward in his control chair and said: "Twenty degrees north, four degrees clockwise, 3000 kilometers negative, then match quasi-velocities and steady as she goes."

"Aye, sir." The pilot repeated the instructions and programmed the computer that operated the hyperdrive.

Flandry kept his attention on the console before him, whose meters and readouts summarized the far more complex data with which the pilot dealt, until he dared say, "Can you hold this course, Citizen Rovian?"

In point of fact, he was asking his executive officer if the destroyer was moving as planned—tagging along after the fleet in order that her wake be drowned in many and that she thus be hidden from pursuit. They both knew, and both knew the master's ritual infallibility must be preserved. Rovian studied the board and said, "Aye, sir," with complete solemnity.

Flandry opened the general intercom. "Now hear this," he intoned. "Captain to all officers and crew. You are aware that our ship has a special mission, highly confidential and of the utmost importance. We are finally embarked on it. For success, we require absolute communications silence. No messages will be received except by Lieutenant Commander Rovian or myself, nor will any be sent without my express authorization. When treason has infected His Majesty's very Navy, the danger of subversion and of ruses must be guarded against." *How's that for casuistry?* he grinned within. "The communications officer will set his circuits accordingly. Carry on."

He switched off. His gaze lifted to the simulacrum of heaven projected on the viewscreens. No spacecraft showed. The greatest of them was lost in immensity, findable only by instruments and esoteric calculations. The stars ignored them, were not touched by the wars and pains of life, were immortal—*No, not that either. They have their own Long Night waiting for them.*

"Outercom circuits ready, sir," Rovian announced after a study of the main panel. He slipped on a headband receiver. Every incoming signal would go there, to be heard by him alone.

"Take the bridge, then." Flandry rose. "I'll interrogate the prisoner. When the time comes to change vectors, notify me immediately but don't wait for me to arrive before you do it."

What he really told Rovian was: Monitor transmissions. Snelund's bound to yell when he learns what's happened. If we're out of hyperwave range by that time, he'll probably send a boat after us. Either way, he'll demand our return, and Pickens might well give in. That could make a delicate situation. The minute it looks like coming about, we're to

42

sheer off and get the devil away. I'd rather be able to prove by the log that I never could have received any order from Pickens, than try to make a court-martial agree I was right in disregarding it.

But those two alone knew the code. Possibly the ratings who had gone to the palace with their exec could have guessed. No matter there. They were tough and close-mouthed and, after what they had seen en route from Terra, callously cheerful about any inconvenience they might have caused His Excellency.

"Aye, sir," said Rovian.

Flandry went down a companionway and along a throbbing passage to his cabin. The door had no chime. He knocked.

"Who is it?" The voice that came through the thin panel was a husky contralto, singingly accented—and how tired, how empty!

"Captain, my lady. May I come in?"

"I can't stop you."

Flandry stepped through and closed the door behind him. His cabin had room for little more than a bunk, a desk and chair, a closet, some shelves and drawers. His bonnet brushed the overhead. A curtain hid a washbasin, toilet, and shower stall. He'd had no chance to install many personal possessions. The sound and vibration and oily-electrical odor of the ship filled the air.

He had not even seen a picture of Kathryn McCormac. Suddenly everything else dissolved around him. He thought afterward he must have given her a courtly bow, because he found his bonnet clutched in his fingers, but he couldn't remember.

She was five standard years older than him, he knew, and in no Terran fashion of beauty. Her figure was too tall, too wide-shouldered and deep-bosomed, too firmly muscled beneath a skin that was still, after her imprisonment, too sun-tanned. The face was broad: across the high cheekbones, between the luminous eyes (gold-flecked green under thick black brows), in the blunt nose and generous mouth and strong chin. Her hair was banged over her forehead, bobbed below her ears, thick and wavy, amber with shadings of gold and copper. She wore the brief nacreous gown and crystaflex sandals in which she had been taken from the palace.

Mother looked sort of like her, Flandry realized.

He hauled his wits back in. "Welcome aboard, my lady." He could feel his smile was a touch unstable. "Permit me to

43

introduce myself." He did. "Entirely at your service," he finished, and held out his hand.

She did not give him hers, either to shake or kiss, nor did she rise from his chair. He observed the darknesses around and behind her eyes, hollowing of cheeks, faint dusting of freckles. . . . "Good day, Commander." Her tone was not warm or cold or anything.

Flandry lowered his bunk and himself onto it. "What may I offer you?" he asked. "We have the regular assortment of drinks and drugs. And would you like a bite to eat?" He extended his opened cigaret case.

"Nothin'."

He regarded her. *Stop skyhooting, son. You've been celibate unrightfully long. She's handsome and*—he dragged it forth—*no doubt you speculated about her possible availability . . . after what's happened to her. Forget it. Save your villainies for the opposition.*

He said slowly: "You don't want to accept hospitality from the Imperium. Correct? Please be sensible, my lady. You know you'll take nourishment to stay alive, as you did in Snelund's house. Why not begin now? My cause isn't necessarily irreconcilable with yours. I had you fetched here, at some risk, intending that we'd discuss matters."

She turned her head. Their glances locked. After a while that seemed lengthy, he saw part of the tension go from her. "Thanks, Commander," she said. Did her lips flutter the ghostliest bit upward? "Coffee and a sandwich 'ud taste well, for truth."

Flandry got on the intercom to the galley. She refused a cigaret but said she didn't mind if he smoked. He inhaled several times before he said, fast:

"I'm afraid an escort destroyer leaves something to be desired in the way of accommodations. You'll have this cabin, of course. I'll move in with the mates; one of them can throw a pad on the deck. But I'll have to leave my clothes and so forth where they are. I hope the steward and I won't disturb you too badly, trotting in and out. You can take your meals here or in the wardroom, as you prefer. I'll see you get some spare coveralls or whatever to wear—sorry I didn't think to lay in a female outfit—and I'll clear a drawer to keep them in. À propos which—" he rose and opened one in his desk—"I'll leave this unlocked. It has the nonsecret items. Including a souvenir of mine." He took out a Merseian war knife. "Know how to handle this cheap and chippy chopper? I can demonstrate. It's not much use if you get in the way of a bullet, a blast, a stun beam, et cetera. But you'd be surprised what it can do at close quarters." Again he caught her gaze. "Do be careful with it, my lady," he said low. "You've nothing to fear on my ship. The situation might alter. But I'd hate to think you'd gotten reckless with my souvenir and bowed out of the universe when there was no real need."

The breath hissed between her teeth. Color and pallor chased each other across her face. The hand she reached out for the knife wavered. She let it fall, raised it back to her eyes, clenched the remaining fist, and fought not to weep.

Flandry turned his back and browsed through a full-size copy of a translated *Genji Monogatori* that he'd brought along to pass the time. The snack arrived. When he had closed the door on the messman and set the tray on his desk, Kathryn McCormac was her own captain again.

"You're a strider, sir," she told him. He cocked his brows. "Aenean word," she explained. "A strong, good man . . . let me say a gentleman."

He stroked his mustache. "A gentleman manqué, perhaps." He sat back down on the bunk. Their knees brushed. "No business discussion over food. Abominable perversion, that." She flinched. "Would you care for music?" he asked hastily. "My tastes are plebeian, but I've been careful to learn what's considered high art." He operated a selector. *Eine Kleine Nachtmusik* awoke in joy.

"That's beautiful," she said when she had finished eating. "Terran?"

"Pre-spaceflight. There's a deal of antiquarianism in the inner Empire these days, revival of everything from fencing to allemands—uh, sport with swords and a class of dances. Wistfulness about eras more picturesque, less cruel and complicated. Not that they really were, I'm sure. It's only that their troubles are safely buried."

"And we've yet to bury ours." She drained her cup and clashed it down on the bare plate. "If they don't shovel us under first. Let's talk, Dominic Flandry."

"If you feel up to it." He started a fresh cigaret.

"I'd better. Time's none too long 'fore you must decide what to do 'bout me." The dark-blonde head lifted. "I feel 'freshed. Liefer attack my griefs than slump."

"Very well, my lady." *Wish I had a pretty regional accent.*

"Why'd you rescue me?" she asked gently.

He studied the tip of his cigaret. "Wasn't quite a rescue," he said.

Once more the blood left her countenance. "From Aaron Snelund," she whispered, "anything's a rescue."

"Bad?"

45

"I'd've killed myself, come the chance. Didn't get it. So I tried to keep sane by plannin' ways to kill him." She strained her fingers against each other until she noticed she was doing so. "Hugh's habit," she mumbled, pulled her hands free and made them both into fists.

"You may win a little revenge." Flandry sat straight. "Listen my lady. I'm a field agent in Intelligence. I was dispatched to investigate Sector Alpha Crucis. It occurred to me you could tell things that nobody else would. That's why you're here. Now I can't officially take your unsupported word, and I won't use methods like hypnoprobing to squeeze the facts out against your will. But if you lie to me, it's worse than if you keep silence. Worse for us both, seeing that I want to help you."

Steadiness had returned to her. She came of a hardy breed. "I'll not lie," she promised. "As to whether I'll speak at all . . . depends. Is it truth what I heard, my man's in revolt?"

"Yes. We're trailing a fleet whose mission is to defeat the rebels, seize and occupy the planets that support them—which includes your home, my lady."

"And you're with the Imperialists?"

"I'm an officer of the Terran Empire, yes."

"So's Hugh. He . . . he never wanted . . . anything but the good of the race—every race everywhere. If you'd think the matter through, I 'spect you yourself 'ud—"

"Don't count on that, my lady. But I'll listen to whatever you care to tell me."

She nodded. "I'll speak what I know. Afterward, when I'm stronger, you can give me a light 'probe and be sure I'm not swittlin'. I believe I can trust you'll use the machine just for confirmation, not for pryin' deeper."

"You can."

In spite of her sorrow, Flandry felt excitement sharpen each sense and riot in his blood. *By Pluto's single icy ball, I am on a live trail!*

She chose words and uttered them, in a flat tone but with no further hesitation. As she spoke, her face congealed into a mask.

"Hugh never planned any treason. I'd've known. He got me cleared for top security so we could also talk together 'bout his work. Sometimes I'd give him an idea. We were both murderin' mad over what Snelund's goons were doin'. Civilized worlds like Aeneas didn't suffer worse'n upratcheted taxes at first. Later, bit by bit, we saw fines, confiscations, political arrests—more and more—and when a secret police was officially installed— But that was mild compared

46

to some of the backward planets. *We* had connections, we could eventu'ly raise a zoosny on Terra, even if Snelund was a pet of the Emperor's. Those poor primitives, though—

"Hugh wrote back. To start with, he got reprimands for interferin' with civilian affairs. But gradu'ly the seriousness of his charges must've percolated through the bureaucracy. He started gettin' replies from the High Admiralty, askin' for more exact information. That was by Naval courier. We couldn't trust the mails any longer. He and I spent this year collectin' facts—depositions, photographs, audits, everything needed to make a case nobody could overlook. We were goin' to Terra in person and deliver the microfile.

"Snelund got wind. We'd taken care, but we were amateurs at sneakery, and you can't dream how poisonous horrible 'tis, havin' secret police 'round, never knowin' when you dare talk free. . . . He wrote offici'ly askin' Hugh to come discuss plans for defendin' the outermost border systems. Well, they had been havin' trouble, and Hugh's not a man who could leave without doin' something for them. I was more scared than him of a bounceplay, but I went along. We always stayed close together, those last days. I did tip the hand to Hugh's chief aide, one of my family's oldest friends, Captain Oliphant. He should stand alert in case of treachery.

"We stayed at the palace. Normal for high-rankin' visitors. Second night, as we were 'bout to turn in, a detachment of militia arrested us.

"I was taken to Snelund's personal suite. Never mind what came next. After a while, though, I noticed he could be gotten to boast. No need for pretendin' I'd changed my mind 'bout him. Contrary: he liked to see me hurtin'. But that was the way to play, then. Show hurt at the right times. I didn't really think I'd ever pass on what he told me. He said I'd leave with my mind scrubbed out of my brain. But hope— How glad I am now for grabbin' that one percent of hope!"

She stopped. Her eyes were reptile dry and did not appear to see Flandry.

"I never imagined he intended his gubernatorial antics for a full-time career," the man said, most softly. "What's his plan?"

"Return. Back to the throne. And become the puppeteer behind the Emperor."

"Hm. Does His Majesty know this?"

"Snelund claimed the two've them plotted it before he left, and've kept in touch since."

Flandry felt a sting. His cigaret had burned down to his fingers. He chucked it into the disposer and started a new

47

one. "I hardly believe our lord Josip has three brain cells to click together," he murmured. "He might have a pair, that occasionally impact soggily. But of course, brother Snelund will have made our lord feel like a monstrous clever fellow. That's part of the manipulation."

She noticed him then. "You said that?"

"If you report me, I could get broken for *lèse majesté*," Flandry admitted. "Somehow I doubt you will."

"Surely not! 'Cause you—" She checked herself.

He thought: *I didn't mean to lead her up any garden paths. But it seems I did, if she thinks maybe I'll join her man's pathetic revolt. Well, it'll make her more cooperative, which serves the Cause, and happier for a few days, if that's doing her any favor.* He said:

"I can see part of the machinery. The Emperor wants dear Aaron back. Dear Aaron points out that this requires extracting large sums from Sector Alpha Crucis. With those, he can bribe, buy elections, propagandize, arrange events, maybe purchase certain assassinations . . . till he has a Policy Board majority on his side.

"*Ergo,* word gets passed from the throne to various powerful, handpicked men. The facts about Snelund's governorship are to be suppressed as much as possible, the investigation of them delayed as long as possible and hampered by every available trick when finally it does roll. Yes. I'd begun to suspect it on my own hook."

He frowned. "But a scandal of these dimensions can't be concealed forever," he said. "Enough people will resign themselves to having Snelund for a gray eminence that his scheme will work—*unless* they understand what he's done out here. Then they might well take measures, if only because they fear what he could do to them.

"Snelund isn't stupid, worse luck. Maybe no big, spectacular warriors or statesmen can topple him. But a swarm of drab little accountants and welfare investigators isn't that easily fended off. He must have a plan for dealing with them too. What is it?"

"Civil war," she answered.

"Huh?" Flandry dropped his cigaret.

"Goad till he's got a rebellion," she said bleakly. "Suppress it in such a way that no firm evidence of anything remains.

"He'd soonest not have this fleet win a clear victory. A prolonged campaign, with planets comin' under attack, would give him his chaos free. But s'posin', which I doubt, your admiral can beat Hugh at a stroke, there'll still be 'pacification' left for his mercenaries, and they'll have their instructions how to go 'bout it.

"Afterward he'll disband them, 'long with his overlord corps. He recruited from the scum of everywhere else in the Empire, and they'll scatter back through it and vanish automatic'ly. He'll blame the revolt on subversion, and claim to be the heroic leader who saved this frontier."

She sighed. "Oh, yes," she finished, "he knows there'll be loose ends. But he doesn't 'spect they'll be important: 'speci'ly as he reckons to supply a lot of them himself."

"A considerable risk," Flandry mused. "But Krishna, what stakes!"

"The Merseian crisis was a grand chance," Kathryn McCormac said. "Attention bent yonder and most of the local fleet gone. He wanted Hugh out of the way 'cause Hugh was dangerous to him, but also 'cause he hoped this'd clear the path for tormentin' Aeneas till Aeneas rose and touched off the fission. Hugh was more'n chief admiral for the sector. He's Firstman of Ilion, which puts him as high on the planet as anybody 'cept the resident. Our Cabinet could only name him an 'expert advisor' under the law, but toward the end he was Speaker in everything save title and led its resistance to Snelund's tools. And Aeneas has tradition'ly set the tone for all human colonies out here, and a good many nonhumans besides."

Life flowed back. Her nostrils flared. "Snelund never looked, though, for havin' Hugh to fight!"

Flandry ground the dropped butt under his heel. Presently he told her, "I'm afraid the Imperium cannot allow a rebellion to succeed, regardless of how well-intentioned."

"But they'll know the truth," she protested.

"At best, they'll get your testimony," he said. "You had a bad time. Frequent drugging and brain-muddling, among other things, right?" He saw her teeth catch her lip. "I'm sorry to remind you, my lady, but I'd be sorrier to leave you in a dream that's due to vaporize. The mere fact that you believe you heard Snelund tell you these schemes does not prove one entropic thing. Confusion—paranoia—deliberate planting of false memories by agents who meant to discredit the governor—any smart advocate, any suborned psychiatrist, could rip your story to ions. You wouldn't carry it past the first investigator screening witnesses for a court of inquiry."

She stared at him as if he had struck her. "Don't you believe me?"

"I want to," Flandry said. "Among other reasons, because your account indicates where and how to look for evidence that can't be tiddlywinked away. Yes, I'll be shooting message capsules with coded dispatches off to various strategic destinations."

"Not goin' home yourself?"

"Why should I, when my written word has better odds of being taken seriously than your spoken one? Not that the odds are much to wager on." Flandry marshalled his thoughts. They were reluctant to stand and be identified. "You see," he said slowly, "bare assertions are cheap. Solid proofs are needed. A mountain of them, if you're to get anywhere against an Imperial favorite and the big men who stand to grow bigger by supporting him. And . . . Snelund is quite right . . . a planet that's been fought over with modern weapons isn't apt to have a worthwhile amount of evidence left on it. No, I think this ship's best next move is to Aeneas."

"What?"

"We'll try a parley with your husband, my lady. I hope you can talk him into quitting. Then afterward they may turn up what's required for the legal frying of Aaron Snelund."

VI

The star Virgil is type F7, slightly more massive than Sol, half again as luminous, with a higher proportion of ultraviolet in its emission. Aeneas is the fourth of its planets, completing an orbit in 1.73 standard years at an average distance of 1.50 astronomical units and thus receiving two-thirds the irradiation that Terra gets. Its mean diameter is 10,700 kilometers, its mass 0.45 Terra, hence gravity on the surface equals 0.635 g. This suffices to retain a humanly breathable atmosphere, comparable on the lowest levels to Denver Complex and on the highest to the Peruvian altiplano. (You must bear in mind that a weak pull means a correspondingly small density gradient, plus orogenic forces insufficient to raise very tall mountains.) Through ages, water molecules have ascended in the thin air and been cracked by energetic quanta; the hydrogen has escaped to space, the oxygen that has not has tended to unite with minerals. Thus little remains of the former oceans, and deserts have become extensive.

The chief original inducement to colonize was scientific: the unique races on the neighbor planet Dido, which itself was no world whereon a man would want to keep his family. Of course, various other kinds of people settled too; but the explorer-intellectuals dominated. Then the Troubles came, and the Aeneans had to survive as best they could, cut off, for generations. They adapted.

The result was a stock more virile and gifted, a society more patriotic and respectful of learning, than most. After civilization returned to the Alpha Crucis region, Aeneas inevitably became its local leader. To the present day, the University of Virgil in Nova Roma drew students and scholars from greater distances than you might expect.

Eventually the Imperium decided that proper organization of this critical sector demanded an end to Aenean independence. Intrigue and judicious force accomplished it. A hundred years later, some resentment lingered, though the ordinary dweller agreed that incorporation had been desirable on the whole and the planet supplied many outstanding men to the Terran armed services.

Its military-intellectual tradition continued. Every Aenean trained in arms—including women, who took advantage of reduced weight. The old baronial families still led. Their titles might not be recognized by the Imperial peerage, but were by their own folk; they kept their strongholds and broad lands; they furnished more than their share of officers and professors. In part this was due to their tendency to choose able spouses, regardless of rank. On its upper levels, Aenean society was rather formal and austere, though it had its sports and holidays and other depressurizing institutions. On its lower levels there was more jollity, but also better manners than you could find on Terra.

Thus a description, cataloguing several facts and omitting the really significant one: that to four hundred million human beings, Aeneas was home.

The sun was almost down. Rays ran gold across the Antonine Seabed, making its groves and plantations a patchwork of bluish-green and shadows, burning on its canals, molten in

51

the mists that curled off a salt marsh. Eastward, the light smote crags and cliffs where the ancient continental shelf of Ilion lifted a many-tiered, wind-worn intricacy of purple, rose, ocher, tawny, black up to a royal blue sky. The outer moon, Lavinia, was a cold small horn on top of that mass.

The wind was cold too. Its whittering blent with the soft roar of a waterfall, the clop of hoofs and creak and jingle of harness as horses wound along a steep upward trail. Those were Aenean horses, shaggy, rangy, their low-gravity gait looking less rapid than it was. Hugh McCormac rode one. His three sons by his first wife accompanied him. Ostensibly they had been hunting spider wolves, but they hadn't found any and didn't care. The unspoken real reason had been to fare forth together across this land that was theirs. They might not have another chance.

A vulch wheeled into view, wings across heaven. John McCormac lifted his rifle. His father glanced behind. "No, don't," he said. "Let it live."

"Save death for the Terries, hey?" asked Bob. At nine years of age—16 standard—he was a bit loud about his discovery that the universe wasn't quite as simple as they pretended in school.

He'll outgrow that, McCormac thought. *He's a good boy. They all are, like their sisters. How could they help being, with Ramona for mother?* "I don't hold with killing anything unnecessarily," he said. "That isn't what war is about."

"Well, I don't know," Colin put in. He was the oldest. Since he would therefore be the next Firstman, family custom had kept him from joining the service. (Hugh McCormac had only succeeded when his elder brother was caught in a sand hell and died childless.) Perhaps his planetographic researches in the Virgilian System had not satisfied every inborn impulse. "You weren't here, Father, when the revolution reached Nova Roma. But I saw crowds—plain, kindly citizens—hound Snelund's political police down the streets, catch them, string them up, and beat them to death. And it felt right. It still does, when you think what they'd done earlier."

"Snelund himself'll be a while dyin', if I catch him," John said hotly.

"No!" McCormac snapped. "You'll not sink yourself to his ways. He'll be killed as cleanly as we kill any other mad dog. His associates will have fair trials. There *are* degrees of guilt."

"If we can find the lice," Bob said.

McCormac thought of the wilderness of suns and worlds

52

where his life had passed, and said, "Probably most will succeed in disappearing. What of it? We'll have more urgent work than revenge."

They rode silent for a while. The trail debouched on one of the steplike plateaus and joined a paved road to Windhome. Soil lay deep, washed down from the heights, and vegetation flourished, in contrast to a few dwarf bushes on the eroded slopes. Trava decked the ground almost as luxuriantly as it did the seabed. Mainly it was fire trava here, the serrated leaves edged with scarlet; but the sword kind bristled and the plume kind nodded. Each type was curling up for the night as temperature dropped, to form a springy heat-conserving mat. Trees grew about, not only the low iron-hard native sorts but imported oak, cedar, and rasmin. The wind carried their fragrances. Some ways to the right, smoke blew from a farmer's stone cottage. Robotized latifundia weren't practical on Aeneas, and McCormac was glad of that; he felt in his bones that a healthy society needed yeomen.

Colin clucked to his horse and drew alongside. His sharp young face looked unhappy. "Father—" He stopped.

"Go ahead," McCormac invited.

"Father . . . do you think . . . do you really think we can pull it off?"

"I don't know," McCormac said. "We'll try like men, that's all."

"But—makin' you Emperor—"

McCormac felt anew how pitifully little chance he'd had to speak with his nearest, since his rescuers brought him home: too much to do, and each scant hour when something wasn't clamoring for attention, the body toppled into sleep. He had actually stolen this one day.

"Please don't imagine I want the job," he said. "You haven't been on Terra. I have. I don't like it. I was never happier than when they reassigned me back where I belong."

Imperial routine, passed over his mind. *Rotate careerists through a series of regions; but in the end, whenever feasible, return them to the sectors they came from. Theory: they'll defend their birthhomes more fiercely than some clutch of planets foreign to them. Practice: when revolt erupted, many Navy personnel, like civilians, discovered that those homes meant more to them than a Terra most of them had never seen. Problem: if I win, should I discontinue the practice, as Josip doubtless will if his admirals win?*

"But why, then?" Colin asked.

"What else could I do?" McCormac replied.

"Well . . . freedom—"

"No. The Empire is not so far decayed that it'll allow itself to be broken apart. And even if it were, I wouldn't. Don't you see, it's the single thing that stands between civilization —our civilization—and the Long Night?

"As for armed protest, it might stimulate policy changes, but the Imperium could not pardon the ringleaders. That'd invite everybody with a grudge to start shooting, and spell the end as clearly as partition would. And besides—" Mc-Cormac's knuckles stood white where he grasped the reins— "it wouldn't get Kathryn back, if any hope remains of that."

"So you aim to preserve the Empire, but take it over," Colin said quickly. His desire to guide his father's thoughts off his stepmother's captivity was so obvious that Mc-Cormac's heart writhed. "I'm with you. You know that. I honestly think you'd give it new life—the best Emperor we've had since Isamu the Great, maybe since Manuel I himself— and I'm layin' not just me, but my wife and son on the board for you—but can it be done?" He waved at the sky. "The Empire's that huge!"

As if at a signal, Virgil went down. The Aenean atmosphere held no twilight worth mentioning. Alpha and Beta Crucis blazed forth, then almost instantly thousands more and the frosty bridge of the Milky Way. The land mass on the right became utterly black, but Lavinia silvered the sea bottom under the left-hand cliffs. A tadmouse piped into the mordant wind.

McCormac said: "The revolution has to have a leader, and I'm its choice. Let's have no false modesty. I control the Cabinet on the principal world of this sector. I can prove by the record I'm the top Naval strategist the Empire has. My men know I'm strict about things that matter, compassionate about the rest, and always try to be fair. So do a hundred planets, human and nonhuman. It'd be no service to anyone if I claimed different."

"But how—" Colin's voice trailed off. Moonlight glimmered along his leather jacket and off his silver-mounted saddle.

"We'll take control of this sector," McCormac told him. "That's largely a matter of defeating the Josipist forces. Once we've done it, every significant community in a ten-parsec radius will come over to us. Afterward . . . I don't like the idea myself, but I know where and how to get barbarian allies. Not the few Darthan ships I've already engaged; no, really wild warriors from well outside the border. Don't worry, I won't let them plunder and I won't let them settle,

54

even if they'll swear allegiance. They'll be hirelings paid from tax monies.

"The whole Imperial fleet can't ever come against us. It has too many other duties. If we work fast and hard, we'll be in shape to throw back whatever does attack.

"Beyond that—I can't predict. I'm hoping we'll have a well-governed region to show. I'm hoping that will underline our message: an end to corruption and tyranny, a fresh start under a fresh dynasty, long-overdue reforms. . . . What we need is momentum, the momentum of a snowball. Then all the guns in the Empire can't stop us: because most of them will be on our side."

Why a snowball? jeered his mind. *Who knows snow on Aeneas, except a thin drift in polar winter?*

They rounded a cluster of trees and spied the castle. Windhome stood on what had once been a cape and now thrust out into air, with a dizzying drop beneath. Lights glowed yellow from its bulk, outlining dark old walls and battlements. The Wildfoss River brawled past in cataracts.

But McCormac did not see this immediately. His eyes had gone to the flat Antonine horizon, far below and far away. Above a last greenish trace of sunset, beneath a wan flicker of aurora, burned pure white Dido, the evening star.

Where Kathryn worked, xenologist in its jungles, till that time I met her, five years ago (no, three Aenean years; have I really been so long in the Empire that I've forgotten the years of our planet?) and we loved and were married.

And you always wished for children of your own, Kathryn, dyuba, and we were going to have them, but there were always public troubles that ought to be settled first; and tonight — He thanked his iron God that the sun of Llynathawr was not visible in these latitudes. His throat was thick with the need to weep. Instead, he spurred his horse to a gallop.

The road crossed cultivated fields before it reached Windhome's portal. A caravan of tinerants had established itself on the meadow in front. Their trucks were parked aside, lost in gloom; light from the castle fell only on gaily striped tents, fluttering flags, half-erected booths. Men, women, children, packed around campfires, stopped their plangent music and stamping dances to give the lord of the manor a hail as he rode by. Tomorrow these tatterdemalion wanderers would open their carnival . . . and it would draw merrymakers from a hundred kilometers around . . . though the fist of the Imperium was already slamming forward.

I don't understand, McCormac thought.

55

Horseshoes rang in the courtyard. A groom caught his reins. He jumped to the ground. Guards were about, the new-come Navy personnel and the liveried family retainers strutting with jealous glances at each other. Edgar Oliphant hurried from the keep. Though McCormac, as Emperor, had raised him to admiral, he hadn't yet bothered to change the captain's star on either shoulder. He had merely added a brassard in the Ilian colors to the tunic that snugged around his stocky form.

"Welcome back, sir!" he exclaimed. "I was 'bout to dispatch a search party."

McCormac achieved a laugh. "Good cosmos, do you think my boys and I can get lost on our ancestral lands?"

"N-no. No, sir. But 'tis, well, if you'll 'scuse me, sir, 'tis foolish for you to run loose with not a single security escort."

McCormac shrugged. "I'll have to endure that later, on Terra. Leave me my privacy a while." Peering closer: "You've something to tell me."

"Yes, sir. Word came in two hours ago. If the admiral, uh, the Emperor will come with me?"

McCormac tried to give his sons a rueful look. He was secretly not sorry to have his awareness taken from the orbit into which it had fallen—again.

The ancient dignity of the Firstman's office had vanished of recent weeks in a clutter of new gear: communication, computation, electronic files and scanners. McCormac sank into a chair behind his battered desk; that at least was familiar. "Well?" he said.

Oliphant closed the door. "The initial report's been confirmed by two more scouts," he said. "The Imperial armada is movin'. 'Twill be here inside three days." It made no difference whether he meant the standard period or the 20-hour rotation of Aeneas.

McCormac nodded. "I didn't doubt the first crew," he said. "Our plans still stand. Tomorrow, 0600 Nova Roma time, I board my flagship. Two hours later, our forces depart."

"But are you certain, sir, the enemy won't occupy Aeneas?"

"No. I would be surprised, though, if he did. What gain? My kinfolk and I won't be around to seize. I've arranged for the enemy to learn that when he arrives. What else can he make a prize of on Aeneas, till the fighting's past? Whoever wins in space can mop up the planets soon enough. Until then, why commit strength badly needed elsewhere, to grip a spearwasp's nest like this world? If he does occupy, then he

56

does. But I expect he'll leave the Virgilian System the instant he discovers we aren't trying to defend it, we're off to grab the real trophy—Satan."

"Your screenin' forces, however—" Oliphant said dubiously.

"Do you mean protection for offplanet bases like Port Frederiksen? A light vessel each, mostly to guard against possible casual destructiveness."

"No, sir. I'm thinkin' of your interplanetary patrols. What effect 'ull they have?"

"They're just Darthan mercenaries. They have no other purpose than to mislead the enemy, gaining time for our fleet," McCormac said. *Have I really not made it clear to him before now? What else have I overlooked since the avalanche hit me?— No, it's all right, he's simply been too engaged with administrative details on the ground.* "A few vessels posted in local space, with orders to attack any Josipist craft they may spot. Those'll be scouts, of course, weakly armed, easily defeated. The survivors among them will carry the news back. I know Pickens' style of thinking. He'll be convinced we intend to make a fight of it at Virgil, and proceed ultra-cautiously, and therefore not detect us on our way off to Beta Crucis." *Oh, good old Dave Pickens, who always brought flowers for Kathryn when we invited you to dinner, must I indeed use against you the things I learned when we were friends?*

"Well, you're the Emperor, sir." Oliphant gestured at the machines hemming them in. "Plenty of business today. We handled it how we could in Staff, but some items seem to require your attention."

"I'll give them a look-over right away, before eating," McCormac said. "Stay available afterward, in case I need to consult."

"Aye, sir." Oliphant saluted and left.

McCormac didn't retrieve the communications at once. Instead, he went out on a balcony. It opened on the cliff and the rich eastern bottomlands. Creusa, the inner moon, was about due to rise. He filled his lungs with dry chill and waited.

Nearly full, the satellite exploded over the horizon. The shadows it cast moved noticeably; and as it hurtled, he could watch the phase change. Drowned in that living white light, the Antonine appeared to get back its vanished waters. It was as if phantom waves ran across those reaches and surf beat once more on the foot of Windhome ness.

57

You used to say that, Kathryn. You loved these moments best, in the whole year of our world. Dyuba, dyuba, will you ever see them again?

VII

When Virgil showed a perceptible disc without magnification, *Asieneuve* went out of hyperdrive and accelerated inward on gravs. Every sensor strained at maximum receptivity; and nothing came through save an endless seething of cosmic energies.

"Not so much as a radio broadcast?" Flandry asked.

"Not yet, sir," Rovian's voice replied.

Flandry turned off the intercom. "I should be on the bridge myself," he muttered. "What am I doing in my—your cabin?"

"Gatherin' intelligence," the woman said with a faint smile.

"If only I were! Why total silence? Has the whole system been evacuated?"

"Hardly. But they must know the enemy'll arrive in a couple days. Hugh's a genius at deployin' scouts. He is at most things."

Flandry's gaze sharpened on her. Too restless to sit, too cramped to pace, he stood by the door and drummed fingers on it. Kathryn McCormac occupied the chair. She appeared almost calm.

But then, she had done little except sleep, between his first talk with her and this one. It had gone far toward healing her in body and, he hoped, at least a small distance toward knitting the wounds that had been torn in her mind. The time had, however, given him a bad case of the crawlies. It had been no easy decision to race ahead of the fleet, the whole way at top quasispeed, bearing his prisoner to the rebel chieftain. He had no hint of authority to negotiate. His action could only be defended on the freest imaginable interpretation of his orders; wouldn't it be valuable to sound out the great insurrectionist, and didn't the wife's presence offer a windfall opportunity to do so?

Why does it bother me to hear love in her voice? Flandry wondered.

He said, "My own genius is in glibness. But that won't get my stern out of the sling if this maneuver doesn't show some kind of profit."

The chrysocolla eyes beneath the amber bangs focused on him. "You'll not make Hugh yield," she warned. "I'd never ask him to, no matter what. They'd shoot him, wouldn't they?"

Flandry shifted his stance. Sweat prickled under his arms. "Well—a plea for leniency—"

He had seldom heard as grim a laugh. "Of your courtesy, Commander, spare us both. I may be a colonial, and I may've spent my adult life 'fore marriage doin' scientific studies on a breed of bein's that're scarcely more concerned with mankind than Ymirites are . . . but I did study history and politics, and bein' the Fleet Admiral's lady did give me a lot to observe. 'Tis not possible for the Imperium to grant Hugh a pardon." Briefly, her tone faltered. "And I . . . 'ud rather see him dead . . . than a brain-channeled slave or a lifelong prisoner . . . a crag bull like him."

Flandry took out a cigaret, though his palate was scorched leather. "The idea, my lady," he said, "is that you'll tell him what you've learned. If nothing else, he may then avoid playing Snelund's game. He can refuse to give battle on or around those planets that Snelund would like to see bombarded."

"But without bases, sources of supply—" She drew a shaken breath. It bulged out the coverall she wore in a way to trouble Flandry. "Well, we can talk, of course," she said in misery. The regained strength fell from her. She half reached toward him. "Commander . . . if you could let me go—"

Flandry looked away and shook his head. "I'm sorry, my lady. You've a capital charge against you, and you've been neither acquitted nor pardoned. The single excuse I could give for releasing you would be that it bought your husband's surrender, and you tell me that's unthinkable." He dragged smoke into his lungs and remembered vaguely that he ought soon to get an anticancer booster. "Understand, you won't be turned back to Snelund. I'd join the rebellion too before permitting that. You'll come with me to Terra. What you can relate of your treatment at Snelund's hands, and his brags to you . . . well, it may cause him difficulty. At a minimum, it ought to gain you the sympathy of men who're powerful enough to protect you."

Glancing her way again, he was shocked to see how the blood had left her face. Her eyes stared blank, and beads of perspiration glittered forth. "My lady!" He flung the cigaret aside, made two steps, and stooped above her. "What's wrong?" he laid a palm on her brow. It was cold. So were her hands, when his slipped as if of themselves down her shoulders and arms. He hunkered in front and chafed them. "My lady—"

Kathryn McCormac stirred. "A stimpill?" she whispered.

Flandry debated calling the ship's medic, decided not to, and gave her the tablet and a tumbler of water. She gulped. When he saw the corpse color going and the breath becoming steady, it rejoiced in him.

"I'm sorry," she said, scarcely audible above the murmur of the ship. "The memory bounced out at me too quick."

"I said the wrong thing," he stammered, contrite.

"Not your fault." She stared at the deck. He couldn't help noticing how long the lashes were against her bronze skin. "Terran mores are different from ours. To you, what happened to me was . . . unfortunate, nasty, yes, but not a befoulin' I'll never quite cleanse me of, not a thing makes me wonder if I really should want to see Hugh ever again. . . . Maybe, though, you'll understand some if I tell you how often he used drugs and brain-scramblers. Time and again, I was trapped in a nightmare where I couldn't think, wasn't me, had no will, wasn't anything but an animal doin' what he told me, to 'scape pain—"

I oughtn't to hear this, Flandry thought. *She wouldn't speak of it if her self-command had entirely returned. How can I leave?*

"My lady," he attempted, "you said a fact, that it wasn't you. You shouldn't let it count. If your husband's half the man you claim, he won't."

She sat motionless a while. The stimulol acted faster than normal on her; evidently she wasn't in the habit of using chemical crutches. At length she raised her head. The countenance was deeply flushed, but the big body seemed in repose. And she smiled.

"You *are* a strider," she said.

"Uh . . . feeling well now?"

"Better, anyways. Could we talk straight business?"

60

Flandry gusted a secret sigh of relief. A touch weak in his own knees, he sat down on the bunk and began another cigaret. "Yes, I rather urgently want to," he said. "For the proverbial nonce, we have common interests, and your information might be what lets us carry on instead of scuttling off for home and mother."

"What d'you need to know? I may not be able to answer some questions, and may refuse to answer others."

"Agreed. But let's try on a few. We've caught no trace of astronautical activity in this system. A fleet the size of Hugh McCormac's should register one way or another. If nothing else, by neutrino emission from powerplants. What's he done? He might be fairly close to the sun, keeping behind it with respect to us; or might be lying doggo a goodly distance out, like half a light-year; or might have hauled mass for some different territory altogether; or— Have you any ideas?"

"No."

"Certain you don't?"

She bridled. "If I did, would I tell?"

"Sizzle it, one destroyer doesn't make a task force! Put it this way: How can we contact him before battle commences?"

She yielded. "I don't know, and that's honest," she said, meeting his stare without wavering. "I can tell you this, whatever Hugh's plannin' 'ull be something bold and unexpected."

"Marvelous," Flandry groaned. "Well, how about the radio silence?"

"Oh, that's easier to 'splain, I think. We don't have many stations broadcastin' with enough power, at the right wavelengths, to be detectable far out. Virgil's too apt to hash them up with solar storms. Mainly we send tight beams via relay satellites. Radiophones're common—isolated villages and steadin's need them—but they natur'ly use frequencies that the ionosphere 'ull contain. Virgil gives Aeneas a mighty deep ionosphere. In short, 'tisn't hard to get 'long without the big stations, and I s'pose they're doin' it so enemy navigators 'ull have extra trouble obtainin' in-system positions."

You understand that principle too—never giving the opposition a free ride, never missing a chance to complicate his life? Flandry thought with respect. *I've known a lot of civilians, including officers' spouses, who didn't.*

"What about interplanetary communications?" he asked. "I assume you do mining and research on the sister worlds. You mentioned having been involved yourself. Think those bases were evacuated?"

61

"N-no. Not the main one on Dido, at least. It's self-supportin', kind of, and there's too big an investment in apparatus, records, relationships with natives." Pride rang: "I know my old colleagues. They won't abandon simply 'cause of an invasion."

"But your people may have suspended interplanetary talk during the emergency?"

"Yes, belike. 'Speci'ly since the Josipists prob'ly won't carry data on where everything is in our system. And what they can't find, they can't wreck."

"They wouldn't," Flandry protested. "Not in mere spite."

She retorted with an acrid: "How do you know what His Ex'lency may've told their admiral?"

The intercom's buzz saved him from devising a reply. He flipped the switch. "Bridge to captain," came Rovian's thick, hissing tones. "A ship has been identified at extreme range. It appears to have started on a high-thrust intercept course to ours."

"I'll be right there." Flandry stood. "You heard, my lady?"

She nodded. He thought he could see how she strained to hold exterior calm.

"Report to Emergency Station Three," he said. "Have the yeoman on duty fit you with a spacesuit and outline combat procedure. When we close with that chap, everyone goes into armor and harness. Three will be your post. It's near the middle of the hull, safest place, not that that's a very glowing encomium. Tell the yeoman that I'll want your helmet transceiver on a direct audiovisual link to the bridge and the comshack. Meanwhile, stay in this cabin, out of the way."

"Do you 'spect danger?" she asked quietly.

"I'd better not expect anything else." He departed.

The bridge viewscreens showed Virgil astonishingly grown. *Asieneuve* had entered the system with a high relative true velocity, and her subsequent acceleration would have squashed her crew were it not for the counteraction of the interior gee-field. Its radiance stopped down in simulacrum, the sun burned amidst a glory of corona and zodiacal light.

Flandry assumed the command chair. Rovian said: "I suppose the vessel was orbiting, generators at minimum, until it detected us. If we wish to rendezvous with it near Aeneas"—a claw pointed at a ruddy spark off the starboard quarter—"we must commence deceleration."

"M-m-m, I think not." Flandry rubbed his chin. "If I were that skipper, I'd be unhappy about a hostile warship close to my home planet, whether or not she's a little one and says she wants to parley. For all he knows, our messages are off

62

tapes and there's nobody here but us machines, boss." He didn't need to spell out what devastation could be wrought, first by any nuclear missiles that didn't get intercepted, finally by a suicide plunge of the ship's multiple tons at perhaps a hundred kilometers a second. "When they've got only one important city, a kamikaze is worth fretting about. He could get a wee bit impulsive."

"What does the captain mean to do, then?"

Flandry activated an astronomical display. The planet-dots, orbit-circles, and vector-arrows merely gave him a rough idea of conditions, but refinements were the navigation department's job. "Let's see. The next planet inward, Dido they call it, past quadrature but far enough from conjunction that there'd be no ambiguity about our aiming for it. And a scientific base . . . cool heads . . . yes, I think it'd be an earnest of pious intentions if we took station around Dido. Set course for the third planet, Citizen Rovian."

"Aye, sir." The directives barked forth, the calculations were made, the engine sang on a deeper note as its power began to throttle down speed.

Flandry prepared a tape announcing his purposes. "If discussion is desired prior to our reaching terminus, please inform. We will keep a receiver tuned on the standard band," he finished, and ordered continuous broadcast.

Time crept by. "What if we are not allowed to leave this system afterward?" Rovian said once in Eriau.

"Chance we take," Flandry replied. "Not too big a risk, I judge, considering the hostage we hold. Besides, in spite of our not releasing her to him, I trust friend McCormac will be duly appreciative of our having gotten her away from that swine Snelund. . . . No, I shouldn't insult the race of swine, should I? His parents were brothers."

"What do you really expect to accomplish?"

"God knows, and He hasn't seen fit to declassify the information. Maybe nothing. Maybe opening some small channel, some way of moderating the war if not halting it. Keep the bridge for ten minutes, will you? If I can't sneak off and get a smoke, I'll implode."

"Can you not indulge here?"

"The captain on a human ship isn't supposed to have human failings, they hammered into me when I was a caydet. I'll have too many explanations to invent for my superiors as is."

Rovian emitted a noise that possibly corresponded to a chuckle.

The hours trickled past. Virgil swelled in the screens. Rovian reported: "Latest data on the other ship indicate it has decided we are bound for Dido, and plans to get there approximately simultaneously. No communication with it thus far, though it must now be picking up our broadcast."

"Odd. Anything on the vessel herself?" Flandry asked.

"Judging from its radiations and our radar, it has about the same tonnage and power as us but is not any Naval model."

"No doubt the Aeneans have pressed everything into service that'll fly, from broomsticks to washtubs. Well, that's a relief. They can't contemplate fighting a regular unit like ours."

"Unless the companion—" Rovian referred to a second craft, detected a while ago after she swung past the sun.

"You told me that one can't make Dido till hours after we do, except by going hyper; and I doubt her captain is so hot for Dido that he'll do that, this deep in a gravitational well. No, she must be another picket, brought in on a just-in-case basis."

Nevertheless, he called for armor and battle stations when *Asieneuve* neared the third planet.

It loomed gibbous before him, a vast, roiling ball of snowy cloud. No moon accompanied it. The regional *Pilot's Manual and Ephemeris* described a moderately eccentric orbit whose radius vector averaged about one astronomical unit; a mass, diameter, and hence surface gravity very slightly less than Terra's; a rotation once in eight hours and 47 minutes around an axis tilted at a crazy 38 degrees; an oxynitrogen atmosphere hotter and denser than was good for men, but breathable by them; a d-amino biochemistry, neither poisonous nor nourishing to humankind—That was virtually the whole entry. The worlds were too numerous; not even the molecules of the reel could encode much information on any but the most important.

When he had donned his own space gear, aside from gauntlets and closing the faceplate, Flandry put Kathryn McCormac on circuit. Her visage in the screen, looking out of the helmet, made him think of warrior maidens in archaic books he had read. "Well?" she asked.

"I'd like to get in touch with your research base," he said, "but how the deuce can I find it under that pea soup?"

"They may not answer your call."

"On the other hand, they may; the more likely if I beamcast so they can tell I've got them spotted. That ship closing with us is maintaining her surly silence, and— Well, if they're old chums of yours on the ground, they ought to respond to *you*."

64

She considered. "All right, I trust you, Dominic Flandry. The base, Port Frederiksen"—a brief white smile—"one of my ancestors founded it—'s on the western end of Barca, as we've named the biggest continent. Latitude 34° 5'18" north. I 'spect you can take it from there with radar."

"And thermal and magnetic and suchlike gizmos. Thanks. Stand by to talk in, oh, maybe half an hour or an hour."

Her look was grave. "I'll speak them truth."

"That'll do till we can think of something better and cheaper." Flandry switched off, but it was as if her countenance still occupied the screen. He turned to Rovian. "We'll assume an approximate hundred-minute orbit till we've identified the base, then move out to a synchronous orbit above it."

The exec switched his space-armored tail. "Sir, that means the rebel ship will find us barely outside atmosphere."

"And it's useful to be higher in a planet's field. Well, didn't you last inform me she's coming in too fast to manage less than a hyperbolic orbit?"

"Yes, sir, unless it can brake much quicker than we can."

"Her master's suspicious. He must intend to whip by in a hurry, lest we throw things at him. That's not unnatural. I'd be nervous of any enemy destroyer myself, if I were in a converted freighter or whatever she is. When he sees we're amiable, he'll take station—by which time, with luck, we'll be another ten or fifteen thousand kilometers out and talking to the scientific lads."

"Aye, sir. Have I the captain's permission to order screen fields extended at full strength?"

"Not till we've located Port Frederiksen. They'd bedbug the instruments. But otherwise, except for the detector team, absolute combat readiness, of course."

Am I right? If I'm wrong— The loneliness of command engulfed Flandry. He tried to fend it off by concentrating on approach maneuvers.

Eventually *Asieneuve* was falling free around Dido. The cessation of noise and quiver was like sudden deafness. The planet filled the starboard screens, dazzling on the dayside, dark when the ship swung around into night, save where aurora glimmered and lightning wove webs. That stormy atmosphere hindered investigation. Flandry found himself gripping his chair arms till he drove the blood from his fingernails.

"We could observe the other ship optically now, sir," Rovian said, "were this disc not in between."

"It would be," Flandry said. The exec's uneasiness had begun to gnaw in him.

65

An intercom voice said: "I think we've found it, sir. Latitude's right, infrared pattern fits a continent to east and an ocean to west, radar suggests buildings, we may actually have gotten a neutrino blip from a nuclear installation. Large uncertainty factor in everything, though, what with the damned interference. Shall we repeat, next orbit?"

"No," Flandry said, and realized he spoke needlessly loud. He forced levelness into his tone. "Lock on radar. Pilot, keep inside that horizon while we ascend. We'll go synchronous and take any further readings from there." *I want to be under thrust when that actor arrives in his deaf-mute role. And, oh, yes,* "Maximum screen fields, Citizen Rovian."

The officer's relief was obvious as he issued commands. The ship stirred back to life. A shifting complex of gravitic forces lifted her in a curve that was nearer a straight line than a spiral. The planet's stormy crescent shrank a little.

"Give me a projection of the rendezvousing craft, soon as you have a line of sight," Flandry said. *I'll feel a lot cheerier after I've eyeballed her.* He made himself lean back and wait.

The vision leaped into the screen. A man yelled. Rovian hissed.

That lean shape rushing down the last kilometers had never been for peaceful use. She was simply, deceptively not of Imperial manufacture. The armament was as complete as *Asieneuve's*, and as smoothly integrated with the hull. Needle nose and rakish fins declared she was meant to traverse atmosphere more often than a corresponding Terran warship . . . as for example on her way to loot a town—

Barbarians, flashed in Flandry. *From some wild country on some wild planet, where maybe a hundred years ago they were still warring with edged iron, only somebody found advantage—military, commercial—in teaching them about spaceflight, providing them with machines and a skeleton education. . . . No wonder they haven't responded to us. Probably not one aboard knows Anglic!*

"White flare," he snapped. " 'Pax' broadcast." They must recognize the signals of peace. Hugh McCormac couldn't have engaged them, as he doubtless had, unless they'd been in some contact with his civilization.

The order was obeyed at once.

Energy stabbed blue-white out of the mercenary. Missiles followed.

Flandry heard a roar of abused metal. He struck the combat button. *Asieneuve's* response was instant. And it was the ship's own. At quarters this close, living flesh could not perceive what went on, let alone react fact enough. Her blaster

66

cannon discharged. Her countermissiles soared to meet what had been sent against her. A second later, tubes opened to release her big birds.

Nuclear detonations raged. Electromagnetic screens could ward off the sleet of ions, but not the heat radiation and X-rays, nor the thrust of energy lances and the assault of material torpedoes. Negagrav forces could slow the latter, but not stop them. Interceptors must do that, if they could.

The barbarian had the immense advantage of high speed and high altitude relative to the planet. She was the harder target to come near, her defenses the harder to penetrate if you did.

Nonetheless, Rovian's work of years bore fruit. Abrupt flame seethed around the enemy. White-hot shrapnel fled from a place where armor plate had been. Twisted, crumpled, blackened, half melted, the rest of the ship whirled off on a cometary path around the world and back toward outer space.

But it was not possible that the Terran escape free. Tactical experts reckoned the life of a destroyer in this kind of fight as less than three minutes. Firebeams had seared and gouged through *Asieneuve's* vitals. No warhead had made the direct hit that would have killed her absolutely; but three explosions were so close that the blast from their shaped charges tore into the hull, bellowing, burning, shattering machines like porcelain, throwing men about and ripping them like red rag dolls.

Flandry saw the bridge crack open. A shard of steel went through Rovian as a circular saw cuts a tree in twain. Blood sheeted, broke into a fog of droplets in the sudden weightlessness, volatilized in the dwindling pressure, and was gone except for spattered stains. Stunned, deafened, his own blood filling nose and mouth, Flandry managed to slam shut the faceplate and draw on the gloves he had forgotten about, before the last air shrieked through the hole.

Then there was a silence. Engines dead, the destroyer reached the maximum altitude permitted by the velocity she had had, and fell back toward the planet.

VIII

~~~~~~~~~

No boat remained spaceworthy. Where destruction was not total, crucial systems had been knocked out. Time was lacking to make repairs or cannibalize. One of the four craft offered a weak hope. Though its fusion generator was inoperative, its accumulators could energize the two drive cones that seemed usable; and the instruments and controls were undamaged. An aerodynamic landing might be possible. Every rated pilot was killed or wounded—but Flandry had flown combat aircraft before he transferred to the Intelligence Corps.

The engineers had barely finished ascertaining this much when it became urgent to abandon ship. They would soon strike atmosphere. That would complete the ruin of the hull. Struggling through airlessness, weightlessness, lightlessness, hale survivors dragged hurt to the boat housing. There wasn't room for all those bodies if they stayed space armored. Flandry pressurized from tanks and, as each man cycled through the airlock, had his bulky gear stripped off and sent out the disposal valve. He managed to find stowage for three suits, including his—which he suddenly remembered he must not wear when everyone else would be unprotected. That was more for the sake of the impellers secured to them than for anything else.

Those worst injured were placed in the safety-webbed chairs. The rest, jammed together down the aisle, would depend for their lives on the gee-field. Flandry saw Kathryn take her stand among them. He wanted wildly to give her the copilot's chair; the field circuits might well be disrupted by the stresses they were about to encounter. But Ensign Havelock had some training in this kind of emergency procedure. His help could be the critical quantum that saved her.

A shudder went through boat and bones, the first impact on Dido's stratosphere. Flandry shot free.

The rest was indescribable: riding a meteorite through incandescence, shock, thunderblast, stormwind, night, mountains and caverns of cloud, rain like bullets, crazy tilting and whirling of horribly onrushing horizon, while the noise roared and battered and vibrations shook brains in skulls and devils danced on the instrument panel.

Somehow Flandry and Havelock kept a measure of control. They braked the worst of their velocity before they got down to altitudes where it would be fatal. They did not skip helplessly off the tropopause nor flip and tumble when they crossed high winds in the lower atmosphere. They avoided peaks that raked up to catch them and a monstrous hurricane, violent beyond anything Terra had ever known, that would have sundered their boat and cast it into the sea. Amidst the straining over meters and displays, the frantic leap of hands over pilot board and feet on pedals, the incessant brutality of sound, heat, throbbing, they clung to awareness of their location.

Their desire was wholly to reach Port Frederiksen. Their descent took them around the northern hemisphere. Identifying what had to be the largest continent, they fought their way to the approximately correct latitude and slanted down westward above it.

They could have made their goal, or come near, had their initial velocity been in the right direction. But the instrumental survey had been expedited by throwing *Asieneuve* into a retrograde orbit. Now the planet's rotation worked against them, forcing extra energy expenditure in the early stages of deceleration. By the time the boat was approaching a safe speed, its accumulators were drained. Overloaded, it had no possibility of a long ballistic glide. There was nothing to do but use the last stored joules for setting down.

Nor could the tail jacks be employed. Unharnessed, men would be crushed beneath their fellows if the gee-field gave way. Flandry picked out an open area surrounded by forest. Water gleamed between hummocks and sedgy clumps. Better marsh than treetops. The keel skids hissed beneath a last rumble of engine; the boat rocked, bucked, slewed around, and came to rest at a steep angle; flying creatures fled upward in clamorous thousands; and stillness was.

A moment's dark descended on Flandry. He pulled out of it to the sound of feeble cheers. "E-e-everybody all right?" he stuttered. His fingers trembled likewise, fumbling with his harness.

"No further injuries, sir," said one voice.

"Maybe not," another responded. "But O'Brien died on the way down."

Flandry closed his eyes. *My man, pierced him. My men. My ship. How many are left? I counted. . . . Twenty-three with only small hurts, plus Kathryn and me. Seventeen—sixteen—seriously wounded. The rest—Those lives were in my hands!*

Havelock said diffidently, "Our radio's out, sir. We can't call for help. What does the captain wish?"

Rovian, I should have collected that chunk, not you. The lives that are left are still in my murderous-clumsy hands.

Flandry forced his lids back up. His ears were ringing almost too loudly for him to hear his own words, but he thought they sounded mechanical. "We can't maintain our interior field long. The final ergs are about to go. Let's get our casualties outside before we have to contend with local pull on a slanted deck." He rose and faced his men. Never had he done anything harder. "Lady McCormac," he said. "You know this planet. Have you any recommendations?"

She was hidden from him by those packed around her. The husky tones were unshaken. "Equalize pressures slowly. If we're anywhere near sea level, that air is half again as thick as Terran. Do you know where we are?"

"We were aiming for the Aenean base."

"If I remember rightly, this hemisphere's in its early summer. S'posin' we're not far below the arctic circle, we'll have more day than night, but not very much more. Bear in mind the short spin period. Don't count on a lot of light."

"Thanks." Flandry issued the obvious commands.

Saavedra, the communications officer, found some tools, took the panel off the radio transceiver, and studied it. "I might be able to cobble something together for signalling the base," he said.

"How long'll that take you?" Flandry asked. A little potency was returning to his muscles, a little clarity to his brain.

"Several hours, sir. I'll have to haywire, and jigger around till I'm on a standard band."

"And maybe nobody'll happen to be listening. And when they do hear us, they'll have to triangulate and—Uh-uh." Flandry shook his head. "We can't wait. Another ship's on her way here. When she finds the derelict we shot up, she'll hunt for us. An excellent chance of finding us, too: a sweep

70

with metal detectors over a planet as primitive as this. I don't want us anywhere near. She's likely to throw a missile."

"What shall we do, then, sir?" Havelock asked.

"Does my lady think we've a chance of marching overland to the base?" Flandry called.

"Depends on just where we are," Kathryn replied. "Topography, native cultures, everything's as variable on Dido as 'tis on most worlds. Can we pack plenty of food?"

"Yes, I imagine so. Boats like this are stocked with ample freeze-dried rations. I assume there's plenty of safe water."

"Is. Might be stinkin' and scummy, but no Didonian bug has yet made a human sick. Biochemistry's that different."

When the lock was opened full, the air turned into a steam bath. Odors blew strange, a hundred pungencies, fragrant, sharp, rotten, spicy, nameless. Men gasped and tried to sweat. One rating started to pull off his shirt. Kathryn laid a hand on his arm. "Don't," she warned. "No matter clouds, enough UV gets past to burn you."

Flandry went first down the accommodation ladder. Weight was hardly changed. He identified a tinge of ozone in the swamp reeks and thought that an increased partial pressure of oxygen might prove valuable. His boots squelched into ankle-deep muck. The sounds of life were coming back: chatter, caw, whistle, wingbeats. They were loud in the dense air, now that his hearing had recovered. Small animals flitted among leaves in the jungle.

It was not like a rain forest on a really terrestroid world. The variety of trees was incredible, from gnarly and thorny dwarfs to soaring slim giants. Vines and fungoids covered many dark trunks. Foliage was equally diverse in its shapes. Nowhere was it green; browns and deep reds predominated, though purples and golds blent in; the same held for the spongy, springy mat on the land. The overall effect was one of somber richness. There were no real shadows, but Flandry's gaze soon lost itself in the gloom under the trees. He saw more brush than he liked to think about pushing his way through.

Overhead the sky was pearl gray. Lower cloud strata drifted across its featurelessness. A vaguely luminous area marked Virgil. Recalling where the terminator was, he knew this district was still at morning. They'd leave before sundown if they worked.

He gave himself to helping. The labor was hard. For that he was grateful. It rescued him from dead men and a wrecked ship.

First the wounded must be borne to higher, drier ground.

71

Their injuries were chiefly broken bones and concussions. If your armor was ripped open in space, that was generally the end of you. Two men did have nasty abdominal gashes from bits of metal whose entry holes had been sufficiently small for them or friends to slap on patches before their air could flee them. One man was unconscious, skin chill, breath shallow, pulse thready. And O'Brien had died.

Luckily, the medical officer was on his feet. He got busy. Arriving with an armful of equipment, Flandry saw Kathryn giving him skilled assistance. He remembered in dull surprise that she'd disappeared for a while. It didn't seem like her not to plunge straight into a task.

By the time the last item had been unloaded, she had finished her nurse's job and supervised a burial party. He glimpsed her doing some of the digging herself. When he slogged to her, O'Brien was laid out in the grave. Water oozed upward around him. He had no coffin. She had covered him with the Imperial flag.

"Will the captain read the service?" she asked.

He looked at her. She was as muddy and exhausted as he, but stood straight. Her hair clung wet to head and cheeks, but was the sole brightness upon this world. Sheathed on a belt around her coverall, he recognized the great blade and knuckleduster half of his Merseian war knife.

Stupid from weariness, he blurted, "Do *you* want me to?"

"He wasn't the enemy," she said. "He was of Hugh's people. Give him his honor."

She handed him the prayerbook. *Me?* he thought. *But I never believed*— She was watching. They all were. His fingers stained the pages as he read aloud the majestic words. A fine drizzle began.

While trenching tools clinked, Kathryn plucked Flandry's sleeve. "A minute, of your courtesy," she said. They walked aside. "I spent a while scoutin' 'round," she told him. "Studied the vegetation, climbed a tree and saw mountains to west —and you wouldn't spy many pteropods at this season if we were east of the Stonewall, so the range ahead of us must be the Maurusian—well, I know roughly where we are."

His heart skipped a beat. "And something about the territory?"

"Less'n I'd wish. My work was mainly in Gaetulia. However, I did have my first season in this general area, more for trainin' than research. Point is, we've got a fair chance of findin' Didonians that've met humans; and the local culture is reasonably high; and if we do come on an entity that knows one of our pidgins, it'll be a version I can talk, and I should

72

be able to understand their lingo after a little practice." The black brows knitted. "I'll not hide from you, better if we'd come down west of the Maurusians, and not just 'cause that'd shorten our march. They have some wild and mean dwellers. However, maybe I can bargain for an escort to the other side."

"Good. You didn't perchance find a trail for us?"

"Why, yes. That's what I was mainly searchin' for. We wouldn't make a kilometer 'fore sundown through muscoid and arrowbush, not if we exhausted our blasters burnin' them. I've found one just a few meters from the swamp edge, aimed more or less our way."

"Sizzle it," Flandry said, "but I wish we were on the same side, you and I!"

"We are," she smiled. "What can you do but surrender at Port Frederiksen?"

His failure rose in him, tasting of vomit. "Doubtless nothing. Let's get loaded and start." He turned on his heel and left her, but could not escape the look that followed him. It burned between his shoulderblades.

The stuff from the boat weighed heavily on men who must also take turns carrying the wounded on improvised stretchers. Besides food, changes of clothing, utensils, handguns, ammunition, ripped-off plastic sheeting for shelters, and other necessities, Flandry insisted on taking the three spacesuits. Havelock ventured to protest: "If the captain please, should we lug them? The impellers could be handy for sending scouts aloft, but they aren't good for many kilometers in planet gravity, nor will their radios reach far. And I don't imagine we'll meet any critters that we have to wear armor to fight."

"We may have to discard things," Flandry admitted, "but I'm hoping for native porters. We'll tote the suits a ways, at least."

"Sir, the men are dead on their feet as is!"

Flandry stared into the blond young face. "Would you rather be dead on your back?" he snapped. His eyes traversed the weary, dirty, stoop-shouldered creatures for whom he was responsible. "Saddle up," he said. "Lend me a hand, Citizen Havelock. I don't intend to carry less than anybody else."

A sighing went among them through the thin sad rain, but they obeyed.

The trail proved a blessing. Twigs and gravel mixed into its dirt—by Didonians, Kathryn said—gave a hard broad surface winding gradually through inwalling forest toward higher country.

73

Dusk fell, layer by layer. Flandry made the group continue, with flashbeams to show the way. He pretended not to hear the *sotto voce* remarks behind his back, though they hurt. Night fell, scarcely cooler than day, tomb black, full of croakings and distant cries, while the men lurched on.

After another nightmare hour, Flandry called a halt. A brook ran across the trail. High trees surrounded and roofed a tiny meadow. His light flew about, bringing leaves and eyes briefly out of murk. "Water and camouflage," he said. "What do you think, my lady?"

"Good," she said.

"You see," he tried to explain, "we have to rest, and daybreak will be soon. I don't want us observed from the air."

She didn't reply. *I rate no answer, who lost my ship,* he thought.

Men eased off their burdens. A few munched food bars before collapsing into sleep with their fellows. The medical officer, Felipe Kapunan, said to Flandry, "No doubt the captain feels he should take first watch. But I'll be busy the next hour or two, seeing to my patients. Dressings need change, they could use fresh enzymes, anti-radiation shots, pain killers—the standard stuff, no help necessary. You may as well rest, sir. I'll call you when I finish."

His last sentence was scarcely heard. Flandry went down and down into miraculous nothingness. His last knowledge was that the ground cover—carpet weed, Kathryn named it, despite its being more suggestive of miniature red-brown sponges—made a damp but otherwise gentle mattress.

The doctor shook him awake as promised and offered him a stimpill. Flandry gulped it. Coffee would have been welcome, but he dared not yet allow a campfire. He circled the meadow, found a seat between two enormous roots, and relaxed with his back against the bole. The rain had paused.

Dawn was stealthy on Dido. Light seemed to condense in the hot rank air, drop by drop, like the mists whose tendrils crawled across the sleepers. Except for the clucking brook and drip of water off leaves, a great silence had fallen.

A footstep broke it. Flandry started to rise, his blaster half out of the sheath. When he saw her, he holstered the weapon and bowed around his shivering heart. "My lady. What . . . what has you awake this early?"

"Couldn't sleep. Too much to think 'bout. Mind if I join you?"

"How could I?"

They sat down together. He contrived his position so that

it was natural to watch her. She looked into the jungle for a space. Exhaustion smudged her eyes and paled her lips.

Abruptly she faced back to him. "Talk with me, Dominic Flandry," she pleaded. "I think 'bout Hugh . . . now I can hope to meet him again. . . . Can I stay with him? Wouldn't there always be that between us?"

"I said," *a cosmic cycle ago,* "that if he'd, well, let a girl like you get away from him, for any cause, he's an idiot."

"Thanks." She reached across and squeezed his hand. He felt the touch for a long while afterward. "Shall we be friends? First-name friends?"

"I'd love that."

"We should make a little ceremony of it, in the Aenean way." Her smile was wistful. "Drink a toast and— But later, Dominic, later." She hesitated. "The war's over for you, after all. You'll be interned. No prison; a room in Nova Roma ought to do. I'll come visit when I can, bring Hugh when he's free. Maybe we'll talk you into joinin' us. I do wish so."

"First we'd better reach Port Frederiksen," he said, not daring anything less banal.

"Yes." She leaned forward. "Let's discuss that. I told you I need conversation. Poor Dominic, you save me from captivity, then from death, now 'tis got to be from my personal horrors. Please talk practical."

He met the green eyes in the wide strong face. "Well," he said, "this is quite a freakish planet, isn't it?"

She nodded. "They think it started out to be Venus type, but a giant asteroid collided with it. Shock waves blew most of the atmosphere off, leavin' the rest thin enough that chemical evolution could go on, not too unlike the Terran—photosynthesis and so forth, though the amino acids that developed happened to be mainly dextro- 'stead of levorotatory. Same collision must've produced the extreme axial tilt, and maybe the high rotation. 'Cause of those factors, the oceans aren't as inert as you might 'spect on a moonless world, and storms are fierce. Lot of tectonic activity: no s'prise, is it? That's believed to be the reason we don't find traces of past ice ages, but do find eras of abnormal heat and drought. Nobody knows for sure, though. In thousands of man-lifetimes, we've barely won a glimpse into the mysteries. This is a whole *world,* Dominic."

"I understand that," he said. "Uh, any humanly comfortable areas?"

"Not many. Too hot and wet. Some high and polar regions aren't as bad as this, and Port Frederiksen enjoys winds off a cold current. The tropics kill you in a few days if

75

you're not protected. No, we don't want this planet for ourselves, only for knowledge. It belongs to the autochthons anyway." Her mood turned suddenly defiant: "When Hugh's Emperor, he'll see that all autochthons get a fair break."

"If he ever is." It was as if someone else sat down at a control console in Flandry's brain and made him say, "Why did he bring in barbarians?"

"He must've gone elsewhere himself and needed them to guard Virgil." She looked aside. "I asked a couple of your men who'd watched on viewscreens, what that ship was like. 'Twas Darthan, from their descriptions. Not truly hostile folk."

"As long as they aren't given the chance to be! We'd offered Pax, and nevertheless they fired."

"They . . . well, Darthans often act like that. Their culture makes it hard for them to believe a call for truce is honest. Hugh had to take what he could get in a hurry. After everything that'd happened, what reason had he to tell them someone might come for parley? He's mortal! He can't think of everything!"

Flandry slumped. "I suppose not, my lady."

A fluting went through the forest. Kathryn waited a minute before she said gently, "You know, you haven't yet spoken my right name."

He replied in his emptiness: "How can I? Men are gone because of what I did."

"Oh, Dominic!" The tears broke forth out of her. He fought to hold back his own.

They found themselves kneeling together, his face hidden against her breasts, his arms around her waist and her left around his neck, her right hand smoothing his hair while he shuddered.

"Dominic, Dominic," she whispered to him, "I know. How well I know. My man's a captain too. More ships, more lives than you could count. How often I've seen him readin' casualty reports! I'll tell you, he's come to me and closed the door so he could weep. He's made his errors that killed men. What commander hasn't? But somebody's got to command. It's your duty. You weigh the facts best's you're able, and decide, and act, and long's you did do your best, you never look back. You needn't. You mustn't.

"Dominic, we didn't make this carnivore universe. We only live here, and have to try and cope.

"Who said you were in error? Your estimate was completely reasonable. I don't believe any board of inquiry 'ud blame you. If Hugh couldn't foresee you'd come with me, how could you foresee—? Dominic, look up, be glad again."

A moment's hell-colored light struck through the eastern leaves. Seconds after, the air roared and a queasy vibration moved the ground.

Men stumbled to their feet. Flandry and Kathryn bounded apart. "What's that?" cried Saavedra.

"That," Flandry yelled into the wind that had arisen, "was the second barbarian ship making sure of our boat."

A minute later they heard the ongoing thunderclap of a large body traveling at supersonic speed. It faded into a terrible whistle and was gone. The gust died out and startled flying creatures circled noisily back toward their trees.

"High-yield warhead," Flandry judged. "They meant to kill within several kilometers' radius." He held a wet finger to the normal dawn breeze. "The fallout's bound east; we needn't worry. I'm stonkerish glad we hiked this far yesterday!"

Kathryn took both his hands. "Your doin' alone, Dominic," she said. "Will that stop your grief?"

It didn't, really. But she had given him the courage to think: *Very well. Nothing's accomplished by these idealistic broodings. Dead's dead. My job is to salvage the living . . . and afterward, if there is an afterward, use whatever tricks I can to prevent my superiors from blaming me too severely.*

No doubt my conscience will. But maybe I can learn how to jettison it. An officer of the Empire is much more efficient without one.

"At ease, men," he said. "We'll spend the next rotation period here, recuperating, before we push on."

IX

~~~~~~~~~

The forest opened abruptly on cleared land. Stepping out, Flandry saw ordered rows of bushes. On three sides the farm was hemmed in by jungle, on the fourth it dropped into a valley full of vapors. The trend of his six Didonian days of travel had been upward.

He didn't notice the agriculture at once. "Hold!" he barked. The blaster jumped into his grasp. *A rhinoceros herd?*

No . . . not really . . . of course not. Lord Advisor Mulele's African preserve lay 200 light-years remote. The half-dozen animals before him had the size and general build of rhinos, though their nearly hairless slate-blue skins were smooth rather than wrinkled and tails were lacking. But the shoulders of each protruded sidewise to make a virtual platform. The ears were big and fanlike. The skull bulged high above a pair of beady eyes, supported a horn on the nose, then tapered to a muzzle whose mouth was oddly soft and flexible. The horn offset that effect by being a great ebony blade with a sawtoothed ridge behind it.

"Wait, Dominic!" Kathryn sped to join him. "Don't shoot. Those're nogas."

"Hm?" He lowered the gun.

"Our word. Humans can't pronounce any Didonian language."

"You mean they are the—" Flandry had encountered curious forms of sophont, but none without some equivalent of hands. What value would an intelligence have that could not actively reshape its environment?

Peering closer, he saw that the beasts were not at graze. Two knelt in a corner of the field, grubbing stumps, while a

78

third rolled a trimmed log toward a building whose roof was visible over a hillcrest. The fourth dragged a crude wooden plow across the newly acquired ground. The fifth came behind, its harness enabling it to steer. A pair of smaller animals rode on its shoulders. That area was some distance off, details hard to make out through the hazy air. The sixth, nearer to Flandry, was not feeding so much as removing weeds from among the bushes.

"C'mon!" Kathryn dashed ahead, lightfoot under her pack.

The trip had been day-and-night trudgery. In camp, he and she had been too occupied—the only ones with wilderness experience—for any meaningful talk before they must sleep. But they were rewarded; unable to mourn, they began to mend. Now eagerness made her suddenly so vivid that Flandry lost consciousness of his surroundings. She became everything he could know, like a nearby sun.

"Halloo!" She stopped and waved her arms.

The nogas halted too and squinted nearsightedly. Their ears and noses twitched, straining into the rank dank heat. Flandry was jolted back to the world. They could attack her. "Deploy," he rapped at those of his men who carried weapons. "Half circle behind me. The rest of you stand at the trailhead." He ran to Kathryn's side.

Wings beat. A creature that had been hovering, barely visible amidst low clouds, dropped straight toward the sixth noga. "A krippo." Kathryn seized Flandry's hand. "I wish I could've told you in advance. But watch. 'Tis wonderful."

The nogas were presumably more or less mammalian, also in their reproductive pattern: the sexes were obvious, the females had udders. The krippo resembled a bird . . . did it? The body was comparable to that of a large goose, with feathers gray-brown above, pale gray below, tipped with blue around the throat, on the pinions, at the end of a long triangular tail. The claws were strong, meant to grab and hang on. The neck was fairly long itself, supporting a head that swelled grotesquely backward. The face seemed to consist mainly of two great topaz eyes. And there was no beak, only a red cartilaginous tube.

The krippo landed on the noga's right shoulder. It thrust a ropy tongue (?) from the tube. Flandry noticed a knot on either side of the noga, just below the platform. The right one uncoiled, revealing itself to be a member suggestive of a tentacle, more than two meters in length if fully outstretched. The krippo's extended equivalent, the "tongue," plunged into a sphincter at the end of this. Linked, the two organisms trotted toward the humans.

79

"We're still lackin' a ruka," Kathryn said. "No, wait." The noga behind the plow had bellowed. "That entity's callin' for one. Heesh's own, ruka has to unharness heesh 'fore heesh can come to us."

"But the rest——" Flandry pointed. Four nogas merely stood where they were.

"Sure," Kathryn said. "Without partners, they're dumb brutes. They won't act, 'cept for the kind of rote job they were doin', till they get a signal from a complete entity. . . . Ah. Here we go."

A new animal dropped from a tree and scampered over the furrows. It was less analogous to an ape than the noga was to a rhinoceros or the krippo to a bird. However, a Terran was bound to think of it in such terms. About a meter tall if it stood erect, it must use its short, bowed legs arboreally by choice, for it ran on all fours and either foot terminated in three well-developed grasping digits. The tail was prehensile. The chest, shoulders, and arms were enormous in proportion, greater than a man's; and besides three fingers, each hand possessed a true thumb. The head was similarly massive, round, with bowl-shaped ears and luminous brown eyes. Like the krippo, this creature had no nose or mouth, simply a nostrilled tube. Black hair covered it, except where ears, extremities, and a throat pouch showed blue skin. It—he—was male. He wore a belt supporting a purse and an iron dagger.

"Is that a Didonian?" Flandry asked.

"A ruka," Kathryn said. "One-third of a Dodonian."

The animal reached the noga closest to the humans. He bounded onto the left shoulder, settled down by the krippo, and thrust out a "tongue" of his own to join the remaining "tentacle."

"You see," Kathryn said hurriedly, "we had to name them somehow. In most Didonian languages, the species are called things answerin' roughly to 'feet,' 'wings,' and 'hands.' But that'd get confusin' in Anglic. So, long's Aenean dialects contain some Russko anyhow, we settled on 'noga,' 'krippo,' 'ruka.'" The tripartite being stopped a few meters off. "Rest your gun. Heesh won't hurt us."

She went to meet it. Flandry followed, a bit dazed. Symbiotic relationships were not unknown to him. The most spectacular case he'd met hitherto was among the Togru-Kon-Tanakh of Vanrijn. A gorilloid supplied hands and strength; a small, carapaced partner had brains and keen eyes; the detachable organs that linked them contained cells for joining the two nervous systems into one. Apparently evolution on Dido had gone the same way.

But off the deep end! Flandry thought. *To the point where the two little types no longer even eat, but draw blood off the big one. Lord, how horrible. Never to revel in a tournedos or a pêche flambée—*

He and Kathryn stopped before the autochthon. A horsey aroma, not unpleasant, wafted down a light, barely cooling breeze. Flandry wondered which pair of eyes to meet.

The noga grunted. The krippo trilled through its nostrils, which must have some kind of strings and resonating chamber. The ruka inflated his throat pouch and produced a surprising variety of sounds.

Kathryn listened intently. "I'm no expert in this language," she said, "but they do speak a related one 'round Port Frederiksen, so I can follow 'long fairly well. Heesh's name is Master Of Songs, though 'name' has the wrong connotations. . . ." She uttered vocables. Flandry caught a few Anglic words, but couldn't really understand her.

I suppose all Didonians are too alien to learn a human tongue, he thought. *The xenologists must have worked out different pidgins for the different linguistic families: noises that a Terran epiglottis can wrap itself around, on a semantic pattern that a Didonian can comprehend.* He regarded Kathryn with renewed marveling. *What brains that must have taken!*

Three voices answered her. *The impossibility of a human talking a Didonian language can't just be a matter of larynx and mouth,* Flandry realized. *A vocalizer would deal with that. No, the structure's doubtless contrapuntal.*

"Heesh doesn't know pidgin," Kathryn told him. "But Cave Discoverer does. They'll assemble heesh for us."

"Heesh?"

She chuckled. "What pronoun's right, in a situation like this? A few cultures insist on some particular sex distribution in the units of an entity. But for most, sex isn't what matters, 'tis the species and individual capabilities of the units, and they form entities in whatever combinations seem best at a given time. So we call a partnership, whether complete or two-way, 'heesh.' And we don't fool 'round inflectin' the word."

The krippo took off in a racket of wings. The ruka stayed aboard the noga. But it was as if a light had dimmed. The two stared at the humans a while, then the ruka scratched himself and the noga began cropping weeds.

"You need all three for full intelligence," Flandry deduced.

Kathryn nodded. "M-hm. The rukas have the most forebrain. Alone, one of them is 'bout equal to a chimpanzee. Is that right, the smartest Terran subhuman? And the noga

81

alone is pretty stupid. A three-way, though, can think as well as you or I. Maybe better, if comparison's possible. We're still tryin' to find tests and measurements that make sense." She frowned. "Do have the boys put away their guns. We're 'mong good people."

Flandry acceded, but left his followers posted where they were. If anything went agley, he wanted that trail held. The hurt men lay there on their stretchers.

The other partnership finished disengaging itself—no, heeshself—from the plow. The earth thudded to the gallop of heesh's noga; krippo and ruka must be hanging on tight! Kathryn addressed this Didonian when heesh arrived, also without result though she did get a response. This she translated as: "Meet Skilled With Soil, who knows of our race even if none of heesh's units have learned pidgin."

Flandry rubbed his chin. His last application of antibeard enzyme was still keeping it smooth, but he lamented the scraggly walrus effect that his mustache was sprouting. "I take it," he said, "that invidi—uh, units swap around to form, uh, entities whose natural endowment is optimum for whatever is to be done?"

"Yes. In most cultures we've studied. Skilled With Soil is evidently just what the phrase implies, a gifted farmer. In other combinations, heesh's units might be part of an outstandin' hunter or artisan or musician or whatever. That's why there's no requirement for a large population in order to have a variety of specialists within a communion."

"Did you say 'communion'?"

"Seems more accurate than 'community,' true?"

"But why doesn't everybody know what anybody does?"

"Well, learnin' does seem to go easier'n for our race, but 'tis not instantaneous. Memory traces have to be reinforced if they're not to fade out; skills have to be developed through practice. And, natur'ly, a brain holds the *kind* of memories and skills 'tis equipped to hold. For instance, nogas keep the botanical knowledge, 'cause they do the eatin'; rukas, havin' hands, remember the manual trades; krippos store meteorological and geographical data. 'Tis not quite that simple, really. All species store some information of every sort—we think—'speci'ly language. But you get the idea, I'm sure."

"Nonetheless—"

"Let me continue, Dominic." Enthusiasm sparkled from Kathryn as Flandry had never seen it from a woman before. "Question of culture. Didonian societies vary as much as ever Terran ones did. Certain cultures let entities form promiscuously. The result is, units learn less from others than they

82

might, for lack of concentrated attention; emotional and intellectual life is shallow; the group stays at a low level of savagery. Certain other cultures are 'stremely restrictive 'bout relationships. For 'sample, the units of an entity are often s'posed to belong to each other 'sclusively till death do them part, 'cept for a grugin' temporary linkage with immature ones as a necessity of education. Those societies tend to be further along technologically, but nowhere beyond the stone age and everywhere esthetically impoverished. In neither case are the Didonians realizin' their full potential."

"I see," Flandry drawled. "Playboys versus puritans."

She blinked, then grinned. "As you will. Anyhow, most cultures—like this one, clearly—do it right. Every unit belongs to a few stable entities, dividin' time roughly equally 'mong them. That way, these entities develop true personalities, broadly backgrounded but each with a maximum talent in heesh's specialty. In addition, less developed partnerships are assembled temporarily at need."

She glanced skyward. "I think Cave Discoverer's 'bout to be created for us," she said.

Two krippos circled down. One presumably belonged to Master Of Songs, the other to Cave Discoverer, though Flandry couldn't tell them apart. Master Of Songs and Cave Discoverer apparently had a noga and ruka in common.

The bird shape in the lead took stance on the platform. The companion flew off to find a noga for itself. More krippos were appearing over the trees, more rukas scampering from the woods or the house. *We'll have a regular town meeting here in a minute,* Flandry anticipated.

He directed his awareness back to Kathryn and Cave Discoverer. A dialogue had commenced between them. It went haltingly at first, neither party having encountered pidgin for some years and the language of this neighborhood not being precisely identical with that which was spoken around Port Frederiksen. After a while, discourse gained momentum.

The rest of the communion arrived to watch, listen, and have the talk interpreted for them—aside from those who were out hunting or gathering, as Flandry learned later. An entity moved close to him. The ruka sprang off and approached, trailing the noga's thick "umbilicus" across a shoulder. Blue fingers plucked at Flandry's clothes and tried to unsheath his blaster for examination. The man didn't want to allow that, even if he put the weapon on safety, but Kathryn might disapprove of outright refusal. Removing his homemade packsack, he spread its contents on the ground. That served to keep the rukas of several curious entities occupied.

83

After he saw they were not stealing or damaging, Flandry sat down and let his mind wander until it got to Kathryn. There it stayed.

An hour or so had passed, the brief day was drawing to a close, when she summoned him with a wave. "They're glad to meet us, willin' to offer hospitality," she said, "but dubious 'bout helpin' us across the mountains. The dwellers yonder are dangerous. Also, this is a busy season in the forest as well as the plowland. At the same time, the communion 'ud surely like the payment I promise, things like firearms and proper steel tools. They'll create one they call Many Thoughts and let heesh ponder the question. Meanwhile we're invited to stay."

Lieutenant Kapunan was especially pleased with that. Such medicines as he had were keeping his patients from getting worse, but the stress of travel hadn't let them improve much. If he could remain here with them while the rest went after help—Flandry agreed. The march might produce casualties of its own, but if so, they ought to be fewer.

Everyone took off for the house. The humans felt dwarfed by the lumbering bulks around them: all but Kathryn. She laughed and chattered the whole way. "Kind of a home-comin' for me, this," she told her companions. "I'd 'most forgotten how 'scitin' 'tis, field work on Dido, and how I, well, yes, love them."

You have a lot of capacity to love, Flandry thought. He recognized it as a pleasing remark that he would have used on any other girl; but he felt shy about flattering this one.

When they topped the ridge, they had a view of the farther slope. It dropped a way, then rose again, forming a shelter for the dwelling place. Artificial channels, feeding into a stream, must prevent flooding. In the distance, above trees, a bare crag loomed athwart the clouds. Thence came the rumble of a major waterfall. Kathryn pointed. "They call this region Thunderstone," she said, " 'mong other things. Places come closer to havin' true names than entities do."

The homestead consisted of turf-roofed log buildings and a rude corral, enclosing a yard cobbled agianst the frequent mudmaking rains. Most of the structures were sheds and cribs. The biggest was the longhouse, impressive in workmanship and carved ornamentation as well as sheer size. Flandry paid more heed at first to the corral. Juveniles of all three species occupied it, together with four adults of each kind. The grownups formed pairs in different combinations, with immature third units. Other young wandered about, dozed, or took nourishment. The cows nursed the noga calves—two adults were lactating females, one was dry, one was male—and were in turn tapped by fuzzy little rukas and fledgling krippos.

"School?" Flandry asked.

"You might say so," Kathryn answered. "Primary stages of learnin' and development. Too important to interrupt for us; not that a partial entity 'ud care anyway. While they grow, the young'll partner 'mong themselves also. But in the end, as a rule, they'll replace units that've died out of established entities."

"Heh! 'If youth knew, if age could.' The Didonians appear to have solved that problem."

"And conquered death, in a way. 'Course, over several generations, a given personality 'ull fade into an altogether new one, and most of the earlier memories 'ull be lost. Still, the continuity—D' you see why they fascinate us?"

"Indeed. I haven't the temperament for being a scientist, but you make me wish I did."

She regarded him seriously. "In your fashion, Dominic, you're as much a filosof as anybody I've known."

My men are a gallant crew, he thought, *and they're entitled to my loyalty as well as my leadership, but at the moment I'd prefer them and their big flapping ears ten parsecs hence.*

The doors and window shutters of the lodge stood open, making its interior more bright and cool than he had awaited. The floor was fire-hardened clay strewn with fresh boughs. Fantastically carved pillars and rafters upheld the roof. The walls were hung with skins, crudely woven tapestries, tools, weapons, and objects that Kathryn guessed were sacred. Built in along them were stalls for nogas, perches for krippos, benches for rukas. Above were sconced torches for night illumination. Fires burned in pits; hoods, of leather stretched on wooden frames, helped draw smoke out through ventholes. Cubs, calves, and chicks, too small for education, bumbled about like the pet animals they were. Units that must be too aged or ill for daily toil waited quietly near the middle of the house. It was all one enormous room. Privacy was surely an idea which Didonians were literally incapable of entertaining. But what ideas did they have that were forever beyond human reach?

Flandry gestured at a pelt. "If they're herbivorous, the big chaps, I mean, why do they hunt?" he wondered.

"Animal products," Kathryn said. "Leather, bone, sinew, grease . . . sh!"

The procession drew up before a perch whereon sat an old

krippo. Gaunt, lame in one wing, he nevertheless reminded Flandry of eagles. Every noga lowered the horn to him. The flyer belonging to Cave Discoverer let go and flapped off to a place of his (?) own. That noga offered his vacated tentacle. The ancient made union. His eyes turned on the humans and fairly blazed.

"Many Thoughts," Kathryn whispered to Flandry. "Their wisest. Heesh'll take a minute to absorb what the units can convey."

"Do that fowl's partners belong to every prominent citizen?"

"Sh, not so loud. I don't know local customs, but they seem to have special respect for Many Thoughts. . . . Well, you'd 'spect the units with the best genetic heritage to be in the best entities, wouldn't you? I gather Cave Discoverer's an explorer and adventurer. Heesh first met humans by seeking out a xenological camp 200 kilometers from here. Many Thoughts gets the vigor and boldness of the same noga and ruka, but heesh's own journeys are of the spirit. . . . Ah, think heesh's ready now. I'll have to repeat whatever information went away with the former krippo."

That conversation lasted beyond nightfall. The torches were lit, the fires stoked, cooking begun in stone pots. While the nogas could live on raw vegetation, they preferred more concentrated and tasty food when they could get it. A few more Didonians came home from the woods, lighting their way with luminous fungoids. They carried basketful of edible roots. No doubt hunters and foragers remained out for a good many days at a stretch. The lodge filled with droning fluting, coughing talk. Flandry and his men had trouble fending curiosity seekers off their injured without acting unfriendly.

At last Kathryn made the best imitation she could of the gesture of deference, and sought out her fellow humans. In the leaping red light, her eyes and locks stood brilliant among shadows. " 'Twasn't easy," she said in exuberance, 'but . argued heesh into it. We'll have an escort—mighty small, but an escort, guides and porters. I reckon we can start in another forty-fifty hours . . . for home!"

"Your home," growled a man.

"Dog your hatch," Flandry ordered him.

X

Centuries before, a rogue planet had passed near Beta Crucis. Sunless worlds are not uncommon, but in astronomical immensity it is rare for one to encounter a star. This globe swung by and receded on a hyperbolic orbit. Approximately Terra-size, it had outgassed vapors in the ardor of its youth. Then, as internal heat radiated away, atmosphere froze. The great blue sun melted the oceans and boiled the air back into fluidity. For some years, appalling violence reigned.

Eventually interstellar cold would have reclaimed its dominion, and the incident would have had no significance. But chance ordained that the passage occur in the old bold days of the Polesotechnic League, and that it be noticed by those who saw an incalculable fortune to be won. Isotope synthesis on the scale demanded by a starfaring civilization had been industry's worst bottleneck. Seas and skies were needed for coolants, continents for dumping of radioactive wastes. Every lifeless body known had been too frigid or too hot or otherwise unsuitable. But here came Satan, warmed to an ideal temperature which the heat of nuclear manufacture could maintain. As soon as the storms and quakes had abated, the planet was swarmed by entrepreneurs.

During the Troubles, ownership, legal status, input and output, every aspect of relationship to the living fraction of the universe, varied as wildly for Satan as for most worlds. For a while it was abandoned. But no one had ever actually dwelt there. No being could survive that poisonous air and murderous radiation background, unless for the briefest of visits with the heaviest of protection. Robots, computers, and automatons were the inhabitants. They continued operating while civilization fragmented, fought, and somewhat reconstructed itself. When at last an Imperial aristocrat sent down a self-piloting freighter, they loaded it from a dragon's hoard.

The defense of Satan became a major reason to garrison and colonize Sector Alpha Crucis.

Its disc hung darkling among the stars in a viewscreen of Hugh McCormac's command room. Beta had long since dwindled to merely the brightest of them, and the machines had scant need for visible light. You saw the sphere blurred by gas, a vague shimmer of clouds and oceans, blacknesses that were land. It was a desolate scene, the more so when you called up an image of the surface—raw mountains, gashed valleys, naked stone plains, chill and stagnant seas, all cloaked in a night relieved only by a rare lamp or an evil blue glow of fluorescence, no sound but a dreary wind-skirl or a rushing of forever sterile waters, no happening throughout its eons but the inanimate, unaware toil of the machines.

For Hugh McCormac, though, Satan meant victory.

He took his gaze from the planet and let it stray in the opposite direction, toward open sapce. Men were dying where those constellations glittered. "I should be yonder," he said. "I should have insisted."

"You couldn't do anything, sir," Edgar Oliphant told him. "Once the tactical dispositions are made, the game plays itself. And you might be killed."

"That's what's wrong." McCormac twisted his fingers together. "Here we are, snug and safe in orbit, while a battle goes on to make *me* Emperor!"

"You're the High Admiral too, sir." A cigar in Oliphant's mouth wagged and fumed as he talked. "You've got to be available where the data flow in, to make decisions in case anything unpredicted happens."

"I know, I know." McCormac strode back and forth, from end to end of the balcony on which they stood. Below them stretched a murmurous complex of computers, men at desks and plotting consoles, messengers going soft-footed in and out. Nobody, from himself on down, bothered with spit-and-polish today. They had too much work on hand, coordinating the battle against Pickens' fleet. It had learned where they were from the ducal guards they chased off and had sought them out. Simply understanding that interaction of ships and energies was beyond mortal capacity.

He hated to tie up *Persei* when every gun spelled life to his outnumbered forces. She was half of the Nova-class dreadnaughts he had. But nothing less would hold the necessary equipment.

"We could do some fighting in addition," he said. "I've operated thus in the past."

"But that was before you were the Emperor," Oliphant replied

McCormac halted and glowered at him. The stout man chewed his cigar and plodded on: "Sir, we've few enough active supporters as is. Most bein's are just prayin' they won't get involved on either side. Why should anybody put everything at stake for the revolution, if he doesn't hope you'll bring him a better day? We could risk our control center, no doubt. But we can't risk you. Without you, the revolution 'ud fall apart 'fore Terran reinforcements could get here to suppress it."

McCormac clenched his fists and looked back at Satan. "Sorry," he mumbled. "I'm being childish."

" 'Tis forgivable," Oliphant said. "Two of your boys in combat—"

"And how many other people's boys? Human or xeno, they die, they're maimed. . . . Well." McCormac leaned over the balcony rail and studied the big display tank on the deck beneath him. Its colored lights gave only a hint of the information—itself partial and often unreliable—that flowed through the computers. But such three-dimensional pictures occasionally stimulated the spark of genius which no known civilization has succeeded in evoking from an electronic brain.

According to the pattern, his tactics were proving out. He had postulated that destruction of the factories on Satan would be too great an economic disaster for cautious Dave Pickens to hazard. Therefore the Josipists would be strictly enjoined not to come near the planet. Therefore McCormac's forces would have a privileged sanctuary. That would make actions possible to them which otherwise were madness. Of course, Pickens might charge straight in anyway; that contingency must be provided against. But if so, McCormac need have no compunctions about using Satan for shield and backstop. Whether it was destroyed or only held by his fleet, its products were denied the enemy. In time, that was sure to bring disaffection and weakness.

But it looked as if Pickens was playing safe—and getting mauled in consequence.

"S'pose we win," Oliphant said. "What next?"

It had been discussed for hours on end, but McCormac seized the chance to think past this battle. "Depends on what power the opposition has left. We want to take over as large a volume of space as possible without overextending ourselves. Supply and logistics are worse problems for us than combat, actually. We aren't yet organized to replace losses or even normal consumption."

"Should we attack Ifri?"

"No. Too formidable. If we can cut it off, the same purpose is better served. Besides, eventually we'll need it ourselves."

"Llynathawr, though? I mean . . . well, we do have information that your lady was removed by some government agent—" Oliphant stopped, seeing what his well-meant speech had done.

McCormac stood alone, as if naked on Satan, for a while. Finally he could say: "No. They're bound to defend it with everything they have. Catawrayannis would be wiped out. Never mind Kathryn. There're too many other Kathryns around."

Can an Emperor afford such thoughts?

A visiscreen chimed and lit. A jubilant countenance looked forth. "Sir—Your Majesty—we've won!"

"What?" McCormac needed a second to understand.

"Positive, Your Majesty. Reports are pouring in, all at once. Still being evaluated, but, well, we haven't any doubt. It's almost like reading their codes."

A piece of McCormac's splintering consciousness visualized that possibility. The reference was not to sophont-sophont but machine-machine communication. A code was more than changed; the key computers were instructed to devise a whole new language, which others were then instructed to learn and use. Because random factors determined basic elements of the language, decipherment was, if not totally impossible, too laborious a process to overtake any prudent frequency of innovation. Hence the talk across space between robots, which wove their ships into a fleet, was a virtually unbreakable riddle to foes, a nearly infallible recognition signal to friends. The chance of interpreting it had justified numerous attempts throughout history at boarding or hijacking a vessel, however rarely they succeeded and however promptly their success caused codes to be revised. If you could learn a language the hostile machines were still using—

No. A daydream. McCormac forced his attention back to the screen. "Loss of *Zeta Orionis* probably decided him. They're disengaging everywhere." *I must get busy. We should harry them while they retreat, though not too far. Tactical improvisations needed.* "Uh, we've confirmed that *Vixen* is untouched. *John's ship.* "No report from *New Phobos*, but no positive reason to fear for her." *Colin's ship. Bob's with me.* "A moment, please. Important datum. . . . Sir, it's confirmed, *Aquilae* suffered heavy damage. She's almost certainly their flagship, you know. They won't be meshing any too well. We can eat them one at a time!" *Dave, are you alive?*

"Very good, Captain," McCormac said. "I'll join you right away on the command deck."

Aaron Snelund let the admiral stand, miserable in blue and gold, while he chose a cigaret from a jeweled case, rolled it in his fingers, sniffed the fragrance of genuine Terra-grown Crown grade marijuana, inhaled it into lighting, sat most gracefully down on his chair of state, and drank the smoke. No one else was in the room, save his motionless Gorzunians. The dynasculps were turned off. The animation was not, but its music was, so that masked lords and ladies danced without sound through a ballroom 200 light-years and half a century distant.

"Superb," Snelund murmured when he had finished. He nodded at the big gray-haired man who waited. "At ease."

Pickens did not relax noticeably. "Sir—" His voice was higher than before. Overnight he had become old.

Snelund interrupted him with a wave. "Don't trouble, Admiral. I have studied the reports. I know the situation consequent on your defeat. One is not necessarily illiterate, even with respect to the Navy's abominable prose, just because one is a governor. Is one?"

"No, Your Excellency."

Snelund lounged back, cross-legged, eyelids drooping. "I did not call you here for a repetition *viva voce* of what I have read," he continued mildly. "No, I wished for a chat that would be candid because private. Tell me, Admiral, what is your advice to me?"

"That's . . . in my personal report . . . sir."

Snelund arched his brows.

Sweat trickled down Pickens' cheeks. "Well, sir," he groped, "our total remaining power must be not greatly inferior to the, the enemy's. If we count what did not go to Satan. We can consolidate a small volume of space, hold it, let him have the rest. The Merseian confrontation can't go on forever. When we have heavy reinforcements, we can go out for a showdown battle."

"Your last showdown was rather disappointing, Admiral."

A tic vibrated one corner of Pickens' mouth. "The governor has my resignation."

"And has not accepted it. Nor will."

"Sir!" Pickens' mouth fell open.

"Be calm." Snelund shifted his tone from delicate sarcasm

91

to kindliness, his manner from idle humor to vigilance. "You didn't disgrace yourself, Admiral. You just had the misfortune to clash with a better man. Were you less able, little would have been salvaged from your defeat. As matters went, you rescued half your force. You lack imagination, but you have competence: a jewel of high price in these degenerate times. No, I don't want your resignation. I want you to continue in charge."

Pickens trembled. Tears stood in his eyes. "Sit down," Snelund invited. Pickens caved into a chair. Snelund kindled another cigaret, tobacco, and let him recover some equilibrium before saying:

"Competence, professionalism, sound organization and direction—you can supply those. I will supply the imagination. In other words, from here on I dictate policies for you to execute. Is that clear?"

His question lashed. Pickens gulped and croaked, "Yes, sir." It had been a precision job for Snelund, these past days, making the officer malleable without destroying his usefulness —an exacting but enjoyable task.

"Good. Good. Oh, by the way, smoke if you wish," the governor said. "Let me make clear what I plan.

"Originally I counted on applying various pressures through Lady McCormac. Then that dolt Flandry disappeared with her." A rage that boiled like liquid helium: "Have you any inkling what became of them?"

"No, sir," Pickens said. "Our Intelligence section hasn't yet succeeded in infiltrating the enemy. That takes time. . . . Er, from what we can piece together, she doesn't seem to have rejoined her husband. But we've had no word about her arrival anywhere else, like maybe on Terra."

"Well," Snelund said, "I don't envy Citizen Flandry once *I* get back." He rolled smoke around in his lungs until coolness returned. "No matter, really. The picture has changed. I've been rethinking this whole affair.

"What you propose, letting McCormac take most of the sector without resistance while we wait for help, is apparently the conservative course. Therefore it's in fact the most deadly dangerous. He must be counting on precisely that. Let him be proclaimed Emperor on scores of worlds, let him marshal their resources and arrange their defenses with that damnable skill he owns—and quite probably, when the Terran task force comes, it won't be able to dislodge him. Consider his short interior lines of communication. Consider popular enthusiasm roused by his demagogues and xenagogues. Consider the likelihood of more and more defections to his side as long as his affairs run smoothly. Consider the virus spreading beyond this sector, out through the Empire, until it may indeed happen that one day he rides in triumph through Archopolis!"

Pickens stuttered, "I, I, I had thought of those things, Your Excellency."

Snelund laughed. "Furthermore, assuming the Imperium can put him down, what do you expect will become of you and, somewhat more significantly from this point of view, me? It will not earn us any medals that we allowed an insurrection and then could not quench it ourselves. Tongues will click. Heads will wag. Rivals will seize the opportunity to discredit. Whereas, if we can break Hugh McCormac unaided in space, clearing the way for my militia to clean out treason on the planets—well, kudos is the universal currency. It can buy us a great deal if we spend it wisely. Knighthood and promotion for you; return in glory to His Majesty's court for me. Am I right?"

Pickens moistened his lips. "Individuals like us shouldn't count. Not when millions and millions of lives—"

"But they belong to individuals too, correct? And if we serve ourselves, we serve the Imperium simultaneously, which we swore to do. Let us have no bleeding-heart unrealism. Let us get on with our business, the scotching of this rebellion."

"What does the governor propose?"

Snelund shook a finger. "Not propose, Admiral. Decree. We will thresh out details later. But in general, your mission will be to keep the war fires burning. True, our critical systems must be heavily guarded. But that will leave you with considerable forces free to act. Avoid another large battle. Instead raid, harass, hit and run, never attack a rebel group unless it's unmistakably weaker, make a special point of preying on commerce and industry."

"Sir? Those are our people!"

"McCormac claims they're his. And, from what I know of him, the fact that he'll be the cause of their suffering distress at our hands will plague him, will hopefully make him less efficient. Mind you, I don't speak of indiscriminate destruction. On the contrary, we shall have to have justifiable reasons for hitting every civilian target we do. Leave these decisions to me. The idea is, essentially, to undermine the rebel strength."

Snelund sat erect. One fist clenched on a chair arm. His hair blazed like a conqueror's brand. "Supply and replacement," he said ringingly. "Those are going to be McCormac's nemesis. He may be able to whip us in a stand-up battle. But he can't whip attrition. Food, clothing, medical supplies, weapons, tools, spare parts, whole new ships, a navy must have them in steady flow or it's doomed. Your task will be to plug their sources and choke their channels."

"Can that be done, sir, well enough and fast enough?" Pickens asked. "He'll fix defenses, arrange convoys, make counterattacks."

"Yes, yes, I know. Yours is a single part of the effort, albeit a valuable one. The rest is to deny McCormac an effective civil service."

"I don't, uh, don't understand, sir."

"Not many do," Snelund said. "But think what an army of bureaucrats and functionaries compose the foundation of any government. It's no difference whether they are paid by the state or by some nominally private organization. They still do the day-to-day work. They operate the spaceports and traffic lanes, they deliver the mail, they keep the electronic communication channels unsnarled, they collect and supply essential data, they oversee public health, they hold crime in check, they arbitrate disputes, they allocate scarce resources. . . . Need I go on?"

He smiled wider. "Confidentially," he said, "the lesson was taught me by experience out here. As you know, I had various changes in policy and administrative procedure that I wished to put into effect. I was only successful to a degree, chiefly on backward planets with no real indigenous civil services. Otherwise, the bureaucrats dragged their feet too much. It's not like the Navy, Admiral. I would press an intercom button, issue a top priority order—and nothing would happen. Memos took weeks or months to go from desk to desk. Technical objections were argued comma by comma. Interminable requests for clarification made their slow ways back to me. Reports were filed and forgotten. It was like dueling a fog. And I couldn't dismiss the lot of them. Quite apart from legalities, I had to have them. There were no replacements for them.

"I intend to give Hugh McCormac a taste of that medicine."

Pickens shifted uneasily. "How, sir?"

"That's a matter I want to discuss this afternoon. We must get word to those planets. The little functionaries must be persuaded that it isn't in their own best interest to serve the rebellion with any zeal. Their natural timidity and stodginess work in our favor. If, in addition, we bribe some, threaten others, perhaps carry out an occasional assassination or bombing—Do you follow? We must plant our agents

94

throughout McCormac's potential kingdom before he can take possession of it and post his guards. Then we must keep up the pressure—agents smuggled in, for example; propaganda; disruption of interstellar transportation by your raiders—Yes, I do believe we can bring McCormac's civil service machinery to a crawling, creaking slowdown. And without it, his navy starves. Are you with me, Admiral?"

Pickens swallowed. "Yes, sir. Of course."

"Good." Snelund rose. "Come along to the conference room. My staff's waiting. We'll thresh out specific plans. Would you like a stimpill? The session will probably continue till all hours."

They had learned of him, first on Venus, then on Terra, then in Sector Alpha Crucis: voluptuary he was, but when he saw a chance or a threat that concerned himself, twenty demons could not outwork him.

XI

Kathryn estimated the distance from Thunderstone to Port Frederiksen as about 2000 kilometers. But that was map distance, the kind that an aircar traversed in a couple of hours, a spacecraft in minutes or seconds. Aground and afoot, it would take weeks.

Not only was the terrain difficult, most of it was unknown to the Didonians. Like the majority of primitives, they seldom ventured far beyond their home territory. Articles of trade normally went from communion to communion rather than cross-country in a single caravan. Hence the three who accompanied the humans must feel their own way. In the mountains especially, this was bound to be a slow process with many false choices.

Furthermore, the short rotation period made for inefficient

95

travel. The autochthons refused to move after dark, and Flandry was forced to agree it would be unwise in strange areas. The days were lengthening as the season advanced; at midsummer they would fill better than seven hours out of the eight and three-quarters. But the Didonians could not take advantage of more than four or five hours. The reason was, again, practical. En route, away from the richer diet provided by their farms, a noga must eat—for three—whatever it could find. Vegetable food is less caloric than meat. The natives had to allow ample time for fueling their bodies.

"Twenty-four of us humans," Flandry counted. "And the sixteen we're leaving behind, plus the good doctor, also have appetites. I don't know if our rations will stretch."

"We can supplement some with native food," Kathryn reassured him. "There're levo compounds in certain plants and animals, same as terrestroid biochemistries involve occasional dextros. I can show you and the boys what they look like."

"Well, I suppose we may as well scratch around for them, since we'll be oysting so much in camp."

"Oystin'?"

"What oysters do. Mainly sit." Flandry ruffled his mustache. "Damn, but this is turning into a loathsome fungus! The two items I did not think to rescue would have to be scissors and a mirror."

Kathryn laughed. "Why didn't you speak before? They have scissors here. Clumsy, none too sharp, but you can cut hair with them. Let me be your barber."

Her hands across his head made him dizzy. He was glad that she let the men take care of themselves.

They were all quite under her spell. He didn't think it was merely because she was the sole woman around. They vied to do her favors and show her courtesies. He wished they would stop, but couldn't well order it. Relationships were strained already.

He was no longer the captain to them, but the commander: his brevet rank, as opposed to his lost status of shipmaster. They cooperated efficiently, but it was inevitable that discipline relaxed, even between enlisted men and other officers. He felt he must preserve its basic forms around himself. This led to a degree of—not hostility, but cool, correct aloofness as regarded him, in distinction to the camaraderie that developed among the rest.

One night, happening to wake without showing it, he overheard a muted conversation among several. Two were declaring their intention not just to accept internment, but to join

McCormac's side if its chances looked reasonable when they got to the base. They were trying to convince their friends to do likewise. The friends declined, for the time being at any rate, but good-naturedly. That was what disturbed Flandry: that no one else was disturbed. He began regular eavesdropping. He didn't mean to report anyone, but he did want to know where every man stood. Not that he felt any great need for moralistic justification. The snooping was fun.

That started well after the party had left Thunderstone. The three Didonians were named by Kathryn as Cave Discoverer, Harvest Fetcher, and, to human amusement, Smith. It was more than dubious if the entities thought of themselves by name. The terms were convenient designations, based on personal qualities or events of past life. The unit animals had nothing but individual signals.

Often they swapped around, to form such combinations as Iron Miner, Guardian Of North Gate, or Lightning Struck The House. Kathryn explained that this was partly for a change, partly to keep fresh the habits and memories which constituted each entity, and partly a quasi-religious rite.

"Oneness is the ideal in this culture, I'm learnin', as 'tis in a lot of others," she told Flandry. "They consider the whole world to be potenti'ly a single entity. By ceremonies, mystic contemplation, hallucinogenic foods, or whatever, they try to merge with it. An everyday method is to make frequent new interconnections. The matin' season, 'round the autumnal equinox, is their high point of the year, mainly 'cause of the ecstatic, transcendental 'speriences that then become possible."

"Yes, I imagine a race like this has some interesting sexual variations," Flandry said. She flushed and looked away. He didn't know why she should react so, who had observed life as a scientist. Associations with her captivity? He thought not. She was too vital to let that cripple her long; the scars would always remain, but by now she had her merriment back. Why, then, this shyness with him?

They were following a ridge. The country belonged to another communion which, being akin to Thunderstone, had freely allowed transit. Already they had climbed above the jungle zone. Here the air was tropical by Terran standards, but wonderfully less wet, with a breeze to lave the skin and caress the hair and carry scents not unlike ginger. The ground was decked with spongy brown carpet weed, iridescent blossoms, occasional stands of arrowbrush, grenade, and lantern tree. A mass of land coral rose to the left, its red and blue the more vivid against the sky's eternal silver-gray.

None of the Didonians were complete. One maintained heesh's noga-ruka linkage, the other two rukas were off gathering berries, the three krippos were aloft as scouts. Separated, the animals could carry out routine tasks and recognize a need for reunion when it arose.

Besides their own ruka-wielded equipment—including spears, bows, and battleaxes—the nogas easily carried the stuff from the spaceboat. Thus liberated, the men could outpace the ambling quadrupeds. With no danger and no way to get lost hereabouts, Flandry had told them to expedite matters by helping the rukas. They were scattered across the hill.

Leaving him alone with Kathryn.

He was acutely conscious of her: curve of breast and hip beneath her coverall, free-swinging stride, locks blowing free and bright next to the sun-darkened skin, strong face, great green-gold eyes, scent of warm flesh. . . . He changed the subject at once. "Isn't the, well, pantheistic concept natural to Didonians?"

"No more than monotheism's natural, inevitable, in man," Kathryn said with equal haste. "It depends on culture. Some exalt the communion itself, as an entity distinct from the rest of the world, includin' other communions. Their rites remind me of human mobs cheerin' an almighty State and its director. They tend to be warlike and predatory." She pointed ahead, where mountain peaks were vaguely visible. "I'm 'fraid we've got to get past a society of that kind. 'Tis one reason why they weren't keen on this trip in Thunderstone. Word travels, whether or not entities do. I had to remind Many Thoughts 'bout our guns."

"People who don't fear death make wicked opponents," Flandry said. "However, I wouldn't suppose a Didonian exactly enjoys losing a unit; and heesh must have the usual desire to avoid pain."

Kathryn smiled, at ease once more. "You learn fast. Ought to be a xenologist yourself."

He shrugged. "My business has put me in contact with various breeds. I remain convinced we humans are the weirdest of the lot; but your Didonians come close. Have you any idea how they evolved?"

"Yes, some paleontology's been done. Nowhere near enough. Why is it we can always find money for a war and're always pinched for everything else? Does the first cause the second?"

"I doubt that. I think people naturally prefer war."

"Someday they'll learn."

"You have insufficient faith in man's magnificent ability to ignore what history keeps yelling at him," Flandry said. Immediately, lest her thoughts turn to Hugh McCormac who wanted to reform the Empire: "But fossils are a less depressing subject. What about evolution on Dido?"

"Well, near's can be told, a prolonged hot spell occurred —like millions of years long. The ancestors of the nogas fed on soft plants which drought made scarce. 'Tis thought they took to hangin' 'round what trees were left, to catch leaves that ancestral rukas tore loose in the course of gatherin' fruit. Belike they had a tickbird relationship with the proto-krippos. But trees were dyin' off too. The krippos could spy forage a far ways off and guide the nogas there. Taggin' 'long, the rukas got protection to boot, and repaid by strippin' the trees.

"At last some of the animals drifted to the far eastern end of the Barcan continent. 'Twas afflicted, as 'tis yet, with a nasty kind of giant bug that not only sucks blood, but injects a microbe whose action keeps the wound open for days or weeks. The ancestral nogas were smaller and thinner-skinned than today's. They suffered. Prob'ly rukas and krippos helped them, swattin' and eatin' the heaviest swarms. But then they must've started sippin' the blood themselves, to supplement their meager diet."

"I can take it from there," Flandry said. "Including hormone exchange, mutually beneficial and cementing the alliance. It's lucky that no single-organism species happened to develop intelligence. It'd have mopped the deck with those awkward early three-ways. But the symbiosis appears to be in business now. Fascinating possibilities for civilization."

"We haven't exposed them to a lot of ours," Kathryn said. "Not just 'cause we want to study them as they are. We don't know what might be good for them, and what catastrophic."

"I'm afraid that's learned by trial and error," Flandry answered. "I'd be intrigued to see the result of raising some entities from birth"—the krippos were viviparous too—"in Technic society."

"Why not raise some humans 'mong Didonians?" she flared.

"I'm sorry." *You make indignation beautiful.* "I was only snakkering. Wouldn't do it in practice, not for anything. I've seen too many pathetic cases. I did forget they're your close friends."

Inspiration! "I'd like to become friends with them myself," Flandry said. "We have a two or three months' trip and buckets of idle time in camp ahead of us. Why don't you teach me the language?"

She regarded him with surprise. "You're serious, Dominic?"

"Indeed. I don't promise to retain the knowledge all my life. My head's overly cluttered with cobwebby information as is. But for the present, yes, I do want to converse with them directly. It'd be insurance for us. And who knows, I might come up with a new scientific hypothesis about them, too skewball to have occurred to any Aenean."

She laid a hand on his shoulder. That was her way; she liked to touch people she cared about. "You're no Imperial, Dominic," she said. "You belong with us."

"Be that as it may—" he said, confused.

"Why do you stand with Josip? You know what he is. You've seen his cronies, like Snelund, who could end by replacin' him in all but name. Why don't you join us, your kind?"

He knew why not, starting with the fact that he didn't believe the revolution could succeed and going on to more fundamental issues. But he could not tell her that, on this suddenly magical day. "Maybe you'll convert me," he said. "Meanwhile, what about language lessons?"

"Why, 'course."

—Flandry could not forbid his men to sit in, and a number of them did. By straining his considerable talent, he soon disheartened them and they quit. After that, he had Kathryn's whole notice for many hours per week. He ignored the jealous stares, and no longer felt jealous himself when she fell into cheerful conversation with one of the troop or joined a campfire circle for singing.

Nor did it perturb him when Chief Petty Officer Robbins returned from an excursion with her in search of man-edible plants, wearing a black eye and a sheepish look. Unruffled, she came in later and treated Robbins exactly as before. Word must have spread, for there were no further incidents.

Flandry's progress in his lessons amazed her. Besides having suitable genes, he had been through the Intelligence Corps' unmercifully rigorous courses in linguistics and metalinguistics, semantics and metasemantics, every known trick of concentration and memorization; he had learned how to learn. Few civilian scientists received that good a training; they didn't need it as urgently as any field agent always did. Inside a week, he had apprehended the structures of Thunderstone's language and man's pidgin—no easy feat, when the Didonian mind was so absolutely alien.

Or was it? Given the basic grammar and vocabulary, Flandry supplemented Kathryn's instruction by talking, mainly with Cave Discoverer. It went ridiculously at first, but after weeks he got to the point of holding real conversations. The Didonian was as interested in him and Kathryn as she was in heesh. She took to joining their colloquies, which didn't bother him in the least.

Cave Discoverer was more adventurous than average. Heesh's personality seemed more clearly defined than the rest, including any others in the party which incorporated heesh's members. At home heesh hunted, logged, and went on rambling explorations when not too busy. Annually heesh traveled to the lake called Golden, where less advanced communions held a fair and Cave Discoverer traded metal implements for their furs and dried fruits. There heesh's noga had the custom of joining with a particular ruka from one place and krippo from another to make the entity Raft Farer. In Thunderstone, besides Many Thoughts, Cave Discoverer's noga and ruka belonged to Master Of Songs; heesh's krippo (female) to Leader Of Dance; heesh's ruka to Brewmaster; and all to various temporary groups.

Aside from educational duties, none of them linked indiscriminately. Why waste the time of a unit that could make part of an outstanding entity, in junction with units less gifted? The distinction was somewhat blurred but nonetheless real in Thunderstone, between "first families" and "proles." No snobbery or envy appeared to be involved. The attitude was pragmatic. Altruism within the communion was so taken for granted that the concept did not exist.

Or thus went Flandry's and Kathryn's impressions. She admitted they might be wrong. How do you probe the psyche of a creature with three brains, each of which remembers its share in other creatures and, indirectly, remembers things that occurred generations before it was born?

Separately, the nogas were placid, though Kathryn said they became furious if aroused. The krippos were excitable and musical; they produced lovely clear notes in intricate patterns. The rukas were restless, curious, and playful. But these were generalizations. Individual variety was as great as for all animals with well-developed nervous systems.

Cave Discoverer was in love with heesh's universe. Heesh looked forward with excitement to seeing Port Frederiksen and wondered about the chance of going somewhere in a spaceship. After heesh got straight the basic facts of astronomy, xenology, and galactic politics, heesh's questions sharpened until Flandry wondered if Didonians might not be inherently more intelligent than men. Could their technological backwardness be due to accidental circumstances that would

101

no longer count when they saw the possibility of making systematic progress?

The future could be theirs, not ours, Flandry thought. *Kathryn would reply, "Why can't it be everybody's?"*

Meanwhile the expedition continued—through rain, gale, fog, heat, strange though not hostile communions, finally highlands where the men rejoiced in coolness. There, however, the Didonians shivered, and went hungry in a land of sparse growth, and, despite their krippos making aerial surveys, often blundered upon impassable stretches that forced them to retrace their steps and try again.

It was here, in High Maurusia, that battle smote them.

XII

The easiest way to reach one pass was through a canyon. During megayears, a river swollen by winter rains had carved it, then shrunken in summer. Its walls gave protection from winds and reflected some heat; this encouraged plant life to spring up every dry season along the streambed, where accumulated soil was kinder to feet than the naked rock elsewhere. Accordingly, however twisted and boulder-strewn, it appeared to offer the route of choice.

The scenery was impressive in a gaunt fashion. The river rolled on the party's left, broad, brown, noisy and dangerous despite being at its low point. A mat of annual plants made a border whose sober hues were relieved by white and scarlet blossoms. Here and there grew crooked trees, deep-rooted, adapted to inundation. Beyond, the canyon floor reached barren: tumbled dark rocks, fantastically eroded pinnacles and mesas, on to the talus slopes and palisades. Gray sky, diffuse and shadowless light, did not bring out color or detail very well; that was a bewildering view. But human lungs found the air mild, dry, exhilarating.

Two krippos wheeled on watch overhead. Harvest Fetcher stayed complete, and every ruka rode a noga. The outworlders walked behind, except for Kathryn, Flandry, and Havelock. She was off to the right, wrapped in her private thoughts. This landscape must have made her homesick for Aeneas. The commander and the ensign kept out of their companions' earshot.

"Damn it, sir, why do we take for granted we'll turn ourselves in at Port Frederiksen without a fight?" Havelock was protesting. "This notion our case is hopeless, it's encouraging treasonable thoughts."

Flandry refrained from saying he was aware of that. Havelock had been less standoffish than the rest; but a subtle barrier persisted, and Flandry had cultivated him for weeks before getting this much confidence. He knew Havelock had a girl on Terra.

"Well, Ensign," he said, "I can't make promises, for the reason that I'm not about to lead us to certain death. As you imply, though, the death may not necessarily be certain. Why don't you feel out the men? I don't want anyone denounced to me," *having a pretty fair idea myself,* "but you might quietly find who's . . . let's not say trustworthy, we'll assume everybody is, let's say enthusiastic. You might, still more quietly, alert them to stand by in case I do decide on making a break. We'll talk like this, you and I, off and on. More off than on, so as not to provoke suspicion. We'll get Kathryn to describe the port's layout, piecemeal, and that'll be an important element in what I elect to do."

You, Kathryn, will be more important.

"Very good, sir," Havelock said. "I hope—"

Assault burst forth.

The party had drawn even with a nearby rock mass whose bottom was screened by a row of crags. From behind these plunged a score of Didonians. Flandry had an instant to think, *Ye devils, they must've hid in a cave!* Then the air was full of arrows. "Deploy!" he yelled. "Fire! Kathryn, get down!"

A shaft went *whoot* by his ear. A noga bugled, a ruka screamed. Bellyflopping, Flandry glared over the sights of his blaster at the charging foe. They were barbarically decorated with pelts, feather blankets, necklaces of teeth, body paint. Their weapons were neolithic, flint axes, bone-tipped arrows and lances. But they were not less deadly for that, and the ambush had been arranged with skill.

103

He cast a look to right and left. Periodically while traveling, he had drilled his men in ground combat techniques. Today it paid off. They had formed an arc on either side of him. Each who carried a gun—there weren't many small arms aboard a warship—was backed by two or three comrades with spears or daggers, ready at need to assist or to take over the trigger.

Energy beams flared and crashed. Slugthrowers hissed, stunners buzzed. A roar of voices and hoofs echoed above the river's clangor. A krippo turned into flame and smoke, a ruka toppled to earth, a noga ran off bellowing its anguish. Peripherally, Flandry saw more savages hit.

But whether in contempt for death or sheer physical momentum, the charge continued. The distance to cover was short; and Flandry had not imagined a noga could gallop that fast. The survivors went by his line and fell on the Thunderstone trio before he comprehended it. One man barely rolled clear of a huge gray-blue body. The airborne flyers barely had time to reunite with their chief partners.

"Kathryn!" Flandry shouted into the din. He leaped erect and whirled around. The melee surged between him and her. For a second he saw how Didonians fought. Nogas, nearly invulnerable to edged weapons, pushed at each other and tried to gore. Rukas stabbed and hacked; krippos took what shelter they could, while grimly maintaining linkage, and buffeted with their wings. The objective was to put an opponent out of action by eliminating heesh's rider units.

Some mountaineer nogas, thus crippled by gunfire, blundered around in the offing. A few two-member entities held themselves in reserve, for use when a ruka or krippo went down in combat. Eight or nine complete groups surrounded the triangular formation adopted by the three from Thunderstone.

No, two and a half. By now Flandry could tell them apart. Harvest Fletcher's krippo must have been killed in the arrow barrage. The body lay transfixed, pathetically small, tailfeathers ruffled by a slight breeze, until a noga chanced to trample it into a smear. Its partners continued fighting, automatically and with lessened skill.

"Get those bastards!" somebody called. Men edged warily toward the milling, grunting, yelling, hammering interlocked mass. It was hard to understand why the savages were ignoring the humans, who had inflicted all the damage on them. Was the sight so strange as not to be readily comprehensible?

Flandry ran around the struggle to see what had become of Kathryn. *I never gave her a gun!* he knew in agony.

104

Her tall form broke upon his vision. She had retreated a distance, to stand beneath a tree she could climb if attacked. His Merseian blade gleamed in her grasp, expertly held. Her mouth was drawn taut but her eyes were watchful and steady.

He choked with relief. Turning, he made his way to the contest.

A stone ax spattered the brains of Smith's ruka. Cave Discoverer's ruka avenged the death in two swift blows—but, surrounded, could not defend his back. A lance entered him. He fell onto the horn of a savage noga, which tossed him high and smashed him underfoot when he landed.

The humans opened fire.

It was butchery.

The mountaineer remnants stampeded down the canyon. Not an entity among them remained whole. A young Terran stood over a noga, which was half cooked but still alive, and gave it the *coup de grace;* then tears and vomit erupted from him. The Thunderstoners could assemble one full person at a time. Of the possible combinations, they chose Guardian Of North Gate, who went about methodically releasing the wounded from life.

The entire battle, from start to finish, had lasted under ten minutes.

Kathryn came running. She too wept. "So much death, so much hurt—can't we help them?" A ruka stirred. He didn't seem wounded; yes, he'd probably taken a stun beam, and the supersonic jolt had affected him as it did a man. Guardian Of North Gate approached. Kathryn crouched over the ruka. "No! I forbid you."

The Didonian did not understand her pidgin, for only heesh's noga had been in Cave Discoverer. But her attitude was unmistakable. After a moment, with an almost physical shrug, heesh had heesh's ruka tie up the animal.

Thereafter, with what assistance the humans could give, heesh proceeded to care for the surviving Thunderstone units. They submitted patiently. A krippo had a broken leg, others showed gashes and bruises, but apparently every member could travel after a rest.

No one spoke aloud a wish to move from the battleground. No one spoke at all. Silent, they fared another two or three kilometers before halting.

In the high latitudes of Dido, nights around midsummer were not only short, they were light. Flandry walked beneath a sky blue-black, faintly tinged with silver, faintly adance

105

with aurora where some of Virgil's ionizing radiation penetrated the upper clouds. There was just sufficient luminance for him not to stumble. Further off, crags and cliffs made blacknesses which faded unclearly into the dusk. Mounting a bluff that overlooked his camp, he saw its fire as a red wavering spark, like a dying dwarf star. The sound of the river belled subdued but clear through cool air. His boots scrunched on gravel; occasionally they kicked a larger rock. An unknown animal trilled somewhere close by.

Kathryn's form grew out of the shadows. He had seen her depart in this direction after the meal she refused, and guessed she was bound here. When he drew close, her face was a pale blur.

"Oh . . . Dominic," she said. The outdoor years had trained her to use more senses than vision.

"You shouldn't have gone off alone." He stopped in front of her.

"I had to."

"At a minimum, carry a gun. You can handle one, I'm sure."

"Yes. 'Course. But I won't, after today."

"You must have seen violent deaths before."

"A few times. None that I helped cause."

"The attack was unprovoked. To be frank, I don't regret anything but our own losses, and we can't afford to lament them long."

"We were crossin' the natives' country," she said. "Maybe they resented that. Didonians have territorial instincts, same as man. Or maybe our gear tempted them. No slaughter, no wounds, if 'tweren't for our travelin'."

"You've lived with the consequences of war," his inner pain said harshly. "And this particular fracas was an incident in your precious revolution."

He heard breath rush between her lips. Remorse stabbed him. "I, I'm sorry, Kathryn," he said. "Spoke out of turn. I'll leave you alone. But please come back to camp."

"No." At first her voice was almost too faint to hear. "I mean . . . let me stay out a while." She seized his hand. "But of your courtesy, don't you skite either. I'm glad you came, Dominic. You understand things."

Do I? Rainbows exploded within him.

They stood a minute, holding hands, before she laughed uncertainly and said: "Again, Dominic. Be practical with me."

You're brave enough to live with your sorrows, he thought, *but strong and wise enough to turn your back on them the first chance that comes, and cope with our enemy the universe.*

He wanted, he needed one of his few remaining cigarets; but he couldn't reach the case without disturbing her clasp, and she might let go. "Well," he said in his awkwardness, "I imagine we can push on, day after tomorrow. They put Lightning Struck The House together for me after you left." All heesh's units had at various times combined with those that had been in Cave Discoverer: among other reasons, for heesh to gain some command of pidgin.

"We discussed things. It'd take longer to return, now, than finish our journey, and the incompletes can handle routine. The boys have gotten good at trailsmanship themselves. We'll bear today's lesson in mind and avoid places where bushwhackers can't be spotted from above. So I feel we can make it all right."

"I doubt if we'll be bothered any more," Kathryn said with a return of energy in her tone. "News'll get 'round."

"About that ruka we took prisoner."

"Yes? Why not set the poor beast free?"

"Because . . . well, Lightning isn't glad we have the potential for just one full entity. There're jobs like getting heavy loads down steep mountainsides which're a deal easier and safer with at least two, especially seeing that rukas are their hands. Furthermore, most of the time we can only have a single krippo aloft. The other will have to stay in a three-way, guiding the incompletes and making decisions, while we're in this tricky mountainland. One set of airborne eyes is damn little."

"True." He thought he heard the rustle of her hair, which she had let grow longer, as she nodded. "I didn't think 'bout that 'fore, too shocked, but you're right." Her fingers tensed on his. "Dominic! You're not plannin' to use the prisoner?"

"Why not? Lightning seems to like the idea. Been done on occasion, heesh said."

"In emergencies. But . . . the conflict, the—the cruelty—"

"Listen, I've given these matters thought," he told her. "Check my facts and logic. We'll force the ruka into linkage with the noga and krippo that were Cave Discoverer's—the strongest, most sophisticated entity we had. He'll obey at gun point. Besides, he has to drink blood or he'll starve, right? A single armed man alongside will prevent possible contretemps. However, two units against one ought to prevail by themselves. We'll make the union permanent, or nearly so, for the duration of our trip. That way, the Thunderstone patterns should go fast and deep into the ruka. I daresay the

107

new personality will be confused and hostile at first; but heesh ought to cooperate with us, however grudgingly."

"Well—"

"We need heesh, Kathryn! I don't propose slavery. The ruka won't be absorbed. He'll give—and get—will learn something to take home to his communion—maybe an actual message of friendship, an offer to establish regular relations —and gifts, when we release him here on our way back to Thunderstone."

She was silent, until: "Audacious but decent, yes, that's you. You're more a knight than anybody who puts 'Sir' in front of his name, Dominic."

"Oh, Kathryn!"

And he found he had embraced her and was kissing her, and she was kissing him, and the night was fireworks and trumpets and carousels and sacredness.

"I love you, Kathryn, my God, I love you."

She broke free of him and moved back. "No. . . ." When he groped toward her, she fended him off. "No, please, please, don't. Please stop. I don't know what possessed me. . . ."

"But I love you," he cried.

"Dominic, no, we've been too long on this crazy trek. I care for you more'n I knew. But I'm Hugh's woman."

He dropped his arms and stood where he was, letting the spirit bleed out of him. "Kathryn," he said, "for you I'd join your side."

"For my sake?" She came close again, close enough to lay hands on his shoulders. Half sobbing, half laughing: "You can't dream how glad I am."

He stood in the fragrance of her, fists knotted, and replied, "Not for your sake. For you."

"What?" she whispered, and let him go.

"You called me a knight. Wrong. I won't play wistful friend-of-the-family rejected suitor. Not my style. I want to be your man myself, in every way that a man is able."

The wind lulled, the river boomed.

"All right," Flandry said to the shadow of her. "Till we reach Port Frederiksen. No longer. He needn't know. I'll serve his cause and live on the memory."

She sat down and wept. When he tried to comfort her, she thrust him away, not hard but not as a coy gesture either. He moved off a few meters and chainsmoked three cigarets.

Finally she said, "I understand what you're thinkin', Dominic. If Snelund, why not you? But don't you see the difference? Startin' with the fact I do like you so much?"

108

He said through the tension in his throat, "I see you're loyal to an arbitrary ideal that originated under conditions that don't hold good any more."

She started to cry afresh, but it sounded dry, as if she had spent her tears.

"Forgive me," Flandry said. "I never meant to hurt you. Would've cut my larynx out first. We won't speak about this, unless you want to. If you change your mind, tomorrow or a hundred years from tomorrow, while I'm alive I'll be waiting."

Which is perfectly true, gibed a shard of him, *though I am not unaware of its being a well-composed line, and nourish a faint hope that my noble attitude will yet draw her away from that bucketheaded mass murderer Hugh McCormac.*

He drew his blaster and pushed it into her cold unsteady clasp. "If you must stay here," he said, "keep this. Give it back to me when you come down to camp. Goodnight."

He turned and left. There went through him: *Very well, if I have no reason to forswear His Majesty Josip III, let me carry on with the plan I'm developing for the discomfiture of his unruly subjects.*

XIII

~~~~~~~~

The group spent most of the next day and night sleeping. Then Flandry declared it was needful to push harder forward than hitherto. The remaining Didonian(s?) formed several successive entities, as was the custom when important decisions were to be reached, and agreed. For them, these uplands were bleak and poor in forage. Worse lay ahead, especially in view of the hurts and losses they had suffered. Best get fast over the mountains and down to the coastal plain.

That was a Herculean undertaking. The humans spent

most of their time gathering food along the way for the nogas. When exhaustion forced a stop, it likewise forced sleep. Kathryn was athletic, but she remained a woman of thirty, trying to match the pace and toil of men in their teens and twenties. She had small chance to talk, with Flandry or anyone, on trail or off.

He alone managed that. His company looked mutinous when he announced that he must be exempted from most of the labor in order to establish communication with the new entity. Havelock jollied them out of their mood.

"Look, you've seen the Old Man in action. You may not like him, but he's no shirker and no fool. Somebody has to get that xeno cooperating. If nothing else, think how we need a guide through this damned arse-over-tip country. . . . Why not Kathryn? Well, she *is* the wife of the man who got us dumped where we are. It wouldn't improve our records, that we trusted her with something this critical. . . . Sure, you'd better think about your records, those of you who plan on returning home."

Flandry had given him a confidential briefing.

At the outset, talk between man and Didonian was impossible. The personality fought itself, captive ruka pouring hate and fear of the whole troop into a noga and krippo which detested his communion. And the languages, habits, attitudes, thought patterns, the whole *Weltanschauungen* were at odds, scarcely comprehensible mutually. Linked under duress, the entity slogged along, sometimes sullen, sometimes dazed, always apt to lash out on a half insane impulse. Twice Flandry had to scramble; the noga's horn missed him by centimeters.

He persevered. So did the two animals which had been in Cave Discoverer. And the noga had had experience with alien partners, the two which had annually joined him to make Raft Farer. Flandry tried to imagine what the present situation felt like, and couldn't. Schizophrenia? A racking conflict of opposed desires, akin to his own as regarded Kathryn McCormac versus the Terran Empire? He doubted it. The being he confronted was too foreign.

He sought to guide its coalescence, initially by his behavior, later by his words. Once the ruka nervous system was freed from expecting imminent torture or death, meshing was natural. Language followed. Part of the Thunderstone vocabulary had died with Cave Discoverer's ruka. But some was retained, and more was acquired when, for a time, the krippo was replaced by the other ruka. The savage unit objected violently—it turned out that his culture regarded a two-species three-way as perverted—but got no choice in the matter. The

110

hookup of neurones as well as blood vessels was automatic when tendrils joined. Flandry exerted his linguistic skills to lead the combinations through speech exercises. Given scientific direction, the inborn Didonian adaptability showed quick results.

By the time the party had struggled across the passes and were on the western slope of the mountains, Flandry could talk to the mind he had called into being.

The entity did not seem especially fond of heeshself. The designation heesh adopted, more by repeated usage than by deliberate selection, was a grunt which Kathryn said might translate as "Woe." She had little to do with heesh, as much because the obvious emotional trouble distressed her as because of weariness. That suited Flandry. Conversing with Woe, alone except for a sentry who did not understand what they uttered, he could build on the partial amnesia and the stifled anger, to make what he would of the Didonian.

"You must serve me," he said and repeated. "We may have fighting to do, and you are needed in place of heesh who is no more. Trust and obey none save me. I alone can release you in the end—with rich reward for both your communions. And I have enemies among my very followers."

He would have told as elaborate, even as truthful a story as required. But he soon found it was neither necessary nor desirable. Woe was considerably less intelligent as well as less knowledgeable than Cave Discoverer. To heesh, the humans were supernatural figures. Flandry, who was clearly their chieftain and who furthermore had been midwife and teacher to heesh's consciousness, was a vortex of *mana*. Distorted recollections of what he and Kathryn had related to Cave Discoverer reinforced what he now said about conflict among the Powers. The ruka brain, most highly developed of the three, contributed its mental set to the personality of Woe, whose resulting suspicion of heesh's fellow units in the group was carefully *not* allayed by Flandry.

When they had reached the foothills, Woe was his tool. Under the influence of noga and krippo, the Didonian had actually begun looking forward to adventuring in his service.

How he would use that tool, if at all, he could not predict. It would depend on the situation at journey's terminus.

Kathryn took him aside one evening. Steamy heat and jungle abatis enclosed them. But the topography was easier and the ribs of the Didonians were disappearing behind regained flesh. He and she stood in a canebrake, screened from the world, and regarded each other.

"Why haven't we talked alone, Dominic?" she asked him.

111

Her gaze was grave, and she had taken both his hands in hers.

He shrugged. "Too busy."

"More'n that. We didn't dare. Whenever I see you, I think of— You're the last person after Hugh that I'd want to hurt."

"After Hugh."

"You're givin' him back to me. No god could do anything more splendid."

"I take it, then," he said jaggedly, "that you haven't reconsidered about us."

"No. You make me wish I could wish to. But—Oh, I'm so grieved. I hope so hard you'll soon find your right woman."

"I've done that," he said. She winced. He realized he was crushing her hands, and eased the pressure. "Kathryn, my darling, we're in the homestretch, but my offer stays the same. Us—from here to Port Frederiksen—and I'll join the revolution."

"That's not worthy of you," she said, whitening.

"I know it isn't," he snarled. "Absolute treason. For you, I'd sell my soul. You have it anyway."

"How can you say treason?" she exclaimed as if he had struck her.

"Easy. Treason, treason, treason. You hear? The revolt's worse than evil, it's stupid. You—"

She tore loose and fled. He stood alone till night entirely surrounded him. *Nu, Flandry,* he thought once, *what ever made you suppose the cosmos was designed for your personal convenience?*

Thereafter Kathryn did not precisely avoid him. That would have been impossible under present circumstances. Nor was it her desire. On the contrary, she often smiled at him, with a shyness that seared, and her tone was warm when they had occasion to speak. He answered somewhat in kind. Yet they no longer left the sight of their companions.

The men were wholly content with that. They swarmed about her at every chance, and this flat lowland gave them plenty of chances. No doubt she sincerely regretted injuring Flandry; but she could not help it that joy rose in her with every westward kilometer and poured from her as laughter and graciousness and eager response. Havelock had no problem in getting her to tell him, in complete innocence, everything she knew about the Aenean base.

"Damn, I hate to use her like that!" he said, reporting to his commander in privacy.

"You're doing it for her long-range good," Flandry replied.

112

"An excuse for a lot of cruelty and treachery in the past."

"And in the future. Yeh. However . . . Tom, we're merely collecting information. Whether we do anything more turns entirely on how things look when we arrive. I've told you before, I won't attempt valorous impossibilities. We may very well go meekly into internment."

"If we don't, though—"

"Then we'll be helping strike down a piece of foredoomed foolishness a little quicker, thereby saving quite a few lives. We can see to it that those lives include Kathryn's." Flandry clapped the ensign's back. "Slack off, son. Figure of speech, that; I'd have had to be more precocious than I was to mean it literally. Nevertheless, slack off, son. Remember the girl who's waiting for you."

Havelock grinned and walked away with his shoulders squared. Flandry stayed behind a while. *No particular girl for me, ever,* he reflected, *unless Hugh McCormac has the kindness to get himself killed. Maybe then—*

Could I arrange that somehow—if she'd never know I had —could I? A daydream, of course. But supposing the opportunity came my way . . . could I?

I honestly can't say.

Like the American Pacific coast (on Terra, Mother Terra), the western end of Barca wrinkled in hills which fell abruptly down to the sea. When she glimpsed the sheen of great waters, Kathryn scrambled up the tallest tree she could find. Her shout descended leaf by leaf, as sunshine does: "Byrsa Head! Can't be anything else! We're less'n 50 kilometers south of Port Frederiksen!"

She came down in glory. And Dominic Flandry was unable to say more than: "I'll proceed from here by myself."

"What?"

"A flit, in one of the spacesuits. First we'll make camp in some pleasant identifiable spot. Then I'll inquire if they can spare us an aircraft. Quicker than walking."

"Let me go 'long," she requested, ashiver with impatience.

You can go 'long till the last stars burn out, if you choose. Only you don't choose. "Sorry, no. Don't try to radio, either. Listen, but don't transmit. How can we tell what the situation is? Maybe bad; for instance, barbarians might have taken advantage of our family squabble and be in occupation. I'll check. If I'm not back in . . . oh . . . two of these small inexpensive days"— *You always have to clown, don't you?*— "Lieutenant Valencia will assume command and use his own judgment." *I'd prefer Havelock. Valencia's too sympathetic to*

113

*the revolt. Still, I have to maintain the senior officer conven-
tion if I'm to lie to you, my dearest, if I'm to have any
chance of harming your cause, my love until I die.*

His reminder dampened hilarity. The troop settled in by a
creek, under screening trees, without fire. Flandry suited up.
He didn't give any special alert to Woe or to his several solid
allies among the men. They had arranged a system of signals
many marches before.

"Be careful, Dominic," Kathryn said. Her concern was a
knife in him. "Don't risk yourself. For all our sakes."

"I won't," he promised. "I enjoy living." *Oh, yes, I expect
to keep on enjoying it, whether or not you will give it any
real point.* "Cheers." He activated the impeller. In a second
or two, he could no longer see her waving goodbye.

He flew slowly, helmet open, savoring the wind and salt
smells as he followed the coastline north. The ocean of
moonless Dido had no real surf, it stretched gray under the
gray sky, but in any large body of water there is always motion and mystery; he saw intricate patterns of waves and
foam, immense patches of weed and shoals of swimming animals, a rainstorm walking on the horizon. To his right the
land lifted from wide beaches, itself a quilt of woods and
meadows, crossed by great herds of grazers and flocks of
flyers. *By and large,* he thought, *planets do well if man lets
them be.*

Despite everything, his pulse accelerated when Port Frederiksen appeared. Here was his destiny.

The base occupied a small, readily defensible peninsula. It
was sufficiently old to have become a genuine community.
The prefab sheds, shelters, and laboratories were weathered,
vine-begrown, almost a part of the landscape; and among
them stood houses built from native wood and stone, in a
breeze-inviting style evolved for this place, and gardens and a
park. Kathryn had said the population was normally a thousand but doubtless far less during the present emergency.
Flandry saw few people about.

His attention focused on the spacefield. If it held a mere
interplanetary vessel, his optimum bet was to surrender. But
no. Hugh McCormac had left this prized outpost a hyperdrive warship. She wasn't big—a Conqueror-class subde-
stroyer, her principal armament a blaster cannon, her principal armor speed and maneuverability, her normal comple-
ment twenty-five—but she stood rakish on guard, and Flandry's heart jumped.

That's my baby! He passed close. She didn't appear to
have more than the regulation minimum of two on duty, to

judge from the surrounding desertion. And why should she? Given her controls, instruments, and computers, a single man could take her anywhere. Port Frederiksen would know of approaching danger in time for her personnel to go aboard. Otherwise they doubtless helped the civilians.

Emblazoned above her serial number was the name *Erwin Rommel*. Who the deuce had that been? Some Germanian? No, more likely a Terran, resurrected from the historical files by a data finder programmed to christen several score thousand of Conquerors.

People emerged from buildings. Flandry had been noticed. He landed in the park. "Hello," he said. "I've had a bit of a shipwreck."

During the next hour, he inquired about Port Frederiksen. In return, he was reasonably truthful. He told of a chance encounter with an enemy vessel, a crash landing, a cross-country hike. The main detail he omitted was that he had not been on McCormac's side.

If his scheme didn't work, the Aeneans would be irritated when they learned the whole truth; but they didn't strike him as the kind who would punish a ruse of war.

Essentially they were caretakers: besides the *Rommel*'s crew, a few scientists and service personnel. Their job was to maintain the fruitful relationship with neighboring Didonians and the fabric of the base. Being what they were, they attempted in addition to continue making studies.

Physically, they were isolated. Interplanetary radio silence persisted, for Josipist ships had raided the Virgilian System more than once. Every month or so, a boat from Aeneas brought supplies, mail, and news. The last arrival had been only a few days before. Thus Flandry got an up-to-date account of events.

From the Aenean viewpoint, they were dismal. Manufacture, logistics, and communications were falling apart beneath Hugh McCormac. He had given up trying to govern any substantial volume of space. Instead, he had assigned forces to defend individually the worlds which had declared for him. They were minimal, those forces. They hampered but could not prevent badgering attacks by Snelund's squadrons. Any proper flotilla could annihilate them in detail.

Against that development, McCormac kept the bulk of his fleet around Satan. If the Josipists gathered in full strength, he would learn of it from his scouts, go meet the armada, and rely on his tactical abilities to scatter it.

"But they know that," Director Jowett said. He stroked his white beard with a hand that trembled. "They won't give our

115

Emperor the decisive battle he needs. I wonder if Snelund 'ull even call for reinforcements when Terra can spare them. He may simply wear us down. I'm sure he'd enjoy our havin' a long agony."

"Do you think we should yield?" Flandry asked.

The old head lifted. "Not while our Emperor lives!"

Folk being starved for visitors, Flandry had no trouble in learning more than he needed to know. They fell in readily with a suggestion he made. Rather than dispatch aircars to fetch his companions, why not use the *Rommel*? No instrumental readings or flashed communication from Aeneas indicated any immediate reason to hold her in condition red. Jowett and her captain agreed. Of course, there wouldn't be room for the whole gang unless most of the crew stayed behind. The few who did ride along could use the practice.

Flandry had sketched alternative plans. However, this simplified his task.

He guided the ship aloft and southward. En route, he called the camp. Somebody was sure to be listening on a helmet radio. "All's fine," he said. "We'll land on the beach exactly west of your location and wait for you. Let me speak with Ensign Havelock. . . . Tom? It's Q. Better have Yuan and Christopher lead off."

That meant that they were to don their armor.

The ship set down. Those who manned her stepped trustfully out onto the sand. When they saw the travelers emerge from the woods, they shouted their welcomes across the wind.

Two gleaming metal shapes hurtled into view above the treetops. A second afterward, they were at hover above the ship, with blasters aimed.

"Hands up, if you please," Flandry said.

"What?" the captain yelled. A man snatched at his sidearm. A beam sizzled from overhead, barely missing him. Sparks showered and steam puffed where it struck.

"Hands up, I repeat," Flandry snapped. "You'd be dead before any shot of yours could penetrate."

Sick-featured, they obeyed. "You're being hijacked," he told them. "You might as well start home at once. It'll take you some hours on shank's mare."

"You Judas." The captain spat.

Flandry wiped his face and answered, "Matter of definition, that. Get moving." Yuan accompanied the group for some distance.

Beforehand, suddenly drawn guns had made prisoners of men whose loyalty was in question. More puzzled than angry,

116

Lightning Struck The House guided the uncoupled units aboard. Woe marched Kathryn up the ramp. When he saw her, Flandry found business to do on the other side of the ship.

With his crew embarked and stations assigned, he hauled gravs. Hovering above the settlement, he disabled the interplanetary transmitter with a shot to its mast. Next he broadcast a warning and allowed the people time to evacuate. Finally he demolished other selected installations.

The Aeneans would have food, shelter, medicine, ground defenses. But they wouldn't be going anywhere or talking to anybody until a boat arrived from Aeneas, and none was due for a month.

"Take her east, Citizen Havelock," Flandry directed. "We'll fetch our chums at Thunderstone and let off the surplus livestock. And, yes, we'll lay in some food for the new Didonian. I think I may have use for heesh."

"Where at, sir?"

"Llynathawr. We'll leave this system cautiously, not to be spotted. When well into space, we'll run at maximum hyperspeed to Llynathawr."

"Sir?" Havelock's mien changed from adoration to puzzlement. "I beg the captain's pardon, but I don't understand. I mean, you've turned a catastrophe into a triumph, we've got the enemy's current code and he doesn't know we do, but shouldn't we make for Ifri? Especially when Kathryn—"

"I have my reasons, " Flandry said. "Never fear, she will not go back to Snelund." His own expression was so forbidding that no one dared inquire further.

XIV

Again the metal narrowness, chemical-tainted air, incessant beat of driving energies, but also the wintry wonder of stars, the steady brightening of a particular golden point among them. From Virgil to Llynathawr, in this ship, the flit was less than two standard days.

Flandry held captain's mast. The wardroom was too cramped for everybody, but audiovisual intercoms were tuned. The crew saw him seated, in whites that did not fit well but were nonetheless the full uniform of his rank. Like theirs, his body was gaunt, the bones standing sharply forth in his countenance, the eyes unnaturally luminous by contrast with a skin burned almost black. Unlike most of them, he showed no pleasure in his victory.

"Listen carefully," he said. "In an irregular situation such as ours, it is necessary to go through various formalities." He took the depositions which, entered in the log, would retroactively legalize his seizure of *Rommel* and his status as her master.

"Some among you were put under arrest," he went on. "That was a precautionary measure. In a civil war, one dares not trust a man without positive confirmation, and obviously I couldn't plan a surprise move with our entire group. The arrest is hereby terminated and the subjects ordered released. I will specifically record and report that their detention was in no way meant to reflect on their loyalty or competence, and that I recommend every man aboard for promotion and a medal."

He did not smile when they cheered. His hard monotone went on: "By virtue of the authority vested in me, and in conformance with Naval regulations on extraordinary recruitment, I am swearing the sophont from the planet Dido, known to us by the name Woe, into His Majesty's armed service on a temporary basis with the rating of common spaceman. In view of the special character of this being, the enrollment shall be entered as that of three new crewpeople."

Laughter replied. They thought his imp had spoken. They were wrong.

"All detection systems will be kept wide open," he continued after the brief ceremony. "Instantly upon contact with any Imperial ship, the communications officer will signal surrender and ask for an escort. I daresay we'll all be arrested when they board us, till our bona fides can be established. However, I trust that by the time we assume Llynathawr orbit, we'll be cleared.

"A final item. We have an important prisoner aboard. I told Ensign Havelock, who must have told the rest of you, that Lady McCormac will not be returned to the custody of Sector Governor Snelund. Now I want to put the reason on fficial though secret record, since otherwise our action ould be grounds for court-martial.

"It is not in the province of Naval officers to make political ecisions. Because of the circumstances about Lady Mc-Cormac, including the questionable legality of her original etention, my judgment is that handing her over to His Excellency would *be* a political decision, fraught with possibly minous consequences. My duty is to deliver her to Naval uthorities who can dispose of her case as they find appropriate. At the same time, we cannot in law refuse a demand for er person by His Excellency.

"Therefore, as master of this vessel, and as an officer of he Imperial Naval Intelligence Corps, charged with an informational mission and hence possessed of discretionary powers with respect to confidentiality of data, et cetera, I classify ady McCormac's presence among us as a state secret. She will be concealed before we are boarded. No one will mention that she has been along, then or at any future date, until uch time as the fact may be granted public release by a ualified governmental agency. To do so will constitute a violation of the laws and rules on security, and subject you to riminal penalties. If asked, you may say that she escaped ust before we left Dido. Is that understood?"

Reverberating shouts answered him.

He sat back. "Very well," he said tiredly. "Resume your tations. Have Lady McCormac brought here for interview."

He switched off the com. His men departed. *I've got them n my pocket,* he thought. *They'd ship out for hell if I were he skipper.* He felt no exaltation. *I don't really want another command.*

He opened a fresh pack of the cigarets he had found mong stocked rations. The room enclosed him in drabness. Under the machine noises and the footfalls outside, silence grew.

But his heart knocked when Kathryn entered. He rose.

She shut the door and stood tall in front of it. Her eyes, alone in the spacecraft, looked on him in scorn. His knife had stayed on her hip.

When she didn't speak and didn't speak, he faltered, "I—I hope the captain's cabin—isn't too uncomfortable."

"How do you aim to hide me?" she asked. The voice had its wonted huskiness, and nothing else.

"Mitsui and Petrović will take the works out of a message capsule. We can pad the casing and tap airholes that won't be noticed. You can have food and drink and, uh, what else

you'll need. It'll get boring, lying there in the dark, bu
shouldn't be longer than twenty or thirty hours."

"Then what?"

"If everything goes as I expect, we'll be ordered into park
ing orbit around Llynathawr," he said. "The code team
won't take much time getting their readouts from our com
puters. Meanwhile we'll be interrogated and the men assigned
temporarily to Catawrayannis Base till extended leave can be
given them. Procedure cut and dried and quick; the Navy'
interested in what we bring, not our adventures while we ob
tained it. Those can wait for the board of inquiry on *Asi
eneuve's* loss. The immediate thing will be to hit the rebel
before they change their code.

"I'll assert myself as captain of the *Rommel,* on detached
service. My status could be disputed; but in the scramble to
organize that attack, I doubt if any bureaucrat will check the
exact wording of regs. They'll be happy to let me have the
responsibility for this boat, the more so when my roving
commission implies that I need the means to rove.

"As master, I'm required to keep at least two hands on
watch. In parking orbit, that's a technicality, no more. And
I've seen to it that technically, Woe is three crewmen. I'm
reasonably confident I can fast-talk my way out of any objections to heesh. It's such a minor-looking matter, a method of
not tying up two skilled spacers who could be useful elsewhere.

"When you're alone, heesh will let you out."

Flandry ran down. He had lectured her in the same way as
he might have battered his fists on a steel wall.

"Why?" she said.

"Why what?" He stubbed out his cigaret and reached for
another.

"I can understand . . . maybe . . . why you did what
you've done . . . to Hugh. I wouldn't've thought it of you, I
saw you as brave and good enough to stand for what's right,
but I can imagine that down underneath, your spirit is small.

"But what I can't understand, can't grasp," Kathryn sighed,
"is that you—after everything—are bringin' me back to enslavement. If you hadn't told Woe to seize me, there's not a
man of your men who wouldn't've turned away while I ran
into the forest."

He could not watch her any longer. "You're needed," he
mumbled.

"For what? To be wrung dry of what little I know? To be
dangled 'fore Hugh in the hope 'twill madden him? To be
made an example of? And it doesn't matter whether 'tis an

120

xample of Imperial justice or Imperial mercy, whatever was
e will die when they kill Hugh." She was not crying, not
eproaching. Peripherally, he saw her shake her head in a
low, bewildered fashion. "I *can't* understand."

"I don't believe I'd better tell you yet," he pleaded. "Too
nany variables in the equation. Too much improvising to do.
ut—"

She interrupted. "I'll play your game, since 'tis the one way
can at least 'scape from Snelund. But I'd rather not be with
ou." Her tone continued quiet. " 'Twould be a favor if you
veren't by when they put me in that coffin."

He nodded. She left. Woe's heavy tread boomed behind
er.

Whatever his shortcomings, the governor of Sector Alpha
Crucis set a magnificent table. Furthermore, he was a charm-
ng host, with a rare gift for listening as well as making
hrewd and witty comments. Though most of Flandry crouched like a panther behind his smile, a part reveled
n this first truly civilized meal in months.

He finished his narrative of events on Dido as noiseless live
servants cleared away the last golden dishes, set forth brandy
and cigars, and disappeared. "Tremendous!" applauded Snelund. "Utterly fascinating, that race. Did you say you
brought one back? I'd like to meet the being."

"That's easily arranged, Your Excellency," Flandry said.
"More easily than you perhaps suspect."

Snelund's brows moved very slightly upward, his fingers
tensed the tiniest bit on the stem of his snifter. Flandry relaxed, inhaled the bouquet of his own drink, twirled it to
enjoy the play of color within the liquid, and sipped in conscious counterpoint to the background lilt of music.

They sat on an upper floor of the palace. The chamber was
not large, but graciously proportioned and subtly tinted. A
wall had been opened to the summer evening. Air wandered
in from the gardens bearing scents of rose, jasmine, and less
familiar blossoms. Downhill glistered the city, lights in constellations and fountains, upward radiance of towers, firefly
dance of aircars. Traffic sounds were a barely perceptible
murmur. You had trouble believing that all around and spill-
ing to the stars, it roared with preparations for war.

Nor was Snelund laying on any pressure. Flandry might
have removed Kathryn McCormac hence for "special interrogation deemed essential to the maximization of success probability on a surveillance mission" in sheer impudence. He
might have lost first his ship and last his prisoner in sheer

121

carelessness. But after he came back with a booty that should allow Admiral Pickens to give the rebellion a single spectacular deathblow, without help from Terra and with no subsequent tedious inspection of militia operations, the governor could not well be aught but courteous to the man who saved his political bacon.

Nevertheless, when Flandry requested a secret talk, it had not been with the expectation of dinner *tête-à-tête*.

"Indeed?" Snelund breathed.

Flandry glanced across the table at him: wavy, fiery hair, muliebrile countenance, gorgeous purple and gold robe, twinkle and shimmer of jewelry. Behind that, Flandry thought, were a bowel and a skull.

"The thing is, sir," he said, "I had a delicate decision to make."

Snelund nodded, smiling but with a gaze gone flat and hard as two stones. "I suspected that, Commander. Certain aspects of your report and behavior, certain orders you issued with a normally needless haste and authoritative ring, were not lost on me. You have me to thank for passing the word that I felt you should not be argued with. I was, ah, curious as to what you meant."

"I do thank Your Excellency." Flandry started his cigar. "This matter's critical to you too, sir. Let me remind you of my dilemma on Dido. Lady McCormac became extremely popular with my men."

"Doubtless." Snelund laughed. "I taught her some unusual tricks."

I have no weapons under this blue and white dress uniform, Aaron Snelund. I have nothing but my hands and feet. And a black belt in karate, plus training in other techniques. Except for unfinished business, I'd merrily let myself be executed, in fair trade for the joy of dismantling you.

Because the creature must recall what her soul had been like when he flayed it open, and might be probing veracity now, Flandry gave him a sour grin. "No such luck, sir. She even refused *my* proposition, which fact I pray you to declare a top secret. But—well, there she was, the only woman handsome, able, bright. Toward the end, most were a touch in love with her. She'd spread the impression that her stay here had been unpleasant. To be frank, sir, I feared a mutiny if the men expected she'd be remanded to you. Bringing in the code was too crucial to risk."

"So you connived at her escape." Snelund sipped. "That's tacitly realized by everyone, Commander. A sound judgment

122

whether or not we dare put it in the record. She can be tracked down later."

"But sir, I didn't."

"What!" Snelund sat bolt erect.

Flandry said fast: "Let's drop the euphemisms, sir. She made some extremely serious accusations against you. Some people might use them to buttress a claim that your actions were what caused this rebellion. I didn't want that. If you've read much history, you'll agree nothing works like a Boadicea—no?—a martyr, especially an attractive female martyr, to create trouble. The Empire would suffer. I felt it was my duty to keep her. To get the men's agreement, I had to convince them she would not be returned here. She'd go to a Naval section, where rules protect prisoners and testimony isn't likely to be suppressed."

Snelund had turned deadpan. "Continue," he said.

Flandry sketched his means of smuggling her in. "The fleet should be assembled and ready to depart for Satan in about three days," he finished, "now that scouts have verified the enemy is still using the code I brought. I'm not expected to accompany it. I am expected, though, by my men, to obtain orders for myself that will send the *Rommel* to Ifri, Terra, or some other place where she'll be safe. They'll have ways of finding out whether I do. You know how word circulates in any set of offices. If I don't—I'm not sure that secrecy will bind every one of those lads. And disclosure would inconvenience you, sir, at this highly critical time."

Snelund drained his brandy glass and refilled it. The little *glug-glug* sounded loud across the music. "Why do you tell me?"

"Because of what I've said. As a patriot, I can't allow anything that might prolong the rebellion."

Snelund studied him. "And she refused you?" he said at length.

Spite etched Flandry's tones. "I don't appreciate that, from third-hand goods like her." With quick smoothness: "But this is beside the point. My obligation . . . to you, Your Excellency, as well as to the Imperium—"

"Ah, yes." Snelund eased. "It does no harm to have a man in your debt who is on his way up, does it?"

Flandry looked smug.

"Yes-s-s, I think we resonate, you and I," Snelund said. "What is your suggestion?"

"Well," Flandry replied, "as far as officialdom knows, *Rommel* contains no life other than my multiple Didonian.

123

And heesh will never talk. If my orders were cut tonight—not specifically to anywhere, let's say, only for 'reconnaissance and report at discretion, employing minimal crew'—a phone call by Your Excellency to someone on Admiral Pickens' staff would take care of that—I could go aboard and depart. My men would relax about Lady McCormac. When they haven't heard news of her in a year or two—well, reassignment will have scattered them and feelings will have cooled. Oblivion is a most valuable servant, Your Excellency."

"Like yourself," Snelund beamed. "I do believe our careers are going to be linked, Commander. If I can trust you—"

"Come see for yourself," Flandry proposed.

"Eh?"

"You said you'd be interested in meeting my Didonian anyway. It can be discreet. I'll give you the *Rommel*'s orbital elements and you go up alone in your flitter, not telling anybody where you're bound." Flandry blew a smoke ring. "You might like to take personal charge of the execution. To make sure it's done in a manner suitable to the crime. We could have hours."

Then he waited.

Until sweat made beads on Snelund's skin and an avid voice said, "Yes!"

Flandry hadn't dared hope to catch the prize for which he angled. Had he failed, he would have made it his mission in life to accomplish the same result by other methods. The fact left him feeling so weak and lightheaded that he wondered vaguely if he could walk out of there.

He did, after a period of conference and arrangement-making. A gubernatorial car delivered him at Catawrayannis Base, where he changed into working garb, accepted his orders, and got a flitter to the *Rommel*.

Time must be allowed for that craft to descend again, lest the pilot notice another and ornate one lay alongside. Flandry sat on the bridge, alone with his thoughts. The viewscreen showed him planet and stars, a huge calm beauty.

Vibration sounded in the metal, as airlocks joined and magnetronic grapples made fast. Flandry went down to admit his guest.

Snelund came through the airlock breathing hard. He carried a surgical kit. "Where is she?" he demanded.

"This way, sir." Flandry let him go ahead. He did not appear to have noticed Flandry's gun, packed in case of bodyguards. There weren't any. They might have gossiped.

Woe stood outside the captain's cabin. Xenological interest

124

or no, Snelund barely glanced at heesh and jittered while Flandry said in pidgin: "Whatever you hear, stay where you are until I command you otherwise."

The noga's horn dipped in acknowledgment. The ruka touched the ax at his side. The krippo sat like a bird of prey.

Flandry opened the door. "I brought you a visitor, Kathryn," he said.

She uttered a noise that would long run through his nightmares. His Merseian war knife flew into her hand.

He wrenched the bag from Snelund and pinioned the man in a grip that was not to be shaken. Kicking the door shut behind him, he said, "Any way you choose, Kathryn. Any way at all."

Snelund began screaming.

XV

Seated at the pilot board of the gig, Flandry pushed controls to slide aside the housing and activate the viewscreens. Space leaped at him. The gloom of Satan and the glitter of stars drifted slowly past as *Rommel* swung around the planet and tumbled along her invariable plane. Twice he identified slivers of blackness crossing the constellations and the Milky Way: nearby warcraft. But unaided senses could not really prove to him that he was at the heart of the rebel fleet.

Instruments had done that as he drove inward, and several curt conversations once he came in range. Even when Kathryn spoke directly with Hugh McCormac, reserve stood between them. Warned by his communications officer what to expect, the admiral had had time to don a mask. How could he know it wasn't a trick? If he spoke to his wife at all, and not to an electronic shadow show, she might be under brainscrub, speaking the words that her operator projected into her middle ear. Her own mostly impersonal sentences, uttered from a visage nearly blank, yet the whole of her unsteady, might lend credence to that fear. Flandry had been astonished. He had taken for granted she would cry forth in joy.

Was it perhaps a simple but strong wish for privacy, or was it that at this ultimate moment and ultimate stress she must fight too hard to keep from flying apart? There had been no chance to ask her. She obeyed Flandry's directive, revealing no secret of his, insisting that the two men hold a closed-door parley before anything else was done; and McCormac agreed, his voice rough and not altogether firm; and then things went too fast—the giving of directions, the study of meters, the maneuvers of approach and orbit matching—for Flandry to learn what she felt.

But while he prepared to go, she came from the cabin to which she had retreated. She seized his hands and looked into his eyes and whispered, "Dominic, I'm prayin' for both of you." Her lips brushed across his. They were cold, like her fingers, and tasted of salt. Before he could respond, she walked quickly away again.

Theirs had been a curious intimacy while they traveled hither. The red gift he had given her; the plan he laid out, and that she helped him perfect after she saw he was not to be moved from it; between times, dreamy talk of old days and far places, much reminiscence about little events on Dido —Flandry wondered if man and woman could grow closer in a wedded lifetime. In one aspect, yes, obviously they could; but that one they both shied off from speaking of.

And here came *Persei* into view and with her, one way or another, an end to everything which had been. The flagship loomed like a moon, mottled with thermostatic paint patterns, hilled with boat nacelles and gun turrets, thrusting out cannon and sensors like crystal forests. Satellite craft glinted around her. Indicator lights glowed on Flandry's board and his receiver said, "We have a lock on you. Go ahead."

He started the gravs. The gig left *Rommel* and surrendered to control from *Persei*. It was a short trip, but tense on both sides of the gap. How could McCormac be positive this was not a way to get a nuclear weapon inside his command vessel and detonate it? *He can't*, Flandry thought. *Especially when I wouldn't allow anyone to come fetch me. Of course that might well have been for fear of being captured by a boarding party, which indeed was partly the case, but just the same— He's courageous, McCormac. I detest him to his inmost cell, but he's courageous.*

126

A portal gaped and swallowed him. He sat for a minute hearing air gush back into the housing. Its personnel valves opened. He left the gig and went to meet the half dozen men who waited. They watched him somberly, neither hailing nor saluting.

He returned the stares. The insurrectionists were as marked by hunger and strain as he, but theirs was a less healthy, a sallowing, faintly grubby condition. "Relax," he said. "Inspect my vessel if you wish. No boobytraps, I assure you. Let's not dawdle, though."

"This way . . . please." The lieutenant who led the squad started off with rapid, stiff strides. Part of the group stayed behind, to check the boat. Those who walked at Flandry's back were armed. It didn't bother him. He had worse dangers to overcome before he could sleep.

They went through metal tunnels and caverns, past hundreds of eyes, in silence hardly broken save for the ship's pulse and breath. At the end, four marines guarded a door. The lieutenant addressed them and passed through. Saluting in the entrance, he said, "Commander Flandry, sir."

"Send him in," replied a deep toneless voice. "Leave us alone but stay on call."

"Aye, sir." The lieutenant stood aside. Flandry went by. The door closed with a soft hiss that betokened soundproofing.

Quiet lay heavy in the admiral's suite. This main room was puritanically furnished: chairs, a table, a couch, a plain rug, the bulkheads and overhead an undraped light gray. A few pictures and animations gave it some personality: family portraits, views from home, scenes of wilderness. So did a chess set and a bookshelf which held both codices and spools, both classics and scientific works. One of the inner doors was ajar, showing an office where McCormac must often toil after his watches. No doubt the bedroom was downright monastic, Flandry thought, the galley and bar seldom used, the—

"Greeting," McCormac said. He stood large, straight, gaunt as his men but immaculate, the nebula and stars frosty on his shoulders. He had aged, Flandry saw: more gray in the dark hair than pictures recorded, still less flesh in the bony countenance and more wrinkles, the eyes sunken while the nose and chin had become promontories.

"Good day." Flandry felt a moment's awe and inadequacy wash over him. He dismissed it with a measure of cold enjoyment.

127

"You might have saluted, Commander," McCormac said quietly.

"Against regulations," Flandry replied. "You've forfeited your commission."

"Have I? Well—" McCormac gestured. "Shall we sit down? Would you care for refreshment?"

"No, thanks," Flandry said. "We haven't time to go through the diplomatic niceties. Pickens' fleet will be on you in less than 70 hours."

McCormac lowered himself. "I am aware of that, Commander. We keep our scouts busy, you know. The mustering of that much strength could not be concealed. We're prepared for a showdown; we welcome it." He glanced up at the younger man and added: "You observe that I give you your proper rank. I am the Emperor of all Terran subjects. After the war, I plan on amnesty for nearly everyone who misguidedly opposed me. Even you, perhaps."

Flandry sat down too, opposite him, crossed ankle over knee, and grinned. "Confident, aren't you?"

"It's a measure of your side's desperation that it sent you in advance to try negotiating, with what you claim is my wife for a hostage." McCormac's mouth tightened. Momentarily, the wrath in him struck forth, though he spoke no louder. "I despise any man who'd lend himself to such a thing. Did you imagine I'd abandon everyone else who's trusted me to save any individual, however dear? Go tell Snelund and his criminals, there will be no peace or pardon for them, though they run to the ends of the universe; but there are ways and ways to die, and if they harm my Kathryn further, men will remember their fate for a million years."

"I can't very well convey that message," Flandry replied, "seeing that Snelund's dead." McCormac half rose. "What Kathryn and I came to let you know is that if you accept battle, you and your followers will be equally dead."

McCormac leaned over and seized Flandry by the upper arms, bruisingly hard. "What is this?" he yelled.

Flandry snapped that grip with a judo break. "Don't paw me, McCormac," he said.

They got back on their feet, two big men, and stood toe to toe. McCormac's fists were doubled. The breath whistled in and out of him. Flandry kept hands open, knees tense and a trifle bent, ready to move out of the way and chop downward. The impasse lasted thirty mortal seconds.

McCormac mastered himself, turned, stalked a few paces

128

off, and faced around again. "All right," he said as if being strangled. "I let you in so I could listen to you. Carry on."

"That's better." Flandry resumed his chair and took out a cigaret. Inwardly he shook and felt now frozen, now on fire. "The thing is," he said, "Pickens has your code."

McCormac rocked where he stood.

"Given that," Flandry said redundantly, "if you fight, he'll take you apart; if you retreat, he'll chivvy you to pieces; if you disperse, he'll snatch you and your bases in detail before you can rally. You haven't time to recode and you'll never be allowed the chance. Your cause is done, McCormac."

He waved the cigaret. "Kathryn will confirm it," he added. "She witnessed the whole show. Alone with her, you'll soon be able to satisfy yourself that she's telling the truth, under no chemical compulsions. You won't need any psych tests for that, I hope. Not if you two are the loving couple she claims.

"Besides, after talking to her, you're welcome to send a team over who'll remove my central computer. They'll find your code in its tapes. That'll disable my hyperdrive, of course, but I don't mind waiting for Pickens."

McCormac stared at the deck. "Why didn't she come aboard with you?" he asked.

"She's my insurance," Flandry said "She won't be harmed unless your side does something ridiculous like shooting at my vessel. But if I don't leave this one freely, my crew will take the appropriate measures."

Which I trust, dear Hugh, you will interpret as meaning that I have trained spacehands along, who'll speed away if you demonstrate bad faith. It's the natural assumption, which I've been careful to do nothing to prevent you from making. The datum that my crew is Woe, who couldn't navigate a flatboat across a swimming pool, and that heesh's orders are to do nothing no matter what happens . . . you're better off not receiving that datum right at once. Among other things, first I want to tell you some home truths.

McCormac lifted his head and peered closely. With the shock ridden out, his spirit and intelligence were reviving fast. "*Your* hostage?" he said from the bottom of his throat.

Flandry nodded while kindling his cigaret. The smoke soothed him the least bit. "Uh-huh. A long story. Kathryn will tell you most of it. But the upshot is, though I serve the Imperium, I'm here in an irregular capacity and without its knowledge."

"Why?"

Flandry spoke with the same chill steadiness as he re-

129

garded the other: "For a number of reasons, including that I'm Kathryn's friend. I'm the one who got her away from Snelund. I took her with me when I went to see what the chance was of talking you out of your lunacy. You'd left the Virgilian System, but one of your lovely barbarian auxiliaries attacked and wrecked us. We made it down to Dido and marched overland to Port Frederiksen. There I seized the warship from which the code was gotten, the same I now command. When I brought it to Llynathawr, my men and I kept Kathryn's presence secret. They think the cosmos of her too, you see. I lured Governor Snelund on board, and held him over a drain while she cut his throat. I'd have done worse, so'd you, but she has more decency in a single DNA strand than you or I will ever have in our whole organisms. She helped me get rid of the evidence because I want to return home. We tossed it on a meteorite trajectory into the atmosphere of an outer planet. Then we headed for Satan."

McCormac shuddered. "Do you mean she's gone over to your side—to you? Did you two—"

Flandry's cigaret dropped from lips yanked into a gorgon's lines. He surged up and across the deck, laid hold of McCormac's tunic, batted defending hands aside with the edge of his other palm and numbing force, shook the admiral and grated:

"Curb your tongue! You sanctimonious son of a bitch! If I had my wish, your pig-bled body would've been the one to burn through that sky. But there's Kathryn. There's the people who've followed you. There's the Empire. Down on your knees, McCormac, and thank whatever smug God you've taken on as your junior partner, that I have to find some way of saving your life because otherwise the harm you've done would be ten times what it is!"

He hurled the man from him. McCormac staggered against a bulkhead, which thudded. Half stunned, he looked upon the rage which stood before him, and his answering anger faded.

After a while, Flandry turned away. "I'm sorry," he said in a dull voice. "Not apologetic, understand. Only sorry I lost my temper. Unprofessional of me, especially when our time is scant."

McCormac shook himself. "I said I'd listen. Shall we sit down and begin over?" Flandry had to admire him a trifle for that.

They descended stiffly to the edges of their chairs. Flandry got out a new cigaret. "Nothing untoward ever happened be-

130

tween Kathryn and me," he said, keeping his eyes on the tiny cylinder. "I won't deny I'd have liked for it to, but it didn't. Her entire loyalty was, is, and forever will be to you. I think I've persuaded her that your present course is mistaken, but not altogether. And in no case does she want to go anyplace but where you go, help in anything but what you do. Isn't that an awesome lot to try to deserve?"

McCormac swallowed. After a moment: "You're a remarkable fellow, Commander. How old are you?"

"Half your age. And yet I have to tell you the facts of life."

"Why should I heed you," McCormac asked, but subduedly, "when you serve that abominable government? When you claim to have ruined my cause?"

"It was ruined anyway. I know how well your opposition's Fabian strategy was working. What we hope to do—Kathryn and I—we hope to prevent you from dragging more lives, more treasure, more Imperial strength down with you."

"Our prospects weren't that bad. I was evolving a plan—"

"The worst outcome would have been your victory."

"What? Flandry, I . . . I'm human, I'm fallible, but *anyone* would be better on the throne than that Josip who appointed that Snelund."

With the specter of a smile, because his own fury was dying out and a measure of pity was filling the vacuum, Flandry replied: "Kathryn still accords with you there. She still feels you're the best imaginable man for the job. I can't persuade her otherwise, and haven't tried very hard. You see, it doesn't matter whether she's right or wrong. The point is, you might have given us the most brilliant administration in history, and nevertheless your accession would have been catastrophic."

"Why?"

"You'd have destroyed the principle of legitimacy. The Empire will outlive Josip. Its powerful vested interests, its cautious bureaucrats, its size and inertia, will keep him from doing enormous harm. But if you took the throne by force, why shouldn't another discontented admiral do the same in another generation? And another and another, till civil wars rip the Empire to shreds. Till the Merseians come in, and the barbarians. You yourself hired barbarians to fight Terrans, McCormac. No odds whether or not you took precautions, the truth remains that you brought them in, and sooner or later we'll get a rebel who doesn't mind conceding them territory. And the Long Night falls."

131

"I could not disagree more," the admiral retorted with vehemence. "Restructuring a decadent polity—"

Flandry cut him off. "I'm not trying to convert you either. I'm simply explaining why I did what I did." *We need not tell you that I'd have abandoned my duty for Kathryn. That makes no difference any more*—interior laughter jangled—*except that it would blunt the edge of my sermon.* "You can't restructure something that's been irreparably undermined. All your revolution has managed to do is get sophonts killed, badly needed ships wrecked, trouble brewed that'll be years in settling—on this critical frontier."

"What should I have done instead?" McCormac disputed. "Leave my wife and myself out of it. Think only what Snelund had already done to this sector. What he would do if and when he won back to Terra. Was there another solution but to strike at the root of our griefs and dangers?"

" 'Root'—*radix*—you radicals are all alike," Flandry said. "You think everything springs from one or two unique causes, and if only you can get at them, everything will automatically become paradisical. History doesn't go that way. Read some and see what the result of every resort to violence by reformists has been."

"Your theory!" McCormac said, flushing. "I . . . we were faced with a fact."

Flandry shrugged. "Many moves were possible," he said. "A number had been started: complaints to Terra, pressure to get Snelund removed from office or at least contained in his scope. Failing that, you might have considered assassinating him. I don't deny he was a threat to the Empire. Suppose, specifically, after your friends liberated you, you'd gotten together a small though efficient force and mounted a raid on the palace for the limited purposes of freeing Kathryn and killing Snelund. Wouldn't that have served?"

"But what could we have done afterward?"

"You'd have put yourselves outside the law." Flandry nodded. "Same as I've done, though I hope to hide the guilt I don't feel. Quite aside from my personal well-being, the fact would set a bad precedent if it became public. Among your ignorances, McCormac, is that you don't appreciate how essential a social lubricant hypocrisy is."

"We couldn't have . . . skulked."

"No, you'd have had to do immediately what you and many others now have to do regardless—get out of the Empire."

"Are you crazy? Where to?"

Flandry rose once more and looked down upon him.

132

"You're the crazy man," he said. "I suppose we are decadent these days, in that we never seem to think of emigration. Better stay home, we feel, and cling to what we have, what we know, our comforts, our assurances, our associations . . . rather than vanish forever into that big strange universe . . . even when everything we cling to is breaking apart in our hands. But the pioneers worked otherwise. There's room yet, a whole galaxy beyond these few stars we think we control, out on the far end of one spiral arm.

"You can escape if you start within the next several hours. With that much lead, and dispersal in addition, your ships ought to be able to pick up families, and leave off the men who don't want to go. Those'll have to take their chances with the government, though I imagine necessity will force it to be lenient. Set a rendezvous at some extremely distant star. None of your craft will likely be pursued much past the border if they happen to be detected.

"Go a long way, McCormac, as far as you possibly can. Find a new planet. Found a new society. Never come back."

The admiral raised himself too. "I can't abandon my responsibilities," he groaned.

"You did that when you rebelled," Flandry said. "Your duty is to save what you can, and live the rest of your life knowing what you wrought here. Maybe the act of leading people to a fresh beginning, maybe that'll console you." *I'm sure it will in time. You have a royal share of self-righteousness.* "And Kathryn. She wants to go. She wants it very badly." He caught McCormac's gaze. "If ever a human being had a right to be taken from this civilization, she does."

McCormac blinked hard.

"Never come back," Flandry repeated. "Don't think of recruiting a barbarian host and returning. You'd be the enemy then, the real enemy. I want your word of honor on that. If you don't give it to me, and to Kathryn, she won't be allowed to rejoin you, whatever you may do to me. *"I lie like a wet rag."* If you do give it, and break it, she will not pardon you.

"In spite of your behavior, you are an able leader. You're the one man who can hope to carry the emigration off, in as short a while as you have to inform, persuade, organize, act. Give me your word, and Kathryn will ride back in my gig to you."

McCormac covered his face. "Too sudden. I can't—"

"Well, let's thresh out a few practical questions first, if you like. I've pondered various details beforehand."

"But—I couldn't—"

133

"Kathryn is your woman, all right," Flandry said bitterly. "Prove to me that you're her man."

She was waiting at the airlock. The hours had circled her like wolves. He wished that his last sight of her could be without that anguish and exhaustion.

"Dominic?" she whispered.

"He agreed," Flandry told her. "You can go to him."

She swayed. He caught her and held her. "Now, now," he said clumsily, nigh to tears. He stroked the bright tousled hair. "Now, now, it's ended, we've won, you and I—" She slumped. He barely kept her from falling.

With the dear weight in his arms, he went to sickbay, laid her down and administered a stimulol injection. Color appeared in seconds, her lashes fluttered, the green eyes found him. She sat erect. "Dominic!" she cried. Weeping had harshened her voice. " 'Tis true?"

"See for yourself," he smiled. "Uh, take care, though. I gave you a minimum shot. You'll have a stiff metabolic price to pay as is."

She came to him, still weary and shaken. Their arms closed. They kissed for a long time.

"I wish," she said brokenly, "I almost wish—"

"Don't." He drew her head into the curve of his shoulder.

She stepped back. "Well, I wish you everything good there'll ever be, startin' with the girl who's really right for you."

"Thanks," he said. "Have no worries on my score. It's been worth any trouble I may have had," *and ever will have.* "Don't delay, Kathryn. Go to him."

She did. He sought the conn, where he could see the boat carry her off and await McCormac's technicians.

XVI

Strange suns enclouded *Persei*. A darkness aft hid the last glimpse of Imperial stars.

McCormac closed the suite door behind him. Kathryn rose. Rest, first under sedation, later under tranquilization, and medicine and nourishment had made her beautiful. She wore a gray shimmerlyn robe somebody had given her, open at throat and calf, sashed at the waist, smooth over the strong deep curves.

He stopped short. "I didn't expect you here yet!" he blurted.

"The medics released me," she answered, "seein' as how I'd come to happy news." Her smile was tremulous.

"Well . . . yes," he said woodenly. "We've verified that we shook those scouts dogging us, by our maneuvers inside that nebula. They'll never find us in uncharted interstellar space. Not that they'd want to, I'm sure. It'd be too risky, sending the power needed to deal with us as far as we're going. No, we're done with them, unless we return."

Shocked, she exclaimed: "You won't! You promised!"

"I know. Not that I mightn't—if—no, don't fear. I won't. Flandry was right, damn him, I'd have to raise allies, and those allies would have to be offered what it would split the Empire to give. Let's hope the threat that I *may* try again will force them to govern better . . . back there."

Her strickenness told him how much remained for her before the old calm strength was regained: "Dyuba, you'd think 'bout politics and fightin' in this hour?"

"I apologize," he said. "Nobody warned me you were coming. And I have been preoccupied."

She reached him, but they did not embrace. "That preoccupied?" she asked.

"Why, why, what do you mean? See here, you shouldn't be standing more than necessary. Let's get you seated. And, er, we'll have to arrange for the sleeping quarters to be remodeled—"

She closed her eyes briefly. When she opened them, she had command of herself. "Poor Hugh," she said. "You're scarred right badly too. I should've thought how you must've hurt."

"Nonsense." He urged her toward the couch.

She resisted in such a manner that his arms went around her. Laying hers about his neck and her cheek against his breast, she said, "Wait. You were tryin' to 'scape thinkin' 'bout us. 'Bout what I can be to you, after everything that was done. 'Bout whether the things I'm leavin' untold concernin' what passed 'tween Dominic and me, if they didn't include— But I've sworn they didn't."

"I cannot doubt you," rumbled through her.

"No, you're too honorable not to try hard to believe me, not to try hard to rebuild what we had. Poor Hugh, you're scared you might not be able."

"Well—associations, of course—" His clasp stiffened.

"I'll help you if you'll help me. I need it bad's you do."

"I understand," he said, gentler.

"No, you don't, Hugh," she replied gravely. "I realized the truth while I was alone, recuperatin', nothin' to do but think in a weird clear way till I'd fall asleep and the dreams came. I'm 'bout as well over what happened to me in the palace as I'll ever be. I'm the one to cure *you* of that. But you'll have to cure me of Dominic, Hugh."

"Oh, Kathryn!" he said into her hair.

"We'll try," she murmured. "We'll succeed, anyhow in part, anyhow enough to live. We must."

Vice Admiral Sir Ilya Kheraskov riffled the papers on his desk. The noise went from end to end of his office. Behind him, the projection screen today held an image of Saturn.

"Well," he said, "I've perused your account, and other relevant data, quite intensely since you arrived home. You were a busy young man, Lieutenant Commander."

"Yes, sir," said Flandry. He had taken a chair, but thought best to give the impression of sitting at attention.

"I regret leave was denied you and you've been made to spend the whole two weeks in Luna Prime. Must have been frustrating, the fleshpots of Terra glowing right overhead. But any number of irregularities had to be checked out."

136

"Yes, sir."

Kheraskov chuckled. "Stop worrying. We'll put you through assorted rituals, but I can tell you in confidence, you're off the hook and your brevet rank of commander will be made permanent. Till your next escapade gets you either broken or promoted, that is. I'd call the odds fifty-fifty."

Flandry leaned back. "Thank you, sir."

"You seem a touch disappointed," Kheraskov remarked. "Did you anticipate more?"

"Well, sir—"

Kheraskov cocked his head and grinned wider. "You ought to be effusive at me. I'm responsible for your getting this much. And I had to work for it!"

He drew breath. "True," he said, "your obtaining the code was an exploit which justifies overlooking a great deal else. But the else is such a very great deal. Besides losing *Asieneuve* on a trip most kindly described as reckless, you staged other performances which were high-handed at best, in gross excess of your authority at worst. Like removing the sector governor's prisoner on your own warrant; and conveying her with you; and concealing her presence on your return; and heading back out with her; and losing her to the enemy. . . . I'm afraid, Flandry, regardless of what rank you may gain, you'll never have another command."

That's no punishment. "Sir," Flandry said, "my report justifies whatever I did as according to regulations. So will the testimony of the men who served under me."

"Taking the most liberal interpretation of your discretionary rights that man, xeno, or computer can conceive of . . . yes, perhaps. But mainly, you rascal, I argued and politicked on your behalf because the Intelligence Corps needs you."

"Again I thank the admiral."

Kheraskov shoved the cigar box forward. "Take one," he said, "and show your gratitude by telling me what really happened."

Flandry accepted. "It's in my report, sir."

"Yes, and I know a weasel when one slinks by me. For instance—I read from the abstract of this wonderful document you wrote—ahem. 'Soon after leaving with Lady McCormac for Terra, with minimal crew for the sake of speed and secrecy as per orders, I was unfortunately noted and overhauled by an enemy cruiser which captured me. Brought to the flagship at Satan, I was surprised to find the rebels so discouraged that, upon learning Admiral Pickens had their code, they decided to flee the Empire. Lady McCormac prevailed

137

upon them to spare me and my Didonian hand, leaving us behind with a disabled vessel. After the loyalists arrived, I discharged and returned home the said Didonian with the promised reward, then set course for Terra—' Well, no matter that." Kheraskov peered over the page. "Now what's the mathematical probability of a prowling cruiser just happening to come in detection range of you?"

"Well, sir," Flandry said, "the improbable has to happen sometimes. It's too bad the rebels wiped the computer's log in the course of removing my ship's hyperdrive. I'd have proof. But my account by itself ought to carry conviction."

"Yes, you build a very solid, interlocking pile of reasons, most of them unverifiable, why you had to do what you did and nothing else. You could spend your whole voyage back from Sector Alpha Crucis developing them. Be honest. You deliberately sought out Hugh McCormac and warned him about the code, didn't you?"

"Sir, that would have been high treason."

"Like doing away with a governor you didn't approve of? It's curious that he was last seen a short while before you cleared for departure."

"Much was going on, sir," Flandry said. "The city was in turmoil. His Excellency had personal enemies. Any one of them could have seen a chance to pay off scores. If the admiral suspects me of wrongdoing, he can institute proceedings to have me hypnoprobed."

Kheraskov sighed. "Never mind. You know I won't. For that matter, nobody's going to search after possible witnesses, rebels who may have elected to stay behind. Too big a job for too small a gain. As long as they keep their noses clean, we'll let them fade back into the general population. You're home free, Flandry. I'd simply hoped— But maybe it's best that I myself don't inquire too deeply. Do light your cigar. And we might send for a real potation. Do you like Scotch?"

"Love it, sir!" Flandry got the tobacco going and inhaled its perfume.

Kheraskov spoke an order on his intercom, leaned forward with elbows on desk, and blew clouds of his own. "Tell me one thing, though, prodigal son," he begged, "in exchange for my wholesale slaughter of fatted calves wearing stars and nebulas. Plain avuncular curiosity on my part. You have extended leave coming as soon as we can tie up the red tape. Where and how does your twisted ingenuity suggest you spend it?"

"Among those fleshpots the admiral mentioned," Flandry replied promptly. "Wine, women, and song. Especially women. It's been a long time."

Aside from such fun and forgetting, he thought while he grinned, *it will be the rest of my life.*

But she's happy. That's enough.

~~~~~~~~

I we remember.

The Feet is old now, slow to travel, aching in flesh when the mists creep around a longhouse that stands at the bottom of a winter night. The Wings that was of Many Thoughts is blind, and sits alone in his head save when a young one comes to learn. The Wings that was of Cave Discoverer and Woe is today in another of Thunderstone. The Hands of Many Thoughts and Cave Discoverer has long left his bones in the western mountains, whereto the Hands that was of Woe has long returned. Yet the memory lives. Learn, young Hands, of those who made oneness before i/we came to being.

It is more than the stuff of song, dance, and rite. No longer may We of this communion feel that Our narrow lands are the whole of the world. Beyond jungle and mountains is the sea; beyond heaven are those stars that Cave Discoverer dreamed of and Woe beheld. And there are the strangers with single bodies, they who visit Us rarely for trade and talk, but of whom We hear ever oftener as We in Our new search for enlightenment explore further among foreign communions. Their goods and their doings will touch Us more and more as the years pass, and will also make changes elsewhere than in Thunderstone, which changes will cause time to stream back across Us in different currents from that steadiness which i/we hitherto found easiest to imagine.

Beyond this and greater: How shall We achieve oneness with the whole world unless We understand it?

Therefore lie down at ease, young Hands, old Feet and Wings. Let wind, river, light, and time flow through. Be at rest, whole, in my/yourself, so gaining the strength that comes from peace, the strength to remember and to seek wisdom.

Be not afraid of the strangers with single bodies. Terrible are their powers, but those We can someday learn to wield like them if we choose. Rather pity that race, who are not beasts but can think, and thus know that they will never know oneness.

A KNIGHT OF
GHOSTS
AND SHADOWS

To
my lady Dorothea of Paravel
and Hal Ravn her lord
(Dorothy and Wilson Heydt)

How shall we tell it, brothers, the tale of Bodin's raid? Whence can we draw the words of wrath and sorrow, the words of valor and vengeance? Who today is a poet such as Andrei Simich, singer of heroes?

For Andrei, words ran to command, baying and belling like a pack of hounds in pursuit through mountains where echoes fly. The words of Andrei thundered like tundra beneath a herd of gromatz, shrieked like wind around the wings of the orlik as it stoops upon its prey, roared like a dyavo hunting—then sounded low and sweet, whether deadly as the call of a vilya or innocent as the song of a guslar in springtime.

Human and zmay together thrilled at the lays of Andrei when he celebrated the olden heroes, Yovan Matavuly who led the Founders the long lightless way to this our Morning Star, Toman Obilich who slew wild Vladimir on the crown of the Glacier, Gwyth who dared the storms of the Black Ocean, Stefan Miyatovich—great ancestor of Gospodar Bodin—who in the depths of the Night Years cast back the reavers from our very homes. Ah, well could Andrei Simich have sung the deeds of Bodin!

But his voice is departed. That the glory of Bodin Miyatovich go not from memory, let us find what poor plain words we may.

7

I

Every planet in the story is cold—even Terra, though Flandry came home on a warm evening of northern summer. There the chill was in the spirit.

He felt a breath of it as he neared. Somehow, talk between him and his son had drifted to matters Imperial. They had avoided all such during their holiday.

Terra itself had not likely reminded them. The globe hung beautiful in starry darkness, revealed by a viewscreen in the cabin where they sat. It was almost full, because they were accelerating with the sun behind them and were not yet close enough to start on an approach curve. At this remove it shone white-swirled blue, unutterably pure, near dewdrop Luna. Nothing was visible of the scars that man had made upon it.

And the saloon was good to be in, bulkheads nacreous gray, benches padded in maroon velvyl, table of authentic teak whereon stood Scotch whisky and everything needed for the use thereof, warm and flawlessly recycled air through which gamboled a dance tune and drifted an odor of lilacs. The *Hooligan*, private speedster of Captain Sir Dominic Flandry, was faster, better armed, and generally more versatile than any vessel of her class had a moral right to be; but her living quarters reflected her owner's philosophy that, if one is born into an era of decadence, one may as well enjoy it while it lasts.

He leaned back, inhaled deeply of his cigarette, took more smokiness in a sip from his glass, and regarded Dominic Hazeltine with some concern. If the frontier was truly that close to exploding—and the boy must go there again ... "Are you sure?" he asked. "What proved facts have you got—proved by yourself, not somebody else?

Why wouldn't I have heard more?"

His companion returned a steady look. "I don't want to make you feel old," he said; and the knowledge passed through Flandry that a lieutenant commander of Naval Intelligence, twenty-seven standard years of age, wasn't really a boy, nor was his father any longer the boy who had begotten him. Then Hazeltine smiled and took the curse off: "Well, I might want to, just so I can hope that at your age I'll have acquired, let alone kept, your capacity for the three basic things in life."

"Three?" Flandry raised his brows.

"Feasting, fighting, and— Wait; of course I haven't been along when you were in a fight. But I've no doubt you perform as well as ever in that department too. Still, you told me for the last three years you've stayed in the Solar System, taking life easy. If the whole word about Dennitza hasn't reached the Emperor—and apparently it's barely starting to—why should it have come to a pampered pet of his?"

"Hm. I'm not really. He pampers with a heavy hand. So I avoid the court as much as politeness allows. This indefinite furlough I'm on—nobody but him would dare call me back to duty, unless I grow bored and request assignment—that's the only important privilege I've taken. Aside from the outrageous amount of talent, capability, and charm with which I was born; and I do my best to share those chromosomes."

Flandry had spoken lightly in half a hope of getting a similar response. They had bantered throughout their month-long jaunt, whether on a breakneck hike in the Great Rift of Mars or gambling in a miners' dive in Low Venusberg, running the rings of Saturn or dining in elegance beneath its loveliness on Iapetus with two ladies expert and expensive. Must they already return to realities?

They'd been more friends than father and son. The difference in age hardly showed. They bore well-muscled height in common, supple movement, gray eyes, baritone voice. Flandry's face stood out in a perhaps overly handsome combination of straight nose, high cheekbones, cleft chin—the result of a biosculp job many years past, which he had never bothered to change again—and trim

10

mustache. His sleek seal-brown hair was frosted at the
temples; when Hazeltine accused him of bringing this
about by artifice, he had grinned and not denied it.
Though both wore civilian garb, Flandry's iridescent puff-
sleeved blouse, scarlet cummerbund, flared blue trousers,
and curly-toed beefleather slippers opposed the other's
plain coverall.

Broader features, curved nose, full mouth, crow's-wing
locks recalled Persis d'Io as she had been when she and
Flandry said farewell on a planet now destroyed, he not
knowing she bore his child. The tan of strange suns, the
lines creased by squinting into strange weathers, had not
altogether gone from Hazeltine in the six weeks since he
reached Terra. But his unsophisticated ways meant only
that he had spent his life on the fringes of the Empire. He
had caroused with a gusto to match his father's. He had
shown the same taste in speech—

("—an itchy position for me, my own admiral looking
for a nice lethal job he could order me to do," Flandry
reminisced. "Fenross hated my guts. He didn't like the rest
of me very much, either. I saw I'd better produce a strat-
agem, and fast."

("Did you?" Hazeltine inquired.

("Of course. You see me here, don't you? It's practically a *sine qua non* of a field agent staying alive, that he
be able to outthink not just the opposition, but his superiors."

("No doubt you were inspired by the fact that 'strat-
agem' spelled backwards is 'megatarts.' The prospect of
counting your loose women by millions should give plenty
of incentive."

(Flandry stared. "Now I'm certain you're my bairn!
Though to be frank, that awesomely pleasant notion escaped me. Instead, having developed my scheme, I confronted a rather ghastly idea which has haunted me ever
afterward: that maybe there's no one alive more intelligent than I.")

—and yet, and yet, an underlying earnestness always remained with him.

Perhaps he had that from his mother: that, and pride.
She'd let the infant beneath her heart live, abandoned her

titled official lover, resumed her birthname, gone from
Terra to Sassania and started anew as a dancer, at last
married reasonably well, but kept young Dominic by her
till he enlisted. Never had she sent word back from her
frontier home, not when Flandry well-nigh singlehanded
put down the barbarians of Scotha and was knighted for
it, not when Flandry well-nigh singlehanded rescued the
new Emperor's favorite granddaughter and headed off a
provincial rebellion and was summoned Home to be rewarded. Nor had her son, who always knew his father's
name, called on him until lately, when far enough along
in his own career that nepotism could not be thought necessary.

Thus Dominic Hazeltine refused the offer of merry
chitchat and said in his burred un-Terran version of Anglic, "Well, if you've been taking what amounts to a long
vacation, the more reason why you wouldn't have kept
trace of developments. Maybe his Majesty simply hasn't
been bothering you about them, and has been quite concerned himself for quite some while. Regardless, I've been
yonder and *I* know."

Flandry dropped the remnant of his cigarette in an ashtaker. "You wound my vanity, which is no mean accom-
plishment," he replied. "Remember, for three or four
years earlier—between the time I came to his notice and
the time we could figure he was planted on the throne too
firmly to have a great chance of being uprooted—I was
one of his several right hands. Field and staff work both,
specializing in the problem of making the marches decide
they'd really rather keep Hans for their Emperor than
revolt all over again. Do you think, if he sees fresh trouble
where I can help, he won't consult me? Or do you think,
because I've been utilizing a little of the hedonism I
fought so hard to preserve, I've lost interest in my old circuits? No, I've followed the news, and an occasional secret
report."

He stirred, tossed off his drink, and added, "Besides,
you claim the Gospodar of Dennitza is our latest problem
child. But you've also said you were working Sector Arcturus: almost diametrically opposite, and well inside those
vaguenesses we are pleased to call the borders of the Em-

pire. Tell me, then—you've been almighty unspecific about your operations, and I supposed that was because you were under security, and didn't pry—tell me, as far as you're allowed, what does the space around Arcturus have to do with Dennitza? With anything in the Taurian Sector?"

"I stayed mum because I didn't want to spoil this occasion," Hazeltine said. "From what Mother told me, I expected fun, when I could get a leave long enough to justify the trip to join you; but you've opened whole universes to me that I never guessed existed." He flushed. "If I ever gave any thought to such things, I self-righteously labeled them 'vice.' "

"Which they are," Flandry put in. "What you bucolic types don't realize is that worthwhile vice doesn't mean lolling around on cushions eating drugged custard. How dismal! I'd rather be virtuous. Decadence requires application. But go on."

"We'll land now, and I'll report back," Hazeltine said. "I don't know where they'll send me next, and doubtless won't be free to tell you. While the chance remains, I'll be honest. I came here wanting to know you as a man, but also wanting to, oh, alert you if nothing else, because I think your brains will be sorely needed, and it's damn hard to communicate through channels."

Indeed, Flandry admitted.

His gaze went to the stars in the viewscreen. Without amplification, few that he could see lay in the more or less 200-light-year radius of that rough and blurry-edged spheroid named the Terran Empire. Those were giants, visible by virtue of shining across distances we can traverse, under hyperdrive, but will never truly comprehend; and they filled the merest, tiniest fragment of the galaxy, far out in a spiral arm where their numbers were beginning to thin toward cosmic hollowness. Yet this insignificant Imperial bit of space held an estimated four million suns. Maybe half of those had been visited at least once. About a hundred thousand worlds of theirs might be considered to belong to the Empire, though for most the connection was ghostly tenuous. . . . It was too much. There were too many environments, races, cultures, lives, messages. No mind, no government could know the whole, let alone cope.

Nevertheless that sprawl of planets, peoples, provinces, and protectorates must somehow cope, or see the Long Night fall. Barbarians, who had gotten spaceships and nuclear weapons too early in their history, prowled the borders; the civilized Roidhunate of Merseia probed, withdrew a little—seldom the whole way—waited, probed again.... Rigel caught Flandry's eye, a beacon amidst the great enemy's dominions. The Taurian Sector lay in that direction, fronting the Wilderness beyond which dwelt the Merseians.

"You must know something I don't, if you claim the Dennitzans are brewing trouble," he said. "However, are you sure what you know is true?"

"What can you tell me about them?" Hazeltine gave back.

"Hm? Why—um, yes, that's sensible, first making clear to you what information and ideas I have."

"Especially since they must reflect what the higher-ups believe, which I'm not certain about."

"Neither am I, really. My attention's been directed elsewhere, Tauria seeming as reliably under control as any division of the Empire."

"After your experience there?"

"Precisely on account of it. Very well. We'll save time if I run barefoot through the obvious. Then you needn't interrogate me, groping around for what you may not have suspected hitherto."

Hazeltine nodded. "Besides," he said, "I've never been in those parts myself."

"Oh? You mentioned assignments which concerned the Merseia-ward frontier and our large green playmates."

"Tauria isn't the only sector at that end of the Empire," Hazeltine pointed out.

Too big, this handful of stars we suppose we know ...
"Ahem." Flandry took the crystal decanter. A refill gurgled into his glass. "You've heard how I happpened to be in the neighborhood when the governor, Duke Alfred of Varrak, kidnapped Princess Megan while she was touring, as part of a scheme to detach the Taurian systems from

the Empire and bring them under Merseian protection—
which means possession. Chives and I thwarted him, or is
'foiled' a more dramatic word?

"Well, then the question arose, what to do next? Let me
remind you, Hans had assumed, which means grabbed, the
crown less than two years earlier. Everything was still in
upheaval. Three avowed rivals were out to replace him by
force of arms, and nobody could guess how many more
would take an opportunity that came along, whether to
try for supreme power or for piratical autonomy. Alfred
wouldn't have made his attempt without considerable support among his own people. Therefore, not only must the
governorship change, but the sector capital.

"Now Dennitza may not be the most populous, wealthy,
or up-to-date human-colonized planet in Tauria. However,
it has a noticeable sphere of influence. And it has strength
out of proportion, thanks to traditionally maintaining its
own military, under the original treaty of annexation. And
the Dennitzans always despised Josip. His tribute assessors
and other agents he sent them, through Duke Alfred, developed a tendency to get killed in brawls, and somehow
nobody afterward could identify the brawlers. When Josip
died, and the Policy Board split on accepting his successor,
and suddenly all hell let out for noon, the Gospodar declared for Hans Molitor. He didn't actually dispatch
troops to help, but he kept order in his part of space, gave
the Merseians no opening—doubtless the best service he
could have rendered.

"Wasn't he the logical choice to take charge of Tauria?
Isn't he still?"

"In spite of Merseians on his home planet?" Hazeltine
challenged.

"Citizens of Merseian descent," Flandry corrected.
"Rather remote descent, I've heard. There are humans
who serve the Roidhunate, too, and not every one has
been bought or brainscrubbed; some families have lived on
Merseian worlds for generations."

"Nevertheless," Hazeltine said, "the Dennitzan culture
isn't Terran—isn't entirely human. Remember how hard
the colonists of Avalon fought to stay in the Domain of
Ythri, way back when the Empire waged a war to adjust

15

that frontier? Why should Dennitzans feel brotherly toward Terrans?"

"I don't suppose they do." Flandry shrugged. "I've never visited them either. But I've met other odd human societies, not to speak of nonhuman. They stay in the Empire because it gives them the Pax and often a fair amount of commercial benefit, without usually charging too high a price for the service. From what little I saw and heard in the way of reports on the Gospodar and his associates, they aren't such fools as to imagine they can stay at peace independently. Their history includes the Troubles, and their ancestors freely joined the Empire when it appeared."

"Nowadays Merseia might offer them a better deal."

"Uh-uh. They've been marchmen up against Merseia far too long. Too many inherited grudges."

"Such things can change. I've known marchmen myself. They take on the traits of their enemies, and eventually—" Hazeltine leaned across the table. His voice harshened. "Why are the Dennitzans resisting the Emperor's decree?"

"About disbanding their militia?" Flandry sipped. "Yes, I know, the Gospodar's representatives here have been appealing, arguing, logrolling, probably bribing, and certainly making nuisances of themselves on governmental levels as high as the Policy Board. Meanwhile he drags his feet. If the Emperor didn't have more urgent matters on deck, we might have seen fireworks by now."

"Nuclear?"

"Oh, no, no. Haven't we had our fill of civil war? I spoke metaphorically. And ... between us, lad, I can't blame the Gospodar very much. True, Hans' idea is that consolidating all combat services may prevent a repetition of what we just went through. I can't say it won't help; nor can I say it will. If nothing else, the Dennitzans do nest way out on a windy limb. They have more faith in their ability to protect themselves, given Navy support, than in the Navy's ability to do it alone. They may well be right. This is too serious a matter—a whole frontier is involved—too serious for impulsive action: another reason, I'm sure, why Hans has been patient, has not dismissed the Gospodar as governor or anything."

16

"I believe he's making a terrible mistake," Hazeltine said.

"What do you think the Dennitzans have in mind, then?"

"If not a breakaway, and inviting the Merseians in—I'm far from convinced that that's unthinkable to them, but I haven't proof—if not that, then insurrection . . . to make the Gospodar Emperor."

Flandry sat still for a while. The ship murmured, the music sang around him. Terra waxed in his sight.

Finally, taking forth a fresh cigarette, he asked, "What gives you that notion? Your latest work didn't bring you within a hundred parsecs of Dennitza, did it?"

"No." Hazeltine's mouth, which recalled the mouth of Persis, drew into thinner lines than ever hers had done. "That's what scares me. You see, we've collected evidence that Dennitzans are engineering a rebellion on Diomedes. Have you heard of Diomedes?"

"Ye-e-es. Any man who appreciates your three primaries of life ought to study the biography of Nicholas van Rijn, and he was shipwrecked there once. Yes, I know a little. But it isn't a terribly important planet to this day, is it? Why should it revolt, and how could it hope to succeed?"

"I wasn't on that team myself. But my unit was carrying out related investigations in the same sector, and we exchanged data. Apparently the Diomedeans—factions among them—hope the Domain of Ythri will help. They've acquired a mystique about the kinship of winged beings. . . . Whether the Ythrians really would intervene or not is hard to tell. I suspect not, to the extent that'd bring on overt conflict with us. But they might well use the potentiality, the threat, to steer us into new orbits. . . . We've barely started tracing the connections."

Flandry scowled. "And those turn out to be Dennitzan?"

"Correct. Any such conspiracy would have to involve members of a society with spaceships—preferably humans—to plant and cultivate the seed on Diomedes, and maintain at least enough liaison with Ythri that the would-be rebels stay hopeful. When our people first got on

17

the track of this, they naturally assumed the humans were Avalonian. But a lucky capture they made, just before I left for Sol, indicated otherwise. Dennitzan agents, Dennitzan."

"Why, on the opposite side of Terra from their home?"

"Oh, come on! You know why. If the Gospodar's planning an uprising of his own, what better preliminary than one in that direction?" Hazeltine drew breath. "I don't have the details. Those are, or will be, in the reports to GHQ from our units. But isn't something in the Empire always going wrong? The word is, his Majesty plans to leave soon for Sector Spica, at the head of an armada, and curb the barbarians there. That's a long way from anyplace else. Meanwhile, how slowly do reports from an obscure clod like Diomedes grind their way through the bureaucracy?"

"When a fleet can incinerate a world," Flandry said bleakly, "I prefer governments not have fast reflexes. You and your teammates could well be quantum-hopping to an unwarranted conclusion. For instance, those Dennitzans who were caught, if they really are Dennitzans, could be freebooters. Or if they have bosses at home, those bosses may be a single clique—may be, themselves, maneuvering to overthrow the Gospodar—and may or may not have ambitions beyond that. How much more than you've told me do you know for certain?"

Hazeltine sighed. "Not much. But I hoped—" He looked suddenly, pathetically young. "I hoped you might check further into the question."

Chives entered, on bare feet which touched the carpet soundlessly though the gee-field was set at Terran standard. "I beg your pardon, sir," he addressed his master. "If you wish dinner before we reach the landing approach zone, I must commence preparations. The tournedos will obviously require a red wine. Shall I open the Château Falkayn '35?"

"Hm?" Flandry blinked, recalled from darker matters. "Why . . . um-m . . . I'd thought of Beaujolais."

"No, sir," said Chives, respectfully immovable. "I cannot recommend Beaujolais to accompany a tournedos such as is contemplated. And may I suggest drinking and smoking cease until your meal is ready?"

Summer evening around Catalina deepened into night. Flandry sat on a terrace of the lodge which the island's owner, his friend the Mayor Palatine of Britain, had built on its heights and had lent to him. He wasn't sleepy; during the space trip, his circadian rhythm had slipped out of phase with this area. Nor was he energetic. He felt—a bit sad?—no, pensive, lonesome, less in an immediate fashion than as an accumulation from the years—a mood he had often felt before and recognized would soon become restlessness. Yet while it stayed as it was, he could wonder if he should have married now and then. Or even for life? It would have been good to help young Dominic grow.

He sighed, twisted about in his lounger till he found a comfortable knees-aloft position, drew on his cigar and watched the view. Beneath him, shadowy land plunged to a bay and, beyond, the vast metallic sheet of a calm Pacific. A breeze blew cool, scented with roses and Buddha's cup. Overhead, stars twinkled forth in a sky that ranged from amethyst to silver-blue. A pair of contrails in the west caught the last glow of a sunken sun. But the evening was quiet. Traffic was never routed near the retreats of noblemen.

How many kids do I have? And how many of them know they're mine? (I've only met or heard of a few.) And where are they and what's the universe doing to them?

Hm. He pulled rich smoke across his tongue. *When a person starts sentimentalizing, it's time either to get busy or to take antisenescence treatments. Pending this decision, how about a woman? That stopover on Ceres was several days ago, after all.* He considered ladies he knew and decided against them, for each would expect personal consideration—which was her right, but his mind was still too full of his son. Therefore: *Would I rather flit to the mainland and its bright lights, or have Chives phone the nearest cepheid agency?*

As if at a signal, his personal servant appeared, a Shalmuan, slim kilt-clad form remarkably humanlike except for 140 centimeters of height, green skin, hairlessness, long prehensile tail, and, to be sure, countless more subtle variations. On a tray he carried a visicom extension, a cup of coffee, and a snifter of cognac. "You have a call, sir," he announced.

How many have you filtered out? Flandry didn't ask. Nor did he object. The nonhuman in a human milieu—or vice versa—commonly appears as a caricature of a personality, because those around him cannot see most of his soul. But Chives had attended his boss for years. "Personal servant" had come to mean more than "valet and cook"; it included being butler of a household which never stayed long in a single place, and pilot, and bodyguard, and whatever an emergency might require.

Chives brought the lounger table into position, set down the tray, and disappeared again. Flandry's pulse bounced a little. In the screen before him was the face of Dominic Hazeltine. "Why, hello," he said. "I didn't expect to hear from you this soon."

"Well"—excitement thrummed—"you know, our conversation— When I came back to base, I got a chance at a general data scanner, and keyed for recent material on Dennitza. A part of what I learned will interest you, I think. Though you'd better act fast."

● II ●

Immediately after the two Navy yeomen who brought Kossara to the slave depot had signed her over to its manager and departed, he told her: "Hold out your left arm." Dazed—for she had been whisked from the ship within an hour of landing on Terra, and the speed of the aircar had blurred the enormousness of Archopolis—she obeyed. He glanced expertly at her wrist and, from a drawer, selected a bracelet of white metal, some three centimeters broad and a few millimeters thick. Hinged, it locked together with a click. She stared at the thing. A couple of sensor spots and a niello of letters and numbers were its only distinctions. It circled her arm snugly though not uncomfortably.

"The law requires slaves to wear this," the manager explained in a bored tone. He was a pudgy, faintly greasy-looking middle-aged person in whose face dwelt shrewdness.

That must be on Terra, trickled through Kossara's mind. *Other places seem to have other ways. And on Denitza we keep no slaves. . . .*

"It's powered by body heat and maintains an audiovisual link to a global monitor net," the voice went on. "If the computers notice anything suspicious—including, of course, any tampering with the bracelet—they call a human operator. He can stop you in your tracks by a signal." The man pointed to a switch on his desk. "This gives the same signal."

He pressed. Pain burned like lightning, through flesh, bone, marrow, until nothing was except pain. Kossara fell to her knees. She never knew if she screamed or if her throat had jammed shut.

21

He lifted his hand and the anguish was gone. Kossara crouched shaking and weeping. Dimly she heard: "That was five seconds' worth. Direct nerve stim from the bracelet, triggers a center in the brain. Harmless for periods of less than a minute, if you haven't got a weak heart or something. Do you understand you'd better be a good girl? All right, on your feet."

As she swayed erect, the shudders slowly leaving her, he smirked and muttered, "You know, you're a looker. Exotic; none of this standardized biosculp format. I'd be tempted to bid on you myself, except the price is sure to go out of my reach. Well . . . hold still."

He did no more than feel and nuzzle. She endured, thinking that probably soon she could take a long, long, long hot shower. But when a guard had conducted her to the women's section, she found the water was cold and rationed. The dormitory gaped huge, echoing, little inside it other than bunks and inmates. The mess was equally barren, the food adequate but tasteless. Some twenty prisoners were present. They received her kindly enough, with a curiosity that sharpened when they discovered she was from a distant planet and this was her first time on Terra. Exhausted, she begged off saying much and tumbled into a haunted sleep.

The next morning she got a humiliatingly thorough medical examination. A psychotech studied the dossier on her which Naval Intelligence had supplied, asked a few questions, and signed a form. She got the impression he would have liked to inquire further—why had she rebelled?—but a Secret classification on her record scared him off. Or else (because whoever bought her would doubtless talk to her about it) he knew from his study how chaotic and broken her memories of the episode were, since the hypnoprobing on Diomedes.

That evening she couldn't escape conversation in the dormitory. The women clustered around and chattered. They were from Terra, Luna, and Venus. With a single exception, they had been sentenced to limited terms of enslavement for crimes such as repeated theft or dangerous negligence, and were not very bright or especially comely.

"I don't suppose anybody'll bid on me," lamented one. "Hard labor for the government, then."

"I don't understand," said Kossara. Her soft Dennitzan accent intrigued them. "Why? I mean, when you have a worldful of machines, every kind of robot—why slaves? How can it . . . how can it pay?"

The exceptional woman, who was handsome in a haggard fashion, answered. "What else would you do with the wicked? Kill them, even for tiny things? Give them costly psychocorrection? Lock them away at public expense, useless to themselves and everybody else? No, let them work. Let the Imperium get some money from selling them the first time, if it can."

Does she talk like that because she's afraid of her bracelet? Kossara wondered. *Surely, oh, surely we can complain a little among ourselves!* "What can we do that a machine can't do better?" she asked.

"Personal services," the woman said. "Many kinds. Or . . . well, economics. Often a slave is less efficient than a machine, but needs less capital investment."

"You sound educated," Kossara remarked.

The woman sighed. "I was, once. Till I killed my husband. That meant a life term like yours, dear. To be quite safe, my buyer did pay to have my mind corrected." A sort of energy blossomed in look and tone. "How grateful I am! I was a murderess, do you hear, a murderess. I took it on myself to decide another human being wasn't fit to live. Now I know—" She seized Kossara's hands. "Ask them to correct you too. You committed treason, didn't you say? Beg them to wash you clean!"

The rest edged away. *Brain-channeled*, Kossara knew. A crawling went under her skin. "Wh-why are you here?" she stammered. "If you were bought—"

"He grew tired of me and sold me back. I'll always long for him . . . but he had the perfect right, of course." The woman drew nearer. "I like you, Kossara," she whispered. "I do hope we'll go to the same place."

"Place?"

"Oh, somebody rich may take you for a while. Likelier, though, a brothel—"

Kossara yanked free and ran. She didn't quite reach a

23

toilet before she vomited. They made her clean the floor. Afterward, when they insisted on circling close and talking and talking, she screamed at them to leave her alone, then enforced it with a couple of skilled blows. No punishment followed. It was dreadful to know that a half-aware electronic brain watched every pulsebeat of her existence, and no doubt occasionally a bored human supervisor examined her screen at random. But seemingly the guardians didn't mind a fight, if no property was damaged. She sought her bunk and curled up into herself.

Next morning a matron came for her, took a critical look, and nodded. "You'll do," she said. "Swallow this." She held forth a pill.

"What's that?" Kossara crouched back.

"A euphoriac. You want to be pretty for the camera, don't you? Go on, swallow." Remembering the alternative, Kossara obeyed.

As she accompanied the matron down the hall, waves of comfort passed through her, higher at each tide. It was like being drunk, no, not drunk, for she had her full senses and command of her body ... like having savored a few glasses with Mihail, after they had danced, and the violins playing yet ... like having Mihail here, alive again.

Almost cheerfully, in the recording room she doffed her gray issue gown, went through the paces and said the phrases designed to show her off, as instructed. She barely heard the running commentary:

"Kossara Vymezal [mispronounced, but a phonetic spellout followed], human female, age twenty-five, virgin, athletic, health and intelligence excellent, education good though provincial. Spirited, but ought to learn subordination in short order without radical measures. Life sentence for treason, conspiracy to promote and aid rebellion. Suffers from hostility to the Imperium and some disorientation due to hypnoprobing. Neither handicap affects her wits or basic emotional stability. Her behavior on the voyage here was cold but acceptable.

"She was born on the planet Dennitza, Zoria III in the Taurian Sector. [A string of numbers] Her family is well placed, father being a district administrator. [Why no mention of the fact Mother was a sister of Bodin Miyatovich,

Gospodar and sector governor? O Uncle, Uncle . . .] As is the rule there, she received military training and served a hitch in the armed forces. She has a degree in xenology. Having done field work on planets near home, several months ago she went to Diomedes [a string of numbers]—quite remote, her research merely a disguise. Most of the report on her has not been made available to us; and as said, she herself is confused and largely amnesiac about this period. Her main purpose was to help instigate a revolt. Before much harm was done, she was detected, arrested, interrogated, and sentenced by court-martial. There being little demand for slaves in that region, and a courier ship returning directly to Terra, she was brought along.

"We rate her unlikely to be dangerous, given the usual precautions, and attractive both physically and person-ally—"

The camera projected back the holograms it had taken, for its operator's inspection, and Kossara looked upon her image. She saw a big young woman, 177 centimeters tall, a bit small in the bosom but robust in shoulders, hips, and long free-striding legs, skin ivory-clear save for a few freckles and the remnant of a tan. The face was wide, high in the cheekbones, snub in the nose, full in the mouth, strong in chin and jawline. Large blue-green eyes stood well apart beneath dark brows and reddish-brown bangs; that hair was cropped below the ears in the manner of both sexes on Dennitza. When she spoke, her voice was husky.

"—will be sullen unless drugged, but given the right training and conditions, ought to develop a high sexual ca-pacity. A private owner may find that kindness will in due course make her loyal and responsive—"

Kossara slipped dreamily away from the words, the room, Terra . . . the whole way home. To Mihail? No, she couldn't quite raise him from the dust between the stars—even now, she dared not. But, oh, just a few years ago, she and Trohdwyr . . .

{She had a vacation from her studies at the Shkola plus

25

a furlough from her ground defense unit in the Narodna
Voyska. Ordinarily she would have spent as much of this
time as *he* could spare with her betrothed. But a space
force had been detected within a few light-years of the
Zorian System which might intend action on behalf of
some other claimant to the Imperium than Hans Molitor
whom the Gospodar supported, or might use such par-
tisanship as an excuse for brigandage. Therefore Bodin
Miyatovich led some of the Dennitzan fleet out to warn
off the strangers, and if necessary fight them off. Mihail
Svetich, engineer on a Meteor-class torpedo craft, had
kissed Kossara farewell.

Rather than fret idle in Zorkagrad, she flitted to her
parents' home. Danilo Vymezal, voivode of the Dubina
Dolyina, was head of council, chief magistrate, and military commander throughout a majestic country at the
northern rim of the Kazan. Soon after she reached the estate, Kossara said she wished for a long hunt. Her father
regarded her for a moment before he nodded. "That will
do you good," he said. "Who would you like for a partner? Trohdwyr?"

She had unthinkingly supposed she would go alone. But
of course he was right; only fools went by themselves so
far into wilderness that no radio relay could pass on a distress call from a pocket transceiver. The old zmay was
welcome company, not least because he knew when to be
silent.

They took an aircar to a meadow on the unpeopled
western slope and set forth afoot. The days and nights, the
leagues and heights, wind, rain, sun, struggle, and sleep
were elixir. More than once she had a clear shot at a soaring orlik or a bull yelen poised on a crag, and forbore;
those wings or those horns were too splendid across the
sky. But at last it was sweet fire in the blood to stand before a charging dyavo, feel the rifle surge back against her
shoulder, see fangs and claws fall down within a meter of
her.

Trohdwyr reproved: "You were reckless, Dama."

"He came at me from his den," Kossara retorted.

"After you saw the entrance and took care to make
much noise in the bushes. Deny it not. I have known you

26

longer than your own memory runs. You learned to walk by clinging to my tail for safety. If I lose you now, your father will dismiss me from his service, and where then shall a poor lorn dodderer go? Back to his birth village to become a fisher again, after these many years? Have mercy, Dama."

She chuckled. They set about making camp. This was high in the bowl of the Kazan, where that huge crater bit an arc from the Vysochina. The view could not have been imagined by anyone who had not seen it, save God before He willed it.

Though treeless, the site bore a dense purple sward of mahovina, springy underfoot and spicy to smell, studded by white and gold wildflowers; and a nearby canebrake rustled in the breeze. Eastward the ringwall sloped down to timberline. Beyond, yellow beams of evening fell on a bluish mistiness of forest, as far as sight could reach, cloven by a river which gleamed like a drawn blade. Westward, not far hence, the rim stood shadowy-sharp athwart rough Vysochina hills. Behind them the snowpeaks of the Planina Byelogorski lifted sungold whiteness into an absolute azure. The purity of sky was not marred by a remote northward thread of smoke from Vulkana Zemlya.

The air grew cold soon after the sun went behind the mountains, cold as the brook which bubbled iron-tasting from a cleft in the crater's lip. Kossara hunched into her jacket, squatted down, held palms forth to the fire. Her breath drifted white through the dusk that rose from the lowlands.

Before he put their meat on a spit above coals and dancing flamelets, Trohdwyr drew a sign and spoke a few words of Eriau. Kossara knew them well: "Aferdhi of the Deeps, Blyn of the Winds, Haawan who lairs on the reefs, by this be held afar and trouble us not in our rest." Hundreds of kilometers and a long lifetime from the Black Ocean, he remained an old-fashioned pagan ychan. Early in her teens, eager in her faith, Kossara had learned it was no use trying to make an Orthochristian of him.

Surely the Pantocrator didn't mind much, and would receive his dear battered soul into Heaven at the last.

She had never thought of him as a zmay. Not that the

word had any particularly bad overtones. Maybe once it
had been a touch contemptuous, four hundred years ago
when the first immigrants arrived from Merseia; but later
it came to mean simply a Dennitzan of such ancestry.
(Did the growth of their original planet into a frightening
rival of Terra have anything to do with that?) However,
from him and his family she had learned Eriau—rather,
the archaic and mutated version they spoke—at the same
time as she was learning Serbic from her parents and Anglic from a governess. When finally prevailed upon to stop
scrambling these three into a private patois, she kept the
habit of referring to Trohdwyr's people by their own name
for themselves, "ychani": "seekers."

For he had been close to the center of her child-uni-
verse. Father and Mother were at its very heart, naturally,
and so for a while were a doll named Lutka, worn into
shapelessness, and a cat she called Butterfeet. Uncle Bodin
approached them when he and Aunt Draga visited, or the
Vymezals went to Zorkagrad and he took her to the zoo
and the merrypark. Three younger siblings, two brothers
and a sister, orbited like comets, now radiant with love,
now off into outer darkness. Trohdwyr never shone quite
as brightly as any of these; but the chief gamekeeper to
three generations of her house moved in an unchangeable
path, always there for her to reach when she needed him.

"Kraich." Having started dinner cooking, he settled
back on the tripod of clawed feet and massive tail.
"You've earned a double drink this evening, Dama. A
regular sundowner, and one for killing the dyavo." He
poured into cups from a flask of shlivovitza. "Though *I*
must skin the beast and carry the hide," he added.

The hoarse basso seemed to hold a note of genuine
complaint. Startled, Kossara peered across the fire at him.

To a dweller in the inner Empire, he might have been
any Merseian. No matter how anthropoid a xenosophont
was, the basic differences usually drowned individuality
unless you knew the species well. Trohdwyr roughly resembled a large man—especially in the face, if you overlooked endless details of its heavy-boned, brow-ridged,
wide-nosed, thin-lipped construction. But he had no external earflaps, only elaborately contoured holes in the skull.

Totally hairless, his skin was pale green and faintly scaled. A sierra of low triangular spines ran from the top of his forehead, down his back to the tail's end. When he stood, he leaned forward, reducing his effective height to tall-human; when he walked, it was not on heels and soles but on his toes, in an alien rhythm. He was warm-blooded; females of his race gave live birth; but he was no mammal—no kind of animal which Terra had ever brought forth.

By a million signs Kossara knew him for Trohdwyr and nobody else, as she knew her kinfolk or Mihail. He had grown gaunt, deep furrows lay in his cheeks, he habitually spurned boots and trousers for a knee-length tunic with many pockets, he wore the same kind of curve-bladed sheath knife with knuckleduster handle which he had given her and taught her to use, years before. . . .

"Why, I'll abandon it if you want," she said, thinking, *Has time begun to wear him down? How hurtful to us both.*

"Oh, no, no, Dama. No need." Trohdwyr grew abashed. "Forgive a gaffer if he's grumpy. I was—well, today I almost saw you ripped apart. There I stood, you in my line of fire, and that beast—Dama, don't do such things."

"I'm sorry," Kossara said. "Though I really don't believe I was taking too big a chance. I know my rifle."

"I too. Didn't you learn from me?"

"But those were lightweight weapons. Because I was a girl? Today I had a Tashta, the kind they've issued me in the Voyska. I was sure it could stop him." Kossara gazed aside, downslope toward the bottom of the Kazan, which night had already filled. "Besides," she added softly, "I needed such a moment. You're right, I did provoke the dyavo to attack."

"To get away from feeling helpless?" Trohdwyr murmured.

"Yes." She could never have opened thus to any human except Mihail, maybe not even to him; but over the years the ychan had heard confessions which she did not give her priest. "My man's yonder." She flung a hand toward the first stars as they twinkled forth, white upon violet above the lowlands. "I have to stay behind in my guard unit—when Dennitza will never be attacked!"

"Thanks to units like yours, Dama," Trohdwyr said.

"Nevertheless, he—" Kossara took her drink in a gulp. It burned the whole way down, and the glow spread fast to every part of her. She held the cup out for a refill. "Why does it matter this much who's Emperor? All right, Josip was foul and his agents did a great deal of harm. But he's dead now; and the Empire did survive him; and I've heard enough from my uncle to know that what really keeps it going is a lot of nameless little officials whose work outlasts whole dynasties. Then why do we fight over who'll sit crowned in Archopolis for the next few years?"

"You are the human, Dama, not I," said Trohdwyr. After a minute: "Yet I can think how on Merseia they would be glad to see another Terran Emperor whose spirit is fear or foolishness. And ... we here are not overly far from Merseia."

Kossara shivered beneath the stars and took a strong sip.

"Well, it'll get settled soon," she declared. "Uncle Bodin told me he's sure it will be. This thing in space is a last gasp. Soon"—she lifted her head—"Mihail and I can travel," *exploring together the infinite marvels on worlds that circle new suns.*

"I hope so, Dama, despite that I'll miss you. Have plenty of young, and let them play and grow around me on the manor as you did, will you?"

Exalted by the liquor—how the smell of the roasting meat awakened hunger!—she blurted: "He wanted me to sleep with him before he left. I said no, we'll wait till we're married. Should I have said yes? Tell me, should I have?"

"You are the human," Trohdwyr repeated. "I can simply answer, you are the voivode's daughter and the Gospodar's niece. But I remember from my cubhood—when folk still lived in Old Aferoch, though already then the sea brought worse and worse floods—a female ychan of that town. I knew her somewhat, since a grown cousin of mine used to come in from our village, courting her—"

The story, which was of a rivalry as fierce as might have stood between two men of different clans in early days on Dennitza, but which ended after a rescue on the water, was oddly comforting: almost as if she were little again, and Trohdwyr rocked her against his warm dry breast and rumbled a lullaby. That night Kossara slept well. Some days afterward she returned happily to Dubina Dolyina. When her leave was up, she went back to Zorkagrad.

There she got the news that Mihail Svetich had been killed in action.

But standing before the slave shop's audiovisual recorders, Kossara did not think of this, nor of what had happened to Trohdwyr himself on cold Diomedes. She remained in that one evening out of the many they had had together.}

The chemical joy wore off. She lay on her bunk, bit her pillow and fought not to yell.

A further day passed.

Then she was summoned to the manager's office. "Congratulations," he said. "You've been bought, luckier than you deserve."

It roared in her. Darkness crossed her eyes. She swayed before his desk. Distantly she heard:

"A private gentleman, and he must really have liked what he saw in the catalogue, because he outbid two different cepheid houses. You can probably do well for yourself—and me, I'll admit. Remember, if he sells you later, he may well go through me again instead of making a deal directly. I don't like my reputation hurt, and I've got this switch here— Anyhow, you'll be wise if you show him your appreciation. His name is Dominic Flandry, he's a captain of Naval Intelligence, a knight of the Imperium, and, I'll tell you, a favorite of the Emperor. He doesn't need a slave for his bed. Gossip is, he's tumbled half the female nobility on Terra, and commoner girls past counting. Like I said, he must think you're special. The more grateful you act, the better your life is likely to be. . . . On your way, now. A matron will groom and gown you."

She also provided a fresh euphoriac. Thus Kossara didn't even mind that the servant who came to fetch her was hauntingly like and unlike an ychan. He too was bald,

31

green, and tailed; but the green was grass-bright, without scales, the tail thin as a cat's, the posture erect, the height well below her own, the other differences unreckonable. "Sir Dominic saw fit to dub me Chives," he introduced himself. "I trust you will find his service pleasant. Indeed, I declined the manumission he offered me, until the law about spy bracelets went into effect on Terra. May I direct you out?"

Kossara went along through rosiness, into an aircar, on across the city and an ocean, eventually to an ornate house on an island which Chives called Catalina. He showed her to a suite and explained that her owner was busy elsewhere but would presently make his wishes known. Meanwhile these facilities were hers to use, within reason.

Kossara fell asleep imagining that Mihail was beside her.

● III ●

It was official: the Emperor Hans would shortly leave
Terra, put himself at the head of an armada, and personally see to quelling the barbarians—war lords, buccaneers,
crusaders for God knew what strange causes—who still
harassed a Sector Spica left weak by the late struggle for
the Imperial succession. He threw a *bon voyage* party at
the Coral Palace. Captain Sir Dominic Flandry was
among those invited. Under such circumstances, one
comes.

Besides, Flandry reflected, *I can't help liking the old
bastard. He may not be the best imaginable thing that
could happen to us, but he's probably the best available.*

The hour was well after sunset in this part of Oceania. A
crescent moon stood high to westward; metrocenter star-
points glinted across its dark side. The constellations threw
light of their own onto gently rolling waves, argent shimmer on sable. Quietness broke where surf growled white
against ramparts. There walls, domes, towers soared aloft
in a brilliance which masked off most of heaven.

When Flandry landed his car and stepped forth, no
clouds of perfume (or psychogenic vapors, as had been
common in Josip's reign) drifted from the palace to soften
salt odors. Music wove among mild breezes, but formal,
stately, neither hypersubtle nor raucous. Flandry wasn't
sure whether it was composed on a colony planet—if so,
doubtless Germania—or on Terra once, to be preserved
through centuries while the mother world forgot. He did
know that a decade ago, the court would have snickered
at sounds this fusty-archaic.

Few servants bowed as he passed among fellow guests,

33

into the main building. More guardsmen than formerly saluted. Their dress uniforms were less ornate than of yore and they and their weapons had seen action. The antechamber of fountains hadn't changed, and the people who swirled between them before streaming toward the ballroom wore clothes as gorgeous as always, a rainbow spectacle. However, fantastic collars, capes, sleeves, cuffs, footgear were passé. Garb was continuous from neck or midbreast to soles, and, while many men wore robes rather than trousers, every woman was in a skirt.

A reform I approve of, he thought. *I suspect most ladies agree. The suggestive rustle of skillfully draped fabric is much more stimulating, really, and easier to arrange, than cosmetics and diadems on otherwise bare areas of interest. For that matter, though it does take more effort, a seduction is better recreation than an orgy.*

There our good Hans goes too far. Every bedroom in the palace locked!

Ah, well. Conceivably he wants his entourage to cultivate ingenuity.

Crown Prince Dietrich received, a plain-faced middle-aged man whose stoutness was turning into corpulence. Though he and Flandry had worked together now and then in the fighting, his welcome was mechanical. Poor devil, he must say a personal hello to each of three or four hundred arrivals important enough to rate it, with no drug except stim to help him. Another case of austere principles overdone, Flandry thought. The younger brother, Gerhart, was luckier tonight, already imperially drunk at a wallside table with several cronies. However, he looked as sullen as usual.

Flandry drifted around the circumference of the ballroom. There was nothing fancy about the lighting, save that it was cast to leave unobscured the stars in the vitryl dome overhead. The floor sheened with diffracted reflections from several score couples who swung through the decorous measures of a quicksilver. He hailed acquaintances when he glimpsed them, but didn't stop till he had reached an indoor arbor where champagne was available. A goblet of tickle in his hand, roses around him, a cheerful melody, a view of pretty women in motion—life could be worse.

It soon was. "Greetin', Sir Dominic."

Flandry turned, and bowed in dismay to the newcomer beneath the leaves. "Aloha, your Grace."

Tetsuo Niccolini, Duke of Mars, accepted a glass from the attendant behind the table. It was obviously not his first. "Haven't seen you for some while," he remarked. "Missed you. You've a way o' puttin' a little spark into a scene, dull as the court is these days." Shrewdly: "Reason you don't come often, what?"

"Well," Flandry admitted, "his Majesty's associates do tend to be a bit earnest and firm-jawed." He sipped. Still, my impression is, your Grace spends a fair amount of time here regardless."

Niccolini sighed. He had never been more than a well-meaning fop; but in these last years, when antisenescence and biosculp could no longer hold wrinkles, baldness, feebleness at bay, he had developed a certain wry perspective. Unfortunately, he remained a bore.

Shadows of petals stirred across a peacock robe as he lifted his drink. "D'you think I should go to my ancestral estates and all that rubbish, set up my own small court along lines I like, eh? No, m'boy, not feasible. I'd get nothin' but sycophants, who'd pluck me while they smiled. My real friends, who put their hearts into enjoyin' life, well, they're dead or fled or sleepin' in an oldster's bed." He paused. " 'Sides, might's well tell you, H.M. gave me t'understand—he makes himself very clear, ha?—gave me t'understand, he'd prefer no Duke o' Mars henceforth visit the planet 'cept for a decent minimum o' speeches an' dedications."

Flandry nodded. *That makes sense,* flickered through him. *The Martians [nonhumans; colonists by treaty arrangement in the time of the Commonwealth; glad to belong to it, but feeling betrayed when it broke down and the Troubles came; dragooned into the Empire] are still restless. Terra can best control them by removing the signs of Terran control. I suspect, after poor tottery Tetty is gone, Hans will buy out his heirs with a gimcrack title elsewhere and a lot of money and make a Martian the next Duke—who may not even know he's a puppet.*

At least, that's what I'd consider doing.

"But we're in grave danger o' seriousness," Niccolini interrupted himself. "Where've you been? Busy at what? Come, come, somethin' amusin' must've happened."

"Oh, just knocking around with a friend." Flandry didn't care to get specific. One reason why he had thus far declined promotion to admiral was that then he'd be too conspicuous, too eagerly watched and sought after, while he remained near the Emperor. He liked his privacy. As a hanger-on who showed no further ambitions—and could therefore in time be expected to lose his energetic patron's goodwill—he drew scant attention.

"Or knockin' up a friend? Heh, heh, heh." The Duke nudged him. "I know your sort o' friends. How was she?"

"In the first place, she was a he," Flandry said. Until he could escape, he might as well reconcile himself to humoring a man who had discovered the secret of perpetual adolescence. "Of course, we explored. Found a new place on Ganymede which might interest your Grace, the Empress Wu in Celestial City."

"No, no." Niccolini waggled his head and free hand. "Didn't y'know? I never go anywhere near Jupiter. Never. Not since the *La Reine Louise* disaster."

Flandry cast his mind back. He couldn't identify— Oh, yes. It had happened five years ago, while he was out of the Solar System. Undeterred by civil war, a luxury liner was approaching Callisto when her screen field generators failed. The trapped radiation which seethes around the giant planet, engulfing its inner moons, killed everybody aboard; no treatment could restore a body burned by so much unfelt fire.

Nothing of the kind had happened for centuries of exploration and colonization thereabouts. Magnetohydrodynamic shields and their backups were supposed to be invulnerable to anything that wouldn't destroy a vehicle or a settlement anyway. Therefore, sabotage? The passenger list had included several powerful people. A court of inquiry had handed down the vaguest finding of "cumulative negligence."

"My poor young nephew, that I inherited the Dukedom from, was among the casualties," Niccolini droned on. "That roused the jolly old instinct o' self-preservation, I can tell you. To blinkin' many hazards as is. Not that I flatter myself I'm a political bull's-eye. Still, one never knows, does one? So tell me 'bout this place you found. If it sounds intriguin', I'll see 'bout gettin' a sensie."

Flandry was saved by a courier in Imperial livery who entered the arbor and bowed. "A thousand pardons, your Grace," she said. "Sir Dominic, there is an urgent message for you. Will you please follow me?"

"With twofold pleasure," Flandry responded, for she was young and well-formed. He couldn't quite place her accent, though he guessed she might be from some part of Hermes. Even when hiring humans, the majordomos of the new Emperor's various households were under orders to get an many non-Terrans as was politic.

Whoever the summons was from, and whether it was terrible or trivial, he was free of the Duke before he could otherwise have disengaged. The noble nodded a vague response to his apology and stood staring after him, all alone.

His Imperial Majesty, High Emperor Hans Friedrich Molitor, of his dynasty the first, Supreme Guardian of the Pax, Grand Director of the Stellar Council, Commander-in-Chief, Final Arbiter, acknowledged supreme on more worlds and honorary head of more organizations than any man could remember, sat by himself in a room at the top of a tower. It was sparsely furnished: a desk and communicator, a couch upholstered in worn but genuine horsehide, a few straightbacked chairs and the big pneumatic that was his. The only personal items were a dolchzahn skin on the floor, from Germania; two portraits of his late wife, in her youth and her age, and one of a blond young man; a model of the corvette that had been his first command. A turret roof, beginning at waist height, was currently transparent, letting this eyrie overlook an illuminated complex of roofs, steeples, gardens, pools, outer walls, attendant rafts, and finally the night ocean.

The courier ushered Flandry through the door and vanished as it closed behind him. He saluted and snapped to attention. "At ease," the Emperor grunted. "Sit. Smoke if you want."

37

Poul Anderson

He was puffing a pipe whose foulness overcame the air 'fresher. In spite of the blue tunic, white trousers, and gold braid with nebula and three stars of a grand admiral, plus the pyrocrystal ring of Manuel the Great, he was not very impressive to see. Yet meditechnics could not account for so few traces of time. The short, stocky frame had grown a kettle belly, bags lay beneath the small dark eyes, the hair was thin and gray on the blocky head: nothing that could not easily be changed by the biocosmetics he scorned to use. Nor had he ever troubled about his face, low forehead, bushy brows, huge Roman nose, heavy jowls, gash of a mouth between deep creases, prow of a chin.

"Thank you, your Majesty." Flandry settled his elegance opposite, flipped out a cigarette case which was a work of art and, at need, a weapon, and established a barrier against the reek around him.

"No foolish formalities," growled the rusty, accented basso. "I must make my grand appearance, and empty chatter will rattle for hours, and at last when I can go I'm afraid I'll be too tired for a nice new wench who's joined the collection, no matter how much I need a little fun."

"A stim pill?" Flandry suggested.

"No. I take too many as is. The price to the body mounts, you know. And ... barely six years on the throne have I had. The first three, fighting to stay there. I need another twenty or thirty for carpentering this jerry-built, dry-rotted Empire into a thing that might last a few more generations, before I can lay down my tools." Hans chuckled coarsely. "Well, let the tool for pretty Thressa wait, recharging, till tomorrow night. You should see her, Dominic, my friend. But not to tell anybody. By herself she could cause a revolution."

Flandry grinned. "Yes, we humans are basically sexual beings, aren't we, sir? If we can't screw each other physically, we'll do it politically."

Hans laughed aloud. He had never changed from a boy who deserted a strait-laced colonial bourgeois home for several years of wild adventure in space, the youth who enlisted in the Navy, the man who rose through the ranks without connections or flexibility to ease his way.

But he had not changed either from the hero of Syrax,

38

where the fleet he led flung back the Merseians and forced a negotiated end to a short undeclared war which had bidden fair to grow. Nor had he changed from the leader who let his personnel proclaim him Emperor—himself reluctantly, less from vainglory than a sense of workmanship, when the legitimate order of succession had dissolved in chaos and every rival claimant was a potential disaster.

A blunt pragmatist, uncultured and unashamed of it, shrewd rather than intelligent, he either appalled Manuel Argos or won a grudging approval, in whatever hypothetical hell or Valhalla the Founder dwelt. The question was academic. His hour was now. How long that hour would be, and what the consequences, were separate puzzles.

Mirth left. He leaned forward. The pipe smoldered between hairy hands clenched upon his knees. "I talk too much," he said, a curious admission from the curtest of the Emperors. Flandry understood, though. Few besides him were left, maybe none, with whom Hans dared talk freely. "Let us come to business. What do you know about Dennitza?"

Inwardly taken aback, Flandry replied soft-voiced, "Not much, sir. Not much about the whole Taurian Sector, in spite of having had the good luck to be there when Lady Megan needed help. Why ask me?"

Hans scowled. "I suppose you do know how the Gospodar, my sector governor, is resisting my defense reorganization. Could be a simple difference of judgment, yes. But ... now information suggests he plans rebellion. And *that*—where he is—will involve the Merseians, unless he is already theirs."

Flandry's backbone tingled. "What are the facts, sir?"

"A wretched planet in Sector Arcturus. Diomedes, it's called. Natives who want to break away and babble of getting Ythrian help. Human agents among them. We would expect such humans would be from the Domain, likeliest Avalon—not true? But our best findings say the Ythrians hold no wish to make trouble for us. And our people discover those humans are Dennitzan. Only one was captured alive, and they had some problems with the hypnoprobing, but it does appear she went to Diomedes under secret official orders."

Hans sighed. "Not till yesterday did this reach me through the damned channels. It never would have before I left, did I not issue strictest orders about getting a direct look at whatever might possibly point to treason. And— *Gott in Himmel,* I am swamped, on top of all else! My computer screens out *lèse-majesté* cases and the rest of such piddle. Nevertheless—"

Flandry nodded. "Aye, sir. You can't give any single item more than a glance. And even if you could pay full attention, you can't send the big clumsy Imperial machine barging into Tauria, disrupting our whole arrangement there, on the basis of a few accusations. Especially in your absence."

"Yes. I must go. If we don't reorder Sector Spica, the barbarians will soon ruin it. But meanwhile Tauria may explode. You see how an uprising in Sector Arcturus would be the right distraction for a traitor Dennitzan before he rebels too."

"Won't Intelligence mount a larger operation?"

"*Ja, ja, ja.* Though the Corps is still in poor shape, after wars and weedings. Also, it has much other business. And ... Dominic, just the Corps by itself is too huge for me to know, for me to control as I should. I need—I am not sure what I need or if it can be had."

Flandry foreknew: "You want me to take a hand, sir?"

"Yes." The wild boar eyes were sighted straight on him. "In your olden style. A roving commission, and you report directly to me. Plenipotentiary authority."

Flandry's pulse broke into a canter. He kept his tone level. "Quite a solo, sir."

"Co-opt. Hire. Bribe. Threaten. Whatever you see fit."

"The odds will stay long against my finding out anything useful—at least, anything the Corps can't, quicker and better."

"You are not good at modesty," Hans said. "Are you unwilling?"

"N-n-no, sir." Surprised, Flandry realized he spoke truth. This could prove interesting. In fact, he knew damn well it would, for he had already involved himself in the affair. His motivation was half curiosity, half kindliness— he thought at the time—though probably, down underneath, the carnivore which had been asleep in him these past three years had roused, pricked up its ears, snuffed game scent on a night breeze. *Was that always my real desire? Not to chase down enemies of the Empire so I could go on having fun in it, but to have fun chasing them down?*

No matter. The blood surged. "I'm happy to accept, sir, provided you don't expect much. Uh, my authority, access to funds and secret data and whatnot ... better be kept secret itself."

"Right." Hans knocked the dottle from his pipe, a ringing noise through a moment's silence. "Is this why you refused admiral's rank? You knew sneaking off someday on a mission would be easier for a mere captain."

Flandry shrugged. "If you'll tip the word to—better be none less than Kheraskov—I'll contact him as soon as may be and made arrangements."

"Have you any idea how you will begin?" Hans asked, relaxing a trifle.

"Well, I don't know. Perhaps with that alleged Dennitzan agent. What became of ... her, did you say?"

"How can I tell? I saw a précis of many reports, remember. What difference, after the 'probe wrung her dry?"

"Sometimes individuals count, sir." Excitement in Flandry congealed to grimness. *I should think the fact she's a niece of the Gospodar—a fact available in the material on her that my son could freely scan from a data bank—would be worth mentioning to the Emperor. I should think such a hostage would not be sold for a slave, forced into whoredom except for the chance that I learned about her when she was offered for sale.*

Better not tell Hans. He'd only be distracted from the million things he's got to do. And anyhow ... something strange here. I prefer to keep my mouth shut and my options open.

"Proceed as you wish," the other said. "I know you won't likely get far. But I can trust you will run a strong race."

His glance went to the picture of the young man. His face sagged. Flandry could well-nigh read his mind: *Ach,*

Otto! If you had not been killed—if I could bring you back, yes, even though I must trade for you dull Dietrich and scheming Gerhart both—we would have an heir to trust.

The Emperor straightened in his seat. "Very well," he rapped. "Dismissed."

The festival wore on. Toward morning, Flandry and Chunderban Desai found themselves alone.

The officer would have left sooner, were it not for his acquired job. Now he seemed wisest if he savored sumptuousness, admired the centuried treasures of static and fluid art which the palace housed, drank noble wines, nibbled on delicate foods, conversed with witty men, danced with delicious girls, finally brought one of these to a pergola he knew (unlocked, screened by jasmine vines) and made love. He might never get the chance again. After she bade him a sleepy goodbye, he felt like having a nightcap. The crowd had grown thin. He recognized Desai, fell into talk, ended in a small garden.

Its base was cantilevered from a wall, twenty meters above a courtyard where a fountain sprang. The waters, full of dissolved fluorescents, shone under ultraviolet illumination in colors more deep and pure than flame. Their tuned splashing resounded from catchbowls to make an eldritch music. Otherwise the two men on their bench had darkness and quiet. Flowers sweetened an air gone slightly cool. The moon was long down; Venus and a dwindling number of stars gleamed in a sky fading from black to purple, above an ocean coming all aglow.

"No, I am not convinced the Emperor does right to depart," Desai said. The pudgy little old man's hair glimmered white as his tunic; chocolate-hued face and hands were nearly invisible among shadows. He puffed on a cigarette in a long ivory holder. "Contrariwise, the move invites catastrophe."

"But to let the barbarians whoop around at will—" Flandry sipped his cognac and drew on his cigar, fragrances first rich, then pungent. He'd wanted to end on a relaxing topic. Desai, who had served the Imperium in many executive capacities on many different planets, owned a hoard of reminiscences which made him worth cultivating. He was on Terra for a year, teaching at the Diplomatic Academy, before he retired to Ramanujan, his birthworld.

The military situation—specifically, Hans' decision to go—evidently bothered him too much for pleasantries. "Oh, yes, that entire frontier needs restructuring," he said. "Not simple reinforcement. New administrations, new laws, new economics: ideally, the foundations of an entire new society among the human inhabitants. However, his Majesty should leave that task to a competent viceroy and staff whom he grants extraordinary powers."

"There's the problem," Flandry pointed out. "Who's both competent and trustworthy enough, aside from those who're already up to their armpits in alligators elsewhere?"

"If he has no better choice," Desai said, "his Majesty should let the Spican sector be ravaged—should even let it be lost, in hopes of regaining the territory afterward—anything, rather than absent himself for months. What ultimate good can he accomplish yonder if meanwhile the Imperium is taken from him? The best service he can render the Empire is simply to keep a grip on its heart. Else the civil wars begin again."

"I fear you exaggerate," Flandry said, though he recalled how Desai was always inclined to understate things. And Dennitzans on Diomedes . . . "We seem to've pacified ourselves fairly well. Besides, why refer to civil wars in the plural?"

"Have you forgotten McCormac's rebellion, Sir Dominic?"

Scarcely, seeing I was involved. Flandry winced at a memory. Lost Kathryn, as well as the irregular nature of his actions at the time, made him glad the details were still unpublic. "No. But that was, uh, twenty-two years ago. And amounted to what? An admiral who revolted against Josip's sector governor for personal reasons. True, this meant he had to try for the crown. The Imperium could never have pardoned him. But he was beaten, and Josip died in bed." *Probably poisoned, to be sure.*

"You consider the affair an isolated incident?" Desai challenged in his temperate fashion. "Allow me to remind

43

you, please—I know you know—shortly afterward I found myself the occupation commissioner of McCormac's home globe, Aeneas, which had spearheaded the uprising. We came within an ångström there of getting a messianic religion that might have burst into space and torn the Empire in half."

Flandry took a hard swallow from his snifter and a hard pull on his cigar. Well had he studied the records of that business, after he encountered Aycharaych who had engineered it.

"The thirteen following years—seeming peace inside the Empire, till Josip's death—they are no large piece of history, are they?" Desai pursued. "Especially if we bear in mind that conflicts have causes. A war, including a civil war, is the flower on a plant whose seed went into the ground long before ... and whose roots reach widely, and will send up fresh growths.... No, Sir Dominic, as a person who has read and reflected for most of a lifetime on this subject, I tell you we are well into our anarchic phase. The best we can do is minimize the damage, and hold outside enemies off until we win back to a scarred kind of unity."

" 'Our' anarchic phase?" Flandry questioned.

Desai misheard his emphasis. "Or our interregnum, or whatever you wish to call it. Oh, we may not always fight over who shall be Emperor; we can find plenty of bones to contend about. And we may enjoy stretches of peace and relative prosperity. I hoped Hans would provide us such a respite."

"No, wait, you speak as if this is something we have to go through, willy-nilly."

"Yes. For about eighty more years, I think—though of course modern technology, nonhuman influences, the sheer scale of interstellar dominion may affect the time-span. Basically, however, yes, a universal state—and the Terran Empire is the universal state of Technic civilization—only gives a respite from the wars and horrors which multiply after the original breakdown. Its Pax is no more than a subservience enforced at swordpoint, or today at blaster point. Its competent people become untrustworthy from their very competence; anyone who can make a decision may make one the Imperium does not like. Incompetence grows with the growing suspiciousness and centralization. Defense and civil functions alike begin to disintegrate. What can that provoke except rebellion? So this universal state of ours has ground along for a brace of generations, from bad to worse, until now—"

"The Long Night?" Flandry shivered a bit in the gentle air.

"I think not quite yet. If we follow precedent, the Empire will rise again . . . if you can label as 'rise' the centralized divine autocracy we have coming. To be sure, if the thought of such a government does not cheer you, then remember that that second peace of exhaustion will not last either. In due course will come the final collapse."

"How do you know?" Flandry demanded.

"The cycle fills the history, yes, the archeology of this whole planet we are sitting on. Old China and older Egypt each went thrice through the whole sorry mess. The Western civilization to which ours is affiliated rose originally from the same kind of thing, that Roman Empire some of our rulers have liked to hark back to for examples of glory. Oh, we too shall have our Diocletian; but scarcely a hundred years after his reconstruction, the barbarians were camping in Rome itself and making emperors to their pleasure. My own ancestral homeland—but there is no need for a catalogue of forgotten nations. For a good dozen cases we have chronicles detailed to the point of nausea; all in all, we can find over fifty examples just in the dust of this one world.

"Growth, until wrong decisions bring breakdown; then ever more ferocious wars, until the Empire brings the Pax; then the dissolution of that Pax, its reconstitution, its disintegration forever, and a dark age until a new society begins in the ruins. Technic civilization started on that road when the Polesotechnic League changed from a mutual-aid organization of free entrepreneurs to a set of cartels. Tonight we are far along the way."

"You've discovered this yourself?" Flandry asked, not as skeptically as he could have wished he were able to.

"Oh, no, no," Desai said. "The basic analysis was made a thousand years ago. But it's not comfortable to live with. Prevention of breakdown, or recovery from it, calls for more thought, courage, sacrifice than humans have yet been capable of exercising for generation after generation. Much easier first to twist the doctrine around, use it for rationalization instead of rationality; then ignore it; finally suppress it. I found it in certain archives, but you realize I am talking to you in confidence. The Imperium would not take kindly to such a description of itself."

"Well—" Flandry drank again. "Well, you may be right. And total pessimism does have a certain bracing quality. If we're doomed to tread out the measure, we can try to do so gracefully."

"There is no absolute inevitability." Desai puffed for a minute, his cigarette end a tiny red pulsar. "I suppose, even this late in the game, we could start afresh if we had the means—more importantly, the will. But in actuality, the development is often aborted by foreign conquest. An empire in the anarchic phase is especially tempting and especially prone to suffer invaders. Osmans, Afghans, Moguls, Manchus, Spaniards, British—they and those like them became overlords of cultures different from their own, in that same way.

"Beyond our borders, the Merseians are the true menace. Not a barbarian rabble merely filling a vacuum we have left by our own political machinations—not a realistic Ythri which sees us as its natural ally—not a pathetic Gorrazani remnant—but Merseia. We harass and thwart the Roidhunate everywhere, because we dare not let it grow too strong. Besides eliminating us as a hindrance to its dreams, think what a furtherance our conquest would be!

"That's why I dread the consequences of the Emperor's departure. Staying home, working to buttress the government and armed force, ready to stamp fast on every attempt at insurrection, he might keep us united, uninvadable, for the rest of his life. Without his presence—I don't know."

"The Merseians would have to be prepared to take quick advantage of any revolt," Flandry argued. "Assuming you're right about your historical pattern, are *they* aware of it? How common is it?"

"True, we don't have the knowledge to say how far it may apply to nonhumans, if at all," Desai admitted. "We should. In fact, it was Merseia, not ourselves, that set me on this research—for the Merseians too must have their private demons, and think what a weapon it would be for our diplomacy to have a generalized mechanic for them as well as us!"

"Hm?" said Flandry, surprised afresh. "Are you implying perhaps they already are decadent? That's not what one usually hears."

"No, it isn't. But what is decadence to a nonhuman? I hope to do more than read sutras in my retirement; I hope to apply my experience and my studies to thought about just such problems." The old man sighed. "Of necessity, this assumes the Empire will not fall prey to its foes before I've made some progress. That may be an unduly optimistic assumption ... considering what a head start they have in the Roidhunate where it comes to understanding us."

"Are you implying they know this theory of human history which you've been outlining to me?"

"Yes, I fear that at least a few minds among them are all too familiar with it. For example, after considering the episode for many years, I think that when Aycharaych tried to kindle a holy war of man against man, starting on Aeneas, he knew precisely what he was doing."

Aycharaych. The chill struck full into Flandry. He raised his eyes to the fading stars. Sol would soon drive sight away from them, but they would remain where they were, waiting.

"I have often wondered what makes him and his kind serve Merseia," Desai mused. "Genius can't really be conscripted. The Chereionites surely have something to win for themselves. But what—from an alien species, an alien culture?"

"Aycharaych's the only one of them I've ever actually met," Flandry said. "I've sometimes thought he's an artist."

"An artist of espionage and sabotage, whose materials are living beings? Well, conceivably. If that's all, he is no more to be envied than you or I."

47

"Why?"

"I'm not sure I can make the reason clear to you, or even very clear to myself. We have not had the good fortune to be born in an era when our society offers us something transcendental to live and die for." Desai cleared his throat. "I'm sorry. I didn't intend to read you a lecture."

"No, I thank you," Flandry said. "Your ideas are quite interesting."

● IV ●

The *Hooligan* sprang from Terra, pierced the sky, and lined out for deep space. A steady standard gravity maintained by her interior fields gave no hint of furious acceleration toward regions sufficiently distant that she could go into hyperdrive and outpace light. Nor did her engine energies speak above an almost subliminal whisper and quiver through the hull. But standing in the saloon before its big viewscreen, Kossara watched the planet shrink, ever faster, a cloudy vastness, a gibbous globe of intricate blue and white, an agate in a diamondful jewel box.

At the back of her mind she wished she could appreciate this sight for which she had left the stateroom assigned her. Terra, Manhome, Maykasviyet; and sheer loveliness— But her heart knocked, her nails bit into wet palms though her tongue was dry and thick, she smelled her harsh sweat.

Yet when her owner entered, calm crystallized in her. By nature and training she met crises coolly, and here was the worst since— As far as she knew, nobody else was aboard but him and his servant. If she could, somehow, kill them—or hogtie the funny, kindly Shalmuan—maybe before he took her—

No. Not unless he grew altogether slack; and she sensed alertness beneath his relaxed manner. He was tall and well built and moved like a hunting vilya. Handsome too, she admitted to herself; then scorn added that anybody could be handsome who bought a biosculpture. A loose lace-trimmed blouse and flowing trousers gathered above sandals matched, in their sheen of expensive fabric, the knee-length gown she had chosen out of the wardrobe she found in her quarters.

49

"Good day, Donna Vymezal," the man said, and bowed. What to do? She jerked a nod.

"Permit self-introduction," he went on. "Hardly to your surprise, I am Captain Sir Dominic Flandry, Intelligence Corps of his Majesty's Navy." He gestured at a bench curved around two sides of a table. "Won't you be seated?"

She stood her ground.

Flandry smiled, placed hands on hips, and drawled: "Please listen. I have no intention of compelling you. None. Not that you don't inspire certain daydreams, Donna. And not that I couldn't make you like it. Drugs, you know. But vanity forbids. I've never needed force or pharmacopoeia, even on those few young ladies I had occasion to buy in the past. Have you noticed your cabin door locks on the inside?"

Strength went from Kossara. She stumbled backward, fell to the bench, rested head in hands while whirling and darkness passed through her.

Presently she grew aware that Flandry stood above. His fingers kneaded her neck and shoulders. As she looked up, he stroked her hair. She gasped and drew aside.

He stepped back. "No offense, Donna." Sternly: "See here, we've a bundle to discuss, none of it very amusing. Do you want a stim pill—or what, to make you operational?"

She shook her head. After two tries, she husked forth, "Nothing, thank you. I am all right now."

"Drink? The liquor cabinet is reasonably well stocked. I'm for Scotch."

"Nothing," she whispered, dreading in spite of his words what might be in a glass he gave her.

He seemed to guess that, for he said, "You'll have to take from my galley in due course if not sooner. We've a long trip ahead of us."

"What? . . . Well, a little wine, please."

He got busy, while she worked to loosen muscles and nerves. When he sat down, not too close, she could meet his eyes. She declined the cigarette he offered, but the claret was marvelous. He streamed smoke from his nostrils before saying, deliberately:

"You might recollect who else was bidding on you." She

felt her face blaze. "And I didn't spend quite a lot of beer money out of chivalry. Your virture is safe as long as you want it to be—while I'm your owner. But I need your co-operation in some rather larger matters. Understood?"

She gulped. "If I can . . . help you, sir—"

"In exchange for manumission and a ticket to Dennitza? Maybe. I haven't the legal right to free you, seeing what you were convicted of. I'd have to petition for a decree. Or I could simply order you to go back where you came from and enjoy yourself." He saw her glance fall to the slave bracelet. "Yes, now we're clear of Terra, I'm permitted to take that off you. But I haven't a key for it, and my tools would damage it, which'd put us through a certain amount of bureaucratic rain dance if we return there. Never mind. Beyond range of the comnet, it's inert." Flandry grinned. "If I were indeed a monster of lust, rather than a staid and hardworking monster, I'd still have taken you into space before commencing. The idea of an audience at any arbitrary time doesn't appeal. Let them invent their own techniques."

Loathing tightened Kossara's throat. "The Terran way of life."

Flandry regarded her quizzically. "You don't have a high opinion of the Empire, do you?"

"I hate it. I would die—be tortured—yes, go into a brothel, if I could pull the rotten thing down around me." Kossara tossed off her wine.

Flandry refilled the glass. "Better be less outspoken," he advised. "I don't mind, but various of my fellow Imperialists might."

She stared. The real horror of her situation shocked home. *"Where are we bound?"*

"Diomedes, for openers at any rate." He nodded. "Yes, I'm investigating what went on, what is going on, whether it threatens the Empire, and how to prevent same."

Kossara rallied. "You have the records of my . . . arrest and interrogation, then," she said fast. "I have no further information. Less, actually, because the hypnoprobe blanked out related memories, including those from Dennitza. What's left is bits, blurry and jumbled together, like

51

barely remembered dreams. So how can I help you—supposing I wanted to?"

"Oh, background and such." Flandry's tone was casual. "Give me the rest of your biography. Explain what your people have against the Imperium. I'll listen. Who knows, you may convert me. I won't hurry you. There's an unsanctified amount of information pumped into the data banks aboard, which I need to study en route. And we've time. Seventeen standard days to destination."

"No more?" In spite of everything, astonishment touched her.

"This boat has legs, albeit not as well turned as yours. Do ease off, Donna. Your culture has a soldierly orientation, right? Consider me your honorable enemy, if nothing else, and the pair of us conducting a parley."

She found little to say. He talked for two, mostly appealing to her xenological interests with tales of sophonts he had met. All were fascinating. A few eventually made her laugh.

Books, musical pieces, shows were available by the thousands, in playback or printout. Kossara grew restless anyhow. Flandry had withdrawn immediately after the first breakfast of the voyage (following a nightwatch wherein she slept unexpectedly well) to concentrate on his briefing material. Interstellar space, seen in the optical-compensating screens, was utter splendor; but however fast the *Hooligan* drove, those immensities changed too slowly for perception. She exercised, prowled around, tried out different hobby kits, at last sought Chives. He was in the galley fixing lunch. "Can I help you?" she offered.

"I regret not, Donna," the Shalmuan answered. "While I have no wish to deprecate your culinary gifts, you can see that Sir Dominic does not willingly trust this excellent chef-machine to prepare his meals, let alone comparative strangers."

She stared at the open-faced sandwiches growing beneath his fingers. Anchovies and pimientos lay across slices of hard-boiled egg on fresh-made mayonnaise, caviar and lemon peel complemented paté de foie gras, cucumber and alfalfa sprouts revitalized cheddar cheese in the dignity of its age ... "No, I couldn't do that," she admitted. "You must be a genius."

"Thank you, Donna. I endeavor to give satisfaction. Although, in candor, Sir Dominic provided my initial training and the impetus to develop further."

Kossara drew a long breath. *A chance to learn about him?* "You were his slave, you said. How did that happen, if I may ask?"

Chives spoke imperturbably, never breaking the rhythm of his work. "My planet of origin has no technologically advanced society, Donna. His late Majesty Josip appointed a sector governor who organized a slave trade in my people, chiefly selling to the barbarians beyond the *limes*. The charges against those captured for this purpose were, shall we say, arguable; but no one argued. When that governor met with misfortune, his successor attempted to right matters. However, this was impossible. Not even victims still within the Empire could be traced, across thousands of worlds. Sir Dominic merely chanced upon me in a provincial market.

"I was not prepossessing, Donna. My owner had put me up for sale because he doubted I could survive more labor in his mercury mine. Sir Dominic did not buy me. He instigated a game of poker which lasted several days and left him in possession of mine and workers alike."

Chives clicked his tongue. "My former master alleged cheating. Most discourteous of him, especially compared to Sir Dominic's urbanity in inviting him out. The funeral was well attended by the miners. Sir Dominic arranged for their repatriation, but kept me since this was far from Shalmu and, besides, I required a long course of chelating drugs to cleanse my system. Meanwhile he employed me in his service. I soon decided I had no wish to return to a society of ... natives ... and strove to make myself valuable to him."

Head cocked, chin in hand, tail switching, Chives studied the lunch layout. "Yes, I believe this will suffice. Akvavit and beer for beverages, needless to say. Since you wish occupation, Donna, you may assist me in setting the table."

She scarcely heard. *"Moze,* if he's a decent man," she

53

blurted, "how can he work for an Empire that lets things like, like your case happen?"

"I have oftener heard Sir Dominic described in such terms as—ah—for example, a slightly overexcited gentleman once called him a cream-stealing tomcat with his conscience in his balls, if you will pardon the expression, Donna. The fact is, he did cheat in that poker game. But as for the Empire, like the proverbial centenarian I suggest you consider the alternative. You will find tableware in yonder cabinet."

Kossara bit her lip and took the hint.

"To the best of my admittedly circumscribed knowledge," Chives said after silver, china, and glass (not vitryl) stood agleam upon snowy linen, "your folk have, on the whole, benefited from the Empire. Perhaps I am misinformed. Would you care to summarize the history for me while the spiced meatballs are heating?"

His slim emerald form squatted down on the deck. Kossara took a bench, stared at her fists resting knotted on her lap, and said dully:

"I don't suppose the details, six hundred years of man on Dennitza, would interest anybody else. That is how long since Yovan Matavuly led the pioneers there. They were like other emigrant groups at the time, hoping not alone for opportunity, room to breathe, but to save traditions, customs, language, race—ethnos, identity, their souls if you like—everything they saw being swallowed up. They weren't many, nor had the means to buy much equipment. And Dennitza . . . well, there are always problems in settling a new planet, physical environment, biochemistry, countless unknowns and surprises that can be lethal—but Dennitza was particularly hard. It's in an ice age. The habitable areas are limited. And in those days it was far from any trade routes, had nothing really to attract merchants of the League—"

Speaking of the ancestors heartened her. She raised head and voice. "They didn't fall back to barbarism, no, no. But they did, for generations, have to put aside sophisticated technology. They lacked the capital, you see. Clan systems developed; feuding, I must admit; a spirit of local independence. The barons looked after their own. That so-

54

cial structure persisted when industrialism began, and affected it." Quickly: "Don't think we were ever ignorant yokels. The Shkola—university and research centrum—is nearly as old as the colony. The toughest backwoodsman respects learning as much as he does marksmanship or battle bravery."

"Do you not have a Merseian element in the population?" Chives asked.

"Yes. Merseian-descended, that is, from about four hundred years ago. You probably know Merseia itself was starting to modernize and move into space then, under fearful handicaps because of that supernova nearby and because of the multi-cornered struggle for power between Vachs, Gethfennu, and separate nations. The young Dennitzan industries needed labor. They welcomed strong, able, well-behaved displaced persons."

"Do such constitute a large part of your citizenry, Donna?"

"About ten percent of our thirty million. And twice as many human Dennitzans live outsystem; since our industry and trade got well underway, we've been everywhere in that part of space. So what is this nonsense I hear about us being Merseian-infiltrated?"

Yet we might be happier in the Roidhunate, Kossara added.

Chives recalled her: "I have heard mention of the Gospodar. Does my lady care to define his functions? Is he like a king?"

"M-m-m, what do you mean by 'king'? The Gospodar is elected out of the Miyatovich family by the plemichi, the clan heads and barons. He has supreme executive authority for life or good behavior, subject to the Grand Court ruling on the constitutionality of what he does. A Court verdict can be reversed by the Skuptshtina—Parliament, I suppose you would say, though it has three chambers, for plemichi, commons, and ychani ... zmayi ... our nonhumans. Domestic government is mainly left to the different okruzhi—baronies? prefectures?—which vary a lot. The head of one of those may inherit office, or may be chosen by the resident clans, or may be appointed by the Gospodar, depending on ancient usage. He—such a nachalnik, I mean—he generally lets townships and rural districts tend their own affairs through locally elected councillors."

"The, ah, ychani are organized otherwise, I take it."

Kossara gave Chives a look of heightened respect. "Yes. Strictly by clans—or better say Vachs—subject only to planetary law unless there's some special fealty arrangement. And while you can find them anywhere on Dennitza, they concentrate on the eastern seaboard of Rodna, the main continent, in the northern hemisphere. Because they can stand cold better than humans, they do most of the fishing, pelagiculture, et cetera."

"Nevertheless, I presume considerable cultural blending has taken place."

"Certainly—"

Recollection rushed in of Trohdwyr, who died on Diomedes whither she was bound; of her father on horseback, a-gallop against a windy autumn forest, and the bugle call he blew which was an immemorial Merseian warsong; of her mother cuddling her while she sang an Eriau lullaby, *"Dwynafor, dwynafor, odhal tiv,"* and then laughing low, "But you, little sleepyhead, you have no tail, do you?"; of herself and Mihail in an ychan boat on the Black Ocean, snowfall, ice floes, a shout as a sea beast magnificently broached to starboard; moonlit gravbelt flight over woods, summer air streaming past her cheeks, a campfire glimpsed, a landing among great green hunters, their gruff welcome; and, "I'm not hungry," Kossara said, and left the saloon before Chives or, worse, Flandry should see her weep.

V

Flandry's office, if that was the right name for it, seemed curiously spare amidst the sybaritic arrangements Kossara had observed elsewhere aboard. She wondered what his private quarters were like. *But don't ask. He might take that as an invitation.* Seated in front of the desk behind which he was, she made her gaze challenge his.

"I know this will be painful to you," he said. "You've had a few days to rest, though, and we must go through with it. You see, the team that 'probed you appears to have made every imaginable blunder and maybe created a few new ones." She must have registered her startlement, for he continued, "Do you know how a hypnoprobe works?"

Bitterness rose in her. "Not really," she said. "We have no such vile thing on Dennitza."

"I don't approve either. But sometimes desperation dictates."

Flandry leaned back in his chair, ignited a cigarette, regarded her out of eyes whose changeable gray became the hue of a winter overcast. His tone remained soft: "Let me explain from the ground up. Interrogation is an unavoidable part of police and military work. You can do it on several levels of intensity. First, simple questioning; if possible, questioning different subjects separately and comparing their stories. Next, browbeating of assorted kinds. Then torture, which can be the crude inflicting of pain or something like prolonged sleep deprivation. The trouble with these methods is, they aren't too dependable. The subject may hold out. He may lie. If he's had psychosomatic training, he can fool a lie detector; or, if he's clever,

57

he can tell only a misleading part of the truth. At best, procedures are slow, especially when you have to cross-check whatever you get against whatever other information you can find.

"So we move on to narcoquiz, drugs that damp the will to resist. Problem here is, first, you often get idiosyncratic reactions or nonreactions. People vary a lot in their body chemistry, especially these days when most of humanity has lived for generations or centuries on worlds that aren't Terra. And, of course, each nonhuman species is a whole separate bowl of spaghetti. Then, second, your subject may have been immunized against everything you have in your medicine chest. Or he may have been deep-conditioned, in which case no drug we know of will unlock his mind."

Between the shoulderblades, Kossara's back hurt from tension. "What about telepathy?" she snapped.

"Often useful but always limited," Flandry said. "Neural radiations have a low rate of information conveyance. And the receiver has to know the code the sender is using. For instance, if I were a telepath, and you concentrated on thinking in Serbic, I'd be as baffled as if you spoke aloud. Or worse, because individual thought patterns vary tremendously, especially in species like ours which don't normally employ telepathy. I might learn to read your mind—slowly, awkwardly, incompletely at best—but find that everybody else's was transmitting gibberish as far as I was concerned. Interspecies telepathy involves still bigger difficulties. And we know tricks for combatting any sort of brain listener. A screen worn on the head will heterodyne the outgoing radiation in a random fashion, make it absolutely undecipherable. Or, again, training, or deep conditioning, can be quite effective."

He paused. Wariness crossed his mobile countenance. "There are exceptions to everything," he murmured, "including what I've said. Does the name Aycharaych mean anything to you?"

"No," she answered honestly. "Why?"

"No matter now. Perhaps later."

"I *am* a xenologist," Kossara reminded him. "You've told me nothing new."

"Eh? Sorry. Unpredictable what somebody else does or does not know about the most elementary things, in a universe where facts swarm like gnats. Why, I was thirty years old before I learned what the Empress Theodora used to complain about."

She stared past his smile. "You were going to describe the hypnoprobe."

He sobered. "Yes. The final recourse. Direct electronic attack on the brain. On a molecular level, bypassing drugs, conditionings, anything. Except—the subject can have been preconditioned, in his whole organism, to die when this happens. Shock reaction. If the interrogation team is prepared, it can hook him into machines that keep the vital processes going, and so have a fair chance of forcing a response. But his mind won't survive the damage."

He ground his cigarette hard against the lip of an ashtaker before letting the stub be removed. "You weren't in that state, obviously." His voice roughened. "In fact, you had no drug immunization. Why weren't you narcoed instead of 'probed? Or were you, to start with?"

"I don't remember—" Astounded, Kossara exclaimed, "How do you know? About me and drugs, I mean? I didn't myself!"

"The slave dealer's catalogue. His medic ran complete cytological analyses. I put the data through a computer. It found you've had assorted treatments to resist exotic conditions, but none of the traces a psychimmune would show."

Flandry shook his head, slowly back and forth. "An overzealous interrogator might order an immediate 'probe, instead of as a last resort," he said. "But why carry it out in a way that wiped your associated memories? True, such things do happen occasionally. For instance, a particular subject might have a low threshold of tolerance; the power level might then be too high, and disrupt the RNA molecules as they come into play under questioning. As a rule, though, permanent psychological effects—beyond those which bad experiences generally leave—are rare. A competent team will test the subject beforehand and establish the parameters."

He sighed. "Well, the civil war and aftermath lopped a lot off the top, in my Corps too. Coprolite-brained characters who'd ordinarily have been left in safe routineering assignments were promoted to fill vacancies. Maybe you had the bad luck to encounter a bunch of them."

"I am not altogether sorry to have forgotten," Kossara mumbled.

Flandry stroked his mustache. "Ah ... you don't think you've suffered harm otherwise?"

"I don't believe so. I can reason as well as ever. I remember my life in detail till shortly before I left for Diomedes, and I'm quite clear about everything since they put me aboard ship for Terra."

"Good." Flandry's warmth seemed genuine. "There are enough unnecessary horrors around, without a young and beautiful woman getting annulled."

He rescued me from the slime pit, she thought. *He has shown me every kindness and courtesy.*

Thus far. He admits—his purpose is to preserve the Empire.

"What pieces do you recall, Kossara?" Flandry had not used her first name before.

She strained fingers against each other. Her pulse beat like a trapped bird. *No. Don't bring them back. The fear, the hate, the beloved dead.*

"You see," he went on, "I'm puzzled as to why Dennitza should turn against us. Your Gospodar supported Hans, and was rewarded with authority over his entire sector. Granted, that's laid a terrible work load on him if he's conscientious. But it gives him—his people—a major say in the future of their region. A dispute about the defense mechanisms for your home system and its near neighbors ... well, that's only a dispute, isn't it, which he may still have some hope of winning. Can't you give me a better reason for him to make trouble? Isn't a compromise possible?"

"Not with the Imperium!" Kossara said out of upward-leaping rage.

"Between you and me, at least? Intellectually? Won't you give me your side of the story?"

Kossara's blood ebbed. "I ... well, speaking for myself, the fighting cost me the man I was going to marry. What use an Empire that can't keep the Pax?"

"I'm sorry. But did any mortal institution ever work perfectly? Hans is trying to make repairs. Besides, think. Why would the Gospodar—if he did plan rebellion—why would he send you, a girl, his niece, to Diomedes?"

She summoned what will and strength she had left, closed her eyes, searched back through time.

{Bodin Miyatovich was a big man, trim and erect in middle age. He bore the broad, snub-nosed, good-looking family face, framed in graying dark-blond hair and close-cropped beard, tanned and creased by a lifetime of weather. He eyes were beryl. Today he wore a red cloak over brown tunic and breeks, gromatz leather boots, customary knife and sidearm sheathed on a silver-studded belt.

Dyavo-like, he paced the sun deck which jutted from the Zamok. In gray stone softened by blossoming creepers, that ancestral castle reared walls, gates, turrets, battlements, wind-blown banners (though the ultimate fortress lay beneath, carved out of living rock) above steep tile roofs and pastel-tinted half-timbered stucco of Old Town houses. Thence Zorkagrad sloped downward; streets changed from twisty lanes to broad boulevards; traffic flitted around geometrical buildings raised in modern materials by later generations. Waterborne shipping crowded docks and bay. Lake Stoyan stretched westward over the horizon, deep blue dusted with glitter cast from a cloudless heaven. Elsewhere beyond the small city, Kossara could from this height see cultivated lands along the shores: green trees, hedges, grass, and yellowing grain of Terran stock; blue or purple where native foliage and pasture remained; homes, barns, sheds, sunpower towers, widely spaced; a glimpse of the Lyubisha River rolling from the north as if to bring greeting from her father's manse. Closer by, the Elena flowed eastward, oceanward; barges plodded and boats danced upon it. Here in the middle of the Kazan, she could not see the crater walls which those streams clove. But she had a sense of them, ramparts against glacier and desert, a chalice of warmth and fertility.

A breeze embraced her, scented by flowers, full of the sweet songs of guslars flitting ruddy to and from their nests in the vines. She sat back in her chair and thought, guilty at doing so, what a pity to spend such an hour on politics.

Her uncle's feet slammed the planks. "Does Molitor imagine we'll never get another Olaf or Josip on the throne?" the Gospodar rumbled. "A clown or a cancer . . . and, once more, Policy Board, Admiralty, civil service bypassed, or terrorized, or corrupted. If we rely on the Navy for our whole defense, what defense will we have against future foolishness or tyranny? Let the foolishness go too far, and we'll have no defense at all."

"Doesn't he speak about preventing any more civil wars?" Kossara ventured.

Bodin spat an oath. "How much of a unified command is possible, in practical fact, on an interstellar scale? Every fleet admiral is a potential war lord. Shall we keep nothing to set against him?" He stopped. His fist thudded on a rail. "Molitor trusts nobody. That's what's behind this. So why should I trust him?"

He turned about. His gaze smoldered at her. "Besides," he said, slowly, far down in his throat, "the time may come . . . the time may not be far off . . . when we need another civil war."}

"No—" she whispered. "I can't remember more than . . . resentment among many. The Narodna Voyska has been a, a basic part of our society, ever since the Troubles. Squadron and regimental honors, rights, chapels, ceremonies—I'd stand formation on my unit's parade ground at sunset—us together, bugle calls, volley, pipes and drums, and while the flag came down, the litany for those of our dead we remembered that day—and often tears would run over my cheeks, even in winter when they froze."

Flandry smiled lopsidedly. "Yes, I was a cadet once." He shook himself a bit. "Well. No doubt your militia intertwines with a lot of civilian matters, social and economic. For instance, I'd guess it doubles as constabulary in some areas, and is responsible for various public works, and—yes. Disbanding it would disrupt a great deal of your lives, on a practical as well as emotional level. His Majesty may not appreciate this enough. Germania doesn't contain your kind of society, and though he's seen a good many others, between us, I wouldn't call him a terribly imaginative man.

"Still, I repeat, negotiations have not been closed. And whatever their upshot, don't you yourself have the imagination to see he means well? Why this fanatical hatred of yours? And how many Dennitzans share it?"

"I don't know," Kossara said. "But personally, after what men of the Empire did to, to people I care about—and later to me—"

"May I ask you to describe what you recall?" Flandry answered. She glared defiance. "You see, if nothing else, maybe I'll find out, and be able to prove to their superiors, those donnickers rate punishment for aggravated stupidity."

He picked up a sheaf of papers on his desk and riffled them. *The report on me must have violated my privacy more than I could ever do myself,* she thought in sudden weariness. *All right, let me tell him what little I can.*

{A cave in the mountains near Salmenbrok held the sparse gear which kept her and her fellows alive. They stood around her on a ledge outside, but except for Trohdwyr shadowy, no real faces or names upon them any more. Cliffs and crags loomed in darkling solidity, here and there a gnarled tree or a streak of snow tinged pink by a reddish sun high in a purple heaven. The wind thrust slow, strong, chill; it had not only an odor but a taste like metal. A cataract, white and green half a kilometer away, boomed loud through thick air that also shifted the pitch and timbre of every sound. Huddled in her parka, she felt how Diomedes drew on her more heavily than Dennitza, nearly two kilograms added to every ten.

Eonan of the Lannachska poised almost clear in her mind. Yellow eyes aglow, wings unfurled for departure, he said in his shrill-accented Anglic: "You understand, therefore, how these things strike at the very life of my folk?

63

And thus they touch our whole world. We thought the wars between Flock and Fleet were long buried. Now they stir again—"

{Both moons were aloft and near the full, copper-colored, twice the seeming size of Mesyatz (or Luna), one slow, one hasty across a sky where few stars blinked and those in alien constellations. The night cold gnawed. Flames sputtered and sparked. Their light fetched Trohdwyr from darkness, where he sat on feet and tail in the cave mouth, roasting meat from the ration box. The smoke bore a sharp aroma. He said to Kossara and her fellow humans: "It's not for an old zmay to tell you wise heads how to handle a clutch of xenos. I'm here as naught but my lady's servant and bodyguard. However, if you want to keep peace among the natives, why not bring some Ythrians to explain Ythri really has no aim of backing any rebellion-minded faction?"

Steve Johnson—no! Stefan Ivanovich. Why in the name of madness should she think of him as Steve Johnson?— replied out of the face she could not give a shape: "That'd have to be arranged officially. The resident can't on his own authority. He'd have to go through the sector governor. And I'm not sure if the sector governor wants Ythri—or Terra—to know how bad the situation is on Diomedes."

"Besides," added -?-, "the effects aren't predictable, except they'd be far-reaching. We do have a full-scale cultural crisis here. Among nonhumans, at that."

"Still," said a third man (woman? And was his/her nose really flat, eyes oblique, complexion tawny?), "whatever instincts and institutions they have, I think we can credit them—enough of them—with common sense. What we will need, however, is a least a partial solution to the Flock's difficulties. Otherwise, dashing their hopes of Ythrian help could drive them to . . . who knows what?"

(If those features were not a mere trick of tattered memory, well, maybe this was a non-Dennitzan whom Uncle Bodin or his agents had engaged.)

"Yes," Kossara opined, "the trick will be to stay on top of events."

Was that the very night when the Imperial marines stormed them?

{Or another night? Trohdwyr shouted, "Let go of my lady!" In the gloom he snatched forth his knife. A stun pistol sent him staggering out onto the ledge, to collapse beneath the moons. After a minute, quite deliberately, the marine lieutenant gave him a low-powered blaster shot in the belly.

No surprise that Kossara didn't remember the fight which killed her companions. She knew only Trohdwyr, stirring awake again. His guts lay cooked below his ribs. After she tore loose from the grip upon her and fell to her knees beside him, she caught the smell. "Trohdwyr, *dragan!*" He coughed, could not speak, maybe could not know her through the pain that blinded him. She raised his head, hugged it close, felt the blunt spines press into her breasts. *"Dwynafor, dwynafor, odhal tiv,"* she heard herself crazily croak.

A man dragged her away. "Come along." She turned on him, spitting, fingers rigid for a karate attack. Another man got a lock on her from behind. The first cuffed her till the world rocked. "All that fuss over a xeno," he complained, and booted Trohdwyr for a while. She couldn't tell whether the ychan felt the blows; but his body jerked like a dropped puppet.

{The office was cramped, its air stale. The commander of Intelligence said, "Nothing slow and easy for you, Vymezal. Treason's too urgent a matter; and traitors deserve no careful handling."

"I am not—"

"We'll soon find out. Take her away, O'Brien. I want her prepared for hypnoprobing."

{Downward whirl through shrieks, thunders, flashes, pain and pain, down toward emptiness, but oh, she cannot reach blessed cool nothing; eternity has her.

The Golden Face, the cinnabar eyes, an indigo plume above, a voice of mercy: "Rest, Kossara. Sleep. Forget." No more.

{She was still dazed, numb, when the drumhead court-martial condemned her to life enslavement.}

Flandry considered the papers in his hands. Her few dry words appeared to have turned him as impersonal, for he said in the same tone, expressionless, "Thank you. Not much left in your mind, is there? No explanation of your hatred for the Empire."

"What do you mean?" exploded from her. "After what I told!"

"Please," he said. "You're a bright, educated, reasonably objective person. Taking your memories as correct—which they may not be; you could be recalling pieces of delirium—you should be able to entertain the possibility that you and your friends had the bad luck to meet fools and brutes such as infest every outfit. You should consider using established procedures to have them identified, traced, penalized. Unless, of course, you're so set in your attitude that this business seems typical, mere confirmation of what you already knew."

He glanced up. "Have you been told exactly what's in this report on you? The Intelligence report, that is."

"No," she got forth.

"I didn't expect you would. It's secret. Let me give you a summary." His vision skimmed the sheets he flipped through as he recited:

"Overtly, you and your attendant Trohdwyr arrived at Thursday Landing for a duly approved xenological research project on behalf of your, um, Shkola, among the Diomedeans of the Sea of Achan area. The declared motivation was that Dennitzans have lately opened trade with a comparable species near home, and want an idea of what to expect from continued impact of high-technology civilization on them. Quite normal. The Imperial resident provided you the customary assistance. He and his household depose that you were a charming guest who gave them no hint of bad intentions. However, you were soon off for the field. They never saw you again.

"Meanwhile, Naval Intelligence was busy throughout that part of space. There was reason to suspect some kind of hostile operation, taking advantage of widespread disorganization caused by the war and not yet amended. Diomedes was certainly a trouble spot, secessionism steadily gaining strength in a principal society of the planet. Those revolutionaries seemed to hope for Ythrian support.

"But other, more reliable sources indicated Ythri had nothing to do with this. Then who were the humans known, from loyal native witnesses, to be active on Diomedes? If not Avalonians, working for the Domain they live in, who?

"With the help of informers, Intelligence agents tracked down a group of these subversives to a mountain hideout. Seeing what they took for a Merseian, they leaped to conclusions . . . not unjustified, it turned out. The gang resisted arrest and, except for you, perished in the fire fight. Blasters in an enclosed space like a cave—the marines were wearing combat armor and your companions were not. The fact that the suspects fought, under those circumstances, seems to prove they were as fanatical as your psychograph says you are.

"Hypnoprobed, you revealed you were the deputy of your uncle the Gospodar, come to check on the progress. His idea was that Dennitzans posing as Avalonians could incite an uprising on Diomedes. This by itself would draw Imperial attention there. The apparent likelihood of Ythri being behind it would decoy considerable of our armed strength, too. Then at the right moment—you quoted your uncle simply as speaking of a 'lever' to use on the Imperium, for getting concessions. But you spilled your belief—and you ought to know—that, if events broke favorably, he'd seize the chance to rebel. Depending on circumstances, he'd either try for the throne, or carry out the same plan as the late Duke Alfred was nursing along, to rip a sizable region loose from the Empire and place it under Merseian protection.

"Which, of course"—Flandry lifted his gaze again—"would give the Roidhunate a bridgehead right in that frontier. Do you wonder that the treatment you got was rough?"

Kossara sprang from her chair. "How crazy do you think we are?" she yelled.

"We're bound for Diomedes to find out," he said.

"Why not straight to Dennitza like an honest man?"

"Others will, never fear. Detective work on an entire nation, or just on its leaders, takes personnel and patience. A singleton like me does best *vis-à-vis* a small operation, as I suppose the one on Diomedes necessarily is."

Flandry's eyes narrowed. "If you want your liberty back, my dear, rather than being resold when I decide you're not worth your keep, you will cooperate," he said. "Think of it not as betraying your folk, but as helping save them from disastrously wrong-headed adventurers.

"We have a libraryful of material on Diomedes aboard. Study it. Ponder it. Something may jog your memory; a lot that you've forgotten is probably not irretrievably lost. Or you should be able to make deductions—you're a smart girl—deductions about likely rendezvous points remaining, where we can snare more agents. Or, better yet, I'd guess: Diomedeans involved in the movement, never identified by our people, they should recognize you, if you show yourself in the proper ways. They should make contact and—do you see?"

"Yes!" she screamed. "And I won't!"

She fled.

The man sat quiet for a while before he said to the empty air, "Very well, if you wish, Chives will bring you your meals in your cabin."

● VI ●

As Flandry conned the *Hooligan*, Diomedes grew huge in the screens before him. Too heavily clouded for oceans and continents to show as anything but blurs, the dayside glowed amber-orange, with tinges of rose and violet, under the light of a dull sun. The nighted part gave pale whiteness back to moons and stars, reflections off ice and snow. When Kossara last came here, equinox was not long past; now absolute winter lay upon fully half the planet.

Flandry's attention was concentrated on piloting. Ordinarily he would have left that to the automatics, or to Chives if no ground-control facilities existed. But this time he must use both skill and the secret data he had commandeered back on Terra, to elude the Imperial space sentries.

Most were small detector-computer units in orbit, such as supervised traffic around any world of the Empire which got any appreciable amount of it, guarding against smugglers, hostiles, recklessness, or equipment failures. Flandry had long since rigged his speedster to evade them without much effort, given foreknowledge of their paths. But surely the unrest on Diomedes, the suspicion of outside interference, had caused spacecraft to be added. Sneaking past these required an artist. He enjoyed it.

Just the same, somewhere at the back of awareness, memory rehearsed what he had learned about his goal. Pictures and passages of text flickered by:

"Among the bodies which men have named Diomedes—among all the planets we know—in many respects, this one is unique.

"Though not unusually old, the system is metal-poor. To explain that, Montoya suggested chemical fractionation of the original cloud of dust and gas by the electromagnetic action of a passing neutron star. . . . As a result, while Diomedes has a mass of 4.75 Terra, the low net density gives it a surface gravity of only 1.10 standard. However, so large an object was bound to generate an extensive atmosphere. Between gravitational potential resulting from a diameter twice Terran, and low temperature and irradiation resulting from the G8 sun, much gas was retained. Life has modified it. Today mean sea-level pressure is 6.2 bars; the partial pressures of oxygen, nitrogen, and carbon dioxide are about the same as on Terra, the rest of the air consisting chiefly of neon. . . .

"Through some cosmic accident, the spin axis of Diomedes, like that of Uranus in the Solar System, lies nearly in the orbital plane. The arctic and antarctic circles thus almost coincide with the equator. In the course of a year 11 percent longer than Terra's, practically the whole of each hemisphere will be sunless for a period ranging from weeks to months. Chill even in summer, land and sea become so frigid in winter that all but highly specialized life-forms must either hibernate or migrate. . . .

"Progressive autochthonous cultures had brought Stone Age technology, the sole kind possible for them, to an astonishing sophistication. Once contacted by humans, they were eager to trade, originally for metals, subsequently for means to build modern industries of their own. Diomedes offers numerous organic substances, valuable for a variety of purposes, cheaper to buy from natives than to synthesize. . . .

"The biochemistry producing these compounds is only terrestroid in the most general sense. It consists of proteins in water solution, carbohydrates, lipids, etc. But few are nourishing to humans and many are toxic. They permeate the environment. A man cannot survive a drink of water or repeated breaths of air, unless he has received thorough immunization beforehand. (Of course, that includes adaptation to the neon, which otherwise at this concentration would have ill effects too.) Short-term visitors prefer to rely on their basic antiallergen, helmets, protective clothing, and packaged rations.

"The Diomedean must be similarly careful about materials from offplanet. In particular, most metals are poisonous to him. That he can use copper and iron anyway, as safely as we use beryllium or plutonium, is a tribute to his intelligence. But the precautions by themselves have inevitably joined those factors which force radical change upon ancient customs. Some cultures have adjusted without extreme stress. Others continue to suffer upheaval. Injustice and alienation bring dissension and violence. . . ."

Although, Flandry thought, *if we Imperials packed up our toys and went home, everybody here would soon be a great deal worse off. There've been too many irreversible changes.*

You can't even sit still in this universe and not make waves.

The sun was never down in summer; but Diomedes' 12½-hour rotation spun it through a circle. At the point in space and time where *Hooligan* landed, sharply rising moutains to the south concealed the disc.

The saloon was warm and scented. Nevertheless, what he saw in the screen made Flandry grimace and give an exaggerated shiver. "Brrr! No wonder climes like this foster Spartan virtues. The inhabitants have to be in training before they can emigrate and dispossess whoever lives on desirable real estate."

"You can't appreciate, can you, here is home for the Lannachska that they only want to keep unruined," Kossara said.

Couldn't she recognize a joke? Maybe not. She'd held aloof since he interviewed her, studying as he urged but saying nothing about what meaning she drew from it.

What a waste, Flandry sighed. *We could have had a gorgeous voyage, you and I.*

His gaze lingered on her. A coverall did not hide the fullness of a tall and supple body. Blue-green eyes, mahogany locks, strongly sculptured countenance had begun to haunt his reveries, and in the last few nightwatches his dreams. Did she really speak in the exact husky contralto of Kathryn McCormac? . . .

She sensed his regard, flushed, and attacked: "We *are*

on Lannach, are we not? I think I recall several of these peaks."

Flandry nodded and gave his attention back to the view. "Yes. Not far south of Sagna Bay." He hoped she'd admire how easily he'd found a particular site on the big island, nothing except maps and navigation to guide him down through the stormy atmosphere. But she registered unmixed anger. *Well, I suppose I shouldn't object to that, seeing how carefully I fueled it.*

Concealed by an overhanging cliff, the ship stood halfway up a mountain, with an overlook down rugged kilometers to a horizon-gleam which betokened sea. Clouds towered in amethyst heaven, washed by faint pink where lightning did not flicker in blue-black caverns. Crags, boulders, waterfalls reared above talus slopes and murky scraps. Thin grasslike growth, gray thornbushes, twisted low trees grew about; they became more abundant as sight descended toward misty valleys, until at last they made forest. Wings cruised on high, maybe upbearing brains that thought, maybe simple beasts of prey. Faint through the hull sounded a yowl of wind.

"Very well," Kossara said grimly. "I'll ask the question you want me to ask. Why are we here? Aren't you supposed to report in at Thursday Landing?"

"I exercised a special dispensation I have," Flandry said. "The Residency doesn't yet know we've come. In fact, unless my right hand has lost its cunning, nobody does."

At least I get a human startlement out of her. He liked seeing expressions cross her face, like clouds and sunbeams on a gusty spring day. "You see," he explained, "if subversive activities are going on, there's bound to be a spy or two around Imperial headquarters. News of your return would be just about impossible to suppress. And since you're in the custody of a Naval officer, it'd alarm the outfit we're after.

"Whereas, if you suddenly reappear by yourself, right in this hotspot, you'll surprise them. They won't have time to get suspicious, I trust. They'll make you welcome—"

"Why should they?" Kossara interrupted. "They'll wonder how I got back."

"Ah, no. Because they won't know you were ever gone."

She stared. Flandry explained: "Your companions died. If rebel observers learned that you lived, they learned nothing else. No matter how idiotically my colleagues behaved toward you, I'm sure they followed doctrine and let out no further information. You vanished into their building, and that was that. You were brought from there to the spaceship in a sealed vehicle, weren't you? . . . Yes, I knew it. . . . The Corpsmen had no reason to announce you'd been condemned and deported, therefore they did not.

"Accordingly, the rest of the gang—human if any are left on Diomedes, and most certainly a lot of natives—have no reason to suppose you haven't just been held incommunicado. In fact, that would be a much more logical thing to do than shipping you off to Terra for purchase by any blabbermouth."

She frowned, less in dislike of him than from being caught up, willy-nilly, by the intellectual problem which his planned deception presented. "But wasn't it a special team that caught and, and processed me? They may well have left the planet by now."

"If so, you can say they gave you in charge of the Intelligence agents stationed here semi-permanently. In fact, that's the safest thing for you to maintain in any event, and quite plausible. We'll work out a detailed story for you. I have an outline already, subject to your criticism. You wheedled a measure of freedom for yourself. That's plausible too, if you don't mind pretending you became the mistress of a bored, lonely commander. At last you managed to steal an aircar. I can supply that; we have two in the hold, one a standard civilian convertible we can set for Diomedean conditions. You fled back here, having enough memories left to know this is where your chances are best of being found by your organization."

She tensed again, and stretched the words out: "What will you do meanwhile?"

Flandry shrugged. "Not having had your preventive-medical treatment, I'm limited in my scope. Let's consult. Tentatively, I've considered making an appearance in a

73

persona I've used before, a harmlessly mad Cosmenosist missionary prospecting for customers on yet another globe. However, I may do best to stay put aboard ship, following your adventures till the time looks ripe for whatever sort of action seems indicated."

Her starkness deepened. "How will you keep track of me?"

From his pocket Flandry took a ring. On its gold band sparkled what resembled a sapphire. "Wear this. If anybody asks, say you got it from your jailer-lover. It's actually a portable transmitter, same as your bracelet was on Terra but with its own power source."

"That little bit of a thing?" She sounded incredulous. "Needing no electronic network around? Reaching beyond line-of-sight? And not detectable by those I spy on?"

Flandry nodded. "It has all those admirable qualities."

"I can't believe that."

"I'm not at liberty to describe the principle. Anyway, nobody ever told me. I've indulged in idle speculations about modulated neutrino emission, but they're doubtless wildly wrong. What I do know is that the thing works." Flandry paused. "Kossara, I'm sorry, but under any circumstances ... before I can release you, before I can even land you again on a prime world like Terra, you'll have to have wiped from your memory the fact that such gadgets exist. The job will be painless and very carefully done."

He held out the ring. She half reached for it, withdrew her hand, flickered her glance about till it came to rest on his, and asked most softly: "Why do you think I'll help you?"

"To earn your liberty," he answered. Each sentence wrenched at him. "Defect, and you're outlaw. What chance would you have of getting home? The orbital watch, the surface hunt would be doubled. If you weren't caught, you'd starve to death after you used up your human-type food.

"And consider Dennitza. Your kin, your friends, small children in the millions, the past and present and future of your whole world. Should they be set at stake, in an era of planet-smasher weapons, for a political point at best,

74

the vainglory of a few aristocrats at worst? You know better, Kossara."

She stood still for a long while before she took the ring from him and put it on her bridal finger.

"Given the support of a dense atmosphere," said a text, "the evolution of large flying organisms was profuse. At last a particular species became fully intelligent.

"Typical of higher animals on Diomedes, it was migratory. Homeothermic, bisexual, viviparous, it originally followed the same reproductive pattern as its less developed cousins, and in most cultures still does. In fall a flock moves to the tropics, where it spends the winter. The exertion during so long a flight causes hormonal changes which stimulate the gonads. Upon arrival, there is an orgy of mating. In spring the flock returns home. Females give birth shortly before the next migration, and infants are carried by their parents. Mothers lactate like Terran mammals, and while they do, will not get pregnant. In their second year the young can fly independently, they have been weaned, their mothers are again ready to breed.

"This round formed the basis of a civilization centered on the islands around the Sea of Achan. The natives built towns, which they left every fall and reentered every spring. Here they carried on sedentary occupations, stoneworking, ceramics, carpentry, a limited amount of agriculture. The real foundation of their economy was, however, herding and hunting. Except for necessary spurts of activity, in their homelands they were an easygoing folk, indolent, artistic, ceremonious, matrilineal—since paternity was never certain—and loosely organized into what they called the Great Flock of Lannach.

"But elsewhere a different practice developed. Dwelling on large oceangoing rafts, fishers and seaweed harvesters, the Fleet of Drak'ho ceased migrating. Oars, sails, nets, windlasses, construction and maintenance work kept the body constantly exercised; year-round sexuality, season-free reproduction, was a direct consequence. Patriarchal monogamy ensued. The distances traveled annually were much less than for the Flock, and home was always nearby. It was possible to accumulate heavy paraphernalia, stores, machines, books. While civilization thus became more wealthy and complex than anywhere ashore, the old democratic organization gave way to authoritarian aristocracy.

"Histories roughly parallel to these have taken place elsewhere on the globe. But Lannach and Drak'ho remain the most advanced, populous, materially well-off representatives of these two strongly contrasted life-orderings. When they first made contact, they regarded each other with mutual horror. A measure of tolerance and cooperation evolved, encouraged by offplanet traders who naturally preferred peaceful conditions. Yet rivalry persisted, sporadically flaring into war, and of late has gained new dimensions.

"At the heart of the dilemma is this: that Lannachska culture cannot assimilate high-energy technology, in any important measure, and survive.

"The Drak'ho people have their difficulties, but no impossible choices. Few of them today are sailors. However, fixed abodes ashore are not altogether different from houses on rafts aforetime. Regular hours of work are a tradition, labor is still considered honorable, mechanical skills and a generally technophilic attitude are in the social atmosphere which members inhale from birth. Though machinery has lifted off most Drak'hoans the toil that once gave them a humanlike libido, they maintain it by systematic exercise (or, in increasingly many cases, by drugs), since the nuclear family continues to be the building block of their civilization.

"As producers, merchants, engineers, industrialists, even occasional spacefarers, they flourish, and are on the whole well content.

"But the cosmos of Lannach is crumbling. Either the Great Flock must remain primitive, poor, powerless, prey to storm and famine, pirates and pestilence, or it must modernize—with all that that implies, including earning the cost of the capital goods required. How shall a folk do this who spend half their lives migrating, mating, or living off nature's summertime bounty? Yet not only is their whole polity founded upon that immemorial cycle. Religion, morality, tradition, identity itself are. Imagine a group of humans, long resident in an unchanged part of Terra, devout churchgoers, for whom the price of progress was that they destroy every relic of the past, embrace atheism, and become homosexuals who reproduce by ectogenesis. For many if not all Lannachska, the situation is nearly that extreme.

"In endless variations around the planet, the same dream is being played. But precisely because the Great Flock has changed more than other nations of its kind, it feels the hurt most keenly, is most divided against itself and embittered at the outside universe.

"No wonder if revolutionary solutions are sought. Economic, social, spiritual secession, a return to the ways of the ancestors; shouts of protest against 'discrimination,' demands for 'justice,' help, subsidy, special consideration of every kind; political secession, no more taxes to the planetary peace authority or the Imperium; seizure of power over the whole sphere, establishment of a sovereign autarky—these are among the less unreasonable ideas afloat.

"There is also Alatanism. The Ythrians, not terribly far away as interstellar distances go, have wings. They should sympathize with their fellow flyers on Diomedes more than any biped ever can. They have their Domain, free alike of Empire and Roidhunate, equally foreign to both. Might it not, are its duty and destiny not to welcome Diomedes in?

"The fact that few Ythrian leaders have even heard of Diomedes, and none show the least interest in crusading, is ignored. Mystiques seldom respond to facts. They are instruments which can be played on. . . ."

Twice had the sun come from the mountains and returned behind them.

"Goodbye, then," Kossara said.

Flandry could find no better words than "Goodbye. Good luck," hoarse out of the grip upon his gullet.

She regarded him for a moment, in the entryroom where they stood. "I do believe you mean that," she whispered.

Abruptly she kissed him, a brief brush of lips which ex-

ploded in his heart. She drew back before he could respond. During another instant she poised, upon her face a
look of bewilderment at her own action.

Turning, she twisted the handle on the inner airlock
valve. He took a following step. "No," she said. "You
can't live out there, remember?" Her body prepared before she left Dennitza, she closed the portal on him. He
stopped where he was. Pumps chugged until gauges told
him the chamber beyond was now full of Diomedean air.

The outer valve opened. He bent over a viewscreen.
Kossara's tiny image stepped forth onto the mountainside.
A car awaited her. She bounded into it and shut its door.
A minute later, it rose.

Flandry sought the control cabin, where were the termi-
nals of his most powerful and sensitive devices. The car
had vanished above clouds. "Pip-ho, Chives," he said tone-
lessly. A hatch swung wide. His Number Two atmospheric
vehicle glided from the hold. It looked little different from
the first, its engine, weapons, and special equipment being
concealed in the teardrop fuselage. It disappeared more
slowly, for the Shalmuan pilot wanted to stay unseen by
the woman whom he stalked. But at last Flandry sat
alone.

*She promised she'd help me. What an inexperienced liar
she is.*

He felt no surprise when, after a few minutes, Chives'
voice jumped at him: "Sir! She is descending. . . . She has
landed in the forest beside a river. I am observing through
a haze by means of an infrared 'scope. Do you wish a
relay?"

"Not from that," Flandry said. Too small, too blurry.
"From her bracelet."

A screen blossomed in leaves and hasty brown water.
Her right hand entered. Off the left, which he could not
see, she plucked the ring, which he glimpsed before she
tossed it into the stream.

"She is running for cover beneath the trees, sir," Chives
reported.

Of course, replied the emptiness in Flandry. *She thinks
that, via the ring, I've seen what she's just done, in the
teeth of every pledge she gave me. She thinks that now, if*

she moves fast, she can vanish into the woods—make her own way afoot, find her people and not betray them, or else die striving.

Whereas in fact the ring was only intended to lull any fears of surveillance she might have after getting rid of it— only a circlet on her bridal finger—and Chives has a radio resonator along to activate her bracelet—the slave bracelet I told her would be blind and deaf outside of Terra.

"I do not recommend that I remain airborne, sir," Chives said. "Allow me to suggest that, as soon as the young lady has passed beyond observing me, I land likewise and follow her on the ground. I will leave a low-powered beacon to mark this site. You can flit here by gravbelt and retrieve the vehicles, sir. Permit me to remind you to wear proper protection against the unsalubrious ambience."

"Same to you, old egg, and put knobs on yours." Flandry's utterance shifted from dull to hard. "I'll repeat your orders. Trail her, and call in to the recorder cum relay 'caster I'll leave here, in whatever way and at whatever times seem discreet. But 'discretion' is your key word. If she appears to be in danger, getting her out of it— whether by bringing me in to help or by taking action yourself—that gets absolute priority. Understand?"

"Yes, sir." Did the high, not quite human accent bear a hint of shared pain? "Despite regrettable tactical necessities, Donna Vymezal must never be considered a mere counter in a game." *That's for personnel and planets, the anonymous billions—and, savingly, for you and me, eh, Chives?* "Will you proceed to the Technic settlement when your preparations are complete?"

"Yes," Flandry said. "Soon. I may as well."

● VII ●

Where the equator crossed the eastern shoreline of a continent men called Centralia, Thursday Landing was founded. Though fertile by Diomedean standards, the country had few permanent residents. Rather, migration brought tides of travelers, northward and southward alternately, to their ancestral breeding grounds. At first, once the sharpest edge was off their sexual appetites, they had been glad to hunt and harvest those things the newcomers wanted from the wilderness, in exchange for portable trade goods. Later this business grew more systematized and extensive, especially after a large contingent of Drak'ho moved to these parts. Descending, Flandry saw a fair-sized town.

Most was man-built, blocky interconnected ferrocrete structures to preserve a human-suitable environment from monstrous rains and slow but ponderous winds. He glimpsed a park, vivid green beneath a vitryl dome, brightened by lamps that imitated Sol. Farther out, widely spaced in cultivated fields, stood native houses: tall and narrow, multiply balconied, graceful of line and hue, meant less to resist weather then to accept it, yielding enough to remain whole. Watercraft, ranging from boats to floating communities, crowded the harbor as wings did the sky.

Yet Flandry felt bleakness, as if the cold outside had reached in to enfold him. Beyond the fluorescents, half the world he saw was land, hills, meadows, dwarfish woods, dim in purple and black twilight, and half was bloodily glimmering ocean. For the sun stood barely above the northern horizon, amidst sulfur-colored clouds. At this place and season there was never true day or honest night.

Are you getting terracentric in your dotage? he gibed at himself. *Here's a perfectly amiable place for beings who belong in it.*

His mood would not go away. *Nevertheless it does feel unreal somehow, a scene from a bad dream. The whole mission has been like that. Everything shadowy, tangled, unstable, nothing what it seems to be ... nor anybody who doesn't carry secrets within secrets. ...*

Myself included. He straightened in the pilot chair. *Well, that's what I'm paid for. I suppose these blue devils of mine come mainly from guilt about Kossara, fear of what may happen to her. O God Who is also unreal, a mask we put on emptiness, be gentle to her. She has been hurt so much.*

Ground Control addressed him, in Anglic though not from a human mouth. He responded, and set *Hooligan* down on the spacefield as directed. The prospect of action heartened him. *Since I can't trust the Almighty not to soldier on the job, let me start my share now.*

He had slipped back into space from Lannach, then returned openly. The sentinel robots detected him, and an officer in a warship demanded identification before granting clearance, at a distance from the planet which showed a thoroughness seldom encountered around fifth-rate outpost worlds. No doubt alarm about prospective rebellion and infiltration had caused security to be tightened. Without the orbital information he possessed, not even a vessel as begimmicked as his could have neared Diomedes unbeknownst.

The image of the portmaster appeared in a comscreen. "Welcome, sir," he said. "Am I correct that you are alone? The Imperial resident has been notified of your coming and invites you to be his house guest during your stay. If you will tell me where your accommodation lock is—frankly, I have never seen a model quite like yours—a car will be there for you in a few minutes."

He was an autochthon, a handsome creature by any standards. The size of a short man, he stood on backward-bending, talon-footed legs. Brown-furred, the slim body ran out in a broad tail which ended in a fleshy rudder; at its middle, arms and hands were curiously anthropoid; above a massive chest, a long neck bore a round head—high, ridged brow, golden eyes with nictitating membranes, blunt-nosed black-muzzled face with fangs and whiskers suggestive of a cat, no external ears but a crest of muscle on top of the skull. From his upper shoulders grew the bat wings, their six-meter span now folded. He wore a belt to support a pouch, a brassard of authority, and, yes, a crucifix.

I'd better stay in character from the beginning. "Many thanks, my dear chap," Flandry replied in his most affected manner. "I say, could you tell the chauffeur to come aboard and fetch my bags? Deuced lot of duffel on these extended trips, don't y' know." He saw the crest rise and a ripple pass along the fur, perhaps from irritation at his rudeness in not asking the portmaster's name.

The driver obeyed, though. He was a husky young civilian who bowed at sight of Flandry's gaudy version of dress uniform. "Captain Ahab Whaling?"

"Right." Flandry often ransacked ancient books. He had documentation aboard for several different aliases. Why risk alerting someone? The more everybody underestimated him, the better. Since he wanted to pump his fellow, he added, "Ah, you are—?"

"Diego Rostovsky, sir, handyman to Distinguished Citizen Lagard. You mentioned baggage? . . . Jumping comets, that much?. . . Well, they'll have room at the Residency."

"Nobody else staying there, what?"

"Not at the moment. We had a bunch for some while, till about a month ago. But I daresay you know that already, seeing as how you're Intelligence yourself." Rostovsky's glance at the eye insigne on Flandry's breast indicated doubt about the metaphorical truth of it.

However, curiosity kept him friendly. When airlocks had decoupled and the groundcar was moving along the road to town, he explained: "We don't fly unnecessarily. This atmosphere plays too many tricks. . . . Uh, they'll be glad to meet you at the Residency. Those officers I mentioned were too busy to be very good company, except for—" He broke off. "Um. And, since they left, the isolation and tension . . . My master and his staff have plenty to keep them occupied, but Donna Lagard always sees the same people, servants, guards, commercial personnel and their families. She's Terran-reared. She'll be happy for news and gossip."

And you judge me the type to furnish them, Flandry knew. *Excellent.* His gaze drifted through the canopy, out over somber fields and tenebrous heaven. *But who was that exception whom you are obviously under orders not to mention?*

"Yes, I imagine things are a bit strained," he said. "Though really, you need have no personal fears, need you? I mean, after all, if some of the tribes revolted, an infernal nuisance, 'speci'lly for trade, but surely Thursday Landing can hold out against primitives."

"They aren't exactly that," was the answer. "They have industrial capabilities, and they do business directly with societies still further developed. We've good reason to believe a great many weapons are stashed around, tactical nukes among them. Oh, doubtless we could fend off an attack and stand siege. The garrison and defenses have been augmented. But trade would go completely to pieces—it wouldn't take many rebels to interdict traffic—which'd hurt the economy of more planets than Diomedes. . . . And then, if outsiders really have been the, uh, the—"

"*Agents provocateurs,*" Flandry supplied. "Or instigators, if y' prefer. Either way; I don't mind."

Rostovsky scowled. "Well, what might their bosses do?"

Martin Lagard was a small prim man in a large prim office. When he spoke, in Anglic still tinged by his Atheian childhood, both his goatee and the tip of his nose waggled. His tunic was of rich material but unfashionable cut, and he had done nothing about partial baldness.

Blinking across his desk at Flandry, who lounged behind a cigarette, the Imperial resident said in a scratchy voice, "Well, I'm pleased to make your acquaintance, Captain Whaling, but frankly puzzled as to what may be the nature of your assignment. No courier brought me any advance word." He sounded hurt.

I'd better soothe him. Flandry had met his kind by the scores, career administrators, conscientious but rule-bound and inclined to self-importance. Innovators, or philosophers like Chunderban Desai, were rare in that service, distrusted by their fellows, destined either for greatness or for ruin. Lagard had advanced methodically, by the book, toward an eventual pension.

He was uncreative but not stupid, a vital cog of empire. How could a planetful of diverse nonhumans be closely governed by Terra, and why should it be? Lagard was here to assist Imperials in their businesses and their problems; to oversee continuous collection of information about this world and put it in proper form to feed the insatiable data banks at Home; to collect from the natives a modest tribute which paid for their share of the Pax; to give their leaders advice as occasion warranted, and not use his marines to see that they followed it unless he absolutely must; to speak on their behalf to those officials of the Crown with whom he dealt; to cope.

He had not done badly. It was not his fault that demons haunted the planet which were beyond his capability of exorcising, and might yet take possession of it.

"No, sir, they wouldn't give notice. Seldom do. Abominably poor manners, but that's policy for you, what?" Flandry nodded at his credentials, where they lay on the desk. " 'Fraid I can't be too explicit either. Let's say I'm on a special tour of inspection."

Lagard gave him a close look. Flandry could guess the resident's thought: Was this drawling clothes horse really an Intelligence officer at work, or a pet relative put through a few motions to justify making an admiral of him? "I will cooperate as far as possible, Captain."

"Thanks. Knew y' would. See here, d'you mind if I bore you for a few ticks? Mean to say, I'd like to diagram the situation as I see it. You correct me where I'm wrong, fill in any gaps, that kind of thing, eh? You know how hard it is to get any proper overview of matters. And then, distances between stars, news stale before it arrives, *n'est-ce pas?*"

"Proceed," Lagard said resignedly.

Flandry discarded his cigarette, crossed legs and bridged fingers. No grav generator softened the pull of Diomedes. He let his added weight flow into the chair's crannies of softness, as if already wearied. (In actuality he did his calisthenics under two gees or more, because thus he shortened the dreary daily time he needed for keeping fit.) "Troublemakers afoot," he said. "Distinct possibility of hostiles taking advantage of the disorganization left by the recent unpleasantness—whether those hostiles be Merseian, Ythrian, barbarian, Imperials who want to break away or even overthrow his Majesty—right? You got hints, various of those troublemakers were active here, fanning flames of discontent and all that sort of nonsense. How'd they get past your security?"

"Not my security, Captain," Lagard corrected. "I've barely had this post five years. I found the sentinel system in wretched condition—expectable, after the Empire's woes—and did my best to effect repairs. I also found our civil strife was doing much to heighten resentment, particularly in the Great Flock of Lannach. It disrupted offplanet commerce, you see. The migrant societies have become more dependent on that than the sedentary ones like Drak'ho which have industry to produce most of what they consume. But please realize, a new man on a strange world needs time to learn its ins and outs, and develop workable programs."

"Oh, quite." Flandry nodded. "At first you'd see no reason to screen visitors from space. Rather, you'd welcome 'em. They might help restore trade, what? Very natural. No discredit to you. At last, however, clues started trickling in. Not every transient was spending his stay in the outback so benignly. Right?

"You asked my Corps to investigate. That likewise takes time. We too can't come cold onto a planet and hope for instant results, y' know. Ah, according to my briefing, it was sector HQ you approached. Terra just got your regular reports."

"Of course," Lagard said. "Going through there would have meant a delay of months."

"Right, right. No criticism intended, sir," Flandry assured him. "Still, we do like to keep tabs at Home. That's what I'm here for, to find out what was done, in more detail than the official report"—*which was almighty sketchy*—"could render. Or, you could say, my superiors want a feel of how the operation went."

Lagard gave the least shrug.

"Well, then," Flandry proceeded. "The report does say a Commander Bruno Maspes brought an Intelligence team, set up shop in Thursday Landing, and got busy interrogating, collating data, sending people out into the field—the usual intensive job. They worked how long?"

"About six months."

"Did you see much of them?"

"No. They were always occupied, often all away from here at once, sometimes away from the whole system. Personnel of theirs came and went. Even those who were my guests—" Lagard stopped. "You'll forgive me, Captain, but I'm under security myself. My entire household is. We've been forbidden to reveal certain items. This clearance of yours does not give you power to override that."

Ah-ha. It tingled in Flandry's veins. His muscles stayed relaxed. "Yes, yes. Perfectly proper. You and yours were bound to spot details—f'r instance, a xenosophont with odd talents—" *Look at his face! Again, ah-ha.* —"which ought not be babbled about. Never fret, I shan't pry.

"In essence, the team discovered it wasn't humans of Ythrian allegiance who were inciting to rebellion and giving technical advice about same. It was humans from Dennitza."

"So I was told," Lagard said.

"Ah . . . during this period, didn't you entertain a Dennitzan scientist?"

"Yes. She and her companion soon left for the Sea of Achan, against my warnings. Later I was informed that they turned out to be subversives themselves." Lagard sighed. "Pity. She was a delightful person, in her intense fashion."

"Any idea what became of her?"

"She was captured. I assume she's still detained."

"Here?"

"Seems unlikely. Maspes and his team left weeks ago. Why leave her behind?"

What would I have done if they were around yet? Flandry wondered fleetingly. *Played that hand in style, I trust.* "They might have decided that was the easiest way to keep the affair under wraps for a bit," he suggested.

"The Intelligence personnel now on Diomedes are simply those few who've been stationed among us for years. I think I'd know if they were hiding anything from me. You're free to talk to them, Captain, but better not expect much."

"Hm." Flandry stroked his mustache. "I s'pose, then, Maspes felt he'd cleaned out the traitors?"

"He said he had a new, more urgent task elsewhere. Doubtless a majority of agents escaped his net, and native sympathizers may well keep any humans among them fed. But, he claimed, if we monitor space traffic carefully, they shouldn't rouse more unrest than we can handle. I hope he was right."

"You're trying to defuse local conflicts, eh?"

"What else?" Lagard sounded impatient. "My staff and I, in consultation with loyal Diomedeans, are hard at work. A fair shake for the migrants is not impossible to achieve, if the damned extremists will let us alone. I'm afraid I'll be a poor host, Captain. Day after tomorrow— Terran, that is—I'm off for Lannach, to lay certain proposals before the Commander of the Great Flock and his councillors. They feel a telescreen is too impersonal."

Flandry smiled. "Don't apologize, sir. I'll be quite happy. And, I suspect, only on this planet a few days anyhow, before bouncing on to the next. You and Maspes seem offhand to've put on a jolly good show."

Gratified, visions of bonuses presumably dancing through his head, the resident beamed at him. "Thank you. I'll introduce you around tomorrow, and you can question or look through the files as you wish, within the limits of security I mentioned. But first I'm sure you'd like to rest. A servant will show you to your room. We'll have apéritifs in half an hour. My wife is eager to meet you."

VIII

At dinner Flandry laid on the wit and sophistication he had preprogrammed, until over the liqueurs Susette Kalehua Lagard sighed, "Oh, my, Captain Whaling, how marvelous you're here! Nobody like you has visited us for ages—they've all been provincials, or if not, they've been so ghastly serious, no sensitivity in them either, except a single one and he wasn't human— Oh!" Her husband had frowned and nudged her. She raised fingers to lips. "No, that was naughty of me. Please forget I said it."

Flandry bowed in his chair. "Impractical, I fear, Donna. How could I forget anything spoken by you? But I'll set the words aside in my mind and enjoy remembering the music." Meanwhile alertness went electric through him. This warm, well-furnished, softly lighted room, where a recorded violin sang and from which a butler had just removed the dishes of an admirable rubyfruit soufflé, was a very frail bubble to huddle in. He rolled curaçao across his tongue and reached for a cigarette.

She fluttered her lashes. "You're a darling." She had had a good bit to drink. "Isn't he, Martin? Must you really leave us in less than a week?"

Flandry shrugged. "Looks as if Distinguished Citizen Lagard hasn't left me much excuse to linger, alas."

"Maybe we can find something. I mean, you can exercise judgment in your mission, can't you? They wouldn't send a man like you out and keep a leash on him."

"We'll see, Donna." He gave a look of precisely gauged meaningfulness. She returned it in kind. The wine had not affected her control in that respect.

His inner excitement became half sardonicism, half a moderately interested anticipation. She was attractive in a buxom fashion, to which her low-cut shimmerlyn gown lent an emphasis that would have raised brows at today's Imperial court—the court she had never seen. Jewels glinted in black hair piled about a round brown countenance. Vivacity had increased in her throughout the meal, till her conversation sounded less platitudinous than it was.

Flandry knew her as he knew her husband, from uncounted encounters: the spouse of an official posted to a distant world of nonhumans. Occasionally such a pair made a team. But oftener the member who did not have the assignment was left to the dismal mercies of a tiny Imperial community, the same homes, bodies, words, games, petty intrigues and catfights for year after year. He or she might develop an interest in the natives, get into adventures and fascinations, even contribute a xenological study or a literary translation. Lady Susette lacked the gift for that. Since she had had no children when she arrived, there would be none for the rest of Lagard's ten-year hitch. The immunizations which let her walk freely outdoors on Diomedes were too deep-going for her organism to accept an embryo, and it would be too dangerous to have them reversed before she departed. What then was Susette Kalehua Lagard, daughter of prosperous and socially prominent Terrans, to do while she waited?

She could terminate the marriage. But a man who had gotten resident's rank was a fine catch. He could expect a subsequent commissionership on a prime human-colonized planet like Hermes, where plenty of glamour was available; in due course, he should become a functionary of some small importance on Terra itself, and perhaps receive a minor patent of nobility. She must feel this was worth her patience. Her eyes told Flandry she did have a hobby.

"Well, if our time's to be short, let's make it sweet," she said. "May I—we call you Ahab? We're Susette and Martin."

"I'm honored." Flandry raised his glass in salute. "And refreshed. Folk on Terra have gotten stiffish these past few years, don't y' know. Example set by his Majesty and the inner circle."

"Indeed?" Lagard asked. "Nuances don't reach us here.

I'd have thought—with due reverence—the present Emperor would be quite informal."

"Not in public," Flandry said. "Career Navy man of Germanian background, after all. I see us generally heading into a puritanical period." *Which, if Desai is right, is not the end of decadence, but rather its next stage.* "Luckily, we've plenty of nooks and crannies for carrying on in the grand old tradition. In fact, disapproval lends spice, what? I remember a while ago—"

His risqué reminiscence had happened to somebody else and the event had lacked several flourishes he supplied. He never let such nigglements hinder a story. It fetched a sour smile from Lagard but laughter and a blush down to the décolletage from Susette.

The staff, assistants, clerks, technical chiefs, Navy and marine personnel, were harried but cooperative, except when Flandry heard: "Sorry, sir. I'm not allowed to discuss that. If you want information, please apply at Sector HQ. I'm sure they'll oblige you there."

Yes, they'll oblige me with the same skeleton account that Terra got. I could make a pest of myself, but I doubt if the secret files have ever contained any mention of what I'm really after. I could check on the whereabouts of Commander Maspes & Co., and make a long trip to find them—no, him, for probably the team's dispersed ... ah, more probably yet, the files will show orders cut for them similar to those in Captain Whaling's papers, and the men have vanished ... maybe to bob up again eventually, maybe never, depending on circumstances.

More deceptions, more phantoms.

He sauntered into the civilian part of town and was quickly on genial terms with factors and employees. Most of them found their work stimulating—they liked the Diomedeans—but were starved for new human contact. And none were under security. The trouble was, there had been no need for it. They knew a special Intelligence force came to search out the roots of the unrest which plagued them in their business. They totally approved, and did not resent not being invited to meet the investigators save for interviews about what they themselves might know. None had seen the entire team together; when not in the field, it kept apart, officers in the Residency, enlisted men in a separate barrack. Yes, rumor said it included a xeno or two. What of that?

Otherwise the community had only heard Lagard's brief announcement after the group was gone. ". . . I am not at liberty to say more than that human traitors have been trying to foment a rebellion among the Lannachska. Fortunately, the vast majority of the Great Flock stayed loyal and sensible. And now the key agents have been killed or captured. A few may still be at large, and information you may come upon concerning these should be reported immediately. But I don't expect they can do serious harm any longer, and I intend to proceed, with your cooperation, to remove the causes of discontent. . . ."

The next Diomedean day, Flandry donned a heated coverall and a dome helmet with an air recycler, passed through pressure change in a lock, and circulated among natives in their part of town. Most knew Anglic and were willing to talk; but none had further news. He wasn't surprised.

Finding a public phone booth, he took the opportunity to call Chives when nobody who chanced to observe him was likely to wonder what a solitary operative was doing there. He used a standard channel but a language he was sure had never been heard on this world. The nearest comsat bucked his words across the ocean to Lannach where, he having paid for the service, they were broadcast rather than beamed. The relay unit he had left under the cliff made contact with the Shalmuan's portable.

"Yes, sir, at present the young lady is eating rations taken from her car before she abandoned it. They should last her as far as the sea, for she is setting a hard pace despite the overgrowth and rugged topography. I must confess I have difficulty following, since I consider it inadvisable to go aloft on my gravbelt. I feel a certain concern for her safety. A fall down a declivity or a sudden tempest could have adverse effects, and she does not let caution delay her."

"I think she can manage," Flandry said. "In any event, you can rescue her. What worries me is what may happen after she gets where she's going. Another twenty-four hours, did you estimate? I'd better try to act fast myself, here."

Susette didn't wish to lose time either. Three hours after she and Flandry had seen Lagard off, she was snuggled against him whispering how wonderful he had been.

"You're no slouch on the couch yourself, m'love," he said, quite honestly. "More, I hope?"

"Yes. As soon and often as you want. And do please want."

"Well, how about a breather first, and getting acquainted? A girl who keeps a bedside beer cooler is a girl whose sound mind I want to know as well as her delectable body." Warm and wudgy, she caressed him while he leaned over to get bottles for them, and stayed in the circle of his free arm when they leaned back against the pillows.

Too bad this can't be a simple romp for me, he thought. *It deserves that. And by the way, so do I. Kossara was making chastity come hard.*

He savored the chill brisk flavor while his glance roved about. The resident's lady had a private suite where, she hinted, the resident was an infrequent caller. This room of it was plushly carpeted, draped, furnished, in rose and white. An incense stick joined its fragrance to her own. A dressing table stood crowded with perfumes and cosmetics. Her garments sheened above his, hastily tossed over a chair. In that richness, her souvenirs of Home—pictures, bric-à-brac, a stuffed toy such as she would have given to a child—seemed as oddly pathetic as the view in the window was grim. Hail dashed against vitryl, thicker and harder than ever fell on Terra, picked out athwart blue-black lightning-jumping violence by an ember sunbeam which stabbed through a rent in the clouds. Past every insulation and heaviness came a ghost of the wind's clamor.

Kossara . . . Yes, Chives is right to fret about her while she struggles through yonder wildwood.

Susette stroked his cheek. "Why do you look sad all of a sudden?" she asked.

"Eh?" He started. "How ridiculous. 'Pensive' is the

word, my imp. Well, perhaps a drop of melancholy, recalling how I'll have to leave you and doubtless never see you again."

She nodded. "Me too. Though are you sure we won't—we can't?"

If I keep any control over events, yes, absolutely! Not that you aren't likable; but frankly, in public you're a bore. And what if Kossara found out?

Why should I care?

Well, she might accept my sporting as such. I get the impression hers is a double-standard society. But I don't believe she'd forgive my cuckolding a man whose salt I've eaten. To plead I was far from unique would get me nowhere. To plead military necessity wouldn't help either; I think she could see (those wave-colored eyes) that I'd have performed the same service free and enjoyed every microsecond.

Hm. The problem is not how to keep a peccadillo decently veiled in hypocrisy. The problem is what to do about the fact that I care whether or not Kossara Vymezal despises me.

"Can't we?" Susette persisted. "The Empire's big, but people get around in it."

Flandry pulled his attention back to the task on hand. He hugged her, smiled into her troubled gaze, and said, "Your idea flatters me beyond reason. I'd s'posed I was a mere escapade."

She flushed. "I supposed the same. But—well—" Defiantly: "I have others. I guess I always will, till I'm too old. Martin must suspect, and not care an awful lot. He's nice to me in a kind of absent-minded way, but he's overworked, and not young, and—you know what I mean. Diego, Diego Rostovsky, he's been the best. Except I know him inside out by now, what there is to know. You come in like a fresh breeze—straight from Home!—and you can talk about things, and make me laugh and feel good, and—" She leaned hard on him. Her own spare hand wandered. "I'd never have thought ... you knew right away what I'd like most. Are you a telepath?"

No, just experienced and imaginative. Aycharaych is the

telepath. "Thank you for your commendation," Flandry said, and clinked his bottle on hers.

"Then won't you stay a while extra, Ahab, and return afterward?"

"I must go whither the vagaries of war and politics require, amorita. And believe me, they can be confoundedly vague." Flandry took a long drink to gain a minute for assembling his next words. "F'r instance, the secrecy Commander Maspes laid on you forces me to dash on to Sector HQ as soon's I've given Diomedes a fairly clean bill of health—which I've about completed. My task demands certain data, you see. Poor communications again. Maspes tucked you under a blanket prohibition because he'd no way of knowing I'd come here, and I didn't get a clearance to lift it because nobody back Home knew he'd been that ultracautious." *If I produced the Imperial writ I do have, that might give too much away.*

Susette's palm stopped on his breast. "Why, your heart's going like a hammer," she said.

"You do that to a chap," he answered, put down his bottle and gathered her to him for an elaborate kiss.

Breathlessly, she asked, "You mean if you had the information you wouldn't be in such a hurry? You could stay longer?"

"I should jolly well hope so," he said, running fingers through her hair. "But what's the use?" He grinned. "Never mind. In your presence, I am not prone to talk shop."

"No, wait." She fended him off, a push which was a caress. "What do you need to know, Ahab?"

"Why—" He measured out his hesitation. "Something you're not allowed to tell me."

"But they'd tell you at HQ."

"Oh, yes. This is a miserable technicality."

"All right," Susette said fast. "What is it?"

"You might—" Flandry donned enthusiasm. "Darling! You wouldn't get in trouble, I swear. No, you'd be expediting the business of the Empire."

She shook her head and giggled. "Uh-uh. Remember, you've got to spend the time you gain here. Promise?"

"On my honor" *as a double agent.*

She leaned back again, her beer set aside, hands clasped behind her neck, enjoying her submission. "Ask me anything."

Flandry faced her, arms wrapped around drawn-up knees. "Mainly, who was with Maspes? Nonhumans especi'lly. I'd better not spell out the reason. But consider. No mind can conceive, let alone remember, the planets and races we've discovered in this tiny offside corner of the solitary galaxy we've explored a little bit. Infiltration, espionage—such things have happened before."

She stared. "Wouldn't they check a memory bank?"

Memory banks can have lies put into them, whenever we get a government many of whose officials can be bought, and later during the confusion of disputed succession, civil war, and sweeping purges. Those lies can then wait, never called on and therefore never suspected, till somebody has need for one of them. "Let's say no system is perfect, 'cept yours for lovemaking. Terra itself doesn't have a complete, fully updated file. Regional bitkeepers don't try; and checking back with Terra seldom seems worth the delay and trouble."

"Golloo!" She was more titillated than alarmed. "You mean we might've had an enemy spy right here?"

"That's what I'm s'posed to find out, sweetling."

"Well, there was only a single xeno on the team." She sighed. "I'd hate to believe he was enemy. So beautiful a person. You know, I daydreamed about going to bed with him, though of course I don't imagine that'd have worked, even if he did look pretty much like a man."

"Who was he? Where from?"

"Uh—his name, Ay ... Aycharaych." She handled the diphthongs better than the open consonants. "From, uh, he said his planet's called Chereion. Way off toward Betelgeuse."

Further, Flandry thought amidst a thrumming.

This time he didn't bother to conceal his right name or his very origin. And why should he? Nobody would check on a duly accredited member of an Imperial Intelligence force—not that the files in Thursday Landing would help anyway—and he could read in their minds that none had ever heard of an obscure world within the Roidhunate—

and the secrecy command would cover his trail as long as he needed, after he'd done his damage and was gone.

When at last, maybe, the truth came out: why, our people who do know a little something about Chereion would recognize that was where he glided from, as soon as they heard his description, regardless of whether he'd given a false origin or not. He might as well amuse himself by leaving his legal signature.

Which I'd already begun to think I saw in this whole affair. Dreams and shadows and flitting ghosts—

"He's about as tall as you are," Susette was saying, "skinny—no, I mean fine-boned and lean—except for wide shoulders and a kind of jutting chest. Six fingers to a hand, extra-jointed, ambery nails; but four claws to a foot and a spur behind, like a sort of bird. And he did say his race comes from a, uh, an analogue of flightless birds. I can't say a lot more about his body, because he always wore a long robe, though usually going barefoot. His face ... well, I'd make him sound ugly if I spoke about a dome of a brow, big hook nose, thin lips, pointed ears, and of course all the, the shapes, angles, proportions different from ours. Actually, he's beautiful. I could've spent days looking into those huge red-brown whiteless eyes of his, if he'd let me. His skin is deep gold color. He has no hair anywhere I saw, but a kind of shark-fin crest on the crown of his head, made from dark-blue feathers, and tiny feathers for eyebrows. His voice is low and ... pure music."

Flandry nodded. "M-hm. He stayed in your house?"

"Yes. We and the servants were strictly forbidden to mention him anywhere outside. When he visited the building his team had taken over—or maybe left town altogether; I can't say—he'd put on boots, a cowl, a face mask, like he came from someplace where men cover up everything in public; and walking slow, he could make his gait pass for human."

"Did you get any hints of what he did?"

"No. They called him a ... consultant." Susette sat upright. "Was he really a spy?"

"I can identify him," Flandry said, "and the answer is no." *Why should he spy on his own companions—subordi-*

nates? And he didn't bring them here to collect information, except incidentally. I'm pretty sure he came to kindle a war.

"Oh, I'm glad," Susette exclaimed. "He was such a lovely guest. Even though I often couldn't follow his conversation. Martin did better, but he'd get lost too when Aycharaych started talking about art and history—of Terra! He made me ashamed I was that ignorant about my own planet. No, not ashamed; really interested, wanting to go right out and learn if only I knew how. And then he'd talk on my level, like mentioning little things I'd never much noticed or appreciated, and getting me to care about them, till this dull place seemed full of wonder and—"

She subsided. "Have I told you enough?" she asked.

"I may have a few more questions later," Flandry said, "but for now, yes, I'm through."

She held out her arms. "Oh, no, you're not, you man, you! You've just begun. C'mere."

Flandry did. But while he embraced her, he was mostly harking back to the last time he met Aycharaych.

● IX ●

{That was four years ago, in the planet-wide winter of eccentrically orbiting Talwin. Having landed simultaneously from the warships which brought them hither, Captain Sir Dominic Flandry and his opposite number, *Qanryf* Tachwyr the Dark, were received with painstaking correctness by the two commissioners of their respective races who administered the joint Merseian-Terran scientific base. After due ceremony, they expressed a wish to dine privately, that they might discuss the tasks ahead of them in frankness and at leisure.

The room for this was small, austerely outfitted as the entire outpost necessarily was. Talwin's system coursed through the Wilderness, that little-explored buffer zone of stars between Empire and Roidhunate; it had no attraction for traders; the enterprise got a meager budget. A table, some chairs and stools, a sideboard, a phone were the whole furniture, unless you counted the dumbwaiter with sensors and extensible arms for serving people who might not wish a live attendant while they talked.

Flandry entered cheerily, 0.88 gee lending bounce to his gait. The Merseian officer waited, half dinosaurian despite a close-fitting silver-trimmed black uniform, bold against snowfields, frozen river, and shrunken sun in crystalline sky which filled a wall transparency behind him.

"Well, you old rascal, how are you?" The man held forth his hand in Terran wise. Tachwyr clasped it between warm dry fingers and leathery palm. They had no further amicable gesture to exchange, since Flandry lacked a tail.

"Thirsty," Tachwyr rumbled. They sought the well-stocked sideboard. Tachwyr reached for Scotch and Flandry for telloch. They caught each other's glances and laughed, Merseian drumroll and human staccato. "Been a long while for us both, *arrach?*"

Flandry noted the inference, that of recent years Tachwyr's work had brought him into little or no contact with Terrans, for whatever it might be worth. Likely that wasn't much. The Empire's mulish attitude toward the aggrandizement of the Roidhunate was by no means the sole problem which the latter faced. Still, Tachwyr was by way of being an expert on *Homo sapiens;* so if a more urgent matter had called him— To be sure, he might have planned his remark precisely to make his opponent think along these lines.

"I trust your wives and children enjoy good fortune," Flandry said in polite Eriau.

"Yes, I thank the God." The formula being completed, Tachwyr went on: "Chydhwan's married, and Gelch has begun his cadetship. I presume you're still a bachelor?" He must ask that in Anglic, for his native equivalent would have been an insult. His jet eyes probed. "Aren't you the gaudy one, though? What style is that?"

The man extended an arm to show off colors and embroideries of his mufti. The plumes bobbed which sprang from an emerald brooch holding his turban together. "Latest fashion in Dehiwala—on Ramanujan, you know. I was there a while back. Garb at home has gotten positively drab." He lifted his glass. "Well, *tor ychwei.*"

"Here's to you," the Merseian responded in Anglic. They drank. The telloch was thick and bitter-fiery.

Flandry looked outdoors. "Brrr!" he said. "I'm glad this time I won't need to tramp through that."

"*Khraich?* I'd hoped we might go on a hunt."

"Don't let me stop you. But if nothing else, my time here is limited. I must get back. Wouldn't have come at all except for your special invitation."

Tachwyr studied Flandry. "I never doubted you are busy these days," he said.

"Yes, jumping around like a probability function in a high wind."

"You do not seem discouraged."

"N-no." Flandry sipped, abruptly brought his gaze

around, and stated: "We're near the end of our troubles. What opposition is left has no real chance."

"And Hans Molitor will be undisputed Emperor." Tachwyr's relaxation evaporated. Flandry, who knew him from encounters both adversary and half friendly since they were fledglings in their services, had rather expected that. A big, faintly scaled hand clenched on the tumbler of whisky. "My reason why I wanted this meeting."

"Your reason?" Flandry arched his brows, though he knew Tachwyr felt it was a particularly grotesque expression.

"Yes. I persuaded my superiors to send your government—Molitor's—the proposal, and put me in charge of our side. However, if you had not come yourself, I imagine the conference would have proved as empty as my *datholch* claimed it would, when I broached the idea to him."

I can't blame the good datholch, *Flandry thought. It does seem ludicrous on the face of it: discussions between Intelligence officers of rank below admiral or* fodaich, *who can't make important commitments—discussions about how to "resolve mutual difficulties" and assure the Imperium that the Roidhunate has never had any desire to interfere in domestic affairs of the Empire—when everybody knows how gleefully Merseian agents have swarmed through every one of our camps, trying their eternally damnedest to keep our family fight going.*

Of course, Molitor's people couldn't refuse, because this is the first overt sign that Merseia will recognize him rather than some rival as our lord, and deal with his agents later on, about matters more real than this farce.

The intention is no surprise, when he's obviously winning. The surprise was the form the feeler took—and Tachwyr's note to me. Neither action felt quite Merseian.

Therefore I had to come.

"Let me guess," Flandry said. "You know I'm close to his Majesty and act as an odd-job man of his. You and your team hope to sound out me and mine about him."

Tachwyr nodded. "If he's to be your new leader, stronger than the past several, we want to know what to expect."

"You must have collected more bits of information on him than there are stars in the galaxy. And he's not a complex man. And no individual can do more than throw a small extra vector or two in among the millions that whipsaw such a big and awkward thing as the Empire toward whatever destiny it's got."

"He can order actions which have a multiplier effect, for war or peace between our folk."

"Oh, come off it, chum! No Merseian has a talent for pious wormwords. He only sounds silly when he tries. As far as you are concerned *vis-à-vis* us, diplomacy is a continuation of war by other means." Flandry tossed off his drink and poured a refill.

"Many Terrans disagree," Tachwyr said slowly.

"My species also has more talent than yours for wishful thinking," Flandry admitted. He waved at the cold landscape. "Take this base itself. For two decades, through every clash and crisis, a beacon example of cooperation. Right?" He leered. "You know better. Oh, doubtless most of the scientists who come here are sincere enough in just wanting to study a remarkable xenological development. Doubtless they're generally on good personal terms. But they're subsidized—they have their nice safe demilitarization—for no reason except that both sides find it convenient to keep a place for secret rendezvous. Neutral domains like Betelgeuse are so public, and their owners tend to be so nosy."

He patted the Merseian's back. "Now let's sit down to eat, and afterward serious drinking, like the cordial enemies we've always been," he urged. "I don't mind giving you anecdotes to pad out your report. Some of them may even be true."

The heavy features flushed olive-green. "Do you imply our attempt—not at final disengagement, granted, but at practical measures of mutual benefit—do you imply it is either idiotic or else false?"

Flandry sighed. "You disappoint me, Tachwyr. I do believe you've grown stuffy in your middle age. Instead of continuing the charade, why not ring up your Chereionite and invite him to join us? I'll bet he and I are acquainted too."

{The sun went down and night leaped forth in stars almost space-bright, crowding the dark, making the winter world glow as if it had a moon. "May I turn off the interior lights?" Aycharaych asked. "The outside is too glorious for them."

Flandry agreed. The hawk profile across the table from him grew indistinct, save for great starlight-catching eyes. The voice sang and purred onward, soft as the cognac they shared, in Anglic whose accent sounded less foreign than archaic.

"I could wish your turban did not cover a mindscreen and powerpack, my friend. Not merely does the field make an ugliness through my nerves amidst this frozen serenity; I would fain be in true communion with you." Aycharaych's chuckle sounded wistful. "That can scarcely be, I realize, unless you join my cause."

"Or you mine," Flandry said.

"And each of your men who might know something I would like to learn is likewise screened against me. Does not that apparatus on their heads make sleep difficult? I warn you in any case, wear the things not overmany days at a stretch. Even for a race like yours, it is ill to keep the brain walled off from those energies which inspirit the universe, behind a screen of forces that themselves must roil your dreams."

"I see no reason for us to stay."

Aycharaych inhaled from his glass. He had not touched the liquor yet. "I would be happy for your company," he said. "But I understand. The consciousness that dreary death will in a few more decades fold this brightly checkered game board whereon you leap and capture—that keeps you ever in haste."

He leaned back, gazed out at a tree turned into a jewel by icicles, and was quiet awhile. Flandry reached for a cigarette, remembered the Chereionite disliked tobacco smoke, and soothed himself with a swallow.

"It may be the root of your greatness as a race," Aycharaych mused. "Could a *St. Matthew Passion* have welled from an immortal Bach? Could a Rembrandt who knew naught of sorrow and had no need for steadfastness in it have brought those things alive by a few daubs of paint? Could a Tu Fu free of loss have been the poet of dead leaves flying amidst snow, cranes departing, or an old parrot shabby in its cage? What depth does the foreknowledge of doom give to your loves?"

He turned his head to face the man. His tone lightened: "Well. Now that poor mortified Tachwyr is gone—most mightily had he looked forward to the sauce which gloating would put on his dinner!—we can talk freely. How did you deduce the truth?"

"Part hunch," Flandry confessed. "The more I thought about that message, the more suggestions of your style I found. Then logic took over. Plain to see, the Merseians had some ulterior motive in asking for a conference as nugatory *per se* as this. It could be just a signal to us, and an attempt at sounding out Molitor's prospective regime a bit. But for those purposes it was clumsy and inadequate. And why go to such trouble to bring *me* here?

"Well, I'm not privy to high strategic secrets, but I'm close enough to him that I must have a fair amount of critical information—the kind which'll be obsolete inside a year, but if used promptly could help Merseia keep our kettle longer on the boil, with that much more harm to us. And I have a freer hand than anybody else who's so well briefed; I could certainly come if I chose. And an invitation from Tachwyr could be counted on to pique my curiosity, if nothing else.

"The whole idea was yours, wasn't it?"

Aycharaych nodded, his crest a scimitar across the Milky Way. "Yes," he said. "I already had business in these parts—*negotium perambulantem in tenebris,* if you like—and saw nothing to lose in this attempt. At least I have won the pleasure of a few hours with you."

"Thanks. Although—" Flandry sought words. "You know I put modesty in a class with virginity, both charming characteristics which should be gotten rid of as fast as puberty allows. However ... why me, Aycharaych? Do you relish the fact I'll kill you, regretfully but firmly, the instant a chance appears? In that respect, there are hundreds like me. True, I may be unusual in having come close, a time or two. And I can make more cultured noises than the average Navy man. But I'm no scholar, no esthete—a dilettante; you can do better than me."

"Let us say I appreciate your total personality." The smile, barely visible, resembled that upon the oldest stone gods of Greece. "I admire your exploits. And since we have interacted again and again, a bond has formed between us. Deny not that you sense it."

"I don't deny. You're the only Chereionite I've ever met—" Flandry stopped.

After a moment he proceeded: "Are you the only Chereionite anybody has ever met?"

"Occasional Merseians have visited my planet, even resided there for periods of study," Aycharaych pointed out.

Yes. Flandry remembered one such, who had endangered him here upon Talwin; how far in the past that seemed, and how immediately near! *I realize why the coordinates of your home are perhaps the best-kept secret in the Roidhunate. I doubt if a thousand beings from offworld know; and in most of them, the numbers have been buried deep in their unconsciousness, to be called forth by a key stimulus which is also secret.*

Secret, secret . . . What do we know about you that is substance and not shadow?

The data fled by, just behind his eyes.

Chereion's sun was dim, as Flandry himself had discovered when he noticed Aycharaych was blind in the blue end of the spectrum though seeing farther into the red than a man can. The planet was small, cold, dry—deduced from Aycharaych's build, walk, capabilities, preferences—not unlike human-settled Aeneas, because he could roam freely there and almost start a holy war to split the Empire, nineteen years ago.

In those days he had claimed that the enigmatic ruins found upon many worlds of that sort were relics of his own people, who ranged and ruled among the stars in an era geologically remote. He claimed. . . . *He's as big a liar as I am, when either of us wants to be. If they did build and then withdraw, why? Where to? What are they upon this night?*.

Dismiss the riddles. Imperial Intelligence knew for certain, with scars for reminders, he was a telepath of extraordinary power. Within a radius of *x* meters, he could read the thoughts of any being, no matter how alien, using any language, no matter how foreign to him. That had been theoretically impossible. Hence the theory was crudely modified (there is scant creativity in a waning civilization) to include suggestions of a brain which with computerlike speed and capacity analyzed the impulses it detected into basic units (binary?), compared this pattern with the one which its own senses and knowledge presented, and by some incredible process of trial and error synthesized in seconds a code which closely corresponded to the original.

It did not seem he could peer far below the surface thoughts, if at all. That mattered little. He could be patient; or in a direct confrontation, he had skill to evoke the memories he wanted. No wonder that the highest Merseian command paid heed to him. The Empire had never had a more dangerous single enemy.

Single—

Flandry grew aware of the other's luminous regard. " 'Scuse me," he said. "I got thinking. Bad habit."

"I can guess what." Aycharaych's smile continued. "You speculate whether I am your sole Chereionite colleague."

"Yes. Not for the first time." Flandry drank again. "Well, are you? What few photographs or eyewitness accounts we've garnered, of a Chereionite among outsiders—never more than one. Were all of them you?"

"You don't expect me to tell you. I will agree to what's obvious, that partakers in ephemeral affairs, like myself, have been rare among my race. They laid such things aside before your kind were aught but apes."

"Why haven't you?"

"In action I find an art; and every art is a philosophical tool, whereby we may seek to win an atom deeper into mystery."

Flandry considered Aycharaych for a silent span before he murmured: "I came on a poem once, in translation—it goes back a millennium or more—that's stayed with me. Tells how Pan—you know our Classical myths—Pan is at a riverside, splashing around, his goat hoofs breaking the lilies, till he plucks a reed and hollows it out, no mat-

ter the agony it feels; then the music he pipes forth en-
chants the whole forest. Is that what you think of yourself
as doing?"

"Ah, yes," Aycharaych answered, "you have the last
stanza in mind, I believe." Low:

> "Yet half a beast is the great god Pan,
> To laugh as he sits by the river,
> Making a poet out of a man:
> The true gods sigh for the cost and pain,—
> For the reed which grows nevermore again
> As a reed with the reeds in the river."

Damn! Flandry thought. *I ought to stop letting him
startle me.*

"My friend," the other went on gently, "you too play a
satanic role. How many lives have you twisted or chopped
short? How many will you? Would you protest me if the
accidents of history had flung Empire rather than
Roidhunate around my sun? Or if you had been born into
those humans who serve Merseia? Indeed, then you might
have lived more whole of heart."

Anger flared. "I know," Flandry snapped. "How often
have I heard? Terra is old, tired, corrupt, Merseia is
young, vigorous, pure. Thank you, to the extent that's
true, I prefer my anomie, cynicism, and existential despair
to counting my days in cadence and shouting huzza—
worse, sincerely meaning it—when Glorious Leader rides
by. Besides . . . the device every conqueror, yes, every al-
truistic liberator should be required to wear on his shield
. . . is a little girl and her kitten, at ground zero."

He knocked back his cognac and poured another. His
temper cooled. "I suspect," he finished, "down inside,
you'd like to say the same."

"Not in those terms," Aycharaych replied. "Sentimental-
ity ill becomes either of us. Or compassion. Forgive me,
are you not drinking a trifle heavily?"

"Could be."

"Since you won't get so drunk I can surreptitiously turn
off your mindscreen, I would be grateful if you stay
clear-headed. The time is long since last I relished dis-

course of Terra's former splendors, or even of her modern pleasures. Come, let us talk the stars to rest."}

In the morning, Flandry told Susette he must scout around the globe a few days, using certain ultrasensitive instruments, but thereafter he would return.

He doubted that very much.

● X ●

Shadow and thunder of wings fell over Kossara. She looked up from the rolling, tawny-begrown down onto which she had come after stumbling from the forest. Against clouds and the plum-colored sky beyond, a Diomedean descended. She halted. Weariness shivered in her legs. Wind slithered around her. It smelled of damp earth and, somehow, of boulders.

An end to my search. Her heart slugged. *But what will I now find? Comrades and trust, or a return to my punishment?*

The native landed, a male, attired in crossbelts and armed with a knife and rifle. He must have been out hunting, when he saw the remarkable sight of a solitary human loose in the wilds, begrimed, footsore, mapless and compassless. He uttered gutturals of his own tongue.

"No, I don't speak that," Kossara answered. The last water she had found was kilometers behind. Thirst roughened her throat. "Do you know Anglic?"

"Some bit," the native said. "How you? Help?"

"Y-yes. But——" *But not from anybody who'll think he should call Thursday Landing and inquire about me.* During her trek she had sifted the fragments of memory, over and over. A name and nonhuman face remained. "Eonan. Bring me Eonan." She tried several different pronunciations, hoping one would be recognizable.

"*Gairath mochra.* Eonan? Wh . . . what Eonan? Many Eonan."

There would be, of course. She might as well have asked a random Dennitzan for Andrei. However, she had expected as much. "Eonan who knows Kossara Vymezal," she said. "Find. Give Eonan this." She handed him a note she had scrawled. "Money." She offered a ten-credit bill from the full wallet Flandry had included in her gear. "Bring Eonan, I give you more money."

After repeated trials, she seemed to get the idea across, and an approximation of her name. The hunter took off northward. God willing, he'd ask around in the bayshore towns till he found the right person; and while this would make the dwellers curious, none should see reason to phone Imperial headquarters. God willing. She ought to kneel for a prayer, but she was too tired; Mary who fled to Egypt would understand. Kossara sat down on what resembled pale grass and wasn't, hugged herself against the bitter breeze and stared across treelessness beneath a wan sun.

Have I really won through?

If Eonan still had his life and liberty, he might have lost heart for his revolution—if, in truth, he had ever been involved; she had nothing more than a dream-vision from a cave. Or if he would still free his people from the Empire, he might be the last. Or if cabals and guerrillas remained, he might not know where they hid. Or if he brought her to them, what could she hope for?

She tossed her head. *A chance to fight. Maybe to win home in the end, likelier to die here: as a soldier does, and in freedom.*

Drowsiness overflowed. She curled herself as best she could on the ground. Heavy garments blunted its hardness, though she hated the sour smell they'd gotten. To be clean again ... Flandry had saved her from the soiling which could never be washed off. He had that much honor—and, yes, a diamond sort of mercy. If she'd done his bidding, tried her best to lead him to whatever was left of her fellows, he would surely have sent her back, manumitted— he'd have the prestige for such a favor to be granted him—unscathed— No! Not whole in her own honor! And release upon a Dennitza lashed to the Empire would be a cruel joke.

Then rest while you can, Kossara. Sleep comes not black, no, blue as a summer sky over the Kazan, blue as the cloak of Mary.... Pray for us, now and in the hour of our death.

A small callused hand shook her awake. Hunger said louder than her watch what a time had passed while the sun brooded nightless. She stared into yellow eyes above a blunt muzzle and quivering whiskers. Half open, bat wings made a stormcloud behind. He carried a blaster.

His face— She sat up, aware of ache, stiffness, cold. "Eonan?"

"Torcha tracked me." Apart from the piping accent, mostly due to the organs of speech, his Anglic came fluent. "But you do not know him, do you?"

She struggled to her feet. "I don't know you either, quite," she got out. "They made me forget."

"Ungn-n-n." He touched the butt of the gun, and his crest erected. Otherwise he stood in taut quietness. She saw he had arrived on a gravsled, no doubt to carry her.

Resolution unfroze him. "I am Eonan Guntrasson, of the Wendru clan in the Great Flock of Lannach. And you are Kossara Vymezal, from the distant planet Dennitza."

Gladness came galloping, and every weakness fled. "I know that, *barem!* And you dared meet me? Then we are not finished yet!"

Eonan drew the membranes over his eyes. "We?"

"The revolution. Yours and mine." She leaned down to grip his upper shoulders. Beneath fur and warmth, the flight muscles stood like rock.

"I must be careful." His tone underlined it. "Torcha said you promised him a reward for fetching me. I paid him myself, not to have him along. Best we go aside and . . . talk. First, in sign of good faith, let me search you."

The place he chose was back in the highlands. Canyon walls rose darkly where a river rang; fog smoked and dripped till Kossara was soaked with chill; at moments when the swirling grayness parted, she glimpsed the black volcanic cone of Mount Oborch.

On the way, Eonan had fed her from a stock of preserved Terran food, and explained he was the factor for Nakamura & Malaysia in the area where he dwelt. This gave him wide contacts and sources of information, as well as an easy excuse to travel, disappearing into the hinterland or across the sea, whenever he wished. Thursday Landing had no suspicion of his clandestine activities. He would not speak about those until she related her story in full.

Then he breathed, "E-e-e-ehhh," and crouched in thought on the gravsled bench. Finally, sharply: "Well, your Terran officer has likeliest concluded you slipped off in search of the cloudflyers—the, keh, the underground. A spacecraft was seen to lift from hereabouts not many sunspins ago. When I heard, I wondered what that meant."

"I imagine he went to warn the resident and start a hunt for me," Kossara said. "He did threaten to, if I deserted." Anxiety touched her. "Yes, and a tightened space watch. Have I caused us trouble?"

"We shall see. It may have been worth it in all events. To learn about that spy device is no slight gain. We shall want your description of the place where you threw the ring away. Perhaps we can safely look for it and take it to study."

"Chances are he's recovered it. But Eonan!" Kossara twisted around toward him. "How are you doing here? How many survive? With what strength, what plans? How can I help?"

Again the third lids blurred his gaze. "Best I keep still. I am just a link. They will answer you in the nest where I have decided to take you."

The hideout was high in a mountainside. Approaching, Kossara felt her eardrums twinge from pressure change and cold strike deep. Snowpeaks, glaciers, ravines, cliffs, crags reached in monstrous confusion between a cloud ocean which drowned the lower slopes, and a sky whose emptiness the sun only seemed to darken. Silence dwelt here, save for air booming over the windshield and a mutter of native language as Eonan radioed ahead.

Why am I not happy? she wondered. *I am about to rejoin my comrades and regain my past—my purpose. What makes me afraid?*

Eonan finished. "Everything will be ready," he informed her. Was he as tense as he looked? She must have come to know Diomedeans well enough during her stay that she could tell; but that had been robbed from her. What had *he* to fear?

"I suppose," she ventured, "this is headquarters for the entire mission. They tucked it away here to make it undiscoverable."

"Yes. They enlarged a cave."

She recalled another cave, where she and Trohdwyr and a few more had huddled. "Were we—those who died when I was captured—were we out in the field—liaison with freedom fighters whose homes were below timberline? Maybe we were betrayed by one of them"—she grimaced—"who'd been caught at sabotage or whatever, and interrogated."

"That sounds plausible."

"But then nobody except us was destroyed! Am I right? Is the liberation movement still healthy?"

"Yes."

Puzzlement: "Why didn't I tell the Impies about our main base when they put me under hypnoprobe?"

"I do not know," Eonan said impatiently. "Please be quiet. I must bring us in on an exact course, or they will shoot."

As the sled glided near, Kossara spied the defense, an energy cannon. It was camouflaged, but military training had enhanced her natural ability to notice things. A great steel door in the bluff behind it would go unseen from above, should anyone fly across this lofty desert. Instruments—infrared sensors, neutrino detectors, magnetometers, gravitometers, atmosphere sniffers, a hundred kinds of robot bloodhound—would expose the place at once. But who would think to come searching?

The door swung aside. The sled passed through and landed in a garage among several aircars. Here were warmth, echoes, a sudden brilliance of light better suited for eyes human or Merseian. Kossara shed her parka before she stepped off. Her pulse raced.

Four stood waiting. Three were men. She was not surprised to see the last was a big green heavy-tailed person, though her heart said *O Trohdwyr*—and for an instant tears stung and blurred.

She rallied herself and walked toward them. Her boots

thudded on the floor; Eonan's claws clicked. Those in front of her were simply clad, shirts, trousers, shoes on the men, a tunic on the zmay. She had expected them to be armed, as they were.

It flashed: *Why did I think zmay, not ychan?* And: *They aren't Dennitzans! None of them!*

She slammed to a halt. The men differed widely, genes from every breed of mankind scrambled in chance combinations. So they could be from Terra—or a colony within the Empire—or—

Eonan left her side. The Merseian drew his pistol. "Hold," he rapped. "You are under arrest."

He called himself Glydh of the Vach Rueth, nicknamed Far-Farer, an *afal* of his navy's Intelligence corps. His immediate assistant was a lanky, sallow, long-nosed man, introduced as Muhammad Snell but addressed by the superior officer as Kluwych. In the middle of wreck, Kossara could flickeringly wonder if the Eriau name had been given him by his parents, when he was born somewhere in the Roidhunate.

They took her to an office. On the way she passed through such space and among such personnel that she estimated the latter numbered about twenty, two or three of them Merseian by species, the rest human. That was probably all there were on Diomedes: sufficient to keep scores of native dupes like Eonan going, who in their turn led thousands.

Though are they dupes? she thought drearily. *Merseia would like to see them unchained from the Empire.*

No. That isn't true. Merseia doesn't give a curse. They're cheap, expendable tools.

The office was cramped and bleak. "Sit," Glydh ordered, pointing to a chair. He took a stool behind a desk. Snell settled on the left; his eyes licked her, centimeter by centimeter and back again.

"*Khraich.*" Glydh laid his hands flat on the desktop, broad and thick, strangler's hands. "An astonishing turn of events. What shall we do with you?" His Anglic was excellent.

113

"Isn't this, uh, Captain Flandry more urgent, sir?" his subordinate asked.

"Not much, I believe," Glydh said. "True, from Vymezal's account via Eonan, he appears to be capable. But what can he know? That she defected, presumably joining a remnant of the underground if she didn't perish *en route*." He pondered. "Maybe he isn't capable, at that—since he let her go, trusting her mere self-interest to keep her on his side."

Hoy? Chives said Flandry is famous. . . . No. How many light-years, how many millions of minds can fame cover before it spreads vanishingly thin?

"Of course, we will have our cell in Thursday Landing keep him under surveillance, and alert our agents globally is he leaves there," Glydh continued. "But I doubt he represents more than a blind stab on the part of somebody in the opposition. I don't think he is worth the risk of trying to kidnap, or even kill."

"We may find out otherwise, sir, when we interrogate Vymezal in detail," said the man. He moistened his lips.

"Maybe. I leave that to you. Co-opt what helpers you need."

"Um-m-m . . . procedures? Treatment? Final disposition?"

"No!" Kossara heard the yell and felt the leaping to her feet, as if from outside her body. This was not real, could not be, must not be, God and saints, no. "I am not a, a Terran agent—I came here to—at least I'm a prisoner of war!"

"Sit!" Glydh's roar, and the gunshot slap of palm on desk, flung her back like a belly blow. She heard his basso through fever-dream distances and humming: "Don't babble about military conventions. You are a slave, property we have acquired. If you do what you are told, there need not be pain. Else there will be, until you are broken to obedience. Do you hear me?"

Snell's fingers twisted together. He breathed fast. "Sir," he said, "it could be a long while before we get a chance to send a report offplanet and ask for instructions about her. So we have to use our own judgment, don't we?"

"Yes," Glydh answered.

"Well, considering what was originally intended for her, and the reason—sir, not a woman among us in this whole region—"

Glydh shrugged. His tone was faintly contemptuous. "Quiz her out first under narco. Afterward do what you like, short of disfiguring damage. Remember, we may find use for her later, and the nearest biosculp laboratory is parsecs hence."

I will make them kill me! Even as she plunged toward Snell, fingernails out to hook his eyeballs, Kossara knew Glydh would seize her and not let her die.

The explosion threw her against a wall. It made a drum of her skull. The floor heaved and cracked. Snell went over backward. Glydh flailed about to keep his balance.

Faintly through the brief deafness that followed, she heard screams, running, bang and hiss of firearms. Ozone drifted acrid to her nostrils, smoke, smells of roastedness.

She was already out of the office, into the central chamber beyond. At its far end, through the passageway which gave on the garage, she saw how the main door lay blown off its trunnions, crumpled and red-hot. Beyond was the ruin of the cannon. Men boiled around or sprawled unmoving.

Enormous shone the bulk of a suit of combat armor. Bullets whanged off it, blaster bolts fountained. The wearer stood where he was, and his own weapon scythed.

As she broke into view—*"Kossara!"* Amplified from the helmet, his voice resounded like God's. His free hand reached beneath a plate that protected his gravbelt. He rose and moved slowly toward her. Survivors fled.

Fingers closed on her arm. Around her shoulder she saw Glydh. He swung her before his body. "That's not nice," the oncoming invader pealed. He spun his blaster nozzle to needle beam, aimed, and fired.

Glydh's brow spurted steam, brains, blood, shattered bone across Kossara. She knew a heartbeat's marvel at that kind of precision shooting. But then the heavy corpse bore her down. Her head struck the floor. Lightning filled the universe.

The armored man reached her, stood over her, shielded

115

her. A spacecraft's flank appeared in the entry. It had sprouted a turret, whose gun sprayed every doorway where an enemy might lurk. Kossara let darkness flow free.

● XI ●

A breath of air cool, pine-scented; all noises gone soft;
a sense of muted energies everywhere around; a lessened
weight—Kossara opened her eyes. She lay in bed, in her
cabin aboard the *Hooligan*. Flandry sat alongside. He
wore a plain coverall, his countenance was haggard and
the gray gaze troubled. Nonetheless he smiled. "Hello,
there," he murmured. "How do you feel?"

Drowsy, altogether at ease, she asked, "Have we left
Diomedes?"

"Yes. We're bound for Dennitza." He took her right
hand between both of his. "Now listen. Everything is all
right. You weren't seriously harmed, but on examination
we decided we'd better keep you under sleep induction
awhile, with intravenous feeding and some medication.
Look at your left wrist." She did. It was bare. "Yes, the
bracelet is off. As far as I'm concerned, you're free, and
I'll take care of the technicalities as soon as possible.
You're going home, Kossara."

Examination— She dropped her glance. A sheer night-
gown covered her. "I'm sorry I never thought to bring
anything more decorous for you to sleep in," Flandry said.
He appeared to be summoning courage. "Chives did the
doctoring, the bathing, et cetera. Chives alone." His mouth
went wry. "You may or may not believe that. It's true,
but hell knows how much I've lied to you."

And I to you, she thought.

He straightened in the chair and released her. "Well,"
he said, "would you like a spot of tea and accompani-
ments? You should stay in bed for another watch cycle or
two, till you get your strength back."

"What happened . . . to us?"

117

"We'd better postpone that tale. First you should rest."
Flandry rose. Almost timidly, he gave her hair a stroke.
"I'll go now. Chives will bring the tea."

Wakefulness returned. When the Shalmuan came to retrieve her tray, Kossara sat propped against pillows, ready
for him. "I hope the refreshments were satisfactory,
Donna," he said. "Would you care for something more?"

"Yes," she replied. "Information."

The slim form showed unease. "Sir Dominic feels—"

"Sir Dominic is not me." She spread her palms. "Chives,
how can I relax in a jigsaw puzzle? Tell me, or ask him to
tell me, what went on in that den. How did you find me?
What did you do after I lost consciousness? Why?"

Chives reached a decision. "Well, Donna, we trust that
in view of results obtained, you will pardon certain earlier
modifications of strict veracity which Sir Dominic deemed
essential. The ring he gave you was a mere ring; no such
device exists as he described, at least within the purview
of Technic civilization." She choked. He continued: "Sir
Dominic, ah, has been known to indulge in what he de-
scribes as wistful fantasizing relevant to his occupation. Instead, the bracelet you wore was slave-driven from an external source of radiated power."

"Slave-driven. A very good word." And yet Kossara
could feel no anger. She imitated it as a duty. Had they
given her a tranquilizing drug which had not completely
worn off?

"Your indignation is natural, Donna." Chives' tail
switched his ankles. "Yet allow me to request you consider
the total situation, including the fact that those whom you
met were not noble liberators but Merseian operatives. Sir
Dominic suspected this from the start. He believed that if
you reappeared, they were sure to contact you, if only to
find out what had transpired. He saw no method short of
the empirical for convincing you. Furthermore, admiration
for your honesty made him dubious of your ability know-
ingly to play a double role.

"Hence I trailed you at a discreet distance while he
went to Thursday Landing to investigate other aspects of
the case. Albeit my assignment had its vexations, I pin-

pointed the spot where you were brought and called Sir Dominic, who by then had returned to Lannach. Underground and surrounded by metal, your bracelet was blocked from us. We concluded immediate attack was the most prudent course—for your sake particularly, Donna. While Sir Dominic flitted down in armor, I blasted the cannon and entrance. Shortly afterward I landed to assist and, if you will excuse my immodesty, took the single prisoner we got. The rest were either dead or, ah, holed up sufficiently well that we decided to content ourselves with a nuclear missile dispatched through the entrance.

"The resultant landslide was somewhat spectacular. Perhaps later you will be interested to see the movie I took.

"Ah ... what he has learned has made Sir Dominic of the opinion that we must speed directly to Dennitza. Nevertheless, I assure you he would in all events have seen to your repatriation at the earliest feasible date."

Chives lifted her tea tray. "This is as much as I should tell you at the present stage, Donna. I trust you can screen whatever you wish in the way of literary, theatrical, or musical diversion. If you require assistance of any kind, please call on the intercom. I will return in two hours with a bowl of chicken soup. Is that satisfactory?"

Stars filled the saloon viewscreen behind Flandry's head. The ship went *hush-hush-hush*, on a voyage which, even at her pseudospeed, would take a Terran month. The whisky he had poured for them glowed across tongue and palate.

"It's a foul story," he warned.

"Does evil go away just because we keep silent?" Kossara answered. Inwardly: *How evil are you, you claw of the Empire?*—but again without heat, a thought she felt obliged to think.

After all, his lean features looked so grim and unhappy, across the table from her. He shouldn't chain-smoke the way he did; anticancer shots, cardiovascular treatments, lungflushes, and everything, it remained a flagellant habit. One could serve a bad cause without being a bad man. Couldn't one?

He sighed and drank. "Very well. A sketch. I got a lot of details from a narcoquiz of our prisoner, but most are

119

simply that, details, useful in hunting down the last of his outfit if and when that seems worthwhile. He did, though, confirm and amplify something much more scary."

Memory prodded her with a cold finger. "Where is he?"

"Oh, I needled him and bunged him out an airlock." Flandry observed her shock. His tone changed from casual to defensive. "We were already in space; this business doesn't allow delays. As for turning him over to the authorities when we arrive—there may not be any authorities, or they may be in full revolt, Merseian-allied. At best, the fact he was alive could trickle across to enemy Intelligence, and give them valuable clues to what we know. This is how the game's played, Kossara." He trailed out smoke before he added, "Happens his name was Muhammad Snell."

Blood beat in temples and cheeks. "He got no chance—I don't need avengers."

"Maybe your people will," he said quietly.

After a second he leaned forward, locked eyes with her, and continued: "Let's begin explanations from my viewpoint. I want you to follow my experiences and reasoning, in hopes you'll then accept my conclusions. You're an embittered woman, for more cause than you know right now. But I think you're also intelligent, fair-minded, yes, tough-minded enough to recognize truth, no matter what rags it wears."

Kossara told herself she must be calm, watchful, like a cat—like Butterfeet when she was little. . . . She drank. "Go on."

Flandry filled his lungs. "The Gospodar, the Dennitzans in general are furious at Hans' scheme to disband their militia and make them wholly dependent on the Navy," he said. "After they supported him through the civil war, too! And we've other sources of friction, inevitable; and thoughts of breaking away or violently replacing the regnant Emperor are no longer unthinkable. Dennitza has its own culture, deep-rooted, virile, alien to Terra and rather contemptuous thereof—a culture influenced by Merseia, both directly and through the, uh, zmay element in your population.

"Aye, granted, you've long been in the forefront of

resistance to the Roidhunate. However, such attitudes can change overnight. History's abulge with examples. For instance, England's rebellious North American colonies calling on the French they fought less than two decades before; or America a couple of centuries later, allied first with the Russians against the Germans, then turning straight around and—" He stopped. "This doesn't mean anything to you, does it? No matter. You can see the workings in your own case, I'm sure. Dennitza is where your loyalties lie. What you do, whom you support, those depend on what you judge is best for Dennitza. Right? Yes, entirely right and wholesome. But damnably misleadable."

"Are you, then, a Terran loyalist?" she demanded.

He shook his head. "A civilization loyalist. Which is a pretty thin, abstract thing to be; and I keep wondering whether we can preserve civilization or even should.

"Well. Conflict of interest is normal. Compromise is too, especially with as valuable a tributary as Dennitza— *provided* it stays tributary. Now we'd received strong accusations that Dennitzans were engineering revolt on Diomedes, presumably in preparation for something similar at home. His Majesty's government wasn't about to bull right in. That'd be sure to bring on trouble we can ill afford, perhaps quite unnecessarily. But the matter had to be investigated.

"And I, I learned a Dennitzan girl of ranking family had been caught at subversion on Diomedes. Her own statements out of partial recollections, her undisguised hatred of the Imperium, they seemed to confirm those accusations. Being asked to look into the questions, what would I do but bring you along?"

He sighed. "A terrible mistake. We should've headed straight for Dennitza. Hindsight is always keen, isn't it, while foresight stays myopic, astigmatic, strabismic, and drunk. But I haven't even that excuse. I'd guessed at the truth from the first. Instead of going off to see if I could prove my hunch or not—" His fist smote the table. "I should *never* have risked you the way I did, Kossara!"

She thought, amazed, *He is in pain about that. He truly is.*

"A-a-ah," Flandry said. "I'm a ruthless bastard. Better hunter than prey, and have we any third choice in these years? Or so I thought. You ... were only another life."

He ground out his cigarette, sprang from the bench, strode back and forth along the cabin. Sometimes his hands were gripped together behind him, sometimes knotted at his sides. His voice turned quick and impersonal:

"You looked like a significant pawn, though. Why such an incredibly bungled job on you? Including your enslavement on Terra. I'd have heard about you in time, but it was sheer luck I did before you'd been thrown into a whorehouse. And how would your uncle the Gospodar react to *that* news if it reached him?

"Might it be intended to reach him?

"Oh, our enemies couldn't be certain what'd happen; but you tilted the probabilities in their favor. They must've spent considerable time and effort locating you. Flandry's Law: 'Given a sufficiently large population, at least one member will fit any desired set of specifications.' The trick is to find that member."

"What?" Kossara exclaimed. "Do you mean—because I was who I was, in the position I was—that's why Dennitza—" She could speak no further.

"Well, let's say you were an important factor," he replied. "I'm not sure just how you came into play, though I can guess. On the basis of my own vague ideas, I made a decoy of you in the manner you've already heard about. That involved first deliberately antagonizing you on the voyage; then deliberately gambling your life, health, sanity—"

He halted in midstride. His shoulders slumped. She could barely hear him, though his look did not waver from hers: "Every minute makes what I did hurt worse."

She wanted to tell him he was forgiven, yes, go take his hands and tell him; but no, he had lied too often. With an effort, she said, "I am surprised."

His grin was wry. "Less than I am." Returning, he flopped back onto the bench, crossed ankle over thigh till he peered across his knee at her, swallowed a long draught from his glass, took out his cigarette case; and when the smoke was going he proceeded:

"Let's next assume the enemy's viewpoint, i.e. what I learned and deduced.

"They—a key one of them, anyhow—he realizes the Terran Empire is in an era when periods of civil war are as expectable as bouts of delirium in chronic umwi fever. I wasn't quite aware of the fact myself till lately. A conversation I had set me thinking and researching. But he knew right along, my opponent. At last I see what he's been basing his strategy on for the past couple of decades. Knowing him, if he believes the theory, I think I will. These days we're vulnerable to fratricide, Kossara. And what better for Merseia, especially if just the right conflict can be touched off at just the right moment?

"We've been infiltrated. They've had sleepers among us for . . . maybe a lifetime . . . notably in my own branch of service, where they can cover up for each other . . . and notably during this past generation, when the chaos first of the Josip regime, then the succession struggle, made it easier to pass off their agents as legitimate colonial volunteers.

"The humans on Diomedes, brewing revolution with the help of a clever Alatanist pitch—thereby diverting some of our attention to Ythri—they weren't Dennitzans. They were creatures of the Roidhunate, posing as Dennitzans. Oh, not blatantly; that'd've been a giveaway. And they were sincerely pushing for an insurrection, since any trouble of ours is a gain for them. But a major objective of the whole operation was to drive yet another wedge between your people and mine, Kossara."

Frost walked along her spine. She stared at him and whispered: "Those men who caught me—murdered Trohdwyr—tortured and sentenced me—they were Merseians too?"

"They were human," Flandry said flatly, while he unfolded himself into a more normal posture. "They were sworn-in members of the Imperial Terran Naval Intelligence Corps. But, yes, they were serving Merseia. They arrived to 'investigate' and thus add credence to the clues about Dennitza which their earlier-landed fellows had already been spreading around.

"Let the Imperium get extremely suspicious of the Gospodar—d'you see? The Imperium will have to act against him. It dare not stall any longer. But this action forces the Gospodar to respond—he already having reason to doubt the goodwill of the Terrans—"

Flandry smashed his cigarette, drank, laid elbows on table and said most softly, his face near hers:

"He'd hear rumors, and send somebody he could trust to look into them. Aycharaych—I'll describe him later —Aycharaych of the Roidhunate knew that person would likeliest be you. He made ready. Your incrimination, as far as Terra was concerned—your degradation, as far as Dennitza was concerned—d'you see? Inadequate by themselves to provoke war. Still, remind me and I'll tell you about Jenkins' Ear. Nations on the brink don't need a large push to send them toppling.

"I've learned something about how you were lured, after you reached Diomedes. The rest you can tell me, if you will. Because when he isn't weaving mirages, Aycharaych works on minds. He directed the blotting out of your memories. He implanted the false half-memories and that hate of the Empire you carry around. Given his uncanny telepathic capabilities, to let him monitor what drugs, electronics, hypnotism are doing to a brain, he can accomplish what nobody else is able to.

"But I don't think he totally wiped what was real. That'd have left you too unmistakably worked over. I think you keep most of the truth in you, disguised and buried."

The air sucked between her teeth. Her fists clenched on the table. He laid a hand across them, big and gentle.

"I hope I can bring back what you've lost, Kossara." The saying sounded difficult. "And, and free you from those conditioned-reflex emotions. It's mainly a matter of psychotherapy. I don't insist. Ask yourself: Can you trust me that much?"

• XII •

Sickbay was a single compartment, but astonishingly well equipped. Kossara entered with tightness in her gullet and dryness on her tongue. Flandry and Chives stood behind a surgical table. An electronic helmet, swiveled out above the pillow, crouched like an ugly arachnoid. The faint hum of driving energies, ventilation, service and life-support devices, seemed to her to have taken on a shrill note.

Flandry had left flamboyancy outside. Tall in a plain green coverall, he spoke unsmiling: "Your decision isn't final yet. Before we go any further, let me explain. Chives and I have done this sort of thing before, and we aren't a bad team, but we're no professionals."

This sort of thing—Muhammad Snell must lately have lain on that mattress, in the dream-bewildered helplessness of narco, while yonder man pumped him dry and injected the swift poison. *Shouldn't I fear the Imperialist? Dare I risk becoming the ally of one who treated a sentient being as we do a meat animal?*

I ought to feel indignation. I don't, though. Nor do I feel guilty that I don't.

Well, I'm not revengeful, either. At least, not very much. I do remember how Trohdwyr died because he was an inconvenience; I remember how Mihail Svetich died, in a war Flandry says our enemies want to kindle anew.

Flandry says—She heard him from afar, fast and pedantic. Had he rehearsed his speech?

"This is not a hypnoprobe here, of course. It puts a human straight into quasisleep and stimulates memory activity, after a drug has damped inhibitions and emotions. In effect, everything the organism has permanently re-

125

corded becomes accessible to a questioner—assuming no deep conditioning against it. The process takes more time and skill than an ordinary quiz, where all that's wanted is something the subject consciously knows but isn't willing to tell. Psychiatrists use it to dig out key, repressed experiences in severely disturbed patients. I've mainly used it to get total accounts, generally from cooperative witnesses— significant items they may have noticed but forgotten. In your case, we'd best go in several fairly brief sessions, spaced three or four watches apart. That way you can assimilate your regained knowledge and avoid a crisis. The sessions will give you no pain and leave no recollection of themselves."

She brought her whole attention to him. "Do you play the tapes for me when I wake?" she asked.

"I could," he replied, "but wouldn't you prefer I wiped them? You see, when our questions have brought out a coherent framework of what was buried, a simple command will fix it in your normal memory. By association, that will recover everything else. You'll come to with full recall of whatever episode we concentrated on."

His eyes dwelt gravely upon her. "You must realize," he continued, "your whole life will be open to us. We'll try hard to direct our questioning so we don't intrude. However, there's no avoiding all related and heavily charged items. You'll blurt many of them out. Besides, we'll have to feel our way. Is such-and-such a scrap of information from your recent, bad past—or is it earlier, irrelevant? Often we'll need to develop a line of investigation for some distance before we can be sure.

"We're bound to learn things you'll wish we didn't. You'll simply have to take our word that we'll keep silence ever afterward . . . and, yes, pass no judgment, lest we be judged by ourselves.

"Do you really want that, Kossara?"

She nodded with a stiff neck. "I want the truth."

"You can doubtless learn enough for practical purposes by talking to the Gospodar, if he's alive and available when we reach Dennitza. And I make no bones: one hope of mine is gaining insight into the *modus operandi* of Merseian Intelligence, a few clear identifications of their agents among us ... for the benefit of the Empire.

"I won't compel you," Flandry finished. "Please think again before you decide."

She squared her shoulders. "I have thought." Holding out her hand: "Give me the medicine."

The first eventide, her feet dragged her into the saloon. Flandry saw her disheveled, drably clad, signs of weeping upon her, against the stars. She had long been in her own room behind a closed door.

"You needn't eat here, you know," he said in his gentlest tone.

"Thank you, but I will," she answered.

"I admire your courage more than I have words to tell, dear. Come, sit down, take a drink or three before dinner." Since he feared she might refuse, lest that seem to herself like running away from what was in her, he added, "Trohdwyr would like a toast to his *manes*, wouldn't he?"

She followed the suggestion in a numb way. "Will the whole job be this bad?" she asked.

"No." He joined her, pouring Merseian telloch for them both though he really wanted a Mars-dry martini. "I was afraid things might go as they went, the first time, but couldn't see any road around. You did witness Trohdwyr's murder, he suffered hideously, and he'd been your beloved mentor your whole life. The pain wasn't annulled just because your thalamus was temporarily anesthetized. Being your strongest lost memory, already half in consciousness, it came out ahead of any others. And it's still so isolated it feels like yesterday."

She settled wearily back. "Yes," she said. "Before, everything was blurred, even that. Now . . . the faces, the whole betrayal—"

{Nobody died in the cave except Trohdwyr. The rest stood by when a mere couple of marines arrived to arrest her. "*You* called them!" she screamed to the one who bore the name Steve Johnson, surely not his own. He grinned. Trohdwyr lunged, trying to get her free, win her a chance

127

to scramble down the slope and vanish. The lieutenant blasted him. The life in his tough old body had not ebbed out, under the red moons, when they pulled her away from him.

Afterward she overheard Johnson: "Why'd you kill the servant? Why not take him along?"

And the lieutenant: "He'd only be a nuisance. As is, when the Diomedeans find him, they won't get suspicious at your disappearance. They'll suppose the Terrans caught you. Which should make them handier material. For instance, if we want any of those who met you here to go guerrilla, our contact men can warn them they've been identified through data pulled out of you prisoners."

"Hm, what about us four?"

"They'll decide at headquarters. I daresay they'll reassign you to a different region. Come on, now, let's haul mass." The lieutenant's boot nudged Kossara, where she slumped wrist-bound against the cold cave wall. "On your feet, bitch!"}

"His death happened many weeks ago," Flandry said. "Once you get more memories back, you'll see it, feel it in perspective—including time perspective. You'll have done your grieving . . . which you did, down underneath; and you're too healthy to mourn forever."

"I will always miss him," she whispered.

Flandry regarded ghosts of his own. "Yes, I know."

She straightened. He saw her features harden, as if bones lent strength to flesh. The blue-green eyes turned arctic. "Sir Dominic, you were right in what you did to Snell. Nobody in that gang was—is—fit to live."

"Well, we're in a war, we and they, the nastier for being undeclared," he said carefully. "What you and I must do, if we can, is keep the sickness from infecting your planet. Or to the extent it has, if I may continue the metaphor, we've got to supply an antibiotic before the high fever takes hold and the eruptions begin."

His brutal practicality worked as he had hoped, to divert her from both sorrow and rage. "What do you plan?" The question held some of the crispness which ordinarily was hers.

"Before leaving Diomedes," he said, "I contacted Lagard's field office on Lannach, transmitted a coded message for him to record, and showed him my authority to command immediate courier service. The message is directly to the Emperor. The code will bypass channels. In summary, it says, 'Hold off at Dennitza, no matter what you hear, till I've collected full information'—followed by a synopsis of all I've learned thus far."

She began faintly to glow in her exhaustion. "Why, wonderful."

"M-m-m, not altogether, I'm afraid." Flandry let the telloch savage his throat. "Remember, by now his Majesty's barbarian-quelling on the Spican frontier. He'll move around a lot. The courier may not track him down for a while. Meantime—the Admiralty on Terra may get word which provokes it to emergency action, without consulting Emperor or Policy Board. It has that right, subject to a later court of inquiry. And I've no direct line there. Probably make no difference if I did. Maybe not even any difference what I counsel Hans. I'm a lone agent. They could easily decide I must be wrong."

He forced a level look at her. "Or Dennitza could in fact have exploded, giving Emperor and Admiralty no choice," he declared. "The Merseians are surely working that side of the street too."

"You hope I—we can get my uncle and the Skupshtina to stay their hands?" she asked.

"Yes," Flandry said. "This is a fast boat. However ... we'll be a month in transit, and Aycharaych & Co. have a long jump on us."

{The resident and his lady made her welcome at Thursday Landing. They advised her against taking her research to the Sea of Achan countries. Unrest was particularly bad there. Indeed, she and her Merseian—pardon, her xenosophont companion—would do best to avoid migratory societies in general. Could they not gather sufficient data among the sedentary and maritime Diomedeans?

Those were more intimate with modern civilization, more accustomed to dealing with offworlders, therefore doubtless more relevant to the problem which had caused her planetary government to send her here.

Striving to mask her nervousness, she met Commander Maspes and a few junior officers of the Imperial Naval Intelligence team that was investigating the disturbances. He was polite but curt. His attitude evidently influenced the younger men, who must settle for stock words and sidelong stares. Yes, Maspes said, it was common knowledge that humans were partly responsible for the revolutionary agitation and organization on this planet. Most Diomedeans believed they were Avalonians, working for Ythri. Some native rebels, caught and interrogated, said they had actually been told so by the agents themselves. And indeed the Alatanist mystique was a potent recruiter.... Yet how could a naïve native distinguish one kind of human from another? Maybe Ythri was being maligned.... He should say no more at the present stage. Had Donna Vymezal had a pleasant journey? What was the news at her home?

Lagard apologized that he must bar her from a wing of the Residency. "A team member, his work's confidential and—well, you are a civilian, you will be in the outback, and he's a xeno, distinctive appearance—"

Kossara smiled. "I can dog my hatch," she said; "but since you wish, I'll leash my curiosity." She gave the matter scant thought, amidst everything else.}

Flandry greeted her at breakfast: *"Dobar yutro, Dama."*

Startled, she asked, "You are learning Serbic?"

"As fast as operant conditioning, electronics, and the pharmacopoeia can cram it into me." He joined her at table. Orange juice shone above the cloth. Coffee made the air fragrant. He drank fast. She saw he was tired.

"I wondered why you are so seldom here when off duty," she said.

"That's the reason."

He gazed out at the stars. She considered him. After a while, during which her pulse accelerated, she said, "No. I mean, if you're studying, there is no need. You must know most of us speak Anglic. You need an excuse to avoid me."

It was his turn for surprise. "Eh? Why in cosmos would I that?"

She drew breath, feeling cheeks, throat, breasts redden. "You think I'm embarrassed at what you've learned of me."

"No—" He swung his look to her. "Yes. Not that I— Well, I try not to, and what comes out regardless shows you clean as a . . . knife blade— But of course you're full of life, you've been in love and—" Abruptly he flung his head back and laughed. "Oh, hellflash! I was afraid you *would* make me stammer like a schoolboy."

"I'm not angry. Haven't you saved me? Aren't you healing me?" She gathered resolution. "I did have to think hard, till I saw how nothing about me could surprise you."

"Oh, a lot could. Does." Their eyes met fully.

"Maybe you can equalize us a little," she said through a rising drumbeat. "Tell me of your own past, what you really are under that flexmail you always wear." She smiled. "In exchange, I can help you in your language lessons, and tell you stories about Dennitza that can't be in your records. The time has been lonely for me, Dominic."

"For us both," he said as though dazed.

Chives brought in an omelet and fresh-baked bread.

{From a dealer in Thursday Landing, Kossara rented an aircamper and field equipment, bought rations and guidebooks, requested advice. She needed information for its own sake as well as for cover. On the long voyage here—three changes of passenger-carrying freighter— —she had absorbed what material on Diomedes the Shkola in Zorkagrad could supply. That wasn't much. It could well have been zero if the planet weren't unusual enough to be used as an interest-grabbing example in certain classes. She learned scraps of astronomy, physics, chemistry, topology, meteorology, biology, ethnology, history, economics, politics; she acquired a few phrases in several different languages, no real grasp of their grammar or semantics; her knowledge was a twig to which she clung above the windy chasm of her ignorance about an entire world.

After a few days getting the feel of conditions, she and Trohdwyr flew to Lannach. The resident had not actually forbidden them. In the towns along Sagna Bay, they went among the gaunt high dwellings of the winged folk, seeking those who understood Anglic and might talk somewhat freely. "We are from a planet called Dennitza. We wish to find out how to make friends and stay friends with a people who resemble you—"

Eonan the factor proved helpful. Increasingly, Kossara tried to sound him out, and had an idea he was trying to do likewise to her. Whether or not he was involved in the subversive movement, he could well fear she came from Imperial Intelligence to entrap comrades of his. And yet the name "Dennitza" unmistakably excited more than one individual, quick though the Diomedeans were to hide that reaction.

How far Dennitza felt, drowned in alien constellations! At night in their camper, she and Trohdwyr would talk long and long about old days and future days at home; he would sing his gruff ychan songs to her, and she would recite the poems of Simich that he loved: until at last an inner peace came to them both, bearing its gift of sleep.}

Flandry always dressed for dinner. He liked being well turned out; it helped create an atmosphere which enhanced his appreciation of the food and wine; and Chives would raise polite hell if he didn't. Kossara slopped in wearing whatever she'd happened to don when she got out of bed. Not to mock her mourning, he settled for the blue tunic, red sash, white trousers, and soft half-boots that were a human officer's ordinary mess uniform.

When she entered the saloon in evening garb, he nearly dropped the cocktail pitcher. Amidst the subdued elegance around her, she suddenly outblazed a great blue star and multitudinously lacy nebula which dominated the viewscreen. Burgundy-hued velvyl sheathed each curve of her tallness, from low on the bosom to silvery slippers. A necklace of jet and turquoise, a bracelet of gold, gleamed against ivory skin. Diamond-studded tiara and crystal earrings framed the ruddy hair; but a few freckles across the snub nose redeemed that high-cheeked, full-mouthed, large-eyed face from queenliness.

"*Nom de Dieu!*" he gasped, and there sang through him, *Yes, God, Whom the believers say made all triumphant beauty. She breaks on me and takes me like a wave of sunlit surf.* "Woman, that's not fair! You should have sent a trumpeter to announce you."

She chuckled. "I decided it was past time I do Chives the courtesy of honoring his cuisine. He fitted me yesterday and promised to exceed himself in the galley."

Flandry shook head and clicked tongue. "Pity I won't be paying his dishes much attention." Underneath, he hurt for joy.

"You will. I know you, Dominic. And I will too." She pirouetted. "This gown is lovely, isn't it? Being a woman again—" The air sent him an insinuation of her perfume, while it lilted with violins.

"Then you feel recovered?"

"Yes." She sobered. "I felt strength coming back, the strength to be glad, more and more these past few days." A stride brought her to him. He had set the pitcher down. She took both his hands—the touch radiated through him—and said gravely: "Oh, I've not forgotten what happened, nor what may soon happen. But life is good. I want to celebrate its goodness ... with you, who brought me home to it. I can never rightly thank you for that, Dominic."

Nor can I rightly thank you for existing, Kossara. In spite of what she had let slip beneath the machine, she remained too mysterious for him to hazard kissing her. He took refuge: "Yes, you can. You can throw off your frontier steadfastness, foresight, common sense, devotion to principle, et cetera, and be frivolous. If you don't know how to frivol, watch me. Later you may disapprove to your heart's contempt, but tonight let's cast caution to the winds, give three-point-one-four-one-six cheers, and speak disrespectfully of the Lesser Magellanic Cloud."

Laughing, she released him. "Do you truly think we Dennitzans are so stiff? I'd call us quite jolly. Wait till you've been to a festival, or till I show you how to dance the luka."

"Why not now? Work up an appetite."

She shook her head. The tiara flung glitter which he noticed only peripherally because of her eyes. "No, I'd rip this dress, or else pop out of it like a cork. Our dances are all lively. Some people say they have to be."

"The prospect of watching you demonstrate makes me admit there's considerable to be said for an ice age."

Actually, the summers where she lived were warm. Farther south, the Pustinya desert was often hot. A planet is too big, too many-sided for a single idea like "glacial era" to encompass.

Through Flandry passed the facts he had read, a parched obbligato to the vividness breathing before him. He would not truly know her till he knew the land, sea, sky which had given her to creation; but the data were a beginning.

Zoria was an F8 sun, a third again as luminous as Sol. Dennitza, slightly smaller than Terra, orbiting at barely more than Terran distance from the primary, should have been warmer—and had been for most of its existence. Loss of water through ultraviolet cracking had brought about that just half the surface was ocean-covered. This, an axial tilt of 32½°, and an 18.8-hour rotation period led to extremes of weather and climate. Basically terrestroid, organisms adapted as they evolved in a diversity of environments.

That stood them in good stead when the catastrophe came. Less than a million years ago, a shower of giant meteoroids struck, or perhaps an asteroid shattered in the atmosphere. Whirled around the globe by enormous forces, the stones cratered dry land—devastated by impact, concussion, radiation, fire which followed—cast up dust which dimmed the sun for years afterward. Worse were the ocean strikes. The tsunamis they raised merely ruined every coast on the planet; life soon returned. But the thousands of cubic kilometers of water they evaporated became a cloud cover that endured for millennia. The energy balance shifted. Ice caps formed at the poles, grew, begot glaciers reaching halfway to the equator. Species, genera, families died; fossil beds left hints that among them had been a kind starting to make tools. New forms arose, winter-hardy in the temperate zones, desperately contentious in the tropics.

Then piece by piece the heavens cleared, sunlight grew brilliant again, glaciers melted back. The retreat of the ice that men found when they arrived, six hundred years later was a rout. The Great Spring brought woes of its own, storms, floods, massive extinctions and migrations to overthrow whole ecologies. In her own brief lifespan, Kossara had seen coastal towns abandoned before a rising sea.

Her birth country lay not far inland, though sheltered from northerly winds and easterly waters—the Kazan, Cauldron, huge astrobleme on the continent Rodna, a bowl filled with woods, farmlands, rivers, at its middle Lake Stoyan and the capital Zorkagrad. Her father was voivode of Dubina Dolyina province, named for the gorge that the Lyubisha River had cut through the ringwall on its way south from the dying snows. Thus she grew up child of a lord close to the people he guided, wilderness child who was often in town, knowing the stars both as other suns and as elven friends to lead her home after dark. . . .

Flandry took her arm. "Come, my lady," he said. "Be seated. This evening we shall not eat, we shall dine."

{At last Eonan told Kossara about a person in the mountain community Salmenbrok who could give her some useful tidings. If she liked, he would take her and Trohdwyr on his gravsled—he didn't trust her vehicle in these airs—and introduce them. More he would not yet say. They accepted eagerly.

Aloft he shifted course. "I bespoke one in Salmenbrok because I feared spies overhearing," he explained. "The truth is, they are four in a cave whom we will visit. I have asked them about you, and they will have you as guests while you explore each other's intents."

She thought in unease that when the Diomedean went back, she and her companion would be left flightless, having brought no gravbelts along. The ychan got the same realization and growled. She plucked up the nerve to shush him and say, "Fine."

The two men and two women she met were not her kind. Racial types, accents, manners, their very gaits belied it. Eonan talked to them and her passionately, as if they really were Dennitzans who had come to prepare the liberation of his folk. She bided in chill and tension, speaking little and nothing to contradict, until he departed. Then she turned on them and cried, "What's this about?" Her hand rested on her sidearm. Trohdwyr bulked close, ready to attack with pistol, knife, tail, foot-claws if they threatened her.

Steve Johnson smiled, spread empty fingers, and replied, "Of course you're puzzled. Please come inside where it's warmer and we'll tell you." The rest behaved in equally friendly wise.

Their story was simple in outline. They too were Imperial subjects, from Esperance. That planet wasn't immensely remote from here. True to its pacifistic tradition, it had stayed neutral during the succession fight, declaring it would pledge allegiance to whoever gave the Empire peace and law again. (Kossara nodded. She had heard of Esperance.) But this policy required a certain amount of armed might and a great deal of politicking and intriguing abroad, to prevent forcible recruitment by some or other pretender. The Esperancians thus got into the habit of taking a more active role than hitherto. Conditions remained sufficiently turbulent after Hans was crowned to keep the habit in tune.

When their Intelligence heard rumors of Ythrian attempts to foment revolution on Diomedes, their government was immediately concerned. Esperance was near the border of Empire and Domain. Agents were smuggled onto Diomedes to spy out the truth—discreetly, since God alone knew what the effect of premature revelations might be. Johnson's party was such a band.

"Predecessors of ours learned Dennitzans were responsible," he said. "Not Avalonian humans serving Ythri, but Dennitzan humans serving their war lord!"

"No!" Kossara interrupted, horrified. "That isn't true! And he's not a war lord!"

"It was what the natives claimed, Mademoiselle Vymezal," the Asian-looking woman said mildly. "We decided to try posing as Dennitzans. Our project had learned enough about the underground—names of various members, for instance—that it seemed possible, granted the autochthons couldn't spot the difference. Their reaction to us does indicate they ... well, they have reason to believe Dennitzans are sparking their movement. We've been, ah, leading them on, collecting information without actually helping them develop paramilitary capabilities. When Eonan told us an important Dennitzan had arrived, openly but with hints she could be more than a straightforward scientist—naturally, we grew interested."

"Well, you've been fooled," burst from Kossara. "I'm here to, to disprove those exact same charges against us. The Gospodar, our head of state, he's my uncle and he sent me as his personal agent. I should know, shouldn't I? And I tell you, he's loyal. *We* are!"

"Why doesn't he proclaim it?" Johnson asked.

"Oh, he is making official representations. But what are they worth? Across four hundred light-years— We need proof. We need to learn who's been blackening us and why." Kossara paused for a sad smile. "I don't pretend I can find out much. I'm here as a, a forerunner, a scout. Maybe that special Navy team working out of Thursday Landing—have you heard about them?—maybe they'll exonerate us without our doing anything. Maybe they already have. The commander didn't act suspicious of me."

Johnson patted her hand. "I believe you're honest, Mademoiselle," he said. "And you may well be correct, too. Let's exchange what we've discovered—and, in between, give you some outdoor recreation. You look space-worn."

The next three darkling springtime days were pleasant. Kossara and Trohdwyr stopped wearing weapons in the cave.}

Flandry sighed. "Aycharaych." He had told her something of his old antagonist. "Who else? Masks within masks, shadows that cast shadows ... Merseian operatives

137

Poul Anderson

posing as Esperancians posing as Dennitzans whose comrades had formerly posed as Avalonians, while other Merseian creatures are in fact the Terran personnel they claim
to be. . . . Yes, I'll bet my chance of a peaceful death that
Aycharaych is the engineer of the whole diablerie."

He drew on a cigarette, rolled acridity over his tongue
and streamed it out his nostrils, as if this mordant would
give reality a fast hold on him. He and she sat side by side
on a saloon bench. Before them was the table, where
stood glasses and a bottle of Demerara rum. Beyond was
the viewscreen, full of night and stars. They had left the
shining nebula behind; an unlit mass of cosmic dust reared
thunderhead tall across the Milky Way. The ship's clocks
declared the hour was late. Likewise did the silence
around, above the hum which had gone so deep into their
bones that they heard it no more.

Kossara wore a housedress whose brevity made him all
too aware of long legs, broad bosom, a vein lifting blue
from the dearest hollow that her shoulderbones made at
the base of her throat. She shivered a trifle and leaned
near him, unperfumed now except for a sunny odor of
woman. "Monstrous," she mumbled.

"N-no . . . well, I can't say." *Why do I defend him?*
Flandry wondered, and knew: *I see in my mirror the
specter of him. Though who of us is flesh and who image?*
"I'll admit I can't hate him, even for what he did to you
and will do to your whole people and mine if he can. I'll
kill him the instant I'm able, but— Hm, I suppose you
never saw or heard of a coral snake. It's venomous but
very beautiful, and strikes without malice. . . . Not that I
really know what drives Aycharaych. Maybe he's an artist
of overriding genius. That's a kind of monster, isn't it?"

She reached for her glass, withdrew her hand—she was
a light drinker—and gripped the table edge instead, till
the ends of her nails turned white. "Can such a labyrinth
of a scheme work? Aren't there hopelessly many chances
for something to go wrong?"

Flandry found solace in a return to pragmatics, regardless of what bitterness lay behind. "If the whole thing
collapses, Merseia hasn't lost much. Not Hans nor any
Emperor can make the Terran aristocrats give up their

138

A Knight of Ghosts and Shadows

luxuries—first and foremost, their credo that eventual
accommodation is possible—and go after the root of the
menace. He couldn't manage anything more than a note
of protest and perhaps the suspension of a few negotiations about trade and the like. His underlings would depose him before they allowed serious talk about singeing
the beard the Roidhun hasn't got."

His cigarette butt scorched his fingers. He tossed it
away and took a drink of his own. The piratical pungency
heartened him till he could speak in detachment, almost
amusement: "Any plotter must allow for his machine losing occasional nuts and bolts. You're an example. Your
likely fate as a slave was meant to outrage every man on
Dennitza when the news arrived there. By chance, I heard
about you in the well-known and deservedly popular nick
of time—I, not someone less cautious—"

"Less noble," She stroked his arm. It shone inside.

Nonetheless he grinned and said, "True, I may lack
scruples, but not warm blood. I'm a truncated romantic. A
mystery, a lovely girl, an exotic planet—could I resist hal-
looing off—"

It jarred through him: —off into whatever trap was
set by a person who knew me? His tongue went on.
"However, prudence, not virtue, was what made me careful to do nothing irrevocable" to you, darling; I praise the
Void that nothing irrevocable happened to you. "And we
did luck out, we did destroy the main Merseian wart on
Diomedes." Was the luck poor silly Susette and her husband's convenient absence? Otherwise I'd have stayed longer at Thursday Landing, playing sleuth—long enough to
give an assassin, who was expecting me specifically, a
chance at me.

No! This is fantastic! Forget it!

"Wasn't that a disaster to the enemy?" Kossara asked.

" 'Fraid not. I don't imagine they'll get their Diomedean
insurgency. But that's a minor disappointment. I'm sure
the whole operation was chiefly a means to the end of
maneuvering Terra into forcing Dennitza to revolt. And
those false clues have long since been planted and let
sprout; the false authoritative report has been filed; in

139

short, about as much damage has been done on the planet as they could reasonably expect."

Anguish: "Do you think . . . we will find civil war?"

He laid an arm around her. She leaned into the curve of it, against his side. "The Empire seldom bumbles fast," he comforted her. "Remember, Hans himself didn't want to move without more information. He saw no grounds for doubting the Maspes report—that Dennitzans were involved—but he realized they weren't necessarily the Gospodar's Dennitzans. That's why I got recruited, to check further. In addition, plain old bureaucratic inertia works in our favor. Yes, as far as the problems created on Diomedes are concerned, I'm pretty sure we'll get you home in time."

"Thanks to you, Dominic." Her murmur trembled. "To none but you."

He did not remind her that Diomedes was not, could never have been the only world on which the enemy had worked, and that events on Dennitza would not have been frozen. This was no moment for reminders, when she kissed him.

Her shyness in it made him afraid to pursue. But they sat together a spell, mute before the stars, until she bade him goodnight.

〔On the tundra far north of the Kazan, Bodin Miyatovich kept a hunting lodge. Thence he rode forth on horseback, hounds clamorous around him, in quest of gromatz, yegyupka, or ice troll. At other times he and his guests boated on wild waters, skied on glacier slopes, sat indoors by a giant hearthfire talking, drinking, playing chess, playing music, harking to blizzard winds outside. Since her father bore her cradle from aircar to door, Kossara had loved coming here.

Though this visit was harshly for business, she felt pleasure at what surrounded her. She and her uncle stood on a slate terrace that jutted blue-black from the granite blocks of the house. Zoria wheeled dazzling through cloudless heaven, ringed with sun dogs. Left, right, and rearward the land reached endless, red-purple mahovina turf, wide-spaced clumps of firebush and stands of windblown plume, here and there a pool ablink. Forward, growth yielded to tumbled boulders where water coursed. In these parts, the barrens were a mere strip; she could see the ice beyond them. Two kilometers high, its cliff stood over the horizon, a worldwall, at its distance not dusty white but shimmering, streaked with blue crevasses. The river which ran from its melting was still swift when it passed near the lodge, a deep brawl beneath the lonesome tone of wind, the remote cries of a sheerwing flock. The air was cold, dry, altogether pure. The fur lining of her parka hood was soft and tickly on her cheeks.

The big man beside her growled, "Yes, too many ears in Zorkagrad. Damnation! I thought if we put Molitor on the throne, we'd again know who was friend and who foe. But things only get more tangled. How many faithful are left? I can't tell. And that's fouler than men becoming outright turncoats."

"You trust me, don't you?" Kossara answered in pride.

"Yes," Miyatovich said. "I trust you beyond your fidelity. You're strong and quick-witted. And your xenological background . . . qualifies you and gives you a cover story . . . for a mission I hope you'll undertake."

"To Diomedes? My father's told me rumors."

"Worse. Accusations. Not public yet. I actually had bloody hard work finding out, myself, why Imperial Intelligence agents have been snooping amongst us in such numbers. I sent men to inquire elsewhere and— Well, the upshot is, the Impies know revolt is brewing on Diomedes and think Dennitzans are the yeast. The natural conclusion is that a cabal of mine sent them, to keep the Imperium amused while we prepare a revolt of our own."

"You've denied it, I'm sure."

"In a way. Nobody's overtly charged me. I've sent the Emperor a memorandum, deploring the affair and offering to cooperate in a full-dress investigation. But guilty or not, I'd do that. How to prove innocence? As thin as his corps is spread, we could mobilize—on desert planets, for instance, without positive clues for them to find."

The Gospodar gusted a sigh. "And appearances are against us. There *is* a lot of sentiment for independence, for turning this sector into a confederacy free of an Empire that failed us and wants to sap the strength we survived by. Those *could* be Dennitzans yonder, working for a faction who plot to get us committed—who'll overthrow me if they must—"

"I'm to go search out the truth if I can," she knew. "Uncle, I'm honored. But me alone? Won't that be like trying to catch water in a net?"

"Maybe. Though at the bare least, you can bring me back ... um ... a feel of what's going on, better than anybody else. And you may well do more. I've watched you from babyhood. You're abler than you think, Kossara."

Miyatovich took her by the shoulders. Breath smoked white from his mouth, leaving frost in his beard, as he spoke: "I've never had a harder task than this, asking you to put your life on the line. You're like a daughter to me. I sorrowed nearly as much as you did when Mihail died, but told myself you'd find another good man who'd give you sound children. Now I can only say—go in Mihail's name, that your next man needn't die in another war."

"Than you think we should stay in the Empire?"

"Yes. I've made remarks that suggested different. But you know me, how I talk rashly in anger but try to act in calm. The Empire would have to get so bad that chaos was better, before I'd willingly break it. Terra, the Troubles, or the tyranny of Merseia—and those racists wouldn't just subject us, they'd tame us—I don't believe we have a fourth choice, and I'll pick Terra."

She felt he was right.}

A part of the *Hooligan*'s hold had been converted to a gymnasium. Outbound, and at first on the flight from Diomedes, Flandry and Kossara used it at separate hours. Soon after her therapy commenced, she proposed they exercise together. "Absolutely!" he caroled. "It'll make calisthenics themselves fun, whether or not that violates the second law of thermodynamics."

In truth, it wasn't fun—when she was there in shorts and halter, sweat, laughter, herself—it was glory.

Halfway to Dennitza, he told her: "Let's end our psychosessions. You've regained everything you need. The rest would be detail, not worth further invasion of your privacy."

"No invasion," she said low. Her eyes dropped, her blood mounted. "You were welcome."

"Chives!" Flandry bellowed. "Get busy! Tonight we do not dine, we feast!"

"Very good, sir," the Shalmuan replied, appearing in the saloon as if his master had rubbed a lamp. "I suggest luncheon consist of a small salad and tea to drink."

"You're the boss," Flandry said. "Me, I can't sit still. How about a game of tennis, Kossara? Then after our rabbit repast we can snooze, in preparation for sitting up the whole nightwatch popping champagne."

She agreed eagerly. They changed into gym briefs and met below. The room was elastic matting, sunlamp fluorescence, gray-painted metal sides. In its bareness, she flamed.

The ball thudded back and forth, caromed, bounced, made them leap, for half an hour. At last, panting, they called time out and sought a water tap.

"Do you feel well?" She sounded anxious. "You missed an awful lot of serves." They were closely matched, her youth against his muscles.

"If I felt any better, you could turn off the ship's powerplant and hook me into the circuits," he replied.

"But why—?"

"I was distracted." He wiped the back of a hand across the salt dampness in his mustache, ran those fingers through his hair and recalled how it was turning gray. Decision came. He prepared a light tone before going on: "Kossara, you're a beautiful woman, and not just because you're the only woman for quite a few light-years around. Never fear, I can mind my manners. But I hope it won't bother you overmuch if I keep looking your way."

She stood quiet awhile, except for the rise and fall of her breasts. Her skin gleamed. A lock of hair clung bronzy to her right cheekbone. The beryl eyes gazed beyond him.

Suddenly they returned, focused, met his as sabers meet in a fencing match between near friends. Her husky voice grew hoarse and, without her noticing, stammered Serbic: "Do you mean—Dominic, do you mean you never learned, while I was under . . . I love you?"

Meteorstruck, he heard himself croak, "No. I did try to avoid—as far as possible, I let Chives question you, in my absence—"

"I resisted," she said in wonder, "because I knew you would be kind but dared not imagine you might be for always."

"I'd lost hope of getting anybody who'd make me want to be."

She came to him.

Presently: "Dominic, darling, please, no. Not yet."

"—Do you want a marriage ceremony first?"

"Yes. If you don't mind too much. I know you don't care, but, well, did you know I still say my prayers every night? Does that make you laugh?"

"Never. All right, we'll be married, and in style!"

"Could we really be? In St. Clement's Cathedral, by Father Smed who christened and confirmed me—?"

"If he's game, I am. It won't be easy, waiting, but how can I refuse a wish of yours? Forgive these hands. They're not used to holding something sacred."

"Dominic, you star-fool, stop babbling! Do you think it will be easy for me?"

XIII

The earliest signs of trouble reached them faintly across distance. Fifty astronomical units from Zoria and well off the ecliptic plane, the *Hooligan* phased out of hyperdrive into normal state. Engines idle, she drifted at low kinetic velocity among stars, her destination sun only the brightest; and instruments strained after traces.

Flandry took readings and made computations. His lips tightened. "A substantial space fleet, including what's got to be a Nova-class dreadnaught," he told Kossara and Chives. "In orbits or under accelerations that fit the pattern of a battle-ready naval force."

The girl clenched her fists. "What can have happened?"

"We'll sneak in and eavesdrop."

Faster-than-light pseudospeed would give them away to detectors. (Their Schrödinger "wake" must already have registered, but no commander was likely to order interception of a single small vessel which he could assume would proceed until routinely checked by a picket craft.) However, in these far regions they could drive hard on force-thrust without anybody observing or wondering why. Nearing the inner system, where ships and meters were thick, Flandry plotted a roundabout course. It brought him in behind the jovian planet Svarog, whose gravitational, magnetic, and radiation fields screened the emissions of *Hooligan*. Amidst all fears for home and kin, Kossara exclaimed at the majestic sight as they passed within three million kilometers—amber-glowing disc, swarming moons—and at the neatness wherewith the planet swung them, their power again turned off, into the orbit Flandry wanted, between its own and that of Perun to sunward.

145

"With every system aboard at zero or minimum, we should pass for a rock if a radar or whatever sweeps us," he explained. "And we'll catch transmissions from Dennitza—maybe intercept a few messages between ships, though I expect those'll be pretty boring."

"How I hope you are right," Kossara said with a forlorn chuckle.

He regarded her, beside him in the control cabin. Interior illumination was doused, heating, weight generator, anything which might betray. They hung loosely harnessed in their seats, bodies if not minds enjoying the fantasy state of free fall. As yet, cold was no more than a nip in the air Chives kept circulating by a creaky hand-cranked fan. Against the clear canopy, stars crowned her head. On the opposite side, still small at this remove, Zoria blazed between outspread wings of zodiacal light.

"They're definitely Technic warcraft," he said, while wishing to speak her praises. "The neutrino patterns alone prove it. From what we've now learned, closer in, about their numbers and types, they seem to match your description of the Dennitzan fleet, though there're some I think must belong to the Imperium. My guess is, the Gospodar has gathered Dennitza's own in entirety, plus such units of the regular Navy as he felt he could rely on. In short, he's reached a dangerous brink, though I don't believe anything catastrophic has happened yet."

"We are in time, then?" she asked gladly.

He could not but lean over and kiss her. "Luck willing, yes. We may need patience before we're certain."

Fortune spared them that. Within an hour, they received the basic information. Transmitters on Dennitza sent broadbeam rather than precisely lased 'casts to the telsats for relay, wasting some cheap energy to avoid the cost of building and maintaining a more exact system. By the time the pulses got as far as *Hooligan*, their dispersal guaranteed they would touch her; and they were not too weak for a good receiver-amplifier-analyzer to reconstruct a signal. The windfall program Flandry tuned in was a well-organized commentary on the background of the crisis.

It broke two weeks ago. *(Maybe just when Kossara and*

I found out about each other? he wondered. *No; meaningless; simultaneity doesn't exist for interstellar distances.*) Before a tumultuous parliament, Bodin Miyatovich announced full mobilization of the Narodna Voyska, recall of units from outsystem duty, his directing the Imperial Navy command for Tauria to maintain the Pax within the sector, his ordering specific ships and flotillas belonging to it to report here for assignment, and his placing Dennitzan society on a standby war footing.

A replay from his speech showed him at the wooden lectern, carved with vines and leaves beneath outward-sweeping yelen horns, from which Gospodar had addressed Skupshtina since the days of the Founders. In the gray tunic and red cloak of a militia officer, knife and pistol on hips, he appeared still larger than he was. His words boomed across crowded tiers in the great stone hall, seemed almost to make the stained-glass windows shiver.

"—Intelligence reports have grown more and more disquieting over the past few months. I can here tell you little beyond this naked fact—you will understand the need not to compromise sources—but our General Staff takes as grave a view of the news as I do. Scouts dispatched into the Roidhunate have brought back data on Merseian naval movements which indicate preparations for action. . . . Diplomatic inquiries both official and unofficial have gotten only assurances for response, unproved and vaguely phrased. After centuries, we know what Merseian assurances are worth. . . .

"Thus far I have no reply to my latest message to the Emperor, and can't tell if my courier has even caught up with him on the Spican frontier. . . . High Terran authorities whom I've been able to contact have denied there is a Merseian danger at the present time. They've challenged the validity of the information given me, have insisted their own is different and is correct. . . .

"They question our motives. Fleet Admiral Sandberg told me to my face, when I visited his command post, he believes our government has manufactured an excuse to marshal strength, not against foreign enemies but against the Imperium. He cited charges of treasonous Dennitzan activity elsewhere in the Empire. He forbade me to act.

Poul Anderson

When I reminded him that I am the sector viceroy, he declared he would see about getting me removed. I think he would have had me arrested then and there"—a bleak half-smile—"if I'd not taken the precaution of bringing along more firepower than he had on hand. . . .

"He revealed my niece, Kossara Vymezal, whom I sent forth to track down the origin of those lies—he claimed she'd been caught at subversion, had confessed under their damnable mind-twisting interrogation—I asked why I was not informed at once, I demanded she be brought home, and learned—" He smote the lectern. Tears burst from his eyes. "She has been sold for a slave on Terra."

The assembly roared.

"Uyak Bodin, *Uyak* Bodin," Kossara herself wept. She lifted her hands to the screen as if to try touching him.

"Sssh," Flandry said. "This is past, remember. We've got to find out what's happening today and what brought it on."

She gulped, mastered her sobs, and gave him cool help. He had a fair grasp of Serbic, and the news analyst was competent, but as always, much was taken for granted of which a stranger was ignorant.

Ostensibly the Merseian trouble sprang from incidents accumulated and ongoing in the Wilderness. Disputes between traders, prospectors, and voortrekkers from the two realms had repeatedly brought on armed clashes. Dennitzans didn't react to overbearingness as meekly as citizens of the inner Empire were wont to. They overbore right back, or took the initiative from the beginning. Several actions were doubtless in a legal sense piracy by crews of one side or the other. Matters had sharpened during the civil war, when there was no effective Imperial control over humans.

Flandry had known about this, and known too that the Roidhunate had asked for negotiations aimed at solving the problem, negotiations to which Emperor Hans agreed on the principle that law and order were always worth establishing even with the cooperation of an enemy. The delegates had wrangled for months.

In recent weeks Merseia had changed its tack and made totally unacceptable demands—for example, that civilian

148

craft must be cleared by its inspectors before entering the Wilderness. "They know that's ridiculous," Flandry remarked. "Without fail, in politics that kind of claim has an ulterior purpose. It may be as little as a propaganda ploy for domestic consumption, or as much as the spark put to a bomb fuse."

"A reason to bring their strength to bear—while most of the Empire's is tied up at Spica—and maybe denounce the Covenant of Alfzar and occupy a key system in the Wilderness?" Kossara wondered.

"Could be . . . *if* Merseia is dispatching warships in this direction," Flandry said. "The Imperium thinks not—thinks Dennitza concocted the whole business to justify mobilization. The Merseians would've been delighted to co-conspire, a behind-the-scenes arrangement with your uncle whereby they play intransigent at the conference. Any split among us is pure gain for them. From the Imperium's viewpoint, Dennitza has done this either to put pressure on it—to get the disbanding decree rescinded and other grievances settled—or else to start an out-and-out rebellion."

He puffed on his cigarette, latest of a chain. "From your uncle's viewpoint—I assume he was honest with you about his opinions and desires—if he believes Merseia may be readying for combat, he dare not fail to respond. Terra can think in terms of settling border disputes by negotiation, even after several battles. Dennitza, though, will be under attack. A tough, proud people won't sit still for being made pawns of. And given the accusations against them, the horrible word about you—how alienated must they not feel?"

The commentator had said: "Is it possible the connivance is between Emperor and Roidhun? Might part of a secret bargain be that Merseia rids the Imperium of troublesomely independent subjects? It would like to destroy us. To it, we are worse than a nuisance, we are the potential igniters of a new spirit within the Empire, whose future leadership may actually come from among us. On the Terran side, the shock of such an event would tend to unite the Empire behind the present bearer of the crown, securing it for him and his posterity. . . ."

Flandry said: "I'm pretty sure that by now, throughout the Dennitzan sphere of influence, a majority favors revolution. The Gospodar's stalling, trying to bide his time in hopes the crisis will slack off before fighting starts. Wouldn't you guess so, love? I suspect, however, if it turns out he doesn't have to resist Merseia, he will then use his assembled power to try squeezing concessions from Terra. His citizens won't let him abstain—and I doubt if he wants to. And . . . any wrong action on the part of the Imperium or its Navy, or any wrong inaction, anywhere along the line, will touch off rebellion."

"We'll go straight to him—" she began.

Flandry shook his head. "Uh-uh. Most reckless thing we could do. Who supplied those Intelligence reports that scared Miyatovich and his staff—reports contradicted by findings of my Corps in separate operations? If the Merseian fleet is making ominous motions, is this a mere show for the Dennitzan scouts they knew would sneak into their space? How did the news about you get here so speedily, when the sale of one obscure slave never rated a word on any Terran newscast? Could barbarian activity in Sector Spica have been encouraged from outside, precisely to draw the Emperor there and leave his officers on this frontier to respond as awkwardly as they've done?"

He sighed. "Masks and mirages again, Kossara. The program we heard showed us only the skin across the situation. We can't tell what's underneath, except that it's surely explosive, probably poisonous. Zorkagrad must be acrawl with Merseian undercover men. I'd be astonished if some of them aren't high and trusted in the Gospodar's councils, fending off any information they prefer he doesn't get. Aycharaych's been at work for a long time."

"What shall we do?" she asked steadily.

Flandry's glance sought for Dennitza. It should be visible here, soft blue against black. But the brightnesses which burned were too many. "Suppose you and I pay a covert visit on your parents," he said. "From there we can send a household servant, seemingly on an ordinary errand, who can find a chance to slip your uncle a word. Meanwhile Chives lands at Zorkagrad port and takes quarters to be our contact in the city. Shalmuan spacers

150

aren't common but they do exist—not that the average person hereabouts ever heard of Shalmu—and I'll modify one of our spare documentations to support his story of being an innocent entrepreneur just back from a long exploration, out of touch, in the Wilderness."

"It seems terribly roundabout," Kossara said.

"Everything is on this mission."

She smiled. "Well, you have the experience, Dominic. And it will give us a little time alone together."

● XIV ●

First the planet loomed immense in heaven, clouds and ice lending it a more than Terran whiteness against which the glimpsed oceans became a dazzlingly deep azure. Then it was no longer ahead, it was land and sea far below. When Flandry and Kossara bailed out, it became a roar of night winds.

They rode their gravbelts down as fast as they dared, while the *Hooligan* vanished southward. The chance of their being detected was maybe slight, but not nonexistent. They need have no great fear of being shot at; as a folk who lived with firearms, the Dennitzans were not trigger-happy. However, two who arrived like this, in time of emergency, would be detained, and the matter reported to military headquarters. Hence Kossara had proposed descending on the unpeopled taiga north of the Kazan. The voivode of Dubina Dolyina must have patrols and instruments active throughout his district.

Even at their present distance from it, she and Flandry could not have left the vessel secretly in an aircraft. The captain of the picket ship which contacted Chives had settled for a telecom inspection of his papers, without boarding, and had cleared him for a path through atmosphere which was a reasonable one in view of his kinetic vector. Yet orbital optics and electronics must be keeping close watch until ground-based equipment could take over.

Hoar in moonlight, treetops rushed upward. The forest was not dense, though, and impact quickly thudded through soles. At once the humans removed their space-suits, stopping only for a kiss when heads emerged from helmets. Flandry used a trenching tool to bury the outfits while Kossara restowed their packs. In outdoor coveralls

152

and hiking boots, they should pass for a couple who had spent a furlough on a trip afoot. Before they established camp for what remained of the night, they'd better get several kilometers clear of any evidence to the contrary.

Flandry bowed. "Now we're down, I'm in your hands," he said. "I can scarcely imagine a nicer place to be."

Kossara looked around, filled her lungs full of chill sweet-scented air, breathed out, *"Domovina"*—home— and began striding.

The ground was soft and springy underfoot, mahovina turf and woodland duff. A gravity seven percent less than Terran eased the burden on backs. Trees stood three or four meters apart, low, gnarly, branches plumed blue-black, an equivalent of evergreens. Shrubs grew in between, but there was no real underbrush; moonlight and shadow dappled open sod. A full Mesyatz turned the sky nearly violet, leaving few stars and sheening off a great halo. Smaller but closer in than Luna, it looked much the same save for brilliance and haste. No matter countless differences, the entire scene had a familiarity eerie and wistful, as if the ghosts of mammoth hunters remembered an age when Terra too was innocent.

"Austere but lovely," the man said into silence. His breath smoked, though the season, late summer, brought no deep cold. "Like you. Tell me, what do Dennitzans see in the markings on their moon? Terrans usually find a face in theirs."

"Why . . . our humans call the pattern an orlik. That's a winged theroid; this planet has no ornithoids." A sad smile flickered over Kossara's night-ivory lips. "But I've oftener thought of it as Ri. He's the hero of some funny ychan fairy tales, who went to live on Mesyatz. I used to beg Trohdwyr for stories about Ri when I was a child. Why do you ask?"

"Hoping to learn more about you and yours. We talked a lot in space, but we've our lifetimes, and six hundred years before them, to explain if we can."

"We'll have the rest of them for that." She crossed herself. "If God wills."

They were laconic thereafter, until they had chosen a sleeping place and spread their bags. By then the crater wall showed dream-blue to south, and the short night of the planet was near an end. Rime glimmered. Flandry went behind a tree to change into pajamas. When he came back, Kossara was doing so. "I'm sorry!" he apologized, and wheeled about. "I forgot you'd say prayers."

She was quiet an instant before she laughed, unsteadily but honestly. "I was forgetful too. Well, look if you wish, darling. What harm? You must have . seen the holograms. . . ." She lifted her arms and made a slow turn before his eyes. "Do you like what you're getting?"

"Sun and stars—"

She stopped to regard him, as if unaware of chill. He barely heard her: "Would it be wrong? Here in these clean spaces, under heaven?"

He took a step in her direction, halted, and grinned his most rueful. "It would not be very practical, I'm afraid. You deserve better."

She sighed. "You are too kind to me, Dominic." She put on her bedclothes. They kissed more carefully than had been their way of late, and got into the bags that lay side by side in the heavy shadow of a furbark tree.

"I'm not sleepy," she told him after a few minutes.

"How could I be?" he answered.

"Was I wanton just now? Or unfair? That would be much worse."

"I was the Fabian this time, not you."

"The what? . . . Never mind." She lay watching the final stars and the first silvery flush before daybreak. Her voice stumbled. "Yes, I must explain. You could have had me if you'd touched me with a fingertip. You can whenever you ask, beloved. Chastity is harder than I thought."

"But it does mean a great deal to you, doesn't it? You're young and eager. I can wait awhile."

"Yes—I suppose that is part of what I feel, the wanting to know—to know you. You've had many women, haven't you? I'm afraid there's no mystery left for me to offer."

"On the contrary," he said, "you have the greatest of all. What's it like to be really man and *wife?* I think you'll teach me more about that than I can teach you about anything else."

She was mute until she could muster the shy words: "Why have you never married, Dominic?"

"Nobody came along whom I couldn't be happy without —what passes for happy in an Imperial Terran."

"Nobody? Out of hundreds to choose from?"

"You exaggerate. . . . Well, once, many years ago. But she was another man's, and left with him when he had to flee the Empire. I can only hope they found a good home at some star too far away for us to see from here."

"And you have longed for her ever since?"

"No, I can't say that I have in any romantic sense, though you are a lot like her." Flandry hesitated. "Earlier, I'd gotten a different woman angry at me. She had a peculiar psionic power, not telepathy but—beings tended to do what she desired. She wished on me that I never get the one I wanted in my heart. I'm not superstitious, I take no more stock in curses or spooks than I do in the beneficence of governments. Still, an unconscious compulsion— Bah! If there was any such thing, which I positively do not think, then you've lifted it off me, Kossara, and I refuse to pursue this morbid subject when I could be chattering about how beautiful you are."

At glaciation's midwinter, a colter of ice opened a gap in the Kazan ringwall. Melt-begotten, the Lyubisha River later enlarged this to a canyon. Weathering of mostly soft crater material lowered and blurred the heights. But Flandry found his third campsite enchanting.

He squatted on a narrow beach. Before him flowed the broad brown stream, quiet except where it chuckled around a boulder or a sandbar near its banks. Beyond, and at his back, the gorge rose in braes, bluffs, coombs where brooks flashed and sang, to ocherous palisades maned with forest. The same deep bluish-green and plum-colored leaves covered the lower slopes, borne on trees which grew taller than the taiga granted. Here and there, stone outcrops thrust them aside to make room for wild-flower-studded glades. A mild breeze, full of growth and soil odors, rustled through the woods till light and shadow danced. That light slanted from a sun a third again as bright as Sol is to Terra, ardent rather than harsh, an evoker of infinite hues.

Guslars trilled on boughs, other wings flew over in their hundreds, a herd of yelen led by a marvelously horned bull passed along the opposite shore, a riba hooked from the water sputtered in Flandry's frying pan while a heap of cloud apples waited to be dessert—no dismally predictable field rations in this meal. He gestured. "How well a planet does if left to its own devices," he remarked.

"Nature could take a few billion years for R & D," Kossara pointed out. "We mortals are always in a hurry."

He gave her a sharp look. "Is something wrong?" she asked.

"N-no. You echoed an idea I've heard before—coincidence, surely." He relaxed, threw a couple of sticks on the fire, turned the fillets over. "I am surprised your people haven't long since trampled this area dead. Such restraint seems downright inhuman."

"Well, the Dolyina has belonged to the Vymezals from olden time, and without forbidding visitors, we've never encouraged them. You've seen there are no amenities, and we ban vehicles. Besides, it's less reachable than many wild lands elsewhere—though most of those are more closely controlled."

Kossara hugged knees to chin. Her tone grew slow and thoughtful. 'We Dennitzans are ... are conservationists by tradition. For generations after the Founding, our ancestors had to take great care. They could not live entirely off native life, but what they brought in could too easily ruin the whole little-understood ecology. The ... *zemly-oradnik* ... the landsman learned reverence for the land, because otherwise he might not survive. Today we could, uh, get away with more; and in some parts of the planet we do, where the new industries are. Even there, law and public opinion enforce carefulness—yes, even Dennitzans who live in neighboring systems, the majority by now, even they generally frown on bad practices. And as for the Kazan, the cradle of mankind out here, haven't heartlands often in history kept old ways that the outer dominions forgot?"

Flandry nodded. "I daresay it helps that wealth flows in

from outside, to support your barons and yeomen in the style to which they are accustomed." He patted her hand. "No offense, darling. They're obviously progressive as well as conservative, and less apt than most people to confuse the two. I don't believe in Arcadian utopias, if only because any that might appear would shortly be gobbled up by somebody else. But I do think you here have kept a balance, a kind of inner sanity—or found it anew—long after Terra lost it."

She smiled. "I suspect you're prejudiced."

"Of course. Common sense dictates acquiring a good strong prejudice in favor of the people you're going to live among."

Her eyes widened. She unfolded herself, leaned on her knuckles toward him, and cried, "Do you mean you'll stay?"

"Wouldn't you prefer that?"

"Yes, yes. But I'd taken for granted—you're a Terran —where you go, I go."

Flandry said straight to her flushed countenance: "At the very least, I'd expect us to spend considerable time on Dennitza. Then why not all, or most? I can wangle a permanent posting if events work out well. Otherwise I'll resign my commission."

"Can you really settle down to a squire's life, a stormbird like you?"

He laughed and chucked her under the chin. "Never fear. I don't imagine you're ambitious either to rise every dawn, hog the slops, corn the shuck, and for excitement discuss with your neighbors the scandalous behavior of Uncle Vanya when he lurched through the village, red-eyed and reeling from liter after liter of buttermilk. No, we'll make a topnotch team for xenology, and for Intelligence when need arises." Soberly: "Need will keep arising."

Graveness took her too. "Imagine the worst, Dominic. Civil war again, Dennitza against Terra."

"I think then the two of us could best be messengers between Emperor and Gospodar. And if Dennitza does tear loose ... it still won't be the enemy. It'll still deserve whatever we can do to help it survive. I'm not that fond of Terra anyway. Here is much more hope."

Flandry broke off. "Enough," he said. "We've had our minimum adult daily requirement of apocalypse, and dinner grows impatient."

The Vymezal estate lay sufficiently far inside the crater that the ringwall cut off little sky—but on high ground just the same, to overlook the river and great reaches of farm and forest. Conducted from an outer gate, on a driveway which curved through gardens and parkscape, Flandry saw first the tile roof of the manor above shading trees, then its half-timbered brick bulk, at last its outbuildings. Situated around a rear court, they made a complete hamlet: servants' cottages, garages, sheds, stables, kennels, mews, workshops, bakery, brewery, armory, recreation hall, school, chapel. For centuries the demesne must have brawled with life.

On this day it felt more silent and deserted than it was. While many of the younger adults were gone to their militia units, many folk of every other age remained. Most of them, though, went about their tasks curt-spoken; chatter, japes, laughter, song or whistling were so rare as to resound ghostly between walls; energy turned inward on itself and became tension. Dogs snuffed the air and walked stiff-legged, ready to growl.

At a portico, the gamekeeper who accompanied Flandry explained to a sentry: "We met this fellow on the riverside lumber road. He won't talk except to insist he has to see the voivode alone. How he got here unbeknownst I couldn't well guess. He *claims* he's friendly."

The soldier used an intercom. Flandry offered cigarettes around. Both men looked tempted but refused. "Why not?" he asked. "They aren't drugged. Nothing awful has happened since mobilization, right?" Radio news received on his minicom had been meager during the seven planetary days of march; entering inhabited country, he and Kossara had shunned its dwellers.

"We haven't been told," the ranger grated. "Nobody tells us a thing. They must be waiting—for what?"

"I'm lately back from an errand in the city," the

guardsman added. "I heard, over and over— Well, can we trust those Impies the Gospodar called in along with our own ships? Why did he? If we've got to fight Terra, what keeps them from turning on us, right here in the Zorian System? They sure throw their weight around in town. What're you up to, Impie?"

A voice from the loudspeaker ended the exchange. Danilo Vymezal would see the stranger as requested. Let him be brought under armed escort to the Gray Chamber.

Darkly wainscoted and heavily furnished like most of the interior, smaller than average, that room must draw its name from rugs and drapes. An open window let in cool air, a glimpse of sunlight golden through the wings of a hovering chiropteroid. Kossara's father stood beside, arms folded, big in the embroidered, high-collared shirt and baggy trousers of his home territory. She resembled her uncle more, doubtless through her mother, but Flandry found traces of her in those weather-darkened craggy features. Her gaze could be as stern.

"*Zdravo, stranac,*" Vymezal said, formal greeting, tone barely polite. "I am he you seek, voivode and nachalnik." Local aristocrat by inheritance, provincial governor by choice of Gospodar and popular assembly. "Who are you and what is your business?"

"Are we safe from eavesdroppers, sir?" Flandry responded.

"None here would betray." Scorn: "This isn't Zorkagrad, let alone Archopolis."

"Nevertheless, you don't want some well-intentioned retainer shouting forth what I'll say. Believe me, you don't."

Vymezal studied Flandry for seconds. A little wariness left him, a little eagerness came in. "Yes, we are safe. Three floors aloft, double-thick door, for hearing confidences." A haunted smile touched his lips. "A cook who wants me to get the father of her child to marry her has as much right to privacy as an admiral discussing plans for regional defense. Speak."

The Terran gave his name and rank. "My first news— your daughter Kossara is unharmed. I've brought her back."

Vymezal croaked a word that might be oath or prayer, and caught a table to brace himself.

He rallied fast. The next half-hour was furiously paced talk, while neither man sat down.

Flandry's immediate declaration was simple. He and the girl lacked accurate knowledge of how matters stood, of what might happen if her return was announced. She waited in the woods for him to fetch her, or guide Vymezal to her, depending on what was decided. Flandry favored the latter course—the voivode only, and a secret word to the Gospodar.

He must spell out his reasons for that at length. Finally the Dennitzan nodded. "Aye," he growled. "I hate to keep the tidings from her mother ... from all who love her ... but if she truly is witness to a galaxy-sized trick played on us—we'll need care, oh, very great care"—he clapped hand on sidearm—"till we're ready to kill those vermin."

"Then you agree Zorkagrad, the planet's government and armed service, must be infested with them?"

"Yes." Vymezal gnawed his mustache. "If things are as you say—you realize I'll see Kossara first, out of your earshot, Captain—but I've small doubt you're honest. The story meshes too well with too much else. Why is our crisis hanging fire? Why— Ha, no more gabble. Tomorrow dawn I'll send ... him, yes, Milosh Tesar, he's trusty, quick of wit and slow of mouth—I'll send him on a 'family matter' as you suggest. Let me see ... my wife's dowry includes property wherein her brother also has an interest—something like that."

"Kossara will have to lie low," Flandry reminded. "Me too. You can call me an Imperial officer who stopped off on his liberty to give you a minor message. Nobody will think or talk much about that. But you'd better squirrel me away."

" 'Squirrel'?" Vymezal dismissed the question. "I understand. Well, I've a cabin in the Northrim, stocked and equipped for times when I want to be unpestered a while. Includes a car. I'll flit you there, telling the household I'm lending it to you. They can't see us land at Kossara's hideout, can they?"

"No. We foresaw—" Flandry stopped, aware of how intent the stare was upon him. "Sir, I've told you she and I aim to get married."

"And aren't yet—and nobody wants a hedge-wedding, not I myself when I don't know you." The voivode sketched a grin. "Thanks, Captain. But if you've told me truth, she needs a marksman more than a chaperone. Anyhow, whatever's between you two must already have happened or not happened. Come, let's go."

● XV ●

The year wanes rapidly on Dennitza. On the morning after Danilo Vymezal had shaken Flandry's hand, kissed Kossara's brow, and left them, they woke to frost on the windows and icy clearness outside. They spent much of the day scrambling around wooded steeps begun to flaunt hues that recalled fall upon ancient Manhome. Flocks of southbound yegyupka made heaven clangorous. Once they heard the cry of a vilya, and savage though the beast was, its voice sang wonderfully sweet. Firebush, spontaneously burning to ripen and scatter its seeds, spread faint pungency through the air. By a waterfall whose spray stung their skins with cold, they gathered feral walnuts. Regardless of what spun around the world beyond its frail blue roof, they often laughed like children.

At dusk they returned to the log building, cooked dinner together, sated huge appetites, and took brandy-laced coffee to the hearth, where they settled down on a shaggy rug, content to let the blaze they had kindled light the room for them. Red flames crackled jokelets of green and blue and yellow, sent warmth in waves, made shadows leap. The humans looked at each other, at the fire, back again, and talked about their tomorrows.

"—we'd better stay around the house hereafter," Flandry said. "Your father's man could scarcely have gotten an appointment today, but he should soon. Your uncle's aides can't all be traitors, assuming I'm right that some are. Two or three, in critical posts, are the most I'd guess possible. And they themselves will see no reason to stall his brother-in-law's personal business. In fact, that'd look too queer. So I expect we'll get word shortly; and Miyatovich may want us to move fast."

162

Highlights crossed Kossara's face above her cheekbones, shone in eyes, glowed in hair. "What do you think he'll do, Dominic?"

"Well, he's tough, smart, and experienced; he may have better ideas than I. But in his place, I'd manufacture an excuse to put myself somewhere more or less impregnable. Like your Nova-class warship; she's the biggest around, Dennitzan or Imperial, and the pride of your fleet damn well ought to have a solidly loyal crew. I'd get the most important persons, including us, there with me. And, oh, yes, a copy of the microfiles on everybody who might be involved in the plot, Imperial officers and locals who've worked themselves close to the Gospodar's hand in the past several years. A clever, widely traveled captain of Naval Intelligence, such as—ahem—could help me get a shrewd notion of whom to suspect. I'd order fleet dispositions modified accordingly, again on an unalarming pretext. When this was done, I'd have the appropriate arrests made, then broadcast a 'hold everything' to the populace, then wait on the *qui vive* to see what the interrogators dig out."

Memory made Kossara wince. Flandry laid an arm about her shoulder. "We've a stiff way yet to go," he said, "but we should be home safe by blossom time."

She thawed, flowed into his embrace, and whispered, "Thanks to you."

"No, you. If you'd lacked courage to visit Diomedes, the strength to stay sane and fight on— Why quibble? We're both magnificent. The species has need of our chromosomes."

"Lots and lots of fat babies," she agreed. "But do you mean it about spring . . . we may have to wait that long?"

"I hope not. The creaking sound you hear is my gentlemanliness. I'm sitting on its safety valve, which is blistering hot."

She touched a corner of his smile. Her own look became wholly serious. "Are your jests always armor?" The question trembled. "Dominic, we may not live till spring."

"We'll take no chances, heart of mine. None. I plan for us to scandalize our respectable grandchildren."

"We'll have to take chances." She drew breath. "I can't

163

become pregnant till my immunity treatment's reversed. Tonight— We'll not deceive Father and Mother. The first chaplain we find can marry us."

"But, uh, your cathedral wedding—"

"I've come to see how little it matters, how little the universe does, next to having you while I can. Tonight, Dominic. Now."

He seized her to him.

A flash went blue-white in the front windows.

They sprang up. The light had not been blinding, but they knew its color.

Flandry flung the door wide and himself out onto the porch. Cold poured over him, sharp liquid in his nostrils. Stars glinted countless. Between shadow-masses that were trees, he saw the craterside shelve away downward into the murk which brimmed its bowl. Distance-dwindled, a fireball yonder lifted and faded. The cloud pillar following appeared against a constellation just as the thunder rumbled faintly in his skull.

"That was home," Kossara said out of numbness.

"A tactical nuke, doubtless fired from an aircraft," responded a machine within Flandry.

The danger to her flogged him aware. He grabbed her arm. "Inside!" She staggered after him. He slammed the door and drew her against his breast. She clung, beginning to shudder.

"My love, my love, my love, we've got to get away from here," he said in a frantic chant. "They must have been after us."

"After you—" She tautened, freed herself, snapped at steadiness and caught it. Her eyes gleamed steel-dry. "Yes. But we'll take a few minutes to pack. Food, clothes, weapons."

Defiant, he also tried phoning the manor. Emptiness hummed reply. They trotted to the shed where the car was, stowed survival gear within, trotted back for more, boarded.

The cabin tumbled from sight. Flandry swept radar around the encompassing darkness. Nothing registered. A traffic safety unit wasn't much use here, of course, but at least this bubble carrying them had a prayer of crawling to safety before the military vessel that did the murder could find it.

If— "Wait a second," Flandry said.

"What?" Kossara asked dully.

He glanced at her, dim in star-glow and wanness off the control panel. She sat hunched into her parka, staring ahead through the canopy. The heater had not yet taken hold and the chill here was no honest outside freeze, but dank. Air muttered around the car body.

He dropped near treetop level and activated the optical amplifier. Its screen showed the wilderness as a gray jumble, above which he zigzagged in search of a secure hiding place. Though belike they had no immediate need of any— "I'll take for granted we were a principal target," he said, quick and toneless. "Snatching us from the household would be too revealing. But if the killers knew where we were, why not come directly to our lodge? If they even suspected we might be there, why not try it first? My guess is, they don't know it exists. However, we're safer in motion regardless."

She bit a knuckle till blood came forth, before she could say: "Everybody died on our account?"

"No, I think not. Your father, at least, had to be gotten rid of, since he knew the truth. And there was no being sure he hadn't told somebody else. I dare hope the enemy thinks we went out with him."

"How did they learn, Dominic?" Through the curbed hardness of her voice, he sensed dread. "Is Aycharaych in Zorkagrad?"

"Conceivable." Flandry's words fell one by one. "But not probable. Remember, we did consider the possibility. If we were to land on the taiga, Chives must proceed to the spaceport, simply to maintain our fiction. Wearing his mindscreen would make him overly conspicuous. Anyhow, Aycharaych wouldn't fail to check on each newcomer, and he knows both Chives and *Hooligan* by sight. I decided the odds were he went to Dennitza from Diomedes, but having made sure the mischief he'd started was proceeding along the lines he wanted, didn't linger. He's no coward, but he knows he's too valuable to risk in a merely warlike action—which this affair has to bring, and soon, or else his efforts have gone for naught. My guess was, he's hanging around Zoria in a wide orbit known only to a few of his most trusted chessmen."

"Yes, I remember now. Talk on. Please, Dominic. I have to be nothing except practical for a while, or I'll fall apart."

"Me too. Well, I still believe my assessment was confirmed when we made such trouble-free contact with your father. Chives had been in Zorkagrad for days. Aycharaych would have found him, read him, and prepared a trap to spring on us the minute we arrived. Anything else would have been an unnecessary gamble." Bleakness softened: "You know, I went into the manor house using every psychotrick they ever drilled into me to keep my knowledge of where you were out of conscious thought, and ready to swallow the old poison pill on the spot should matters go awry."

"What?" She turned her head toward him. "Why, you ... you told me to leave the rendezvous if you didn't return by sunset—but— Oh, Dominic, no!"

Then she did weep. He comforted her as best he could. Meanwhile he found a place to stop, a grove on the rim beneath which he could taxi and be sheltered from the sky.

She gasped back to self-mastery and bade him tell her the rest of his thoughts. "I feel certain what caused the attack tonight was the capture of your father's courier," he said. "He must have been interrogated hastily. Aycharaych would have found out about our cabin, whether or not your father explicitly told his man. But a quick narcoquiz by nontelepaths—" He scowled into murk. "The problem is, what made the enemy suspicious of him? He wasn't carrying any written message, and his cover story was plausible. Unless—"

He leaned forward, snapped a switch. "Let's try for news."

"The next regular 'cast is in about half an hour," Kossara said in a tiny voice, "if that hasn't changed too."

He tuned in the station she named. Ballet dancers moved to cruelly happy music. He held her close and murmured.

A woman's countenance threw the program out. Terror

distorted it. "Attention!" she screeched. "Special broadcast! Emergency! We have just received word from a spokesman of the Zamok—officers of the Imperial Navy have arrested Gospodar Miyatovich for high treason. Citizens are required to remain calm and orderly. Those who disobey can be shot. And ... and weather satellites report a nuclear explosion in the Dubina Dolyina area—neighborhood of the voivode's residence—attempts to phone there have failed. The voivode was, is ... the Gospodar's brother-in-law.... No announcement about whether he was trying to rebel or— Stay calm! Don't move till we know more! Ex-except ... the city police office just called in—blast shelters will be open to those who wish to enter. I repeat, blast shelters will be open—"

Repetition raved on for minutes. Beneath it, Flandry snarled, "If ever they hope to provoke their war, they've reckoned this is their last and maybe their best chance."

The newsroom vanished. "Important recorded announcement," said a man in Dennitzan uniform. "A dangerous agent of Merseia is at large in Zorkagrad or vicinity." What must be a portrait from some xenological archive, since it was not of Chives, flashed onto the screen. "He landed eight days ago, posing as a peaceful traveler. Four days ago" (the computer must redub every 18.8 hours) "he was identified, but fought his way free of arrest and disappeared. He is of this species, generally known as Shalmuan. When last seen he wore a white kilt and had taken a blaster from a patrolman after injuring the entire squad. I repeat, your government identifies him as a Merseian secret agent, extremely dangerous because of his mission as well as his person. If you see him, do not take risks. Above all, do not try talking with him. If he cannot safely be killed, report the sighting to your nearest military post. A reward of 10,000 gold dinars is offered for information leading to his death or capture. Dead or alive, he himself is worth a reward of 50,000—"

Air hissed between Kossara's teeth. Flandry sat moveless for minutes before he said stonily, "That's how. Somebody, in some fashion, recognized Chives. That meant I was around, and most likely you. That meant—any contact between your family and the Gospodar—yes."

167

Kossara wept anew, in sorrow and in rage.

Yet at the end it was she who lifted her head and said, hoarse but level-toned, "I've thought of where we might go, Dominic, and what we might try to do."

● XVI ●

Clouds and a loud raw wind had blown in across the ocean. Morning along the Obala, the east coast of Rodna, was winterlike, sky the color of lead, sea the colors of iron and gunmetal. But neither sky nor sea was quiet. Beneath the overcast a thin smoky wrack went flying; surf cannonaded and exploded on reefs and beaches.

All Nanteiwon boats were in, big solid hulls moored behind the jetty or tied at the wharf. Above the dunes the fisher village huddled. Each house was long and wide as an ychan family needed, timbers tarred black, pillars that upheld the porch carved and brightly painted with ancestral symbols, blue-begrown sod roof cable-anchored against hurricanes, a spacious and sturdy sight. But there were not many houses. Beyond them reached the flatlands the dwellers cultivated, fields harvested bare and brown, trees a-toss by roadsides, on the horizon a vague darkening which betokened the ringwall of the Kazan. The air smelled of salt and distances.

Inside the home of Ywodh were warmth, sun-imitating fluorescents, musky odor of bodies, growls to drown out the piping at the windows. Some forty males had crowded between the frescoed walls of the mootroom, while more spilled throughout the building. They wore their common garb, tunic in bright colors thrown over sinewy green frame and secured by a belt which held the knuckleduster knife. But this was no common occasion. Perched on tails and feet, muscles knotted, they stared at the three on the honor-dais.

Two were human. One they knew well, Kossara Vymezal. She used to come here often with Trohdwyr, brother to Khwent, Yffal, drowned Qythwy.... How

169

weary she looked. The other was a tall man who bore a mustache, frosted brown hair, eyes the hue of today's heaven.

Ywodh, Hand of the Vach Anochrin, steadcaptain of Nanteiwon, raised his arms. "Silence!" he called. "Hark." When he had his desire, he brought his gaunt, scarred head forward and told them:

"You have now heard of the outrages done and the lies proclaimed. Between dawn, when I asked you to keep ashore today, and our meeting here, I was in phonetalk up and down the Obala. Not an ychan leader but swore us aid. We know what Merseian rule would bring.

"Let us know, too, how empty of hope is a mere rebellion against rebellion. We have boats, civilian aircars, sporting guns; a revolutionary government would have military flyers and armored groundcars, spacecraft, missiles, energy weapons, gases, combat shielding. The plotters have ignored us partly because they took for granted we care little about a change of human overlords and might welcome Merseians—untrue—but mainly because they see us as well-nigh powerless against their crews—true.

"Can we then do aught? These two have made me believe it. Rebellion can be forestalled. Yet we've netted a flailfish. We need care as much as courage.

"To most of us, what's gone on of late in Zorkagrad and in space has been troubling, even frightening, and not understandable, like an evil dream. Therefore we went about our work, trusting Gospodar Miyatovich and his councillors to do what was right for Dennitza. Last night's tale of his arrest as a traitor stunned us. We'd have stood bewildered until too late for anything—this was intended—had not Kossara Vymezal and Dominic Flandry come to us in our darkness.

"The whole planet must be in the same clubbed state, and likewise its fighting forces. What to do? Where is truth? Who is friend and who is foe? Everyone will think best he wait a few days, till he has more knowledge.

"In that brief span, a small band of well-placed illwishers, who know exactly what they are at, can put us on the tack they want, too hard over to come about: unless, in the same span, we go up against them, knowing what *we* do.

"This day, leaders will meet in Novi Aferoch and decide on a course for us. This morning along the Obala, other meetings hear what I tell you: Stand fast with your weapons, speak to no outsiders, keep ready to move."

Father. Mother. Ivan. Gyorgye. Little, little Natalie.

Mihail. Trohdwyr. And every soul who perished in our home, every living thing that did.

Father of Creation, receive them. Jesus, absolve them. Mary, comfort them. Light of the Holy Spirit, shine upon them forever.

I dare not ask for more. Amen.

Kossara signed herself and rose. The boulder behind which she had knelt no longer hid Nanteiwon. It looked very small, far down the beach between gray sea and gray sky. Lutka her doll and Butterfeet her cat might take shelter in those houses from the wind that blew so cold, so cold.

Strange she should think of them when their loss belonged to her childhood and most of her dead were not a day old. She turned from the village and walked on over the strand. It gritted beneath her boots. Often an empty shell crunched, or she passed a tangle of weed torn from the depths and left to dry out. On her right, a hedge of cane barred sight of autumn fields, rattling and clicking. Waves thundered in, rushed out, trundled hollowly back again. Wind shrilled, thrust, smacked her cheeks and laid bitterness across her lips.

Do I comprehend that they are gone?

If only things would move. They had hours to wait, safest here, before the ychan chiefs could be gathered together. Flandry had offered her medicines from his kit, for sleep, for calm and freedom from pain, but when she declined, he said, "I knew you would. You'll always earn your way," and when she told him she would like to go out for a while, he saw she needed aloneness. He saw deeper than most, did her Dominic, and covered the hurt of it with a jape. If only he did not see right past God.

171

In time? I'll never preach at him, nor admit outright that I pray for him. But if we are given time—

They had had no end to their plans. A house in the Dubina Dolyina country, an apartment in Zorkagrad; they could afford both, and children should have elbow room for body and mind alike. Quests among the stars, wild beauties, heart-soaring moment of a new truth discovered, then return to the dear well-known. Service, oh, nothing too hazardous any more, staff rather than field Intelligence —nonetheless, swordplay of wits in the glad knowledge that this was for the future, not the poor wayworn Empire but a world he too could believe in, the world of their own blood. Ideas, investments, enterprises to start; the things they might undertake had sparkled from them like fireworks. . . .

It had all gone flat and blurred, unreal. What she could still hold whole in her daze were the small hopes. She shows him an overlook she knows in the Vysochina highlands. He teaches her the fine points of winetasting. She reads aloud to him from Simich, he to her from *Genji*. They attend the opera in Zorkagrad. They join in the dances at a land festival. They sail a boat across Lake Stoyan to a café beneath flowering viyenatz trees on Garlandmakers' Island. They take their children to the zoo and the merrypark.

If we prevail.

She stopped. Her body ached, but she straightened, faced into the wind, and told it, *We will. We will. I can borrow strength and clarity from his medicines. The repayment afterward will simply be a time of sleep, a time of peace.* She wheeled and started back. As she fared, her stride lengthened.

Novi Aferoch climbed from the docks at the Elena River mouth, up a hill from whose top might be spied the ruins of Stari Aferoch when they jutted from the sea at low tide. There stood Council Hall, slate-roofed, heavy-timbered, colonnaded with carven water monsters. In the main chamber was a table made three hundred years ago from timbers out of Gwyth's ship. Around it perched the steadcaptains of the Obala. At its head stood their mootlord Kyrwedhin, Hand of the Vach Mannoch, and the two humans.

A storm hooted and dashed rain on windowpanes. Inside, the air was blue and acrid from the pipes whereon many had been puffing. Anger smoldered behind obsidian eyes, but the leathery visages were moveless and not a tailtip twitched. These males had heard what the voivode's daughter had to tell, and roared their curses. The hour had come to think.

Kyrwedhin addressed them in quick, precise words. He was short for an ychan, though when he was younger it had not been wise to fight him. He was the wealthy owner of seareaping and merchant fleets. And ... he held a degree from the Shkola, a seat in the Skupshtina, a close experience of great affairs.

"For myself I will merely say this," he declared in Eriau. (Flitting from Zorkagrad after receiving Ywodh's urgent, argot-phrased call, he had been pleased to learn Flandry was fluent in the language, at least its modern Merseian version. His own Serbic was excellent, his Anglic not bad, but that wasn't true of everybody here.) "The ideas of our Terran guest feel right. We in the House of the Zmayi have doubtless been too parochial where the Empire was concerned, too narrowly aimed at Dennitzan matters—much like the House of the Folk. However, we have always kept a special interest in our mother world, many of us have gone there to visit, some to study, and the inhabitants are our species. Thus we have a certain sense for what the Roidhunate may or may not do. And, while I never doubted its masters wish us harm, what news and clues have reached me do not suggest current preparations for outright war. For instance, I've corresponded for years with Korvash, who lately became Hand of the Vach Rueth there. If an attack on us were to be mounted soon, he would know, and he must be more cunning than I believe for this not to change the tone of his letters.

"No proof, I agree. A single bit of flotsam in the maelstrom. I will give you just one more out of many, given me by Lazar Ristich, voivode of Kom Kutchki. Like most members of the House of the Lords, he takes close interest in Imperial business and is familiar with several prime parts of the inner Empire; he had friends on Terra itself, where he's spent considerable time. He told me the story we heard about Kossara Vymezal could not be right. Whether truly accused because she belonged to an overzealous faction among us, or falsely accused for a twisted political reason elsewhere, a person of her rank would not be shipped off to shame like any common criminal. That could only happen through monumental incompetence—which he felt sure was unlikely—or as a deliberate provocation—which he felt sure the present Imperium itself would not give us, though a cabal within it might. He wanted to discuss this with her uncle. The Zamok kept putting him off, claiming the Gospodar was too busy during the crisis.

"Well, both Ristich and I know Bodin Miyatovich of old. Such was not his way. It had to be the doing of his staff. Expecting we'd get a chance at him somehow, soon —since he was never one to closet himself in an office— we did not press too hard. We should have. For now he is captive."

Kyrwedhin halted. The wind shrilled. Finally Kossara said, tone as uncertain as words, "I can't find out what's really happened to him. Do you know?"

"Nobody does except the doers," he answered. "There are—were—Imperial liaison officers about, and their aides. Bodin had explained publicly why he, as sector governor, called in chosen craft that serve the Emperor directly, as well as those of the Voyska. Besides their guns, should Merseia attack, he wanted to demonstrate our reluctance to break with Terra.

"Spokesmen for the Zamok—the Castle," he added to Flandry; "the executive center and those who work there— spokesmen for the Zamok have said they aren't sure either. Apparently a party of Imperials got Bodin alone, took him prisoner, and spirited him away to a ship of theirs. Which vessel is not revealed. None have responded to beamed inquiries."

"They wouldn't," Flandry observed.

Kyrwedhin nodded his serrated head. "Naturally not. Imperial personnel still on the ground deny any knowledge. Thus far we have nothing except the statement that

174

a high Terran officer contacted Milutin Protich, informed
him Bodin Miyatovich was under arrest for treason, and
demanded Dennitza and its armed forces give immediate
total obedience to Admiral da Costa. He's the ranking Imperial in the Zorian System at the moment, therefore can
be considered the Emperor's representative."

"And who is, m-m, Milutin Protich?"

"A special assistant to the Gospodar. According to the
announcement, he was the first important man in the
Zamok whom the Terrans managed to get in touch with."
Kyrwedhin pondered. "Yes-s-s. He isn't Dennitzan-born—
from a nearby system where many families from here
have settled. He arrived several years back, entered administrative service, did brilliantly, rose fast and far.
Bodin had much faith in him."

Flandry drew forth a cigarette. "I take it everybody's
been pretty well paralyzed throughout today," he said.

"Aye. We must decide what to do. And we've fiendish
little information to go on, half of it contradicting the
other half. Were the Imperialists essentially right to seize
our Gospodar, or was this their next step in subjugating
us, or even getting us destroyed? Should we declare independence—when Merseia lurks in the wings? The Imperials can't prevent that; our ships vastly outnumber theirs
hereabouts. But if fighting starts, they could make us pay
heavily."

"You Dennitzans, human and zmay—ychan—you
don't strike me as hesitant people," Flandry remarked.
"As we say in Anglic, 'He who dithers is diddled.' The
newscasts have been forgivably confused. But am I right
in my impression that your parliament—Skupshtina—
meets tomorrow?"

"Yes. In the Gospodar's absence, the Chief Justice will
preside."

"Do you think the vote will go for secession?"

"I had no doubt of it ... until I heard from Dama
Vymezal and yourself."

The captains gripped their pipes, knife handles, the edge
of the table, hard. They would have their own words to
say later on; but what they heard in the next few minutes
would be their compass.

175

"If you rise and tell them—" Flandry began.

Kossara cut him off. "No, dear. That's impossible."

"What?" He blinked at her.

She spoke carefully, clearly. The stim she had taken made vigor shine pale through flesh and eyes. "The Skupshtina's no controlled inner-Empire congress. It's about five hundred different proud individuals, speaking for as many different proud sections of land or walks of life. It's often turbulent—fights have happened, yes, a few killings—and tomorrow it'll be wild. Do you think our enemy hasn't prepared for the climax of his work? I know the Chief Justice; he's honest but aged. He can be swayed about whom he recognizes. And if somebody did get the floor, started telling the whole truth—do you imagine he'd live to finish?"

"She's right," Kyrwedhin said.

Flandry drew on his cigarette till his face creased before he replied, "Yes, I'd supposed something like that must be the case. Assassination's easy. A few concealed needle guns, spotted around—and as a backup, maybe, some thoroughly armed bully boys hidden away in buildings near the Capitol. If necessary, they seize it, proclaim themselves the Revolutionary Committee ... and, given the spadework the enemy's done over the years, they can probably raise enough popular support to commit your people beyond any chance of turning back."

"If you have thought of this and not despaired," Kyrwedhin said, "you must have a plan."

Flandry frowned. "I'd rather hear what you have in mind. You know your establishment."

"But I am taken by surprise."

Kossara spoke against storm-noise: "*I* know. If you and I, Dominic—especially I—if we appear before them, suddenly, in person—why, killing us would be worse than useless."

Kyrwedhin's tail smacked the floor. "Yes!" he cried. "My thoughts were headed your same way. Though you can't simply walk in from Constitution Square. You'd never pass the Iron Portal alive. What you need is an escort, bodies both shielding and concealing you, on your way right into the Union Chamber."

"How?" snapped from a village chief.

Kossara had the answer: "Ychani have always been the Peculiar People of Dennitza. The House of the Zmayi has never entirely spoken for them; it's a human invention. If, in a desperate hour, several hundred Obala fishers enter Zorkagrad, march through Square and Portal into the Chamber, demanding their leaders be heard—it won't be the first time in history. The enemy will see no politic way to halt that kind of demonstration. They may well expect it'll turn to their advantage; outsiders would naturally think Merseian-descended Dennitzans are anti-Terran, right? Then too late—" She flung her hands wide, her voice aloft. "Too late, they see who came along!"

Beneath the surf of agreement, Flandry murmured to her: "My idea also. I kept hoping somebody would have a better one."

● XVII ●

Just before their car set down, Flandry protested to
Kossara, "God damn it, *why* does your parliament have to
meet in person? You've got holocom systems. Your politicians could send and receive images ... and we could've
rigged untraceable methods to call them and give them the
facts last night."

"Hush, darling." She laid a hand across his fist. "You
know why. Electronics will do for ornamental relics. The
Skupshtina is alive, it debates and decides real things, the
members need intimacies, subtleties, surprises."

"But you, you have to go among murderers to reach
them."

"And I fear for you," she said quietly. "We should both
stop."

He looked long at her, and she at him, in the seat they
shared. Beryl eyes under wide brow and bronze hair,
strong fair features though her smile quivered the least bit,
height, ranginess, fullness, the warmth of her clasp and the
summery fragrance of herself: had she ever been more
beautiful? The vitality that surged in her, the serenity
beneath, were no work of a drug; it had simply let her put
aside shock, exhaustion, grief for this while and be altogether Kossara.

"If there is danger today," she said, "I thank God He
lets me be in it with you."

He prevented himself from telling her he felt no gratitude. They kissed, very briefly and lightly because the car
was crammed with ychans.

It landed in a parking lot at the edge of Zorkagrad.
None farther in could have accommodated the swarm of
battered vehicles which was arriving. Besides, a sudden ap-

pearance downtown might have provoked alarm and a quick reaction by the enemy. A march ought to have a calming effect. Flandry and Kossara donned cowled cloaks, which should hide their species from a cursory glance when they were surrounded by hemianthropoid xenos, and stepped outside.

A west wind skirled against the sun, whose blaze seemed paled in a pale heaven. Clouds were brighter; they scudded in flocks, blinding white, their shadows sweeping chill across the world, off, on, off, on. Winged animals wheeled and thinly cried. Trees around the lot and along the street that ran from it—mostly Terran, oak, elm, beech, maple—cast their outer branches about, creaked, soughed Delphic utterances though tongue after fire-tongue ripped loose to scrittle off over the pavement. Rainpuddles wandered and wandered. All nature was saying farewell.

The ychans closed in around the humans. They numbered a good four hundred, chosen by their steadcaptains as bold, cool-headed, skilled with the knives, tridents, harpoons, and firearms they bore. Ywodh of Nanteiwon, appointed their leader by Kyrwedhin before the parliamentarian returned here, put them in battle-ready order. They spoke little and showed scant outward excitement, at least to human eyes or nostrils; such was the way of the Obala. They did not know the ins and outs of what had happened, nor greatly care. It was enough that their Gospodar had been betrayed by the enemy of their forefathers, that his niece had come home to speak truth, and that they were her soldiers. The wind snapped two standards in their van, star white on blue of Yovan Matavuly, ax red on gold of Gwyth.

"All set," Ywodh reported. A shout: "Forward!" He took the lead. Flandry and Kossara would fain have clasped hands as they walked, but even surrounded must clutch their cloaks tight against this tricksy air. The thud of their boots was lost amidst digitigrade slither and click.

At first it was predictable they would encounter nobody. Here was a new district of private homes and clustered condominium units, beyond the scope of forcefield generators that offered the inner city some protection. Residents had sought safer quarters. An occasional militia squad, on patrol to prevent looting, observed the procession from a distance but did not interfere.

Farther on, buildings were older, higher, close-packed on streets which had narrowed and went snakily uphill: red tile roofs, stucco walls of time-faded gaudiness, signs and emblems hung above doorways, tenements, offices, midget factories, restaurants, taverns, amusements, a bulbous-domed parish church, a few big stores and tiny eccentric shops by the score, the kind of place that ought to have pulsed with traffic of vehicles and foot, been lively with movement, colors, gestures broad or sly, words, laughter, whistling, song, sorrow, an accordion or a fiddle somewhere, pungencies of roast corn and nuts for sale to keep the passerby warm, oddments in display windows, city men, landmen, offworlders, vagabonds, students, soldiers, children, grannies, the unforgettably gorgeous woman whom you know you will never glimpse again.... A few walkers stepped aside, a few standers poised in doorways or leaned on upper-story sills, warily staring. Now and then a groundcar detoured. A civilian policeman in brown uniform and high-crowned hat joined Ywodh; they talked; he consulted his superiors via minicom, stayed till an aircar had made inspection from above, and departed.

"This is downright creepy," Flandry murmured to Kossara. "Has everybody evacuated, or what?"

She passed the question on. Untrained humans could not have conveyed information accurately in that wise; but soon she told Flandry from Ywodh: "Early this morning—the organizers must have worked the whole night—an *ispravka* started against Imperial personnel. That's when ordinary citizens take direct action. Not a riot or lynching. The people move under discipline, often in their regular Voyska units; remember, every able-bodied adult is a reservist. Such affairs seldon get out of control, and may have no violence at all. Offenders may simply be expelled from an area. Or they may be held prisoner while spokesmen of the people demand the authorities take steps to punish them. A few *ispravkai* have brought down governments. In this case, what's happened is that Terrans and others who serve the Imperium were rounded up into certain buildings: hostages for the Gospodar's release and the good behavior of their Navy ships. The Zamok denounced the action as illegal and bound to increase tension, demanded the crowds disperse, and sent police. The people stand fast around those buildings. The police haven't charged them; no shots have yet been fired on either side."

"I've heard of worse customs," Flandry said.

Puzzled, she asked, "Shouldn't the plotters be pleased?"

Flandry shrugged. "I daresay they are. Still, don't forget the vast majority of your officials must be patriotic, and whether or not they prefer independence, consider civil war to be the final recourse. The top man among them issued that cease-and-desist order." He frowned. "But, um, you know, this nails down a lot of our possible helpers, both citizens and police. The enemy isn't expecting us. However, if too many parliament members refuse to board the secession railroad, he'll have a clear field for attempting a *coup d'état*. Maybe the firebrand who instigated that, uh, *ispravka* is a Merseian himself, in human skin."

The wind boomed between walls.

A minor commotion occurred on the fringes of the troop. Word flew back and forth. "Chives!" Kossara gasped.

The ychans let him through. He also went cloaked to muffle the fact of his race from any quick glance. Emerald features were eroded from spare to gaunt; eyes were more fallow than amber; but when Flandry whooped and took him by the shoulders, Chives said crisply, "Thank you, sir. Donna Vymezal, will you allow me the liberty of expressing my sympathy at your loss?"

"Oh, you dear clown!" She hugged him. Her lashes gleamed wet. Chives suffered the gesture in embarrassed silence. Flandry sensed within him a deeper trouble.

They continued through hollow streets. A fighter craft passed low above chimneys. Air whined and snarled in its wake. "What've you been doing?" Flandry asked. "How'd you find us?"

"If you have no immediate statement or directive for me, sir," the precise voice replied, "I will report chronologically. Pursuant to instructions, I landed at the spaceport and submitted to inspection. My cover story was approved and I given license, under police registry, to remain here for a stated period as per my declared business. Interested in exotics, many townspeople conversed with me while I circulated among them in the next few planetary days. By pretending to less familiarity with *Homo sapiens* than is the case, I gathered impressions of their individual feelings as respects the present imbroglio. At a more convenient time, sir, if you wish, I will give you the statistical breakdown.

"I must confess it was a complete surprise when a Naval patrol entered my lodgings and declared an intention to take me in custody. Under the circumstances, sir, I felt conformity would be imprudent. I endeavored not to damage irreparably men who wore his Majesty's uniform, and in due course will return the borrowed blaster you observe me wearing. Thereupon I took refuge with a gentleman I suspected of vehement anti-Terran sentiments. May I respectfully request his name and the names of his associates be omitted from your official cognizance? Besides their hospitality and helpfulness toward me, they exhibited no more than a misguided zeal for the welfare of this planet, and indeed I was the occasion of their first overt unlawful act. They sheltered me only after I had convinced them I was a revolutionary for my own society, and that my public designation as a Merseian agent was a calumny which the Imperialists could be expected to employ against their kind too. They were persuaded rather easily; I would not recommend them for the Intelligence Corps. I got from them clothes, disguise materials, equipment convertible to surveillance purposes, and went about collecting data for myself.

"They do possess a rudimentary organization. Through this, via a phone call, my host learned that a large delegation of zmays was moving on the Capitol. Recalling Donna Vymezal's accounts of her background, and trusting she and you had not perished after all, I thought you might be here. To have this deduction confirmed was ... most gratifying, sir."

Flandry chewed his lip for a while before he said,

"Those were Imperials who came to arrest you? Not Dennitzans?"

"No, sir, not Dennitzans. There could be no mistake." Chives spoke mutedly. His thin green fingers hauled the cowl closer around his face.

"You went unmolested for days, and then in a blink—" Flandry's speech chopped off. They were at their goal.

Well into Old Town, the party passed between two many-balconied mansions, out onto a plateau of Royal Hill. Constitution Square opened before them, broad, slate-flagged, benches, flowerbeds, trees—empty, empty. In the middle was a big fountain, granite catchbasin, Toman Obilich and Vladimir locked in bronze combat, water dancing white but its sound and spray borne off by the wind. Westward buildings stood well apart, giving a view down across roofs to Lake Stoyan, metal-bright shimmer and shiver beyond the curve of the world. Directly across the square was the Capitol, a sprawling, porticoed marble mass beneath a gilt dome whose point upheld an argent star. A pair of kilometers further on, a rock lifted nearly sheer, helmeted with the battlements and banners of the Zamok.

Flandry's gaze flickered. He identified a large hotel, office buildings, cafés, fashionable stores, everything antiquated but dignified, the gray stones wearing well; how many Constitution Squares had he known in his life? But this lay deserted under wind, chill, and hasty cloud shadows. A militia squad stood six men on the Capitol verandah, six flanking the bottom of the stairs; their capes flapped, their rifles gleamed whenever a sunbeam smote and then went dull again. Aircraft circled far overhead. Otherwise none save the newcomers were in sight. Yet surely watchers waited behind yonder shut doors, yonder blank panes: proprietors, caretakers, maybe a few police—a few, since the turmoil was elsewhere in town and no disturbance expected here. Who besides? He walked as if through a labyrinth of mirages. Nothing was wholly what he sensed, except the blaster butt under his hand and a stray russet lock of Kossara's hair.

She had no such dreads. As they trod into the plaza, he

heard her whisper, "Here we go, my brave beloved. They'll sing of you for a thousand years."

He shoved hesitation out of his mind and readied himself to fight.

But no clash came. Despite what they told him when the move was being planned, he'd more or less awaited behavior like that when a gaggle of demonstrators wanted to invade a legislative session on any human planet he knew—prohibition, resistance, then either a riot or one of the sides yielding. If officialdom conceded in order to avoid the riot, it would be grudgingly, after prolonged haggling; and whatever protesters were admitted would enter under strict conditions, well guarded, to meet indignant stares.

Dennitza, though, had institutionalized if not quite legalized procedures like the *ispravka*. Through the officer he met on the way, Ywodh had explained his band's intent. Word had quickly reached the Chief Justice. Four hundred zmays would not lightly descend on Zorkagrad, claiming to represent the whole Obala; they could be trusted to be mannerly and not take an unreasonable time to make their points; urged by Kyrwedhin, a majority in the third house of the Skupshtina endorsed their demand. No guns greeted them, aside from those of the corporal's guard at the entrance; and they bore their own arms inside.

Up the stairs—past armored doors that recalled the Troubles—through an echoful lobby—into a central chamber where the parliament in joint session waited— Flandry raked his glance around, seeking menaces to his woman and shelters for her.

The room was a half ellipsoid. At the far-end focus, a dais bore the Gospodar's lectern, a long desk, and several occupied chairs. To right and left, tiers held the seats of members, widely spaced. Skylights cast fleetingness of weather into steadiness of fluorescents, making the polished marble floor seem to stir. On gilt mural panels were painted the saints and heroes of Dennitza. The lawmakers sat according to their groupings, Lords in rainbow robes, Folk in tunics and trousers or in gowns, Zmayi in leather and metal. After the outdoors, Flandry breathed an air which felt curdled by fear and fury.

A Knight of Ghosts and Shadows

Banners dipped to an old man in black who sat behind the lectern. Slowly the fishers advanced, while unseen telescanners watched on behalf of the world. In the middle of the floor, the ychans halted. Silence encompassed them. Flandry's pulse thuttered.

"*Zdravo*," said the Chief Justice, and added a courteous Eriau "*Hydhref*." His hand forgot stateliness, plucked at his white beard. "We have ... let you in ... for unity's sake. My understanding is, your delegation wishes to speak relevantly to the present crisis—a viewpoint which might else go unheard. You in turn will, will understand why we must limit your time to fifteen minutes."

Ywodh bowed, palms downward, tail curved. Straightening, he let his quarterdeck basso roll. "We thank the assembly. I'll need less than that; but I think you'll then want to give us more." Flandry's eyes picked out Kyrwedhin. Weird, that the sole Dennitzan up there whom he knew should bear Merseian genes. "Worthies and world," Ywodh was saying, "you've heard many a tale of late: how the Emperor wants to crush us, how a new war is nearly on us because of his folly or his scheming to slough us off, how his agents rightly or wrongly charged the Gospodar's niece Kossara Vymezal with treason and—absolutely wrongly—sold her for a slave, how they've taken the Gospodar himself prisoner on the same excuse, how they must have destroyed the whole homestead of his brother-in-law the voivode of Dubina Dolyina to grind out any spark of free spirit, how our last choices left are ruin or revolution— You've heard this.

"I say each piece of it is false." He flung an arm in signal. With a showmanship that humans would have had to rehearse, his followers opened their ranks. "And here to gaff the lies is Kossara Vymezal, sister's daughter to Bodin Miyatovich our Gospodar!"

She bounded from among them, across the floor, onto the dais, to take her place between the antlers of the lectern. A moan lifted out of the benched humans, as if the fall wind had made entry; the zmayi uttered a surflike rumble. "What, what, what is this?" quavered the Chief Justice. Nobody paid him heed. Kossara raised her head and cried forth so the room rang:

185

"Hear me, folk! I'm not back from the dead, but I am back from hell, and I bear witness. The devils are not Terrans but Merseians and their creatures. My savior was, is, not a Dennitzan but a Terran. Those who shout, 'Independence!' are traitors not to the Empire but to Dennitza. Their single wish is to set humans at each other's throats, till the Roidhun arrives and picks our bones. Hear my story and judge."

Flandry walked toward her, Chives beside him. He wished it weren't too disturbing to run. Nike of Samothrace had not borne a higher or more defenseless pride than she did. They took stance beneath her, facing the outer door. Her tones marched triumphant:

"—I escaped the dishonor intended me by the grace of God and the decency of this man you see here, Captain Sir Dominic Flandry of his Majesty's service. Let me tell what happened from the beginning. Have I your leave, worthies?"

"*Aye!*"

Gunshots answered. Screams flew ragged. A blaster bolt flared outside the chamber.

Flandry's weapon jumped free. The tiers of the Skupshtina turned into a yelling scramble. Fifty-odd men pounded through the doorway. Clad like ordinary Dennitzans, all looked hard and many looked foreign. They bore firearms.

"Get down, Kossara!" Flandry shouted. Through him ripped: *Yes, the enemy did have an emergency force hidden in a building near the square, and somebody in this room used a minicom to bring them. The Revolutionary Committee—they'll take over, they'll proclaim her an impostor—*

He and Chives were on the dais. She hadn't flattened herself under the lectern. She had gone to one knee behind it, sidearm in hand, ready to snipe. The attackers were deploying around the room. Two dashed by either side of the clustered, bewildered fishers.

Their blaster beams leaped, convergent on the stand. Its wood exploded in flame, its horns toppled. Kossara dropped her pistol and fell back.

Chives pounced zigzag. A bolt seared and crashed

within centimeters of him. He ignored it; he was taking aim. The first assassin's head became a fireball. The second crumpled, grabbed at the stump of a leg, writhed and shrieked a short while. Chives reached the next nearest, wrapped his tail around that man's neck and squeezed, got an elbow-beaking single-arm lock on another, hauled him around for a shield and commenced systematic shooting.

"I say," he called through the din to Ywodh, "you chaps might pitch in a bit, don't you know."

The steadcaptain bellowed. His slugthrower hissed. A male beside him harpooned a foeman's belly. Then heedless of guns, four hundred big seafarers joined battle.

Flandry knelt by Kossara. From bosom to waist was seared bloody wreckage. He half raised her. She groped after him with hands and eyes. "Dominic, darling," he barely heard, "I wish—" He heard no more.

For an instant he imagined revival, life-support machinery, cloning. . . . No. He'd never get her to a hospital before the brain was gone beyond any calling back of the spirit. Never.

He lowered her. *I won't think yet. No time. I'd better get into that fight. The ychans don't realize we need a few prisoners.*

Dusk fell early in fall. Above the lake smoldered a sunset remnant. Otherwise blue-black dimness drowned the land. Overhead trembled a few stars; and had he looked from his office window aloft in the Zamok, Flandry could have seen city lights, spiderwebs along streets and single glows from homes. Wind mumbled at the panes.

Finally granted a rest, he sat back from desk and control board, feeling his chair shape its embrace to his contours. Despite the drugs which suppressed grief, stimulated metabolism, and thus kept him going, weariness weighted every cell. He had turned off the fluoros. His cigarette end shone red. He couldn't taste the smoke, maybe because the dark had that effect, maybe because tongue and palate were scorched.

Well, went his clockwork thought, *that takes care of the main business.* He had just been in direct conversation with Admiral da Costa. The Terran commander appeared

187

reasonably well convinced of the good faith of the provisional government whose master, for all practical purposes, Flandry had been throughout this afternoon. Tomorrow he would discuss the Gospodar's release. And as far as could be gauged, the Dennitzan people were accepting the fact they had been betrayed. They'd want a full account, of course, buttressed by evidence; and they wouldn't exactly become enthusiastic Imperialists; but the danger of revolution followed by civil war seemed past.

So maybe tomorrow I can let these chemicals drain out of me, let go my grip and let in my dead. Tonight the knowledge that there was no more Kossara reached him only like the wind, an endless voice beyond the windows. She had been spared that, he believed, had put mourning quite from her for the last span, being upheld by urgency rather than a need to go through motions, by youth and hope, by his presence beside her. *Whereas I—ah, well, I can carry on. She'd've wanted me to.*

The door chimed. *What the deuce?* His guards had kept him alone among electronic ghosts. Whoever got past them at last in person must be authoritative and persuasive. He waved at an admit plate and to turn the lights back on. Their brightness hurt his eyes.

A slim green form in a white kilt entered, bearing a tray where stood teapot, cup, plates and bowls of food. "Your dinner, sir," Chives announced.

"I'm not hungry," said the clockwork. "I didn't ask for—"

"No, sir. I took the liberty." Chives set his burden down on the desk. "Allow me to remind you, we require your physical fitness."

Her planet did. "Very good, Chives." Flandry got down some soup and black bread. The Shalmuan waited unobtrusively.

"That did help," the man agreed. "You know, give me the proper pill and I might sleep."

"You—you may not wish it for the nonce, sir."

"What?" Flandry sharpened his regard. Chives had lost composure. He stood head lowered, tail a-droop, hands hard clasped: miserable.

"Go on," Flandry said. "You've gotten me nourished. Tell me."

The voice scissored off words: "It concerns those personnel, sir, whom you recall the townsmen took into custody."

"Yes. I ordered them detained, well treated, till we can check them out individually. What of them?"

"I have discovered they include one whom I, while a fugitive, ascertained had come to Zorkagrad several days earlier. To be frank, sir, this merely confirmed my suspicion that such had been the case. I must have been denounced by a party who recognized your speedster at the port and obtained the inspectors' record of me. This knowledge must then have made him draw conclusions and recommend actions with respect to Voivode Vymezal."

"Well?"

"Needless to say, sir, I make no specific accusations. The guilt could lie elsewhere than in the party I am thinking of."

"Not measurably likely, among populations the size we've got." Beneath the drumhead of imposed emotionlessness, Flandry felt his body stiffen. "Who?"

Seldom did he see Chives' face distorted. "Lieutenant Commander Dominic Hazeltine, sir. Your son."

• XVIII •

Two militiamen escorted the prisoner into the office. "You may go," Flandry told them.

They stared unsurely from him, standing slumped against night in a window, to the strong young man they guarded. "Go," Flandry repeated. "Wait outside with my servant. I'll call on the intercom when I want you."

They saluted and obeyed. Flandry and Hazeltine regarded each other, mute, until the door had closed. The older saw an Imperial undress uniform, still neat upon an erect frame, and a countenance half Persis' where pride overmastered fear. The younger saw haggardness clad in a soiled coverall.

"Well," Flandry said at last. Hazeltine extended a hand. Flandry looked past it. "Have a seat," he invited. "Care for a drink?" He indicated bottle and glasses on his desk. "I remember you like Scotch."

"Thanks, Dad." Hazeltine spoke as low, free of the croak in the opposite throat. He smiled, and smiled again after they had both sat down holding their tumblers. Raising his, he proposed, "Here's to us. Damn few like us, and they're all dead."

They had used the ancient toast often before. This time Flandry did not respond. Hazeltine watched him a moment, grimaced, and tossed off a swallow. Then Flandry drank.

Hazeltine leaned forward. His words shook. "Father, you don't believe that vapor about me. Do you?"

Flandry took out his cigarette case. "I don't know what else to believe." He flipped back the lid. "Somebody who knew Chives and the *Hooligan* fingered him. The date of your arrival fits in." He chose a cigarette. "And thinking

190

back, I find the coincidence a trifle much that you called my attention to Kossara Vymezal precisely when she'd reached Terra. I was a pretty safe bet to skyhoot her off to Diomedes, where she as an inconvenient witness and I as an inconvenient investigator could be burked in a way that'd maximize trouble." He puffed the tobacco into lighting, inhaled, streamed smoke till it veiled him, and sighed: "You were overeager. You should have waited till she'd been used at least a few days, and a reputable Dennitzan arranged for to learn about this."

"I didn't— No, what are you saying?" Hazeltine cried.

Flandry toyed with the case. "As was," he continued levelly, "the only word which could be sent, since the Gospodar would require proof and is no fool . . . the word was merely she'd been sold for a slave. Well, ample provocation. Where were you, between leaving Terra and landing here? Did you maybe report straight to Aycharaych?"

Hazeltine banged his glass down on the chair arm. "Lies!" he shouted. Red and white throbbed across his visage. "Listen, I'm your *son*. I swear to you by—"

"Never mind. And don't waste good liquor. If I'd settled on Dennitza as I planned, the price we'd've paid for Scotch—" Flandry gave his lips a respite from the cigarette. He waved it. "How were you recruited? By the Merseians, I mean. Couldn't be brainscrub. I know the signs too well. Blackmail? No, implausible. You're a bright lad who wouldn't get suckered into that first mistake they corral you by—a brave lad who'd sneer at threats. But sometime during the contacts you made in line of duty—"

Hazeltine's breath rasped. "I didn't! How can I prove to you, Father, I didn't?"

"Simple," Flandry said. "You must have routine narco immunization. But we can hypnoprobe you."

Hazeltine sagged back. His glass rolled across the floor.

"The Imperial detachment brought Intelligence personnel and their apparatus, you know," Flandry continued. "I've asked, and they can take you tomorrow morning. Naturally, any private facts which emerge will stay confidential."

Hazeltine raised an aspen hand. "You don't know—I —I'm deep-conditioned."

"By Terra?"

"Yes, of course, of course. I can't be 'probed ... without my mind being . . . destroyed—"

Flandry sighed again. "Come, now. We don't deep-condition our agents against giving information to their own people, except occasional supersecrets. After all, a 'probe can bring forth useful items the conscious mind has forgotten. Don't fear if you're honest, son. The lightest treatment will clear you, and the team will go no further."

"But—oh, no-o-o—"

Abruptly Hazeltine cast himself on his knees before Flandry. Words burst from his mouth like the sweat from his skin. "Yes, then, yes, I've been working for Merseia. Not bought, nothing like that, I thought the future was theirs, should be theirs, not this walking corpse of an Empire— Merciful angels, can't you see their way's the hope of humankind too?—" Flandry blew smoke to counteract the reek of terror. "I'll cooperate. I will, I will. I wasn't evil, Dad. I had my orders about you, yes, but I hated what I did, and Aycharaych doubted you'd really be killed, and I knew I was supposed to let that girl be bought first by somebody else before I told you but when we happened to arrive in time I couldn't make myself wait—" He caught Flandry by the knees. "Dad, in Mother's name, let my mind live!"

Flandry shoved the clasp aside, rose, stepped a couple of meters off, and answered, "Sorry. I could never trust you not to leave stuff buried in your confession that could rise to kill or enslave too many more young girls." For a few seconds he watched the crouched, spastic shape. "I'm under stim and heavy trank," he said. "A piece of machinery. I've a far-off sense of how this will feel later on, but mostly that's abstract. However . . . you have till morning, son. What would you like while you wait? I'll do my best to provide it."

Hazeltine uncoiled. On his feet, he howled, "You cold devil, at least I'll kill you first! And then myself!"

He charged. The rage which doubled his youthful strength was not amok; he came as a karate man, ready to smash a ribcage and pluck out a heart.

Flandry swayed aside. He passed a hand near the other.

Razor-edged, the lid of the cigarette case left a shallow red gash in the right cheek. Hazeltine whirled for a renewed assault. Flandry gave ground. Hazeltine followed, boxing him into a corner. Then the knockout potion took hold. Hazeltine stumbled, reeled, flailed his arms, mouthed, and caved in.

Flandry sought the intercom. "Come remove the prisoner," he directed.

Day broke windless and freezing cold. The sun stood in a rainbow ring and ice crackled along the shores of Lake Stoyan. Zorkagrad lay silent under bitter blue, as if killed. From time to time thunders drifted across its roofs, arrivals and departures of spacecraft. They gleamed meteoric. Sometimes, too, airships whistled by, armored vehicles rumbled, boots slammed on pavement. About noon, one such vessel and one such march brought Bodin Miyatovich home.

He was as glad to return unheralded. Too much work awaited him for ceremonies—him and Dominic Flandry. But the news did go out on the 'casts; and that was like proclaiming Solstice Feast. Folk ran from their houses, poured in from the land, left their patrols to shout, dance, weep, laugh, sing, embrace perfect strangers; and every church bell pealed.

From a balcony of the Zamok he watched lights burn and bob through twilit streets, bonfires in squares, tumult and clamor. His breath smoked spectral under the early stars. Frost tinged his beard. "This can't last," he muttered, and stepped back into the office.

When the viewdoor closed behind him, stillness fell except for chimes now muffled. The chill he had let in remained a while. Flandry, hunched in a chair, didn't seem to notice.

Miyatovich gave the Terran a close regard. "You can't go on either," he said. "If you don't stop dosing yourself and let your glands and nerves function normally, they'll quit on you."

Flandry nodded. "I'll stop soon." From caverns his eyes observed a phonescreen.

The big gray-blond man hung up his cloak. "I'll admit I

193

couldn't have done what got done today, maybe not for weeks, maybe never, without you," he said. "You knew the right words, the right channels; you had the ideas. But we *are* done. I can handle the rest."

He went to stand behind his companion, laying fingers on shoulders, gently kneading. "I'd like to hide from her death myself," he said. "Aye, it's easier for me. I'd thought her lost to horror, and learned she was lost in honor. While if you and she— Dominic, listen. I made a chance to call my wife. She's at our house, not our town house, a place in the country, peace, woods, cleanness, healing. We want you there." He paused. "You're a very private man, aren't you? Well, nobody will poke into your grief."

"I'm not hiding," Flandry replied in monotone. "I'm waiting. I expect a message shortly. Then I'll take your advice."

"What message?"

"Interrogation results from a certain Mers— Roidhunate agent we captured. I've reason to think he has some critical information."

"Hoy?" Miyatovich's features, tired in their own right, kindled. He cast himself into an armchair confronting Flandry. It creaked beneath his weight.

"I'm in a position to evaluate it better than anyone else," the Terran persisted. "How long does da Costa insist on keeping his ships here 'in case we need further help'? —Ah, yes, five standard days, I remember. Well, I'll doubtless need about that long at your house; I'll be numb, and afterward—

"I'll take a printout in my luggage, to study when I'm able. Your job meanwhile will be to . . . not suppress the report. You probably couldn't; besides, the Empire needs every drop of data we can wring out of what enemy operatives we catch. But don't let da Costa's command scent any special significance in the findings of this particular 'probe job."

The Gospodar fumbled for pipe and tobacco pouch. "Why?"

"I can't guarantee what we'll learn, but I have a logical

suspicion— Are you sure you can keep the Dennitzan fleet mobilized, inactive, another couple of weeks?"

"Yes." Miyatovich grew patient. "Maybe you don't quite follow the psychology, Dominic. Da Costa wants to be certain we won't rebel. The fact that we aren't dispersing immediately makes him leery. He hasn't the power to prevent us from whatever we decide to do, but he thinks his presence as a tripwire will deter secessionism. All right, in five Terran days his Intelligence teams can establish it's a bogeyman, and he can accept my explanation that we're staying on alert for a spell yet in case Merseia does attack. He'll deem us a touch paranoid, but he'll return to base with a clear conscience."

"You have to give your men the same reason, don't you?"

"Right. And they'll accept it. In fact, they'd protest if I didn't issue such an order, Dennitza's lived too many centuries by the abyss; this time we nearly went over."

Miyatovich tamped his pipe bowl needlessly hard. "I've gotten to know you well enough, I believe, in this short while, that I can tell you the whole truth," he added. "You thought you were helping me smooth things out with respect to the Empire. And you were, you were. But my main reason for quick reconciliation is ... to get the Imperials out of the Zorian System while we still have our own full strength."

"And you'll strike back at Merseia," Flandry said.

The Gospodar showed astonishment. "How did you guess?"

"I didn't guess. I knew—Kossara. She told me a lot."

Miyatovich gathered wind and wits. "Don't think I'm crazy," he urged. "Rather, I'll have to jump around like sodium in the rain, trying to keep people and Skupshtina from demanding action too loudly before the Terrans leave. But when the Terrans do—" His eyes, the color of hers, grew leopard-intent. "We want more than revenge. In fact, only a few of us like myself have suffered what would have brought on a blood feud in the old days. But I told you we live on the edge. We have got to show we aren't safe for unfriends to touch. Otherwise, what's next?"

"Nemo me impune lacessit," Flandry murmured.

"Hm?"

"No matter. Ancient saying. Too damned ancient; does nothing ever change at the heart?" Flandry shook his head. The chemical barriers were growing thin. "I take it, then, in the absence of da Costa or some other Imperial official—who'd surely maintain anything as atavistic as response to aggression is against policy and must in all events be referred to the appropriate authorities, in triplicate, for debate—in the absence of that, as sector governor you'll order the Dennitzan fleet on a retaliatory strike."

Miyatovich nodded. "Yes."

"Have you considered the consequences?"

"I'll have time to consider them further, before we commit. But ... if we choose the target right, I don't expect Merseia will do more than protest. The fact seems to be, at present they are not geared for war with Terra. They were relying on a new civil war among us. If instead they get hit, the shock ought to make them more careful about the whole Empire."

"What target have you in mind?"

Miyatovich frowned, spent a minute with a lighter getting his pipe started, finally said, "I don't yet know. The object is not to start a war, but to punish behavior which could cause one. The Roidhunate couldn't write off a heavily populated planet. Nor would I lead a genocidal mission. But, oh, something valuable, maybe an industrial center on a barren metal-rich globe—I'll have the War College study it."

"If you succeed," Flandry warned, "you'll be told you went far beyond your powers."

"That can be argued. Those powers aren't too well defined, are they? I like to imagine Hans Molitor will sympathize." The Gospodar shrugged. "If not, what becomes of me isn't important. I'm thinking of the children and grandchildren."

"Uh-huh. Well, you've confirmed what— Hold on." The phone buzzed. Flandry reached to press accept. He had to try twice before he made it.

A countenance half as stark as his looked from the

screen. "Lieutenant Mitchell reporting, sir. Hypnoprobing of the prisoner Dominic Hazeltine has been completed."

"Results?" The question was plane-flat.

"You predicted aright, sir. The subject was deep-conditioned." Mitchell winced at a recollection unpleasant even in his line of work. "I'd never seen or heard of so thorough a treatment. He went into shock almost at once. In later stages, the stimuli necessary were—well, he hasn't got a forebrain left to speak of."

"I want a transcript in full," Flandry said. "Otherwise, you're to seal the record, classified Ultimate Secret, and your whole team will keep silence. I'll give you a written directive on that, authorized by Governor Miyatovich."

"Yes, sir." Mitchell showed puzzlement. He must be wondering why the emphasis. Intelligence didn't make a habit of broadcasting what it learned. Unless— "Sir, you realize, don't you, this is still raw material? More incoherent than usual, too, because of the brain channeling. We did sort out his basic biography, details of his most recent task, that kind of thing. Offhand, the rest of what we got seems promising. But to fit the broken, scrambled association chains together, interpret the symbols and find their significance—"

"I'll take care of that," Flandry snapped. "Your part is over."

"Yes, sir." Mitchell dropped his gaze. "I'm ... sorry ... on account of the relationship involved. He really did admire you. Uh, what shall we do about him now?"

Flandry fell quiet. Miyatovich puffed volcanic clouds. Outside, the bells caroled.

"Sir?"

"Let me see him," Flandry said.

Interlinks flickered. In the screen appeared the image of a young man, naked on a bed, arms spreadeagled to meet the tubes driven into his veins, chest and abdominal cavities opened for the entry of machines that kept most cells alive. He stared at the ceiling with eyes that never moved nor blinked. His mouth dribbled. *Click, chug*, it said in the background, *click, chug.*

Flandry made a noise. Miyatovich seized his hand.

After a while Flandry stated, "Thank you. Switch it off."

They held Kossara Vymezal in a coldvault until the Imperials had left. This was by command of the Gospodar, and folk supposed the reason was she was Dennitza's, nobody else's, and said he did right. As many as were able would attend her funeral.

The day before, she was brought to the Cathedral of St. Clement, though none save kin were let near. Only the four men of her honor guard were there when Dominic Flandry came.

They stood in uniform of the Narodna Voyska, heads lowered, rifles reversed, at the corners of her bier. He paid them no more mind than he did the candles burning in tall holders, the lilies, roses, viyenatz everywhere between, their fragrance or a breath of incense or the somehow far-off sound of a priest chanting behind the iconostasis, which filled the cool dim air. Alone he walked over the stones to her. Evening sunlight slanted through windows and among columns, filtered to a domed ceiling, brought forth out of dusk, remote upon gold and blue, the Twelve Apostles and Christ Lord of All.

At first he was afraid to look, dreading less the gaping glaring hideousness he had last seen—that was only what violent death wrought—than the kind of rouged doll they made when Terran bodies lay in state. Forcing himself, he found that nothing more had been done than to cleanse her, close the eyes, bind the chin, gown and garland her. The divided coffin lid showed her down to the bosom. The face he saw was hers, hers, though color was gone and time had eased it into an inhuman serenity.

This makes me a little happier, dear, he thought. *I didn't feel it was fitting that they mean to build you a big tomb on Founders' Hill. I wanted your ashes strewn over land and sea, into sun and wind. Then if ever I came back here I could dream every brightness was yours. But they understand what they do, your people.* A corner of his mouth bent upward. *It's I who am the sentimental old fool. Would you laugh if you could know?*

He stooped closer. *You believed you would know, Kos-*

sara. If you do, won't you help me believe too—believe that you still are?

His sole answer was the priest's voice rising and falling through archaic words. Flandry nodded. He hadn't expected more. He couldn't keep himself from telling her, *I'm sorry, darling.*

And I won't kiss what's left, I who kissed you. He searched among his languages for the best final word. *Sayonara.* Since it must be so. Stepping back a pace, he bowed three times very deeply, turned, and departed.

Bodin Miyatovich and his wife waited outside. The weather was milder than before, as if a ghost of springtime flitted fugitive ahead of winter. Traffic boomed in the street. Walkers cast glances at the three on the stairs, spoke to whatever companions they had, but didn't stop; they taught good manners on Dennitza.

Draga Miyatovich took Flandry by the elbow. "Are you well, Dominic?" she asked anxiously. "You've gone pale."

"No, nothing," he said. "I'm recovering fast, thanks to your kindness."

"You should rest. I've noticed you hour after hour poring over that report—" She saw his expression and stopped her speech.

In a second he eased his lips, unclamped his fists, and raised memory of what he had come from today up against that other memory. "I'd no choice," he said. To her husband: "Bodin, I'm ready to work again. With you. You see, I've found your target."

The Gospodar peered around. "What? Wait," he cautioned.

"True, we can't discuss it here," Flandry agreed. "Especially, I suppose, on holy ground ... though she might not have minded."

She'd never have been vindictive. But she'd have understood how much this matters to her whole world: that in those broken mutterings of my son's I found what I thought I might find, the coordinates of Chereion, Aycharaych's planet.

• XIX •

The raiders from Dennitza met the guardians of the red sun, and lightning awoke.

Within the command bridge of the *Vatre Zvezda*, Bodin Miyatovich stared at a display tank. Color-coded motes moved around a stellar globe to show where each vessel of his fleet was—and, as well as scouts and instruments could learn, each of the enemy's—and what it did and when it died. But their firefly dance, of some use to a life-long professional, bewildered an unskilled eye; and it was merely a sideshow put on by computers whose real language was numbers. He swore and looked away in search of reality.

The nearest surrounded him in metal, meters, intricate consoles, flashing signal bulbs, dark-uniformed men who stood to their duties, sat as if wired in place, walked back and forth on rubbery-shod feet. Beneath a hum of engines, ventilators, a thousand systems throughout the great hull, their curt exchanges chopped. To stimulate them, it was cool here, with a thunderstorm tang of ozone.

The Gospodar's gaze traveled on, among the view-screens which studded bulkheads, overhead, deck—again, scarcely more than a means for keeping crew who did not have their ship's esoteric senses from feeling trapped. Glory brimmed the dark, stars in glittering flocks and Milky Way shoals, faerie-remote glimmer of nebulae and a few sister galaxies. Here in the outer reaches of its system, the target sun was barely the brightest, a coal-glow under Bellatrix. At chance moments a spark would flare and vanish, a nuclear burst close enough to see. But most were too distant; and never another vessel showed, companion or foe. Such was the scale of the battle.

200

And yet it was not large as space combats went. Springing from hyperdrive to normal state, the Dennitzan force—strong, but hardly an armada—encountered Merseian craft which sought to bar it from accelerating inward. As more and more of the latter drew nigh and matched courses with invaders, action spread across multimillions of kilometers. Hours passed before two or three fighters came so near, at such low relative speeds, that they could hope for a kill; and often their encounter was the briefest spasm, followed by hours more of maneuver. Those gave time to make repairs, care for the wounded, pray for the dead.

"They've certainly got protection," Miyatovich growled. "Who'd have expected this much?"

Scouts had not been able to warn him. The stroke depended altogether on swiftness. Merseian observers in the neighborhood of Zoria had surely detected the fleet's setting out. Some would have gone to tell their masters, others would have dogged the force, trying to learn where it was bound. (A few of those had been spotted and destroyed, but not likely all.) No matter how carefully plotted its course, and no matter that its destination was a thinly trafficked part of space, during the three-week journey its hyperwake must have been picked up by several travelers who passed within range. So many strange hulls together, driving so hard through Merseian domains, was cause to bring in the Navy.

If Miyatovich was to do anything to Chereion, he must get there, finish his work, and be gone before reinforcements could arrive. Scouts of his, prowling far in advance near a sun whose location seemed to be the Roidhunate's most tightly gripped secret, would have carried too big a risk of giving away his intent. He must simply rush in full-armed, and hope.

"We can take them, can't we?" he asked.

Rear Admiral Raich, director of operations, nodded.

"Oh, yes. They're outnumbered, outgunned. I wonder why they don't withdraw."

"Merseians aren't cowards," Captain Yulinatz, skipper of the dreadnaught, remarked. "Would you abandon a trust?"

201

"If my orders included the sensible proviso that I not contest lost cases when it's possible to scramble clear and fight another day—yes, I would," Raich said. "Merseians aren't idiots either."

"Could they be expecting help?" Miyatovich wondered. He gnawed his mustache and scowled.

"I doubt it," Raich replied. "We know nothing significant can reach us soon." He did keep scouts far-flung throughout this stellar vicinity, now that he was in it. "They must have the same information to base the same conclusions on."

Flandry, who stood among them, his Terran red-white-and-blue gaudy against their indigo or gray, cleared his throat. "Well, then," he said, "the answer's obvious. They do have orders to fight to the death. Under no circumstances may they abandon Chereion. If nothing else, they must try to reduce our capability of damaging whatever is on the planet."

"Bonebrain doctrine," Raich grunted.

"Not if they're guarding something vital," Miyatovich said. "What might it be?"

"We can try for captures," Yulinatz suggested: reluctantly, because it multiplied the hazard to his men.

Flandry shook his head. "No point in that," he declared. "Weren't you listening when he talked *en route?* Nobody lands on Chereion except by special permission which is damn hard to get—needs approval of both the regional tribune and the planet's own authorities, and movements are severely restricted. I don't imagine a single one of the personnel we're killing and being killed by has come within an astronomical unit of the globe."

"Yes, yes, I heard," Yulinatz snapped. "What influence those beings must have."

"That's why we've come to hit them," the Gospodar said in his beard.

Yulinatz's glance went to the tank. A green point blinked: a cruiser was suffering heavily from three enemy craft which paced her. A yellow point went out, and quickly another: two corvettes lost. His tone grew raw. "Will it be worth the price to us?"

"That we can't tell till afterward." Miyatovich squared

his shoulders. "We could disengage and go home, knowing we've thrown a scare into the enemy. But we'd never know what opportunity we did or did not forever miss. We will proceed."

In the end, a chieftain's main duty is to say, "On my head be it."

"Gentlemen."

Flandry's word brought their eyes to him. "I anticipated some such quandary," he stated. "What we need is a quick survey—a forerunner to get a rough idea of what is on Chereion and report back. Then we can decide."

Raich snorted. "We need veto rights over the laws of statistics too."

"If the guard is this thick at this distance," Yulinatz added, "what chance has the best speedster ever built for any navy of getting anywhere near?"

Miyatovich, comprehending, swallowed hard.

"I brought along my personal boat," Flandry said. "She was not built for a navy."

"No, Dominic," Miyatovich protested.

"Yes, Bodin," Flandry answered.

Vatre Zvezda unleashed a salvo. No foes were close. None could match a Nova-class vessel. She was huge, heavy-armored, intricately compartmented, monster-powered in engines, weapons, shielding fields, less to join battle than to keep battle away from the command posts at her heart. Under present conditions, it was not mad, but it was unreasonable that she fired at opponents more than a million kilometers distant. They would have time to track those missiles, avoid them or blow them up.

The reason was to cover *Hooligan*'s takeoff.

She slipped from a boat lock, through a lane opened momentarily in the fields, outward like an outsize torpedo. Briefly in her aft-looking viewscreens the dreadnaught bulked, glimmering spheroid abristle with guns, turrets, launch tubes, projectors, sensors, generators, snatchers, hatches, watchdomes, misshapen moon adrift among the stars. Acceleration dwindled her so fast that Yovan Vymezal gasped, as if the interior were not at a steady

Dennitzan gravity but the full unbalanced force had crushed the breath from him.

In the pilot's chair, Flandry took readings, ran off computations, nodded, and leaned back. "We won't make approach for a good three-quarters of an hour," he said, "and nothing's between us and our nominal target. Relax."

Vymezal—a young cadre lieutenant of marines, Kossara's cousin and in a sturdy male fashion almost unendurably like her—undid his safety web. He had been invited to the control cabin as a courtesy; come passage near the enemy destroyer they were aimed at, he would be below with his dozen men, giving them what comfort he could in their helplessness, and Chives would be here as copilot. His question came hesitant, not frightened but shy: "Sir, do you really think we can get past? They'll know pretty soon we're not a torp, we're a manned vessel. I should think they won't be satisfied to take evasive action, they'll try for a kill."

"You volunteered, didn't you? After being warned this is a dangerous mission."

Vymezal flushed. "Yes, sir. I wouldn't beg off if I could. I was just wondering. You explained it's not necessarily a suicide mission."

The odds are long that it is, my boy.

"You said," the earnest voice stumbled on, "your oscillators are well enough tuned that you can go on hyperdrive deep into a gravity well—quite near the sun. You planned to make most of our transit that way. Why not start at once? Why first run straight at hostile guns? I'm just wondering, sir, just interested."

Flandry smiled. "Sure you are," he replied, "and I'm sorry if you supposed for a minute I suppose otherwise. The reason is simple. We've a high kinetic velocity right now with respect to Chereion. You don't lose energy of relativistic motion merely because for a while you quantum-hop around the light-speed limit. Somewhere along the line, we have to match our vector to the planet's. That's better done here, where we have elbow room, than close in, where space may be crammed with defenses. We gain time—time to increase surprise at the far end—by posing as a missile while we adjust our velocity. But a missile should logically have a target. Within the cone of feasible directions, that destroyer seemed like our best bet. Let me emphasize, the operative word is 'bet.' "

Vymezal eased and chuckled. "Thank you, sir. I'm a dice addict. I know when to fade."

"I'm more a poker player." Flandry offered a cigarette, which was accepted, and took one for himself. It crossed his mind: how strange he should still be using the box which had snapped shut on his son, and give it no particular thought.

Well, why throw away a tool I'd want duplicated later? I've been taught to avoid romantic gestures except when they serve a practical demagogic purpose.

Vymezal peered ahead at the ruby sun. Yes, his profile against the star-clouds of Sagittarius was as much like Kossara's as young Dominic's had been like Persis'.

What can I write to Persis? Can I?

Maybe my gesture is to carry this cigarette case in my pocket for the rest of my days.

"What information have we?" the lieutenant almost whispered.

"Very little, and most we collected personally while we approached," Flandry said. "Red dwarf star, of course; early type, but still billions of years older than Sol or Zoria, and destined to outlive them. However, not unduly metal-poor," *as Diomedes is where I put her at stake for no more possible win than the damned Empire.* "Distribution of higher elements varies a good bit in both space and time. The system appears normal for its kind, whatever 'normal' may mean: seven identified planets, Chereion presumably the only vitafer. We can't predict further; life has no such thing as a norm. I do expect Chereion will be, m-m, interesting."

And not an inappropriate place to leave my bones.

Flandry inhaled acridity and gazed outward. With all the marvels and mysteries yonder, he wasn't seeking death. In the last few weeks, his wounds had scarred over. But scar tissue is not alive. He no longer minded the idea of death.

He wished, though, it had been possible to leave Chives behind, and Kossara's cousin.

A magnifying screen emblazoned the Merseian destroyer, spearhead on a field of stars.

"Torpedo coming, sir," Chives stated. "Shall I dispose of it?" His fingers flicked across the gun control board before him. A firebolt sprang hell-colored. Detector-computer systems signaled a hit. The missile ceased accelerating. Either its drive was disabled or this was a programmed trick. In the second case, if *Hooligan* maintained the same vector, a moment's thrust would bring it sufficiently close that radiation from the exploding warhead could cripple electronics, leave her helpless and incidentally pass a death sentence on her crew.

"Keep burning till we're sure," Flandry ordered. That required a quick change of course. Engines roared, steel sang under stress, constellations whirled. He felt his blood tingle and knew he was still a huntsman.

Flame fountained. A crash went through hull and flesh. The deck heaved. Shouts came faintly from aft.

Gee-fields restabilized. "The missile obviously had a backup detonator," Chives said. "It functioned at a safe remove from us, and our force screens fended off a substantial piece of débris without harm. Those gatortails are often inept mechanicians, would you not agree, sir?" His own tail switched slim and smug.

"Maybe. Don't let that make you underestimate the Chereionites." Flandry studied the readouts before him.

His pulse lifted. They were matched to their goal world. A few minutes at faster-than-light would bring them there, and—

"Stand by," he called.

● XX ●

The eeriest thing was that nothing happened.

The planet spun in loneliness around its ember sun. Air made a thin bordure to its shield, shading from blue to purple to the winter sky of space. Hues were iron-rusty and desert-tawny, overlaid by blue-green mottlings, hoar polar caps, fierce glint off the few shrunken seas which remained. A small, scarred moon swung near.

It had to be the world of Flandry's search. No other was possible. But who stood guard? War raved through outer space; here his detectors registered only a few automatic traffic-control stations in orbit, easily bypassed. Silence seeped through the hull of his vessel and filled the pilot's cabin.

Chives broke it: "Analysis indicates habitability for us is marginal, sir. Biotypes of the kind which appear to be present—sparsely—have adapted to existing conditions but could not have been born under them. Given this feeble irradiation, an immense time was required for the loss of so much atmosphere and hydrosphere." He paused. "The sense of age and desolation is quite overwhelming, sir."

Flandry, his face in the hood of a scannerscope, muttered, "There are cities. In good repair, fusion powerplants at work ... though putting out very little energy for complexes their size. ... The deserts are barren, the begrown regions don't look cultivated—too saline, I'd guess. Maybe the dwellers live on synthetic food. But why no visible traffic? Why no satellite or ground defenses?"

"As for the former, sir," Chives ventured, "the inhabitants may generally prefer a contemplative, physically austere existence. Did not Aycharaych intimate that to you on various occasions? And as for the latter question,

207

Merseian ships have maintained a cordon, admitting none except an authorized few."

"That is"—the tingle in Flandry sharpened—"if an intruder like us ever came this close, the game would be up anyway?"

"I do not suggest they have no wiles in reserve, sir."

"Ye-e-es. The Roidhunate wouldn't keep watch over pure philosophers." Decision slammed into Flandry like sword into sheath. "We can't learn more where we are, and every second we linger gives them an extra chance to notice us and load a trap. We're going straight down!"

He gave the boat a surge of power.

Nonetheless, his approach was cautious. If naught else, he needed a while to reduce interior air pressure to the value indicated for the surface ahead of them. (Sounds grew muffled; pulse quickened; breast muscles worked enough to feel. Presently he stopped noticing much, having always taken care to maintain a level of acclimation to thin air. But he was glad that gravity outside would be weak, about half a gee.) Curving around the night hemisphere, he studied light-bejeweled towers set in the middle of rock and sand wastes, wondered greatly at what he saw, and devised a plan of sorts.

"We'll find us a daylit place and settle alongside," he announced on the intercom. "If they won't talk to us, we'll maybe go in and talk to them." For his communicator, searching all bands, had drawn no hint of—

No! A screen flickered into color. He looked at the first Chereionite face he could be certain was not Aycharaych's. It had the same spare beauty, the same deep calm, but as many differences of sculpture as between one human countenance and the next. And from the start, even before speech began, he felt a . . . heaviness: nothing of sardonic humor or flashes of regret.

"Talk the conn, Chives," he directed. A whistling had begun, and the badlands were no longer before but below him. *Hooligan* was an easier target now than she had been in space; she had better be ready to dodge and strike back.

"You are not cleared for entry," said the screen in Eriau which was mellow-toned but did not sing like Aycharaych's. "Your action is forbidden under strict penalties, by command of the Roidhun in person, renewed in each new reign. Can you offer a justification?"

Huh? jabbed through Flandry. *Does he assume this is a Merseian boat and I a Merseian man?* "Em—emergency," he tried, too astonished to invent a glib story. He had expected he would declare himself as more or less what he was, and hold his destination city hostage to his guns and missiles. Whether or not the attempt could succeed in any degree, he had no notion. At best he'd thought he might bear away a few hints about the beings who laired here.

"Have you control over your course?" inquired the voice.

"Yes. Let me speak to a ranking officer."

"You will go approximately five hundred kilometers northwest of your immediate position. Prepare to record a map." The visage vanished, a chart appeared, two triangles upon it. "The red apex shows where you are, the blue your mandatory landing site, a spacefield. You will stay inboard and await instructions. Is this understood?"

"We'll try. We, uh, we have a lot of speed to kill. In our condition, fast braking is unsafe. Can you give us about half an hour?"

Aycharaych would not have spent several seconds reaching a decision. "Permitted. Be warned, deviations may cause you to be shot down. Proceed." Nor would he have broken contact with not a single further inquiry.

Outside was no longer black, but purple. The spacecraft strewed thunder across desert. "What the *hell*, sir?" Chives exploded.

"Agreed," said Flandry. His tongue shifted to an obscure language they both knew. "Use this lingo while that channel's open."

"What shall we do?"

"First, play back any pictures we got of the place we're supposed to go." Flandry's fingers brushed a section of console. On an inset screen came a view taken from nearby space under magnification. His trained eyes studied it and a few additional. "A spacefield, aye, standard Merseian model, terminal and the usual outbuildings. Modest-sized, no vessels parked. And way off in wilderness." He twisted his mustache. "You know, I'll bet that's where every visitor's required to land. And then he's brought in a closed car to a narrowly limited area which is all he ever sees."

"Shall we obey, sir?"

"Um, 'twould be a pity, wouldn't it, to pass by that lovely city we had in mind. Besides, they doubtless keep heavy weapons at the port; our pictures show signs of it. Once there, we'd be at their mercy. Whereas I suspect that threat to blast us elsewhere was a bluff. Imagine a stranger pushing into a prohibited zone on a normal planet —when the system's being invaded! Why aren't we at least swarmed by military aircraft?"

"Very good, sir. We can land in five minutes." Chives gave his master a pleading regard. "Sir, must I truly stay behind while you debark?"

"Somebody has to cover us, ready to scramble if need be. We're Intelligence collectors, not heroes. If I call you and say, 'Escape,' Chives, you will escape."

"Yes, sir," the Shalmuan forced out. "However, please grant me the liberty of protesting your decision not to wear armor like your men."

"I want the full use of my senses." Flandry cast him a crooked smile and patted the warm green shoulder. "I fear I've often strained your loyalty, old chap. But you haven't failed me yet."

"Thank you, sir." Chives stared hard at his own busy hands. "I ... endeavor ... to give satisfaction."

Time swooped past.

"Attention!" cried from the screen. "You are off course! You are in absolutely barred territory!"

"Say on," Flandry jeered. He half hoped to provoke a real response. The voice only denounced his behavior.

A thump resounded and shivered. The tone of wind and engines ceased. They were down.

Flandry vaulted from his chair, snatched a combat helmet, buckled it on as he ran. Beneath it he already wore a mindscreen, as did everybody aboard. Otherwise he was attired in a gray coverall and stout leather boots. On his back and across his chest were the drive cones and controls of a grav unit. His pouchbelt held field rations, medical supplies, canteen of water, ammunition, blaster, slugthrower, and Merseian war knife.

At the head of his dozen Dennitzan marines, he bounded from the main personnel lock, along the extruded gangway, onto the soil of Chereion. There he crouched in what shelter the hull afforded and glared around, fingers on weapons.

After a minute or two he stepped forth. Awe welled in him.

A breeze whispered, blade-sharp with cold and dryness. It bore an iron tang off uncounted leagues of sand and dust. In cloudless violet, the sun stood at afternoon, bigger to see than Sol over Terra, duller and redder than the sun over Diomedes; squinting, he could look straight into it for seconds without being blinded, and through his lashes find monstrous dark spots and vortices. It would not set for many an hour, the old planet turned so wearily.

Shadows were long and purple across the dunes which rolled cinnabar and ocher to the near horizon. Here and there stood the gnawed stump of a pinnacle, livid with mineral hues, or a ravine clove a bluff which might once have been a mountain. The farther desert seemed utterly dead. Around the city, wide apart, grew low bushes whose leaves glittered in rainbows as if crystalline. The city itself rose from foundations that must go far down, must have been buried until the landscape eroded from around them and surely have needed renewal as the ages swept past.

The city—it was not a giant chaos such as besat Terra or Merseia; nothing on Chereion was. An ellipse defined it, some ten kilometers at the widest, proportioned in a rightness Flandry had recognized from afar though not knowing how he did. The buildings of the perimeter were single-storied, slenderly colonnaded; behind them, others lifted ever higher, until they climaxed in a leap of slim towers. Few windows interrupted the harmonies of colors and iridescence, the interplay of geometries that called forth visions of many-vaulted infinity. The heart rode those lines and curves upward until the whole sight became a silent music.

Silent . . . only the breeze moved or murmured.

A time passed beyond time.

"Milostiv Bog," Lieutenant Vymezal breathed, "is it Heaven we see?"

"Then is Heaven empty?" said another man as low.

Flandry shook himself, wrenched his attention away, sought for his purposefulness in the ponderous homely shapes of their armor, the guns and grenades they bore. "Let's find out." His words were harsh and loud in his ears. "This is as large a community as any, and typical insofar as I could judge." *Not that they are alike. Each is a separate song.* "If it's abandoned, we can assume they all are."

"Why would the Merseians guard ... relics?" Vymezal asked.

"Maybe they don't." Flandry addressed his minicom. "Chives, jump aloft at the first trace of anything untoward. Fight at discretion. I think we can maintain radio contact from inside the town. If not, I may ask you to hover. Are you still getting a transmission?"

"No, sir." That voice came duly small. "It ceased when we landed."

"Cut me in if you do.... Gentlemen, follow me in combat formation. Should I come to grief, remember your duty is to return to the fleet if possible, or to cover our boat's retreat if necessary. Forward."

Flandry started off in flat sub-gee bounds. His body felt miraculously light, as light as the shapes which soared before him, and the air diamond clear. Yet behind him purred the gravity motors which helped his weighted troopers along. He reminded himself that they hugged the ground to present a minimal target, that the space they crossed was terrifyingly open, that ultimate purity lies in death. The minutes grew while he covered the pair of kilometers. Half of him stayed cat-alert, half wished Kossara could somehow, safely, have witnessed this wonder.

The foundations took more and more of the sky, until at last he stood beneath their sheer cliff. Azure, the material resisted a kick and an experimental energy bolt with a hardness which had defied epochs. He whirred upward, over an edge, and stood in the city.

A broad street of the same blue stretched before him,

flanked by dancing rows of pillars and arabesque friezes
on buildings which might have been temples. The farther
he scanned, the higher fountained walls, columns, tiers, cu-
polas, spires; and each step he took gave him a different
perspective, so that the whole came alive, intricate, simple,
powerful, tranquil, transcendental. But footfalls echoed
hollow.

They had gone a kilometer inward when nerves twanged
and weapons snapped to aim. "Hold," Flandry said. The
man-sized ovoid that floated from a side lane sprouted
tentacles which ended in tools and sensors. The lines and
curves of it were beautiful. It passed from sight again on
its unnamed errand. "A robot," Flandry guessed. "Fully
automated, a city could last, could function, for—millions
of years?" His prosiness felt to him as if he had spat on
consecrated earth.

No, damn it! I'm hunting my woman's murderers.

He trod into a mosaic plaza and saw their forms.

Through an arcade on the far side the tall grave shapes
walked, white-robed, heads bare to let crests shine over
luminous eyes and lordly brows. They numbered perhaps a
score. Some carried what appeared to be books, scrolls,
delicate enigmatic objects; some appeared to be in discourse, mind to mind; some went alone in their medita-
tions. When the humans arrived, most heads turned observ-
ingly. Then, as if having exhausted what newness was there,
the thoughtfulness returned to them and they went on
about their business of—wisdom?

"What'll we do, sir?" Vymezal rasped at Flandry's ear.

"Talk to them, if they'll answer," the Terran said.
"Even take them prisoner, if circumstances warrant."

"Can we? Should we? I came here for revenge, but—
God help us, what filthy monkeys we are."

A premonition trembled in Flandry. "Don't you mean,"
he muttered, "what animals we're intended to feel like . . .
we and whoever they guide this far?"

He strode quickly across the lovely pattern before him.
Under an ogive arch, one stopped, turned, beckoned, and
waited. The sight of gun loose in holster and brutal forms
at his back did not stir the calm upon that golden face.
"Greeting," lulled in Eriau.

Flandry reached forth a hand. The other slipped easily aside from the uncouth gesture. "I want somebody who can speak for your world," the man said.

"Any of us can that," sang the reply. "Call me, if you wish, Liannathan. Have you a name for use?"

"Yes. Captain Sir Dominic Flandry, Imperial Navy of Terra. Your Aycharaych knows me. Is he around?"

Liannathan ignored the question. "Why do you trouble our peace?"

The chills walked faster along Flandry's spine. "Can't you read that in my mind?" he asked.

"Sta pakao," said amazement behind him.

"Hush," Vymezal warned the man, his own tone stiff with intensity; and there was no mention of screens against telepathy.

"We give you the charity of refraining," Liannathan smiled.

To and fro went the philosophers behind him.

"I . . . assume you're aware . . . a punitive expedition is on its way," Flandry said. "My group came to . . . parley."

Calm was unshaken. "Think why you are hostile."

"Aren't you our enemies?"

"We are enemies to none. We seek, we shape."

"Let me talk to Aycharaych. I'm certain he's somewhere on Chereion. He'd have left the Zorian System after word got beamed to him, or he learned from broadcasts, his scheme had failed. Where else would he go?"

Liannathan curved feathery brows upward. "Best you explain yourself, Captain, to yourself if not us."

Abruptly Flandry snapped off the switch of his mindscreen. "Read the answers," he challenged.

Liannathan spread graceful hands in gracious signal. "I told you, knowing what darkness you must dwell in, for mercy's sake we will leave your thoughts alone unless you compel us. Speak."

Conviction congealed in Flandry, iceberg huge. "No, you speak. What are you on Chereion? What do you tell the Merseians? I already know, or think I know, but tell me."

The response rang grave: "We are not wholly the last of an ancient race; the others have gone before us. We are those who have not yet reached the Goal; the bitter need of the universe for help still binds us. Our numbers are few, we have no need of numbers. Very near we are to those desires that lie beyond desire, those powers that lie beyond power." Compassion softened Liannathan's words. "Terran, we mourn the torment of you and yours. We mourn that you can never feel the final reality, the spirit born out of pain. We have no wish to return you to nothingness. Go in love, before too late."

Almost, Flandry believed. His sense did not rescue him; his memories did. "Yah!" he shouted. "You phantom, stop haunting!"

He lunged. Liannathan wasn't there. He crashed a blaster bolt among the mystics. They were gone. He leaped in among the red-tinged shadows of the arcade and peered after light and sound projectors to smash. Everywhere else, enormous, brooded the stillness of the long afternoon.

The image of a single Chereionite flashed into sight, in brief white tunic, bearing though not brandishing a sidearm, palm uplifted—care-worn, as if the bones would break out from the skin, yet with life in flesh and great garnet eyes such as had never burned in those apparitions which were passed away. Flandry halted. "Aycharaych!"

He snatched for the switch to turn his mindscreen back on. Aycharaych smiled. "You need not bother, Dominic," he said in Anglic. "This too is only a hologram."

"Lieutenant," Flandry snapped over his shoulder, "dispose your squad against attack."

"Why?" said Aycharaych. The armored men gave him scant notice. His form glimmered miragelike in the gloom under that vaulted roof, where sullen sunlight barely reached. "You have discovered we have nothing to resist you."

You're bound to have something, Flandry did not reply. *A few missiles or whatever. You're just unwilling to use them in these environs. Where are you yourself, and what were you doing while your specters held us quiet?*

As if out of a stranger's throat, he heard: "Those weren't straightforward audiovisuals like yours that we met, were they? No reason for them to put on a show of being present, of being real, except that none of them ever

215

were. Right? They're computer-generated simulacrums, will-o'-the-wisps for leading allies and enemies alike from the truth. Well, life's made me an unbeliever.

"Aycharaych, you are in fact the last Chereionite alive. The very last. Aren't you?"

Abruptly such anguish contorted the face before him that he looked away. "What did they die of?" he was asking. "How long ago?" He got no answer.

Instead: "Dominic, we share a soul, you and I. We have both always been alone."

For a while I wasn't; and now she is; she is down in the aloneness which is eternal. Rage ripped Flandry. He swung back to see a measure of self-command masking the gaunt countenance. "You must have played your game for centuries," he grated. "Why? And ... whatever your reason to hide that your people are extinct ... why prey on the living? You, you could let them in and show them what'd make your Chereionites the ... Greeks of the galaxy—but you sit in a tomb or travel like a vampire— Are you crazy, Aycharaych? Is that what drives you?"

"No!"

Flandry had once before heard the lyric voice in sorrow. He had not heard a scream: "I am not! Look around you. Who could go mad among these? And arts, music, books, dreams—yes, more, the loftiest spirits of a million years —they lent themselves to the scanners, the recorders— If you could have the likenesses to meet whenever you would ... of Gautama Buddha, Kung Fu-Tse, Rabbi Hillel, Jesus the Christ, Rumi ... Socrates, Newton, Hokusai, Jefferson, Gauss, Beethoven, Einstein, Ulfgeir, Manuel the Great, Manuel the Wise—would you let your war lords turn these instruments to their own vile ends? *No!*"

And Flandry understood.

Did Aycharaych, half blinded by his dead, see what he had given away? "Dominic," he whispered hastily, shakily, "I've used you ill, as I've used many. It was from no will of mine. Oh, true, an art, a sport—yours too—but we had our services, you to a civilization you know is dying, I to a heritage I know can abide while this sun does. Who has the better right?" He held forth unsubstantial hands.

"Dominic, stay. We'll think how to keep your ships off and save Chereion—"

Almost as if he were again the machine that condemned his son, Flandry said, "I'd have to lure my company into some kind of trap. Merseia would take the planet back, and the help it gives. Your shadow show would go on. Right?"

"Yes. What are a few more lives to you? What is Terra? In ten thousand years, who will remember the empires? They can remember you, though, who saved Chereion for them."

Candle flames stood around a coffin. Flandry shook his head. "There've been too many betrayals in too many causes." He wheeled. "Men, we're returning."

"Aye, sir." The replies shuddered with relief.

Aycharaych's eidolon brought fingers together as if he prayed. Flandry touched his main grav switch. Thrust pushed harness against breast. He rose from the radiant city, into the waning murky day. Chill flowed around him. Behind floated his robot-encased men.

"Brigate!" bawled Vymezal. "Beware!"

Around the topmost tower flashed a score of javelin shapes. Firebeams leaped out of their nozzles. *Remote-controlled flyer guns,* Flandry knew. *Does Aycharaych still hope, or does he only want revenge?* "Chives," he called into his sender, "come get us!"

Sparks showered off Vymezal's plate. He slipped aside in midair, more fast and nimble than it seemed he could be in armor. His energy weapon, nearly as heavy as the assailants, flared back. Thunders followed brilliances. Bitterness tinged air. A mobile blast cannon reeled in midflight, spun downward, crashed in a street, exploded. Fragments ravaged a fragile façade.

"Shield the captain," Vymezal boomed.

Flandry's men ringed him in. Shots tore at them. The noise stamped in his skull, the stray heat whipped over his skin. Held to his protection, the marines could not dodge about. The guns converged.

A shadow fell, a lean hull blocked off the sun. Flames reaped. Echoes toned at last to silence around smoking ruin down below. Vymezal shouted triumph. He waved his warriors aside, that Flandry might lead them through the open lock, into the *Hooligan*.

Wounded, dwindled, victorious, the Dennitzan fleet took orbits around Chereion. Within the command bridge, Bodin Miyatovich and his chieftains stood for a long while gazing into the viewscreens. The planet before them glowed among the stars, softly, secretly, like a sign of peace. But it was the pictures they had seen earlier, the tale they had heard, which made those hard men waver.

Miyatovich even asked through his flagship's rustling stillness: "Must we bombard?"

"Yes," Flandry said. "I hate the idea too."

Qow of Novi Aferoch stirred. Lately taken off his crippled light cruiser, he was less informed than the rest. "Can't sappers do what's needful?" he protested.

"I wish they could," Flandry sighed. "We haven't time. I don't know how many millennia of history we're looking down on. How can we read them before the Merseian navy arrives?"

"Are you sure, then, the gain to us can justify a deed which someday will make lovers of beauty, seekers of knowledge, curse our names?" the zmay demanded. "Can this really be the center of the opposition's Intelligence?"

"I never claimed that," Flandry said. "In fact, obviously not. But it must be important as hell itself. We here can give them no worse setback than striking it from their grasp."

"Your chain of logic seems thin."

"Of course it is! Were mortals ever certain? But listen again, Qow.

"When the Merseians discovered Chereion, they were already conquest-hungry. Aycharaych, among the ghosts those magnificent computers had been raising for him— computers and programs we today couldn't possibly invent —he saw they'd see what warlike purposes might be furthered by such an instrumentality. They'd bend it wholly to their ends, bring their engineers in by the horde, ransack, peer, gut, build over, leave nothing unwrecked except a few museum scraps. He couldn't bear the thought of that.

"He stopped them by conjuring up phantoms. He made them think a few million of his race were still alive, able to give the Roidhunate valuable help in the form of staff work, while he himself would be a unique field agent—if they were otherwise left alone. We may never know how he impressed and tricked those tough-minded fighter lords; he did, that's all. They believe they have a worldful of enormous intellects for allies, whom they'd better treat with respect. He draws on a micro part of the computers, data banks, stored knowledge beyond our imagining, to generate advice for them ... excellent advice, but they don't suspect how much more they might be able to get, or by what means.

"Maybe he's had some wish to influence them, as if they learned from Chereion. Or maybe he's simply been biding his time till they too erode from his planet."

Flandry was quiet for a few heartbeats before he finished: "Need we care which, when real people are in danger?"

The Gospodar straightened, walked to an intercom, spoke his orders.

There followed a span while ships chose targets. He and Flandry moved aside, to stand before a screen showing stars that lay beyond every known empire. "I own to a desire for vengeance," he confessed. "My judgment might have been different otherwise."

Flandry nodded. "Me too. That's how we are. If only— No, never mind."

"Do you think we can demolish everything?"

"I don't know. I'm assuming the things we want to kill are under the cities—some of the cities—and plenty of megatonnage will if nothing else crumble their caverns around them." Flandry smote a fist hurtfully against a bulkhead. "I told Qow, we don't ever have more to go on than guesswork!"

"Still, the best guess is, we'll smash enough of the system—whether or not we reach Aycharaych himself—"

"For his sake, let's hope we do."

"Are you that forgiving, Dominic? Well, regardless, Intelligence is the balance wheel of military operations. Merseian Intelligence should be . . . not broken, but badly knocked askew. . . . Will Emperor Hans feel grateful?"

"Yes, I expect he'll defend us to the limit against the nobles who'll want our scalps." Flandry wolf-grinned. "In fact, he should welcome such an issue. The quarrel can force influential appeasers out of his regime.

"And . . . he's bound to agree you've proved your case for keeping your own armed forces."

"So Dennitza stays in the Empire—" Miyatovich laid a hand on his companion's shoulder. "Between us, my friend, I dare hope myself that what I care about will still be there when the Empire is gone. However, that scarcely touches our lifetimes. What do you plan to do with the rest of yours?"

"Carry on as before," Flandry said.

"Go back to Terra?" The eyes which were like Kossara's searched him. "In God's name, why?"

Flandry made no response. Shortly sirens whooped and voices crackled. The bombardment was beginning.

A missile sprang from a ship. Among the stars it flew arrow slim; but when it pierced air, hurricane furies trailed its mass. That drum-roar rolled from horizon to horizon beneath the moon, shook apart wind-carven crags, sent landslides grumbling to the bottoms of canyons. When it caught the first high dawnlight, the missile turned into a silver comet. Minutes later it spied the towers and treasures it was to destroy, and plunged. It had weapons ready against ground defenses; but only the spires reached gleaming for heaven.

The fireball outshone whole suns. It bloomed so tall and wide that the top of the atmosphere, too thin to carry it further, became a roof; therefore it sat for minutes on the curve of the planet, ablaze, before it faded. Dust then made a thick and deadly night above a crater full of molten stone. Wrath tolled around the world.

And more strikes came, and more.

Flandry watched. When the hour was ended, he answered Miyatovich: "I have my own people."

In glory did Gospodar Bodin ride home.

Maidens danced to crown him with flowers. The songs of their joy rang from the headwaters of the Lyubisha to the waves of the Black Ocean, up the highest mountains and down the fairest glens; and all the bells of Zorkagrad pealed until Lake Stoyan gave back their music.

Springtime came, never more sweet, and blossoms well-nigh buried the tomb which Gospodar Bodin had raised for St. Kossara. There did he often pray, in after years of his lordship over us; and while he lived, no foeman troubled the peace she brought us through his valor. Sing, poets, of his fame and honor! Long may God give us folk like these!

And may they hearten each one of us. For in this is our hope.

Amen

ABOUT THE AUTHOR

A former president of the Science Fiction Writers of America, Poul Anderson was born in 1926 of Scandinavian parents. Married to writer Karen Kruse, they have one daughter and reside in the San Francisco Bay area, where he pursues his hobbies of mountaineering, gardening, and cartooning.

Mr. Anderson has published over 50 books and more than 200 shorter pieces, the latter in periodicals as diverse as *Analog, Saturday Review, Boys' Life, Playboy, and National Review.* He is the winner of five Hugo awards and two Nebula awards for his science fiction works. His books for NAL include THE PEOPLE OF THE WIND, THE QUEEN OF AIR AND DARKNESS, THERE WILL BE TIME, THE DANCER FROM ATLANTIS, A CIRCLE OF HELLS, THE HORN OF TIME, THE BYWORLDER, BEYOND THE BEYOND, and THE DAY OF THEIR RETURN.

SIGNET Science Fiction You'll Enjoy

Great Science Fiction by Robert Adams from SIGNET

Recommended Reading from SIGNET

The Best in Fiction From SIGNET